Ethel E. Pollock.

PRAISE AT MORNING

MILDRED MASTERSON McNEILLY

Praise *at* Morning

PEOPLES BOOK CLUB
Chicago

This is a special edition published exclusively for the members of the PEOPLES BOOK CLUB, P. O. BOX 6570A, Chicago, Illinois. It was originally published by William Morrow and Co.

MANUFACTURED IN THE UNITED STATES OF AMERICA

To Glenn D. McNeilly

Some Praise At Morning
what they blame at night,
But always think
the last opinion right.

—ALEXANDER POPE, *Essay on Criticism*

CHAPTER I

FOR THE second time that day Matthew Steel flung open the door of his room in Mrs. Anne Doughty's Boarding House for Seamen, and shouted for Lexie. The first time had been before seven o'clock in the morning, and when that slattern had appeared in her eager, shuffling half-run, he had thrust his shaving mug at her and demanded hot water—and quickly.

Now it was nearing six o'clock in the evening and darkness had already blotted out even the little light that filtered into the musty halls in mid-day. Lexie Small, who was half-heartedly attempting to clean a room fouled by a four-day debauch of a Liverpool seaman and his women, dropped her dirty rag into the black water of her scrubbing bucket, and leaped to her feet. Even near the end of her fifteen-hour day, Lexie Small responded with alacrity to a summons by Matthew Steel.

The soles of Lexie's shoes were loose and they flapped as she hurried in her peculiar, flat-footed gait down the hall toward Steel's door. She shoved back the greasy strings of her hair with a wet, grimy paw and wiped her hands on her skirts. Lexie's front teeth had rotted off at the gums, but she grinned ingratiatingly as she approached.

The light in his room outlined Matthew Steel as he stood in the doorway waiting for Lexie. He was a tall, powerful man, and young. He had taken off his coat and in the dusk his white shirt gleamed. Lexie feasted her eyes upon it. His collar was open and folded under neatly, baring a strong, brown neck. His hair was black, crisp and straight and it had been newly trimmed. It was clipped close in the back as was the fashion in the early fall of 1854, and the skin thus revealed was several shades lighter than the smooth, heavily tanned neck below it. It looked clean and young.

He wore neither mustache nor side-whiskers; his forehead was lined above his heavy, straight black brows, and though he was in his middle twenties there were small lines at the corners of his eyes as well, etched there by sun and spray and wind. He had a seaman's eyes, used to distances; they were very dark, almost black, and they were bold, direct and very clear. His nose was strong and straight and his mouth a little large, his lips hard over even teeth. He stood well over six feet and his wide shoulders almost filled the narrow doorway. He was frowning impatiently and Lexie twisted her thin body down in its shapeless, spotted garments, fawning, tucking her chin down and looking up at him coyly.

His hand sought his pocket and he tossed her a coin and handed her his shaving mug.

"Water, Lexie. Make it hot, and hurry," he said, not unkindly.

Lexie caught the coin and lifted her skirt shamelessly, baring a bony limb to her thigh. She put the coin into a small bag suspended from a string at her waist and dropped her dress, her eyes gleaming. She took the shaving mug, her dirty fingers managing to touch Steel's own.

"Law, Mr. Steel, and thank ye, now!" she giggled. "But you shaved this morning! I declare, you don't need it again, for all your heavy beard."

Steel stroked his chin. It was a good chin and it could harden easily as it did now. His eyes narrowed ever so little. He did not raise his voice.

"Get on, you lazy slut."

Lexie scuttled down the hall, turning slightly sideways as she passed Steel. But Steel, unlike Mrs. Doughty's other roomers, neither pinched nor slapped her backside as she passed and Lexie glanced over her shoulder, disappointed. Matthew Steel had gone back into his room, leaving the door ajar.

She did not knock when she returned with the water. She pushed open the door and stared hungrily at Steel as she placed the mug on the dresser before him. Then she drew back a little, into the shadows, still watching him avidly. Matthew Steel's room was the best Mrs. Doughty's Boarding House had to offer, and Lexie kept it in better order than the rest. The previous tenant had been ousted without ceremony a week before, when Matthew Steel had appeared, his sea-bag over his shoulder. Mrs. Doughty herself, though not one to show affection, had thrown both fat arms about Steel, and over his shoulder told Lexie to ready the second floor front room for him. It was a larger room than most, and two windows, overlooking Cherry Street, were unevenly curtained with limp, worn lace. On the bed were Mrs. Doughty's own sheets and one good, gray blanket, which had come from Steel's sea-bag lying on the bare floor beside it. On a peg on the wall hung a pair of seaman's trousers, a bright red shirt, and beneath them stood a pair of boots, much worn. Carefully draped over the back of a straight wooden chair, to keep it free from wrinkles, was a new well-tailored coat in a conservative tan woolen, and on the chair seat an expensive beaver hat, also new, a silk cravat, and a pair of light, soft gloves.

Steel bent toward the cracked mirror and began to shave. There was no gentleness in the face that looked back at him. There was keen intelligence; there was courage, there was stubborness, there was a damn-your-eyes, thick-skinned Irish toughness about it. It was a fighter's face, young and undefeated, a fighter in his prime and quietly aware of it, one who would welcome and revel in battle. But it was also the closed, controlled face of a man who has learned early not to reveal by his expression any inner thought or emotion, though the mouth suggested a capacity for humor. It was a gambler's face, saved from sharpness by its strength.

He shaved deliberately, with great care. He dried his face carefully and turned up his collar, examining the fine broadcloth to be sure it was not soiled. Lexie watched him, twisting her apron, her eyes darting over his back, down the long, lean, hardened muscles of his arms and legs and back to the mirror again. She leaped to hand him his cravat and he knotted it painstakingly. Lexie picked up his coat but he turned and took a waistcoat from beneath it first and buttoned it across his chest.

"Law, Mr. Steel, but you do look fine now!" she said breathlessly. He took his coat from her and she slunk back into the shadows, twisting coquettishly. "Must be a lady, a fine lady, Mr. Steel, that you are goin' to see?

Matthew Steel stood motionless for an instant, then he turned slowly and pinned her to the wall with his glance.

"No one on the waterfront ever gained by meddling, Lexie," he said meaningly. "Did they, now?"

She shook her head swiftly, in quick agreement. Steel picked up his hat and gloves.

"There wouldn't be anyone asking you questions, Lexie, about Matthew Steel?"

Again Lexie shook her head quickly. Matthew eyed her for a minute and then grinned.

"A pretty wench like you," he said wickedly, "could get herself into a heap of trouble talking too much." Lexie giggled. Steel motioned with his head and she slid out of the room. He locked the door behind him and dropped the key in his pocket. Lexie watched him as he swung down the narrow, bare stairs. He moved lightly and quickly for so large a man. She heard the door that let him out on Cherry Street slam behind him.

Outside, by force of habit, Matthew Steel looked up at the sky appraisingly and took a deep breath. Through the dusk he could see low clouds scudding eastward, a good wind, he thought, and promise of a fair day ahead. But the odors of Cherry Street weighted the breeze that struck his face. The wind carried the odor of the New York waterfront, two blocks to the south, the smell of old timbers rotting in East River, of mud and sewage and crowded ships and wet ropes, of high-piled, bamboo-wrapped cargoes on the wharves. It scooped up a little dust and dried horse-dung from the crowded streets, was thickened with the rank smell of clogged gutters. It gathered up the boarding-house scents of pungent foods cooking, scallions and cabbage and beef and mutton, of steam and a little smoke, and stirred it with the sour stench of cheap liquor and old, untended buildings. It was lightened only by the clean fresh fragrance of new lumber in the lumber yard directly across the street from Mrs. Doughty's. It all blended into the familiar Cherry Street smell, and Matthew Steel's nostrils flared a little, repelling it.

He turned to his right, toward Market Street, walking in long, easy strides, erect and alert, a magnificent young giant of a man who knew where he was going. He knew Cherry Street well. It had changed little in the fourteen years since he had first seen it. It still drained its livelihood from the waterfront. There were a few business establishments, like the lumber yard, which contributed their products to the shipyards. But mostly the places existed by feeding on the needs, the weaknesses, the vices of the men who sailed the ships and worked the cargoes.

He passed a store front on which was painted in large gold letters "Segars," and then there was Rebecca Lachman's boarding house. A servant girl, almost indistinguishable from Lexie, came from the Lachman establishment as he passed, carried a slop bucket to the street and emptied it into the gutter. With the approach of darkness Cherry Street was awakening. Down flights of rickety stairs, behind dirty windows, lights were beginning to show in cellar dives; there was a woman's shrill laugh from a bagnio on the corner and traffic had thickened on Market Street.

Drays were returning from the waterfront, empty. Drivers shouted at one another in greeting, whips cracked, harness and wheels creaked and the teamsters leered insolently at pedestrians waiting to cross. Steel kept walking and behind him a respectable gray-haired woman scurried, availing herself of his unwitting protection from horses and wheels. She smiled timidly and gratefully at him as she completed the crossing safely. Steel went on, never changing his gait, through the crowds.

All this day Steel's stomach muscles had been tight with nervous tension. He found himself gripping his gloved fist now and he deliberately forced himself to relax. Scarcely an hour away from the most important interview of his life, he must not betray his inner excitement. He must keep his wits and his senses sharp and under perfect control. He could afford no mistakes tonight.

Near the corner an old Irishman sat, sawing on a wheezing fiddle; beside him his mangy mongrel dog danced uncertainly on his hind legs. Steel looked at the pathetic, eager performer and the aged, hunched fiddler and dropped a coin into the beggar's cup. The old fellow smiled toothlessly, his pink, bare gums glistening, his face, with its stubble of white whiskers, breaking into a thousand wrinkles. A big Scandinavian sailor lurched toward them, stopped to cling to a lamppost for support, staring at them, unseeing, his eyes glazed, a trickle of saliva drawing a line from the corner of his loose mouth down his chin. Steel glanced from him to the panting dog and grinned.

"Drunk as a fiddler's bitch, eh, Old Dan?" he said. The old fiddler dropped his bow and cackled with mirth, bending double, his face hidden in his rags for an instant, only the sparse gray strings of his hair showing over his collar. He straightened again, eyes watery, empty, sunken old mouth working with delight. He pointed a shaking finger at the unsteady sailor and cackled again, overcome with merriment.

"Not since the ould country have I heard the likes a that!" he shrilled. His dog crowded against him and the old hand rubbed the animal's head in pleasure. "A gentleman and a wit ye are, sir! The blessings of Jasus and the Holy Mother—" He strained his weak eyes, peering at Steel, and then he slapped his thigh in surprise and delight. "By the living God, it's Matthew Steel himself and Ould Dan didn't know ye! Back from the sea, again, are ye, son? From where ye come, this voyage?"

"Around the Horn, Old Dan, from San Francisco. We docked a week today, at the foot of Maiden Lane."

"And with coins in ye pocket—'s God's truth! Ye always was a one to put your hand to a dollar, Matthew Steel. I mind the time—"

"I'll see you soon again, Old Dan."

"God's peace on you, boy-o. And guard your money well—let no trull get her claws on 't!"

He cackled again and Steel passed on.

The women of the town were coming out after a day of sleep. They sauntered, eyes wary, they sat on the steps or in the windows, lewd, jaded, the muddy, unhealthy skin of their faces frankly painted. A girl in a scarlet dress and shining black boots leaned in an open doorway, posturing, watching Matthew Steel approach, her eyes speculative. As he passed her she fell into step beside him, smiling up at him in invitation. His eyes traveled over her, inch by inch, and he caught the heavy body odor, not hidden by her cheap perfume. He shook his head and went on. She dropped out of step, her lip curling, and went back to her doorway. The walk was more crowded now, and there were more lights from the windows of the boarding houses on both sides of the street; from the grogshops tucked among them came the hum of voices, doors opening and closing, the clink of bottles and mugs and glasses. An old bawd backed out of a doorway of a dimly lit den, screaming obscenities at someone within and a hairy longshoreman with a slant-eyed girl on his arm nodded briefly to Matthew Steel and moved aside a little to let him pass.

At Catharine Street Steel stopped. There were private carriages and hired cabs on Catharine Street, with fine horses, taking businessmen to the Brooklyn ferry. There would be carriages for hire at the ferry slip on South Street, at the foot of Catharine, at this hour, carriages released by the ship-owners, ship-builders, merchants and brokers and bankers, moneyed men who controlled the waterfront, going home to their great houses on Brooklyn Heights.

Matthew Steel turned down Catharine Street toward the ferry slip, watching for a carriage for hire, but a hand on his arm halted him. He glanced at the hand first, barely touching him, not restraining him, friendly, asking only his attention. He knew that touch well. It was a slender hand and smooth. Before looking into the owner's face he said: "Hello, Tessa. On your way to work?"

"Yes, Matthew Steel," Tessa Dunn answered. "You are dressed so fine. I hardly knew you."

Tessa's voice was very deep for a girl's and she spoke lazily, as though she had all the time in the world. She was a tall girl and slight. Her face, upturned to Steel's, was a perfect oval, the skin white and flawless, the cheeks hollowed ever so little. Her eyes, more green than blue, seeemed small, for they were always half-closed, sleepily, guarded by heavy, shining lashes. Her mouth was sensuous, not pretty; the lower lip too full, giving her a permanent pout, half-sullen, half-scornful. But the most striking thing about Tessa Dunn was her hair. It was flame-colored, rippling, curling, and pins and combs would never stay fast in its crackling aliveness for long. She wore no head covering now and in the dusk her hair glittered. Tessa was not a pretty girl but she was a conspicuous one, and there was facination in her slow, flowing grace. She was perhaps twenty years old, but her assurance, her cool defiance, was that of a much older woman. There was no girlish gaiety or childish innocence in Tessa's face or manner, nor any sign that there had ever been; only brooding, moody, lazy disinterest. Those who saw Tessa Dunn felt instinctively that burning hate, murderous rage and acid bitterness were no strangers to her; but happiness and tenderness could make her a rare beauty.

She dropped her hand now. She did not ask Matthew where he was going. She was sparing, always, with her words. She smiled a little, her slow, amused, secret smile, taking in his smoothshaven face, his starched shirt front, the well-fitting coat, his gloved hands.

"Good luck, Matthew Steel."

She started to move away but Matthew caught her wrist. He drew her back out of the sidewalk crowds, close to a store front. He did not release her.

"Why did you say that, Tessa?" His eyes were searching her face. She laughed shortly, half teasingly, and shrugged slightly. His grip on her wrist tightened. She made no move to free herself.

"No reason. I just thought—you must be on an errand of some importance. You are dressed for the Astor House Bar—or Fifth Avenue, perhaps. Not South Street and the Cock and Bull."

"Go on," he said.

She lifted her eyebrows slightly and laughed again, fearlessly. "Don't be so harsh with me, Matthew Steel," she said coolly. "I know nothing. I only guess."

"And you guess what?" His voice was very low.

Her glance flicked around the sidewalk crowds and her voice dropped almost to a whisper. She swayed toward him, her lips close to his chin, her eyes on his face.

"Your errand tonight. It might have something to do with the ship that came last night to Brighton's repair yard—near Corlear's Hook?"

"You guess a great deal, Tessa Dunn." A grin played around

Steel's lips, and Tessa laughed again, triumphantly. "And why do you think that?"

"Oh-h, many reasons," she said vaguely. "Last night I watched you at the Cock and Bull while I was singing. The stevedore, Big Wayne, was at the bar beside you and you talked, and after a while you took a table together. You were deep in conversation —too deep to hear my song. And then you left."

"And what has that to do with the ship at Brighton's?"

"Big Wayne did not leave as early as you. We talked."

Steel dropped her wrist. He had found out what he wanted to know and his laugh had relief in it and admiration. "You are smart, Tessa Dunn. You were always one to ferret out my plans. So it is not common talk along the waterfront?"

"No. I think no one but I—and Big Wayne—know that you are trying to buy that ship."

"And no one else must know tonight, Tessa." He looked about them again. The crowds moved on, glancing at the man and the red-haired girl with only passing interest. He tried to think of convincing words that would show her the need of secrecy. "Listen. South Street has never been so busy, nor so prosperous. The big companies—with more capital than I—" his white teeth flashed— "are buying anything that will float. Perhaps you know that." Tessa nodded. "And what they do not buy the foreigners do—the British and the French and the Russians. The Russian Navy is bottled up in her own ports, and it takes plenty of British ships to keep them there. It is hard now, damned near impossible, to get a ship, Tessa; yet times were never better for shipping and trading. It's harder still to get a ship as good as that one in Brighton's yards, and for a price. I won't have such a chance again, Tess. I want her—bad."

"You've seen her, then, and she is the one you want?"

"She's sorely damaged. She struck a rock outside Canton and was poorly repaired, and she's been bad used in a hard trip around the Horn. But she's built right and she's well-balanced, stout and fast. It will cost twelve thousand dollars at least, to make her fit to sail. But Tess, once she's overhauled and painted and her rigging blacked, she'll be as good as any—and better far than most!"

"And the first to carry the house flag of Matthew Steel?"

Matthew took a deep breath and grinned. "That's right, Tess. But the moneyed men will be after her by morning. As soon as South Street knows she is to be sold I'll be outbid. That means tomorrow, Tessa. She'll be sold for sure, before nightfall tomorrow. The owner, Captain Brenner, is mortal sick, and sick in heart as well. I routed him out of bed last night and made an offer. He gives me till noon tomorrow to raise the money. He's not been ashore yet. He doesn't know there's money to burn and offers a-plenty waiting him on South Street."

Tessa put her hand on his arm again and this time his closed over it warmly, joining them. Her voice was still a whisper.

"And where are you going to get the price, Matthew Steel? Big Wayne says it will take a fortune."

"Not a fortune, Tess, but enough. I have some. I picked up a little on the Barbary Coast. A faro table."

"With a woman dealer, no doubt." Tessa's eyes were narrow slits.

"A charming little Frenchwoman, to be exact. And then I doubled in on a bet—I put my money on a Yankee clipper over an English ship in a run from Good Hope to Java Head."

"And won, of course."

Tessa was laughing with him now, Steel's eagerness and excitement mirrored in her face.

"Yes, but not enough. The rest—you have heard of Thaddeus Blake?"

"And who has not?" Then her face sobered suddenly. "But Matthew—Blake himself has need of ships. He's in the cotton trade, rumor has it."

"He's a banker, Tessa, and has an interest in many ventures. But cotton shipping—are you sure?"

"That's the talk."

"Hm-m." Matthew frowned in thought. "At any rate, I've seen him once. I saw him early this morning, in his office. I did not tell him what ship I wished to buy, or where she lay, but I swore she was worth far more than the price. I gave him names of those who would tell him my character and my skill as seaman. I promised him good returns on a trip to San Francisco; no matter if the trade is falling off, it is still to be had! And laid a course thence to the China seas. It can't miss, Tessa! He listened, with interest, too. And he knows there is need for haste. We talked a long while. He gave me no answer then. But he asked me to meet with him again tonight, at seven o'clock, at his home. For dinner, he said, and afterwards we would discuss it further."

Tessa's eyes were proud and her lips were soft. "So you are going to the home of Thaddeus Blake as guest and equal. You are ready at last for your own command, Captain Steel?"

"I like the sound of that, Captain Steel. Wish me luck again, Tessa."

"Good luck, Captain Steel."

Her fingers gripped his briefly, firm and friendly as another man's and she moved away. Matthew watched her go, watching the gleaming mass of her hair, the slight sway of her hips, saw other men turn to stare after her. He had known Tessa Dunn since she was a hungry, bitter child. She stemmed from beginnings not unlike his own and she was and had always been of his world. He knew she meant it when she wished him luck. He was glad to have her good wishes go with him tonight, and she would guard his secret well. Odd, he thought, half-smiling, how it gave a woman pleasure to have a hand, however small, in a man's work. Matthew Steel was not one given to confidences, but he realized it had done him good to talk to Tessa. It had eased the tension within him a little, sharing it with someone, and of all those on South Street Tessa was the one whom he could trust.

He came to the intersection where Catharine Street ended in South Street, New York's waterfront, the street unlike any other, the street he knew and loved best in all the world. He watched the carriages discharging their passengers, and he glanced beyond them, up and down South Street. Yes, it was always the same, though it was busier and more crowded now than he had ever seen it; a great noisy wave of activity, a welter of color and movement, of shifting lights and hoarse voices, of pungent smells and harsh sounds, of poverty and wealth, of permanence and change. Its contrasts were its fascination.

One side of South Street was lined, as streets should be, in orthodox fashion with stores and warehouses, office buildings and gin palaces, small shops and coffee houses, and Matthew knew them all, both ways from Catharine Slip—the famous names of the shipowners, whose house flags were known in every major world port, and the obscure ones, too, the sailmakers, the tugboat owners, the hotel proprietors, the grocers, and ship chandlers, the fancy ladies, the sweating stevedores and the runners for the seamen's boarding houses and brothels.

Yes, he knew where to find Patrick Draddy, the junk dealer, and Mr. Lethbridge, the shipping merchant; Abraham Fardon, dealer in sail duck, and Mr. Tooker, the tailor. Mr. Oliver, who ran the best porter house on South Street, was quick to reach across the bar to shake his hand when he came back from every voyage, and Hite and Morton, owners of the Cock and Bull, welcomed him like a son. Cromwell, master carver, near Market Slip, was always ready to give him news of the waterfront. All of them were a part of South Street, the part that changed but little from year to year, their shops and offices walling the land side of the street.

But the other side of South Street did change, for it was fluid, walled only with ships, great ships, made temporarily fast in their berths in the East River, their great bowsprits pushed out over the strand as though they attempted to leave behind for a little while the vast loneliness of the seas and to crowd as closely as possible to the great pulsing city and the solid safe earth on which it stood. Their huge bulks, and above them the bare spars, like a burned-over forest, stretched along the street as far as a man—or a boy—could see.

The ships were there, always, but they changed in size and shape; the figureheads differed from day to day, and their flags, and the color of them, and their age and their newness; the little knots of immigrants who left the ships, hesitatingly, and gathered on the street beneath the bowsprits, alien and hopeful, were not the same groups from year to year, but upon them was an identical stamp. The cargoes piled on the wharves, tobacco from Virginia, rugs of Smyrna, sugar and molasses from the Barbados, coffee from Rio de Janeiro, teas from China, rum from Curacao, apples from the Hudson Valley—they were not the same, but the smells were as they had always been; and the straining backs of the stevedores, their grunts and short breaths of effort, were not different. The gangs of boys who threaded their way from one side of South Street to the other—from the permanent, safe, unchanging land side, to the fluctuating, moving side linked with the seas and other worlds beyond, were not the same lads, perhaps, but they had about them the same look of hungry eagerness and nimbleness and curiosity and desire.

Matthew Steel squared his shoulders. As it had always done, South Street made his heart beat faster. It was in his blood, like the love of a woman. The fascination of it gripped him, aroused him, strengthened him now for the interview that lay ahead.

Years ago Matthew Steel had pledged himself that one day he would be a power on South Street. Never, in all the time between, had he lost sight of that goal for a single instant. It was to that end that he had made friends with Patrick Draddy, with Abraham Fardon, with Mrs. Doughty, with Lethbridge and Cromwell and Oliver and Tooker, even with Old Dan, the fiddling beggar, and with Big Wayne, the stevedore, and already those friendships had aided him. Toward his goal he had done other things too, just as deliberate, just as calculated, for always, it seemed to him, the end would justify the means. He had paid with sweat, suffering and denial for meager wages in coin and greater experience. He had smashed his bare fists into men's faces, taken their blows on his own and on the hardened, trained muscles of his body, for a price. He had shared stinking forecastles with men of every age and race, brutal men, broken men, beasts and dreamers. He had learned navigation on a tramp trader, fast sailing on an opium smuggler; he had learned the various merits of white oak and locust and cedar as apprentice to a builder, and in the mold lofts he had pored over designs and he knew which ships would have speed and which would carry the greatest cargo. He had spent six months of land-locked labor in a counting house, learning about foreign exchange and duties and laws governing international trade; he knew, as only post graduates knew, that despite their materials and their designs some ships were erratic and undependable, and some would respond to one captain and not to another, and some ships were ill-fated and some sailed under a lucky star.

It seemed to Matthew Steel now that he had always been in a hurry, gulping experience and training, storing away information and tricks and solid knowledge, readying himself for this day when he would take a major step toward the position he had set for himself—master of South Street and the parasitical streets about it.

Yes, a new house flag would appear on South Street. It would become familiar in every corner of the globe. The crowds of tattered urchins who ducked like cats beneath the cargo slings, who followed the masters of the sailing vessels to swinging saloon doors, would trail after the greatest master of them all—Matthew Steel. Shipping notices would list the record runs of Steel's vessels, and his name would be listed with the aristocracy of the United States' greatest ports, in equal rank with the Beekmans, the Setons, the De Peysters and Ludlows.

Matthew Steel brought his attention back to the present merchant dictators of the waterfront, alighting from their carriages and dismissing the drivers. These men had built their homes in Brooklyn, overlooking the traffic of the East River. Others like them had built in Washington Square, and in the newer area above it. The greatest fortunes of all New York had been made on the waterfront. Others would be made there as well, though competition was keener and profits less than in past decades. But it could be done. Matthew Steel would be one of the wealthy. He would be, in time, the most powerful of them all.

The carriages, empty of fares, were moving back up Catharine Street and draymen shouted and swore and argued with the coachmen at the intersection. A carriage drew up to the walk in response to Matthew's summons. He stepped inside it. It was a mile and a half, perhaps, or a little more, from South Street to the home of Thaddeus Blake. But, Matthew thought, it was, in reality, much farther than that. It took years, and money and power, truly to bridge that distance.

He leaned back against the cushions and took a deep breath and his chin firmed as it always did, unconsciously, when Matthew Steel was going into battle.

"Fifth Avenue and Fourteenth Street," he said.

[2]

THE driver had a large, red face, with a prominent nose, heavily veined, and he seemed too heavy for the light seat on which he perched. He eased his rig skillfully into the stream of traffic, and they moved up Catharine Street toward the Bowery. He glanced over his shoulder once at Matthew, inquisitive, about to speak, and then he seemed to think better of it and looked straight ahead. He held his whip at the proper angle, he drove smoothly; but the lapels of his green coat, once part of a handsome livery, were spotted with food droppings, and the two lower buttons of his waistcoat were unfastened for further comfort over his swelling stomach.

They left Catharine Street and were passing the Bowery Theater when the driver glanced over his shoulder at his fare again. Matthew was deep in thought and did not notice. He was thinking about Tessa Dunn's statement that Thaddeus Blake was himself in need of ships. Thaddeus Blake had probably not been idle this afternoon, since his first meeting with Matthew Steel. It was not unlikely that the banker had his men scouring the waterfront, trying to locate the vessel Steel said he could buy. Thaddeus Blake, for all his conservatism and excellent reputation, was not one to pass up good and legitimate opportunities for profit.

Blake had made several smooth efforts during their first talk to learn the whereabouts of the vessel and Steel had parried them with equal smoothness. They had understood each other perfectly.

Now Steel began to wonder about his wisdom in appealing to Thaddeus Blake. For many years he had heard of him. He was said to have financed many South Street ventures, and to have an interest in numerous vessels. He was a staunch Whig, very highly respected, even among those whom he had bested in business, for they admitted that Blake was a wizard in finance and that he fought fairly.

Matthew Steel had found him courteous and impersonal. He had listened to Matthew's proposition without interruption, and then he had asked questions, pointed, direct and intelligent, without once tipping his own hand. Matthew admired him. His Wall

Street office was impressive, with thick carpets and heavy, well-rubbed furniture. Thaddeus Blake himself was impeccably dressed; he wore side-whiskers and his hair, thinning and brushed close to his fine head, was beginning to gray; a pince-nez on a fine ribbon about his neck rested on his waistcoat, which was edged with a fold of snowy white pique. But it did not give him the appearance of being a foppish man, nor a man interested in trifles; instead, he was distinguished, established; his eyes, of faded blue, were keen and they were also kind; his handshake was firm and warm.

Going back over every phase of their interview, Matthew Steel sought for a sign that would foretell Thaddeus Blake's decision. He had given him no encouragement in words, but he had asked him to come tonight for further discussion. Matthew did not believe it was Thaddeus Blake's custom to invite business acquaintances to his home for an evening's talk unless he had something to say, or they had something he wanted very much to hear.

He ran his finger around the inside of his collar, and hoped he would not start sweating so it would go limp and he would face the banker red-faced and moist as a schoolboy. He had not been awed by Blake's surroundings today, nor by the man himself, for he had his mind on the business at hand. But meeting him in his home was a little different matter. There were the social amenities to be observed, and while Steel was adept enough in a business interview, at thrust and parry, or in a rough-and-tumble scramble for business, he was not so sure of himself in a banker's home across a dinner table. He wondered if Blake had intended to throw him off guard; but, searching his memory again, he could not recall any malice in the banker's words or manner. In fact, he realized that with true natural courtesy Blake had put him immediately at ease. It must mean that he was interested in Steel's proposition.

It was a good one, too, for both the banker and himself, Matthew thought, encouraged. He had asked for $30,000, half the cost of the ship plus her repairs. The ship itself was worth much more on today's market than the asking price of $40,000. But Steel had not offered an interest in the ship and the outcome of its trading ventures. He had asked for an outright loan with the ship as security, or nothing. He wanted no strings on him, when he put to sea on his own. He wanted no landsman governing his schedules or his cargoes. He intended to snatch cargoes out from under the noses of other shipping men simply by fast sailing; time was the most important commodity of the day, and a day or so sliced from an ocean crossing meant the difference between profit and loss.

He could command higher freight rates with a faster ship. He'd take his chances on securing cargoes, once he had a ship like the one in Brighton's yards, that could streak her way along the sea-lanes faster than the next one. He was willing any time to sacrifice cargo space for speed, and he knew that he could safely crowd on more sail than less daring, less skillful seamen. But he must be free so he alone could dictate the routes and schedules, so he could bargain and compete on cargoes and freight rates, so he alone could pick his crew.

He let his thoughts jump ahead. Suppose he owned the ship. The next job would be to put her into shape to sail, and then to pick his men. He would defy South Street custom when he hand-picked his men. He would not rely on any runner to supply his crews for him, a drunken, drugged lot, flung aboard at sailing time like so many cattle, at so much per head. It meant making enemies on South Street when he deliberately flaunted that well-established practice—vicious enemies, who would stop at nothing to destroy the man who invaded their tightly controlled, highly profitable business. Nevertheless, he'd prefer enemies in South Street's underworld to a mutinous, unskilled crew. He had to outsail and out-trade many rivals in his fight for cargoes and markets, if he were to survive and prosper. He knew the men he wanted, rugged, experienced, loyal men who would work with him as a unit. He would raid other crews to get them. But first he had to get his ship.

The driver cleared his throat and made up his mind to speak. Steel looked up. They were traveling very slowly, behind a horse-drawn car of the Harlem Railroad.

"Begging your pardon, sir, but it would not be the Thaddeus Blake residence to which you are going, by any chance?"

Matthew swore softly. Was everyone in New York watching him, sharing his efforts to buy the ship in Brighton's yards?

"And if I am?" he asked, curtly.

The driver chuckled. "I was just going to say, sir," he said slyly, "if you are the Blake's dinner guest tonight, then there is no need to hurry."

The driver's voice was deep, but it broke into a startling falsetto at the end of his speech and without warning. Matthew studied the back of his fat neck, frowning, and then a light of recognition broke over his face.

"Why do you say that?" he asked.

"Well, dinner at the Blakes' will be late tonight, sir." He was proud of his knowledge, and he cocked his eyebrow as he turned his face sideways to speak to Steel, but he kept his bleary eyes on the street ahead of him.

"You seem to know a great deal about the Blakes."

The driver chuckled again. He was a garrulous old gossip, Steel remembered, and he had also recently had a mug or two of ale to loose his tongue still more.

"Well, it's like this, sir. You see, I've known the Blakes for a long while. Just this afternoon I heard they were to have a dinner guest—a business acquaintance of Mr. Blake, so I heard tell." He spoke mysteriously, savoring his knowledge. "But the fact is, the young ones, they will be a little late for dinner. That is, Mr. Cass and Miss Loyalty. It would help them a mite, sir, if you was to be a little late yourself."

"Yes?"

"Mr. Cass—you don't know the young people, sir?"

"No."

"No harm in my telling you then, and might do them a bit of good! There are three, sir. Miss Serena, she's the oldest—ah, and a lovely girl she is, too—and then Mr. Cass. Charming young gentleman, quite a beau, very handsome you know, but he does love his drink, sir. He is high-spirited, don't you know, nothing vicious, because of course the whole family is quality—none better! Just likes his fun and pranks. And then there is Miss Loyalty. Ah, there's a one!" He shook his head in pleasure.

"And their mother?"

"There is no mother. More's the pity. Miss Serena, she is mistress of the house now their mother's gone, and has been these many years, and a lively house it is, too, with all the young people about. Miss Loyalty, beautiful as stars at midnight—only sixteen she is, but what a minx! Prettiest girl in all New York, I've heard many say, young and old, and the beaux she has! And does she lead them a merry chase. But Loyalty is a good name for her, for she is loyal to that rascal brother, Mr. Cass. Always helping him out of a jam and getting herself into them, too, and mind you, if she was a boy, she'd be worse than Cass himself with her love of fun and deviltry. Spoiled, I suppose you might say, for she has a way of getting everything she wants—and who could deny her? But for all her spirit she is innocent and sweet as a babe in arms."

Steel bent forward, clasping his hands between his knees. This was unexpected information about the household into which he was going and he sought in it something which might be of value to him. He had not considered Blake's family. He had supposed the banker and perhaps his wife, probably a quiet, aristocratic woman, would be present at the evening meal. To enter a house full of young people was disturbing. He would have to watch his tongue and his manners, he thought wryly, with ladies present. His talk might lapse into terms fit only for the waterfront, and such a move might alienate Blake completely. He cursed again, softly. Why the devil could not business be kept in offices and on the streets where it belonged?

"So dinner will be late," he encouraged the driver.

"Yes, sir. You see, Mr. Blake sent word this afternoon there would be this dinner guest—you, sir." The man hooked his thumb over his thick shoulder. "And he said he would like especially for Mr. Cass to be on hand. He is trying to interest the young man in business, I believe, sir, but Mr. Cass is more interested in pretty girls." He laughed lewdly. "Hee, hee, hee! But along about four o'clock Mr. Cass had not come home. So Miss Loyalty slips out and sends a boy for me. She doesn't like to use their own carriages, you can understand that, sir, when she's on an errand of some secrecy, and she knows I am her friend. So she sends for me. I stable in Washington Mews."

Matthew nodded. His lips straightened. Washington Mews. It conjured up many memories, things he did not want to remember.

He glanced about him. They were passing the Eighth Street intersection and at the next corner the driver would turn west, toward Fifth Avenue, north of Washington Square. There were few carriages on Fourth Avenue now, but at the cross street the odor of livery stables was heavy and Matthew recognized the block in which the horses of the stage lines and Harlem Railroad were housed. Pigs were rooting in the gutter, hunting out garbage thrown there by the housewives in the poor tenements that lined the railroad street.

As they started to turn the corner on Ninth Street a boy darted in front of them and the driver stood and jerked up his horse. He cursed in anger but the child did not look at him. The boy was chasing some chickens and the fowl flapped beneath the horse's hoofs as the driver shouted. They freed themselves finally and boy and birds disappeared back into an alley as quickly as they had come. The carriage moved on slowly, along Ninth Street and toward Broadway and University Place.

Matthew sucked his breath through his teeth. It had been a long time since he had been in this neighborhood. He had vowed once he would never come back. The boy chasing the chickens, the pigs in the gutter, the smell of the stable blocks, were too familiar, and they touched a chord that had long been still.

They crossed Broadway. Off to his left would be the Episcopal Church, he thought, near Clinton Place. University Place was just ahead. He could have clicked off the names down that street as well as he could those on South Street, and he was surprised that they all came back to him so clearly. Frederick Roe, stables, at Number Two. The Union Theological Seminary. Nearer Washington Square was Mr. H. F. Ketchum, dealer in liquors, and Mary Meekers' school, and Ann Day's. Down there was where Mr. Cranch, an artist, had lived, and a cabinet maker—what was his name? And Edward Dannum, the barber.

He passed his hand over his face. He did not want to remember. He wanted to look ahead, to tomorrow, next week, next year, not backwards, ever again.

"So Miss Loyalty sent for you," he prompted the driver.

"Indeed she did. And we went downtown and first she sent

me into the Astor House and Mr. Cass was not there. She was nervous, because of course ladies do not go below Canal Street unescorted—expecially after four o'clock. Then we tried the New York Hotel. No sign of Mr. Cass. Miss Loyalty was furious, I tell you. So then we started on the places south of Washington Square, and I found him, finally, in the House of Lords on Houston Street. He was in a sorry state!"

"And you got him home all right—but not without a stop on the way?" Steel said dryly.

"We did not stop on the way, sir. Miss Loyalty would have none of that! We took him home and turned him over to the butler at the servants' entrance, and he will put him in shape for dinner. Last I saw of Miss Loyalty was the swish of her skirts as she ran in the back entrance, and up the back stairs straight to her room, no doubt! Henry Austin, the one of her squires most in her favor, is also to be a guest tonight, and Miss Loyalty does not like to dress in haste. But it was quite late, then—we barely arrived before the master! I took a fare to the Catharine Ferry then, sir, and that is where I picked you up—so you see it has not been long. Mr. Cass always scolds his sister for sending for him, but if she did not fetch him, sir, there'd be the devil to pay! Miss Loyalty is very fond of her father, same as she is of Mr. Cass, and she hates for there to be trouble between them, nor does she wish to worry Miss Serena. Not that Mr. Cass is always in his cups, mind you, as I say, they are quality, but he just has himself a bit of fun. But that is why I say it is apt to be a little past the regular hour, sir. You, being young yourself, might understand, sir—all a prank, you know."

They turned on Fifth Avenue. The horse's hoofs rang against the clean, heavy Belgian paving blocks. Upper Fifth Avenue had changed a good deal since Matthew Steel had seen it last. There had been no houses above Ninth Street then, but now it was built up, to Fourteenth and even beyond, great houses of varying shades and styles, of light marble, of sandstone, redstone, brownstone and brick, Colonial houses, Victorian houses, some with turrets and some square, dignified blocks, all of them huge, imposing and still. There was not a shop as far as one could see on Fifth Avenue, not even a greengrocer's. The street was wide and clean, and it was bordered with elms and ailanthus trees. A lamp-lighter was making his rounds, coming toward them, and a policeman, swinging his unlighted lantern, paced leisurely, his leather helmet pushed far back on his head. The air was fresh and clear and only a few carriages marred the pleasant, empty, spacious orderliness of the street. A victoria met and passed them; it was drawn by a pair of handsome bright bays. Their coats shone like satin and the silver trappings on their harness glittered. The white buckskin breeches of the coachman gleamed in the lamp light; the footman beside him glanced without recognition at the hired carriage in which Matthew Steel rode. They flashed past, and were gone.

"That's the Austin carriage, sir," the driver volunteered. "One of them." The carriage slowed and stopped. "This is the Blake house, sir." There was respect in the driver's tone.

The mansion was of light-colored stone and from its upper windows soft lights gleamed. The lower windows, recessed and barred, castle-like, in thick walls, were discreetly shaded from the street with heavy hangings.

Steel stepped to the walk and looked up at the solid, rectangular block of Blake's home. It looked substantial, impregnable, as firmly secure as its master. Steel glanced up at the doorbell handle, protruding from the side of the door frame at the wide entrance. In a minute he would mount the steps and pull it. He knew exactly what would happen. He could almost hear it now, the great jangling in the servants' quarters. There, along with the front doorbell, a row of brass bells would hang high up on springs on the wall and a maid, or cook or butler would watch to see which bell was ringing, and then one of them would run to answer.

Memories swept over Matthew Steel as he stood and looked at the doorbell handle, and he wondered for an instant if he could force himself to pull it, to start that harsh, demanding summons down in the servants' quarters. But he must not forget why he was here. He must not allow sour, sick memories to interfere with his mission. He brought his mind back to the business at hand, forcibly. The driver was waiting. Matthew reached in his pocket for money and he handed it to the old fellow and faced him squarely. Light from a street lamp fell on Matthew Steel's face.

"You always did talk too damned much, Bennett," he said coolly. He turned away and mounted the steps and deliberately he reached for the bell pull.

Behind him the driver held his hat in his hands, crushing it, his eyes protruding, his mouth hanging loose. He saw the heavy door open. A butler in full livery stepped quickly aside and Matthew Steel strode within.

Bennett still stood, unable for a minute to clamber back upon the box.

"Jesus, Joseph and Mary!" he said wonderingly. He gathered up the reins and began his cumbersome ascent. "Jesus, Joseph and Mary," he repeated, as he turned his carriage in the middle of the street. "That's Mary Steel's son!"

[3]

MATTHEW STEEL was born in a dank, unaired, ugly room in a tenement in Five Points, the foulest slum of New York. The building stood near the intersection, where Worth, Baxter and Pearl Streets came together, almost in the shadow of the prison itself, and the noise and grind of the great city came clearly through the thin old walls to Mary Steel, awaiting the birth of her son.

Mary, nineteen, recently widowed and penniless, had stepped ashore on South Street just a few hours before Matthew's birth. She had come from Valencia, Ireland, aboard the immigrant packet, *Ocean Queen,* with only a little oatmeal and a tiny packet of rice tucked in her bundle to sustain her on the four-week ocean crossing. It had been her plan and that of her husband, a gay, husky young Scotch seaman, that their child should be born in America. And when Matthew's father was knifed in the back, murdered for the money he carried which was to pay for Mary's passage to the promised land of the United States, Mary determined that she would still carry out their plans. She had no money. But she persuaded Captain Carter of the *Ocean Queen* to grant her the privilege he gave many male immigrants—to take her to New York and to permit her to pay for her passage with money she earned after her arrival.

That same indomitable spirit which had brought impoverished, grief-striken Mary Steel across the stormy Atlantic in the ancient, rickety *Ocean Queen*, in a stubborn effort for a new and better life for her son, took her quickly out of Five Points. Famine had lain like a blight over all Ireland and the new land looked to Mary —as it did to hundreds of abused and downtrodden and hungry immigrants—like all the promises of plenty of which she had heard and dreamed. It was Mary's earnestness and persistence that found her a place almost immediately as a domestic, for she was determined also to keep her son with her. Strange this country might be; unfamiliar and unfriendly were many of the faces in the employment bureaus she visited, and harsh was the unsolicited advice that petulant, prospective employers gave to her. But Mary's ramrod-straight back and the polite firmness in her lovely, rich Irish voice finally convinced them. Mary Steel would not give up her child and Mary would work.

And so Matthew Steel's first memories were of Washington Mews. It was often not yet light when a sharp rap on the door roused Mary Steel from her short sleep and she hurried to dress before the cold of their cellar room crept clear through to her bones. The room was below stairs in one of Washington Square's finest mansions, but there was no heat until they emerged to the servants' dining room. Sometimes Matthew, his face raw and smarting from the cold water which Mary splashed on him from the china pitcher in their room, slipped silently into a corner of the big kitchen, hungrier for the warmth of the glowing stoves than he was for food. But as soon as he was fed he knew he must leave the house by the back entrance and go to the stables.

Mary would keep one eye on him while she arranged breakfast trays, her starched skirts swishing as she hurried about the kitchen, one eye on the bells near the ceiling. First one and then another would ring and Mary would run at their bidding, her neat black shoes making a quick little patter on the long stairs. Sometimes when she returned her face would be drawn with worry and weariness, for Mary was never truly rested; or her lips would be a tight, straight line and she would speak seldom all that day. Then Matthew knew that someone above stairs in the rich warm beauty of the great house had spoken petulantly or harshly to his mother and resentment smoldered within him. Mary grew thinner through the years, but her hands, bony as they were, were gentle whenever they touched Matthew, and there was strength in them. She had no time to stop to caress him, beyond running her hand over his dark head, but her eyes and her voice were warm for him, and the pleasure of it went with him as he left the kitchen. He would go out into the chill, unpleasant morning and idle a little on his way to the stables. Once there, even when he was very small, he would find himself at once with a chamois in his hand, and he would begin mechanically to polish the side of a gleaming brougham. He rubbed till he could see his reflection, a serious child with direct dark eyes, a firm-chinned youngster with a promise of height and strength.

Matthew's hands would chap and crack as he worked in the cold. With brushes or flat sticks he scraped mud from the wheels of the carriages and he hated it, thick and odorous with street filth. He watched the wagons come and haul away the straw and refuse from the stables, dogs running between the wheels, chickens squawking stupidly in their path. He listened to the talk of footmen and coachmen, grooms and stable boys, but he spoke little. He polished silver buckles as he was told and shined the carriages and sometimes, when his hands were clean enough, removed the small velvet cushions from the floors of the victorias and dusted them, then put them back carefully in their proper positions, waiting for a lady's slippers. The cushions were tiny and soft and they matched the tan or green or maroon trimmings of the carriages and he thought they were very beautiful. Once he tried to fold a lap robe in neat creases and it was too big for him and it dragged in the dust. The footman, Dunlap, fetched him a blow that tossed him halfway across the stable floor and made his ear ring for hours after.

The Follett family coachman was Bennett, properly obese and

pompous. He had a great fondness for Mary Steel, but it did not extend to her son. Mary would have none of him, though it was said that Bennett had actually proposed marriage to her in spite of the boy and was truly hurt at her refusal. Bennett wore a buff livery; his high black boots had a four-inch cuff and sometimes when he came in he sat down carefully so as not to split his tight trousers and tossed the boots to Matthew to polish. Then Bennett would take off his high collar and loose his cravat and sit panting for a moment, red-faced. He would fan himself with his high silk hat and talk to Dunlap about their duties or about the horses of other owners, and comment slightingly on the liveries and the demeanor of other coachmen. Sometimes apprentices came to Bennett for instruction, and Matthew, slowly rubbing a breast chain, would watch Bennett show them how to hold the whip, exactly two feet from the butt, which would rest on his right leg.

The carriages of all the mansions of Washington Square stabled in Washington Mews and some public carriages as well. The drivers of the vehicles for hire were looked down upon by the men who were engaged by wealthy families. Their rigs were not expensive and often shabbily kept and the drivers grew careless of their own appearance. Sometimes Bennett, thirsty and sighing, would say he envied the men who worked only when they were in the mood and were not at the beck and call of a large family. But Matthew knew that Bennett was jealously proud of his position and held in greatest respect the pomp and ceremony of his calling. It was a symbol, he explained to Matthew, of elegance and quality. There were rigid rules and customs governing a superior coachman, and a man had to be bred to it or train for it from childhood like any other first-class craftsman.

Matthew was eight years old when he began to disappear, silently, from Washington Mews, for short intervals. Bennett started him. Bennett had a thirst and he would send the boy to the liquor dealers, or to the back door of a saloon for a bucket of beer, and Matthew learned to take his time in coming back. Finally he did not wait to be sent on an errand. He learned to hurry with his work and then to disappear, returning only when the carriages would be coming in at evening and his absence noted.

At first he wandered only about the square. Sometimes he saw coachmen and footmen whom he knew, but when they were on the box they never recognized him; they faced straight ahead, though their eyes roved. Bennett sat like a squat toad, balancing his hat squarely, his red face uncomfortable above the stiff collar. Dunlap would run lightly to the doorway and ring the bell and wait for the ladies and gentlemen to appear. He would help them into the carriage, arrange the velvet cushions for their feet so only the very tips of the ladies' slippers showed; he would place the robe reverently across their knees and then he would leap nimbly up beside Bennett, and, like a wooden soldier, stare ahead while Bennett took over and started the carriage with never a jerk nor jostle. Matthew, small and unnoticed, watched them, and his lip curled. In the stables they were different beings. He began to wonder why they must always jump to the bidding of their employers. He began to resent and finally to hate violently the tinkling bells in the kitchen that were absolute dictators over every waking hour of his mother.

He wandered a little farther than Washington Square and he met other boys homeless and curious and uncontrolled. Then one day he found suddenly that his wanderings were circumscribed, not by Mary, who was too busy to notice, nor by the men in the stables, but by a gang of other boys who ruled the district south of Washington Square.

It was a spring day, a bright and golden day with the promise of summer and a still sharp breeze, remnant of the winter just past, a perfect day for exploring and adventuring. Matthew had drifted as far as Houston Street, reveling in his freedom, pleased to escape the confines of smelly, narrow Washington Mews. Houston Street was a street of saloons and except to a small boy there was little of absorbing interest about it. Yet Matthew liked the activity, the noise, the crowds who passed him and let him go, unnoticed. But at the corner of Mercer Street he found his path blocked by another boy.

The youth was older and larger than Matthew Steel and he stood squarely in Matthew's path, his chin jutting, his nostrils flaring, and behind him were two of his followers, eyes bright with anticipation. Matthew, uncertain, started to move around him but the boy stepped quickly before him.

In the sharp exchange of words that followed, Matthew learned that the boy's name was Mike Globinsky; that he was head of the gang that roamed Houston Street south to Canal Street, a good half mile; that no boys from other districts entered his area without his permission or unless they could best him in battle. Matthew Steel was herded into an alley and he got his first lesson in street fighting.

Matthew was whipped. It was his first and last defeat.

Deliberately he learned to use his fists. He practiced with stable boys, and he fought, too, at the public school which Mary insisted he attend. And a year to the day from his first fight he met Mike again. It was a short, sharp, bitter engagement. But after it Matthew could roam Mike's territory at will.

And then, at ten, too old for his years, he fought his way through to South Street, New York's street of ships. It seemed to him it was the place for which he had always searched.

He did not stop now at the prison or Five Points or City Hall Park. As soon as he was free he hurried straight for the water front. All the pageantry and excitement of a twenty-four hour show were there, all the adventure and color a boy could hope for. He took it by slow bits at first, racing as fast as he could to the Astor House, down narrow Ann Street, into Fulton, and then as he came to South Street his steps slowed and he savored it all with delight.

At first it seemed to him a carnival of confusion and activity. There were smartly uniformed men whom he was later to recognize as seamen from the British mail brigs. There were longshoremen, grouped together at various spots on the broken sidewalk, kneeling about a dice game, waiting to be summoned to work. There were spruce, sharp-eyed, baize-coated men, small and quick as ferrets, whom he later recognized as scalpers for the tow companies. There were frock-coated men in and out of the Tontine Coffee House, their faces creased, absorbed masks of concentration, whom he came to identify as executives in the sailing-packet lines. There were boys no older than himself, petty thieves who harassed shippers and exasperated the police by stealing small articles from cargo shipments on the wharves. There were shifty-eyed men, lounging against the brick fronts of the great warehouses, eyeing passers-by speculatively, later identified for him as procurers for the side-street bagnios catering to deepwater sailors.

But the ships themselves were enough to make a boy's heart swell to bursting. There were foreign ships with foreign flags, from which immigrants disembarked. There were the smart British brigs that sailed with passengers and cargo by way of Halifax and Bermuda, and the names rang sweetly in Matthew's ears. Smartest of all were the American packets, bluff-bowed, but still more audacious, more jaunty and light-hearted, he thought, than the British ships; they carried gold and silver shipments to Liverpool and Havre and to the boy they were treasure ships, themselves gilded with excitement and adventure. He learned to recognize the coasting vessels, and the names of the cotton ports—Charleston, Savannah, Mobile—were round and smooth to roll upon his tongue.

Once a Baltimore clipper came in to a South Street pier; she was the first he had ever seen, and she was breath-takingly beautiful beside the tiny, busy, officious, puffing tugboats that accompanied her. Matthew's heart fairly stopped when he saw her. Her bowsprit thrust out farther over the quay than any other and with her clean, sharp lines she was the aristocrat of all seagoing craft in the world. He liked to wander down the strand, just to look at the printing on the cargoes themselves, great bales of cotton, seeming to him still to carry the warmth of the southland; coffee and fruits, bearing the addresses of New York's biggest merchants; and outgoing cargoes, turpentine and new lumber. There were spices then, and rum, and once he followed a seaman who carried a sea-chest on his shoulder. The man was just back from a China voyage and in a grogshop back room he opened the chest and Matthew saw lacquers and porcelains, silks and jade.

Anything could happen on South Street. A man of the sea was not confined to stationary streets and walks, to little districts ruled jealously by small tyrants. A man of the sea had all the world to roam in.

After a while he began to make some order of the seeming confusion of the waterfront. He learned at which slips the various ships docked, the coasting vessels, the foreign ships, the packets of the various lines. He knew the insignia on the fore topsails of the sailing packets and he knew their schedules, too, and whether they had a hard crossing or had made a record run. He loitered around the tow-company offices and on one memorable day he was allowed aboard and they puffed their way out to Sandy Hook. It was not all fun. The men aboard the vessel they met had grinned down at them, tiny and busy beside the big ocean-going craft, and laughed at a boat powered by steam instead of sail. In spite of his pleasure in the voyage, his first on water, Matthew Steel could understand their ridicule. There was something majestic and clean and noble about harnessing the winds which was lacking on the little steam-driven tugs. But he was proud of the part his tug played in shepherding the larger vessel safely into East River and, with a busy flourish, into her berth.

His speech was laced with the terms of seamen, he read the shipping notices and speculated about the length of the voyage around the Cape of Good Hope and into the Indian Ocean. He talked of Sunda Strait and Valparaiso and Smyrna.

Mary Steel, seeing his father in him, listened patiently to him talk of monsoons, typhoons, Nor'westers. He began to dream by day of ships and sea, over his slates and sums, and his school work went hard for him. But Mary told him of the counting houses, and the work of estimating tonnage and figuring freight rates—things quite beyond the ken of a woman, but not a boy and student such as Matthew. And so the dry columns of figures became the capacities of schooners and brigs, or the costs of transporting coffee and sugar, cranberries and wool. The first time he heard an anchor chantey when a ship docked he thought he would surely weep with delight and the tune rang in his head for days on end. He marched to it. In the stables he sang it to himself as he polished carriages and the sweeps of his arms became pulls on halyards and anchor ropes.

Sometimes he attended auctions on South Street near Wall; he knew the Custom House as well as he knew Washington Mews. He was quick to run errands and do small favors for sailing men. He followed ships' captains to the doors of the City Hotel, looking for a chance to do them a favor and receive their notice. Once he watched a fight between a first mate and a seaman, settling ashore a feud begun at sea, and when it was over he picked up a knife that had slid from the mate's belt and handed it to him.

The man said "Thank'ee, boy," and reached in his pocket for a coin, shoving the knife back in its place. The sweat was running in little trickles down his scarred, rugged face, and rents in his shirt revealed his powerful shoulders and swelling biceps. He held out a coin to Matthew but the boy clasped his hands behind his back and took a deep breath.

"Instead, sir, could you please let me go aboard the ship?"

So for the first time Matthew Steel set foot on the deck of an ocean-going vessel. He saw it all, the forecastle, even the galley; he was allowed to touch the wheel itself. His hands were eager, caressing, and he was lost in a new world. The very smell of the ship, the smooth, holystoned deck beneath his feet, the heavy, neatly coiled ropes, the lifeboats, suggesting unknown dangers, all seemed to him familiar and good.

He roamed the strand from the Battery to James Slip and on to Corlear's Hook. He knew the piers by number and by name, Whitehall, Exchange, Coenties. . . . He found it pleasurable to carry messages into the warehouse, and back to the wharves, and to watch the day-by-day progress of the ships a-building at William H. Webb's or Smith and Dimon's yards, growing, taking shape, to the rhythmic beat of mallets. He saw the deepwater vessels warped into the docks one day, moved to repair yards the next, and stripped and overhauled and painted and turned out again as good as new; he listened to the workmen: "She struck a sunken rock out of Foochow. . . . She took a heavy head-sea over the bow rounding the Horn." To Matthew Steel they were magic words, far out of the workaday world in which the rest of New York city moved, for the delicate odors of the cargoes hung over the vessels from the Orient and the scarred old hulls were mute evidence of a battle with the sea, a battle which the ship and good seamanship had won.

He was prowling one day, north of Market Slip, staring at the ship's instruments in the display windows, watching a little Maine lumberman making her way to a pier, thinking he might go to watch the woodcarvers at work on ship's figureheads, when he was deliberately shoved from the walk by a swaggering, sallow-faced boy. The boy had his fingers hooked in his belt and he used only his shoulders to push and he was grinning.

Matthew stepped back on the walk. The boy glanced over his shoulder and walked on. Matthew sized him up, running his tongue carefully over his lips and then he followed.

At the intersection of South Street and Market the boy stopped and looked back. It was a busy spot on South Street, and music from a concertina from a tavern on the corner came out to Matthew clearly. It might as well have been a bagpipe, urging his Scottish blood to battle.

"You," Matthew said, clearly. "Who do you think you are?"

The boy sneered. "I'm cabin boy aboard the *Monarch*. Who are you, wharf rat?"

Matthew's teeth came together, hard. "Nobody shoves me," he said.

The boy laughed. "I shove who I please," he answered. He took his hands out of his belt.

Two men standing in the doorway of the grogshop turned to look and one winked at the other. The boys were of a height but the cabin boy was heavier. One of the men, the shorter, stouter of the two, put his hand in his pocket.

"A dollar on the cabin boy," he said. His friend laughed.

"You'd have to give me odds," he answered.

"Two to one, then."

"Taken."

The cabin boy was raising his fists. Matthew's head was down. He stepped forward, quick as a cat. The boy feinted. Matthew's quick left landed and he crossed with his right, with the rhythmic, fast, powerful swing of a professional. He stood ready to resume the fight if the boy wanted more but the heavy hand of the law landed on his shoulder. He knew it well. He glanced around swiftly and noticed that a crowd had gathered; from the doorway of one of the few missions that faced South Street a dark-coated man was marching. Matthew smelled trouble. Fear that he would be banned from South Street, memories of the stories he had heard of orphanages into which roaming boys were placed, chilled him. But his opponent had picked himself up now and his face was twisted with rage and his fists went into action again. Matthew jerked away from the policeman's grasp, he dodged and ducked and awaited his chance. His fists worked like hammers and he put his weight behind each blow, aiming, calculatingly for the tender spots, taking blows harmlessly on his shoulders and chest, following every advantage. The boy went down on one knee and the hand was heavy again on Matthew's arm, this time not to be shaken off.

Only then did Matthew hear the cheers. He glanced about the ring of delighted faces and then up at the policeman and he said nothing. Keep your mouth shut, wait, he kept telling himself. Once the grip was relaxed he'd dive through the mob and disappear. He was poised, ready for it. He knew, somehow, that the people of South Street would close in after him, make pursuit unprofitable. The faces were unmistakably friendly. He was part of South Street. This was home.

His nose was bleeding a little and he wiped it on his sleeve. Unexpectedly a man's hearty voice spoke close to him and he looked up to see the two who had stood in the doorway of the grogshop at the beginning of the fight.

"Let him go, officer," one of the men was saying. "I'll be responsible." He was a thick-featured, jug-shaped man, in high good humor. The policeman, too, was grinning a little.

"Can't have street-fighting, you know, Hite," the officer mumbled good-naturedly.

"Come with me, boy," the man addressed as Hite said. Matthew saw something pass from Hite's hand to the policeman, and then he was hustled through the crowd toward the tavern.

In its dim interior he saw the sailor with the concertina and as he entered the musician struck up a lively tune again. Matthew began to feel better. The man called Hite was friendly enough. His companion, thin, razor-faced and sallow, followed them. Neither of the men looked like members of the Committee for Neglected and Vicious Children, and the black-coated man from the Mission had been lost in the crowd. The policeman was gone and the cabin boy; only Hite and his companion remained, looking down at Matthew. The thin one shoved a chair toward the boy and motioned to the bartender. He set a glass of ale before each of them.

"Do you good, boy, after a fight."

Matthew glanced at the tankard but he made no move to touch it. He had never seen a man whom drink improved. Nor was he used to getting something for nothing. He looked at the men suspiciously.

"Ever see a cock fight, boy?"

"Sure."

"What's your name?"

"Why?"

The men exchanged glances. "Smart lad, aren't you? Well, I'll tell you why. We like the way you fight. We need fighters. We run cock fights and other contests, around the waterfront. People pay to see them. We stage some matches for boys."

Matthew's eyes narrowed. He had watched grown men fight often enough when he was able to squirm his way close enough to the blocked-out square where the matches were held. They fought with bare fists and no rules that he could make out and sometimes they came out of it with their faces butchered, groggy and staggering.

"I don't fight for fun," he said, finally.

"Plenty of coins tossed to a good fighter," the short man suggested. Matthew looked at him guardedly. The thin man took a long drink of ale and set down the mug and smacked his lips.

"What's your name?" he asked again.

"Matthew Steel," the boy said, after consideration.

"Live around here?"

"Not far."

"How'd you like to fight tonight—another lad your size?"

"For money?"

"All the coins the crowd throws to you."

"How much do you think?"

"Some fighters, the good ones, pick up as much as a dollar a fight. Maybe more. Depends on how the crowd likes you."

"Where?"

"Cock and Bull. Near Fulton Street. We run the place."

"I know where that is," Matthew said.

"My name's Hite," the short man said. "His is Morton. Come around to the Cock and Bull about eight o'clock and ask the bartender for us. You can make yourself some money, boy." He looked at his companion and laughed. "And so can we."

"Where did you learn to fight, Steel?" Morton asked.

Matthew was silent. The men exchanged glances and nodded.

"Well, will you come or not?" Morton asked. Matthew stood up. He hiked up his trousers. For a dollar he would fight a battering ram, but he would not let Hite or Morton know that.

"I'll come," he said laconically, and left.

After that Matthew Steel appeared often in the back room of the Cock and Bull and in other waterfront taverns and warehouses, slugging his way to money and popularity. South Street gave him a welcome he had never known in any other place. It seemed to recognize him as one of its own. He picked up more money than most boys his age had ever seen and he counted it and saved it jealously. He had need of money and he intended to make a lot of it before he was through.

Not Wall Street, nor the City Hall, but South Street, to Matthew Steel, was the beating, throbbing heart of New York upon which all else was dependent. Slowly the idea grew in his mind. A man who was a power on South Street, who owned ships, who dealt in cargoes, who commanded crews of seamen, who owned warehouses, was a power in New York, in the world. South Street grew on him, permeated his blood, fascinated him so he loved it and yearned to master it all at the same time. He could see his own houseflag, flying at proud masts; he could see crowds of boys at his heels, he could see himself pointed out and admired, entering the Tontine Coffee House, the City Hotel, the Astor House, wined and dined and feted at the return of a voyage with a record crossing. He would puff on a cheroot, and tell how he had come home from China against a monsoon—

It was in 1842, in mid-winter, when Matthew was twelve years old and ships coming in to South Street were heavy and cumbersome and phantasmal with ice, that Mary Steel took ill. She said nothing but her step slowed a little and her voice was husky and her cough so frequent that the others in the household almost became used to it. She talked to Matthew, repeating again the story of his father and her crossing on the *Ocean Queen*, trying to tell him why she had come. She admonished him again to control his temper, to fight fair, and never to give up. He kept telling her that soon he would make enough money so she might rest, so she would have fine clothes and a house of her own. She urged him to tell her of South Street, and when he spoke of the immigrant packets she smiled.

But when Matthew came home one night and slipped into the great house to see his mother she was not there. A housemaid, her eyes wide with awe, told him. Mary Steel had simply crumpled, silent and unconscious. Mrs. Follett had ordered her removed to the Fever Hospital at once. Matthew ran for Dunlap but he could not find the footman. All the carriages had been put up for the night, for it was snowing. The boy began to walk then, never noticing the cold and the snow, half-running, half-stumbling, to Fourth Avenue. He found a lone carriage there with a driver he knew and the man took the boy to 26th Street, and then block after deserted block, where there was not even a wheel track in the new snow, toward the East River. The bulk of the Fever Hospital and the Alms House next it were only darker blotches in the gloom. Matthew entered the building; it was strange and silent, smelling of sickness and pestilence and death, and his stomach twisted and tightened with fear.

When he came out again he climbed back into the rig beside the waiting driver, quiet, seeming smaller than when he went in. They drove back to Washington Mews, and Matthew helped the man to unhitch the horses and rub the animals down. There was no need for words. The boy worked mechanically, his eyes staring. After he was through with his work, as payment for the long ride, he went to the room he shared with other stable boys and he picked up his blanket. He had an extra shirt, a jacket, a pair of trousers and a cap that Mary had knitted for him. He hesitated, thinking, going back over the possessions of Mary Steel in the cold little cellar room. There was nothing there of his mother's that he would take with him. He could not force himself to go into that room again, nor into the Follett house. He could not look at those gay, horrible tinkling bells which had drained her strength, nor feel the clammy, dank coldness of her room. His heart was as icy cold and numb as the ice on the streets, and tears that he could not shed crushed his throat and pressed behind his eyes. He knew what would happen to him if he stayed in Washington Mews. First an orphanage, and when he was old enough he would be sent inland, to an Illinois farm.

Matthew Steel tiptoed quietly down the stairs and out into the street. He was leaving Washington Mews for the last time. He slung his bundle over his back. He began to walk southward, keeping a wary eye out for the swinging lanterns of the police. He kept shoving back the words that kept repeating themselves in horrible monotony over and over to the rhythm of his feet on the snow, the words the woman at the hospital had said:

"Mary Steel died this morning. She had the fever and by orders of the officials she was buried tonight. They fear an epidemic and all fever victims . . ." She had spoken casually, without expression or compassion, not looking at the boy but at a little card she held in her hand.

Washington Mews was behind him, and Houston Street, and still he walked on. When at last he neared the waterfront he felt safer, and weariness and grief began to make his stomach churn; he went into an alley and was very sick and he leaned against a wall and took deep breaths of the cold, wet air that seemed to touch his very lungs with frost. He was shaking violently. The sounds of the waterfront at night, the music, the voices, the laughter, floated about him dimly. He felt darkness closing over him, his feet were slipping beneath him and he knew he was falling into the snow, slipping down, slowly, like a drunk.

He shook his head as he did in a fight to clear it after a stinging blow. Then he picked up his small bundle again and made his way to the Cock and Bull.

He walked through the barroom, past the musicians, saying nothing to the greetings of the dancehall girls, to the waiters and patrons who crowded the noisy, garish place thickly. He walked past the table where Hite and Morton sat, not seeing them. He went into the back room where he sometimes fought, deserted now and dark, except for slits of light that filtered through the cracks from the outer room. The music of "La Paloma" drifted in to him. He pulled two benches together and put his bundle upon them. He sat down, then, leaning his head upon his hands.

A week later Matthew Steel was a cabin boy on a ship bound for China.

[4]

MATTHEW STEEL stood in the entrance hall of the home of Thaddeus Blake and pulled off his gloves slowly. The hall was larger than his room at Mrs. Doughty's Boarding House for Seamen. It slashed deep into the big house and double doors opened off it at regular intervals along each side. It was high-ceilinged; the walls were of light-colored wood, beautifully grained and softly polished, and the floor was covered with a rich, ruby-red carpet. The rug shimmered like the folds of a lady's gown, shading from light to dark, and it was very thick and very soft beneath Matthew's feet. It stretched down the broad, long hall, and swept on up a wide, gently curving staircase.

The hall was pleasantly warm and despite its size the light and color and the few beautiful furnishings, evidence of Thaddeus Blake's widespread influence, made it friendly and gracious. There was a pleasant smell of comfort and luxury, a faint whiff of fine tobacco, perhaps the perfume of some girl who had just passed, and of burning wood from the fireplaces in adjoining rooms. The size of the entrance, the spacious, graceful staircase, the thickness of the carpets, the solidity of the wood paneling, and the immaculate, shining, gleaming order of it spoke wealth and security. A man would feel safe in a house like this, Matthew thought, surrounded by beauty. A proud house and at the same time a friendly place where a man could go and close the door behind him, shutting himself away from the rest of the world and its worries. Matthew was surprised to find himself thinking thus; it was the first time since childhood that he had thought much about owning a home. A house had seemed to him something to tie one to one place, more of a burden than a pleasure. But this house was different.

There was something else, slightly familiar, very pleasant; he sought for it and then he knew. Only a year ago he lay over for several weeks in St. Petersburg while his ship was being repaired. As usual when he was in a port he explored the city carefully, trying to find out all he could about it. He had sailed often with Russian sailors and he knew their language well, for he put his facility with foreign tongues to good and frequent use. He had many friends among the Russians and he liked and understood their hard-hitting, hard-drinking, literal trading. In St. Petersburg he had fallen in with some young naval officers, newly returned to Kronstadt and full of rumors of war to come in the Crimea. One of the men was young Segonov, whose home was in St. Petersburg, and he was delighted to find an American who spoke his language well. He took Matthew Steel home with him, and in that huge, merry household Steel had made friends.

The Segonov family was a very old one and their massive, rambling house was full of heavy silver and other family heirlooms, carpets and pictures, tapestries and icons, samovars, powder and snuff boxes, swords and sidearms. At table the entire family, from an aged, spirited grandmother down to small, mischievous children, had lined the heavily laden board and there was much good talk and laughter. Matthew Steel had a feeling that the Segonov family would go on for a long time in just that way, in the same house, with the same surroundings, regardless of war or panic or epidemic. It was unshakable, ancestral, and it was good to know there were families and homes like that some place in the world, though afterwards he was a little lonely, too. For the first time in America, in Thaddeus Blake's house, Matthew had that same feeling. It was warming to the heart of a man with no roots. A home like this would give a man confidence, Matthew thought. There was neither age nor tradition about many American families for the country itself was new, but there was quality, permanence, a solid, sure foundation about the Blake house, and Matthew Steel, his senses highly trained to catch the feeling of his surroundings, felt it at once.

The butler took his hat and gloves and led the way down the hall. The door to his left was open, and within firelight flickered over row after row of books, their leather bindings in brown and black and red. They went on and then the butler stepped back from a doorway and pronounced his name.

Blake came with hand outstretched. In his left hand he held a slender stemmed glass of a light golden wine. Behind him, leaning on the mantelpiece, was a tall young man, slightly built and light-complexioned, with a small blond mustache and a too-thin, sensitive face.

"Glad to see you again, Steel," Blake said easily. He turned to present his guest. "Henry Austin, Junior, son of an old friend of mine-attorney, of whom you may have heard. Henry is also reading law. We consider him one of the family. Matthew Steel, the young man I was telling you about."

The men shook hands and their eyes met. Austin was several years younger than Steel and his hand was narrow, but his handclasp was firm. He was at ease, very polished, his eyes frankly curious. He had an intelligent face, well-bred, but Matthew thought the mustache a boyish affectation which weakened it. This was the man who had arrived in the fine carriage they had met, the one Bennett said was beau to one of the Blake daughters. Apparently Thaddeus Blake approved of him, too. Matthew dropped his hand and turned his attention to Thaddeus Blake. Here was the man whom he had come to see.

"And my daughter, Serena," Blake was saying.

There was a faint rustle of silk at the doorway, a hint of a delicate perfume, and Serena Blake entered. She was a slender girl, tall and blond; she wore a white gown, modestly cut, almost too plain, and her hair was smooth, drawn back from her face and fastened in a heavy, gleaming roll on the back of her neck. There was a look of the Madonna about Serena, untouched and innocent; her wide brown eyes, flecked with gold, were soft and grave.

Matthew bowed over her hand. It was very small and very

smooth. It was easy to smile at Serena, for she had a wistful, little-girl quality about her as though she wanted very much for everyone to like her. Her answering smile broke across her face with all the delightful unexpectedness of a sudden beam of sunlight, transforming her, emphasizing the full sweetness of her mouth.

"We are glad to have you here, Mr. Steel," she said.

"It is a great privilege, Miss Blake." She turned to Austin and he, too, bowed over her hand. Steel accepted a glass of wine, waiting, replying briefly to Blake's questions, trying to orient himself to these new surroundings.

There were quick feet on the stairs, muffled by the carpet, and another young man entered the room. He bore a resemblance to Serena, but his hair was dark and curling and he had an almost olive skin. He was of medium height and expensively, almost foppishly dressed. He was newly shaven and a faint odor of lilac water about him might deceive one who did not know he had been in his cups only a few hours before. His eyes were slightly bloodshot; he had a likable, handsome face, an amused, disarming grin and he was holding himself very erect. Cass Blake, Matthew decided, was a light-hearted fellow, completely irresponsible, and undoubtedly he enjoyed his easy life to the full. He shook hands with Matthew and took a glass of wine and raised it, whimsically, to his father. The older Blake smiled at him a little grudgingly.

"Where's your sister, Cass?" the father asked. He glanced at a clock, slight annoyance on his face. He's as eager as I to have this over with and get down to business, Matthew thought.

"Coming, I think. Isn't she, Serena?" Cass's voice was innocent.

"She was to follow me at once, Father," Serena answered. She looked at Cass a little uneasily.

"You have just returned from a voyage, Mr. Steel?" Austin asked smoothly.

"A week since. From San Francisco." Matthew's quick ear caught the sound of running feet on the stairs—feet that slowed as they neared the doorway.

"Ah! And what is it like there now, with the gold-rush excitement dying—"

Austin's question broke off. He was facing the entrance and he seemed to forget, suddenly, what he was saying. Loyalty Blake, appearing without warning, was sensational enough to throw any man off guard. She stood in the doorway for an instant and all four men stared at her, delighted with the picture she made.

"My God, she's beautiful!" For a minute Matthew was afraid that he had spoken aloud. Austin put down his glass and went to meet her. Cass sipped his wine and a grin played about his lips. Serena smiled a little in relief. Thaddeus Blake looked at his lovely younger daughter and his face softened.

Loyalty Blake's eyes flicked first to Cass, questioningly, and then, reassured, to her father.

"I'm sorry I'm late, Father," she said sweetly. She smiled up at Austin. "Hello, Henry." She put her small hand on his arm and entered the room. She was like a flame in the dark, Matthew thought, and could go unnoticed just as easily. She was small and beautifully, exquisitely made. Her hair was as black and polished as a piece of satin; it was carefully imprisoned with small jeweled pins which held it back from her face, but the rippling, waving mass escaped in a pile of curls at the back of her head. Her skin was white as milk, a startling contrast to the black of her hair. Her cheeks were highly flushed and Matthew Steel smiled, thinking of the mad dash she must have made about her room in her hurry to dress, her running feet on the stairs, and then her demure, unhurried entrance into the drawing room, sure of her welcome and sure of her father's forgiveness for being late. Her eyes were gray and heavily lashed and her lips were red and full and sweet, perfectly molded. There was a dimple in one cheek, impish and lovable. Her gown, of gleaming, rustling, very fine raspberry-colored silk was made for her black-haired, white-skinned beauty. A black velvet ribbon ran through a lace edging about the low, square neckline, like a charcoal mark against her skin, and quite naturally it attracted Matthew's eye. Her small waist, above the flaring hoopskirts, was tightly laced and it also was encircled by a black ribbon which accented it becomingly. She certainly used no artificial padding to fill out her bodice, Matthew noticed appreciatively. It was impossible to fake that young and lovely line. The tip of a very small black satin slipper and a bit of the rosette that adorned it peeped from beneath the wide skirt.

Almost mature, Loyalty Blake had the attraction that only a woman both very sensuous and completely innocent can have. She was untouched, without a blemish, a protected, cherished bit of perfection, dangerously lovely. She was color and movement and light and gaiety, all youth and eagerness, as she came forward, her eyes sparkling, her hair shining, her small teeth gleaming as she smiled, irresistible, glittering beside the paler Serena, vital beside the lazy Cass.

Her knowing eyes rested on Matthew Steel and for an instant their glances crossed and then her long lashes lowered modestly. The sixteen-year-old beauty acknowledged her father's introduction, and then, in the midst of her bow, she deliberately glanced up at Matthew, sidewise, appraisingly, in daring invitation. Matthew caught himself in time and suppressed a grin. She was a born coquette. It came as naturally to her as breathing. She had a lovely hairline and a smooth forehead, he noted, looking down at her, and her black eyebrows were fairy-light brush strokes. He had a great desire to touch them, to run his finger over her smooth, rosy, dimpled cheek, to feel the velvet of her skin, to be sure that she was real. Her cheek would be warm and alive and her lips, parted a little, were fresh and a little moist.

He wanted to stand and stare at her but instead he let his eyes slide away from her, dismissing her. It was a difficult thing to do and he knew, instinctively, that he had, in less than a minute, their first minute of meeting, thereby infuriated Loyalty Blake.

As he looked away from her his eyes met Austin's and he was startled to see that that young man's face had reddened slightly with anger. So that is it, Steel thought wryly. Austin is jealous enough at this point to do murder. I'm doing well. I already have two enemies in the Blake household—Loyalty, for ignoring her smile; Austin, for receiving it. He finished his wine and turned to Thaddeus.

"A very fine Manzanilla sherry, sir," he said, and knew that Blake was pleased.

He was glad that dinner was announced almost immediately.

At the table he deliberately kept his eyes away from Loyalty Blake but he was nevertheless very conscious of her presence. Though apparently ignoring her he knew the candlelight was playing beautifully upon her face; she was outlined against the light wainscoting of the wall behind her and he memorized every line of her proud, small figure. Her hands, handling the heavy silver and delicate china, were very graceful and appealing. Matthew forced himself to pay close attention to Thaddeus, who attemped to draw Cass into the conversation. The talk roamed from the formation of the new Republican Party at Jackson, Michigan, to a discussion of the Know-Nothings, and then they covered the latest reports on the Crimean War. Austin quoted liberally from the *Liberator* and the *Tribune*. Matthew was led skillfully into an account of the countries he had visited and the talk was easy and pleasant. The food was excellent, but Matthew was hardly aware of what he ate. In the back of his mind he was resenting Henry Austin, so welcome and accepted in the Blake house. Austin was not the man for that madcap daughter, he thought. She needed a strong hand, someone who would teach her not to smile at every man she met. Some day some man would answer her invitation and would not give her a chance to withdraw it when the chase became exciting. It would teach her a good lesson. She was smoldering now and when he glanced casually past her to her brother he noticed she was pouting a little. It was a delightful pout and it amused him, but he had sense enough to be cautious. He was in no position for a flirtation with the daughter of Thaddeus Blake, delightful as it might be.

Only once did the talk become personal.

"Is your home in New York, Mr. Steel?" Serena asked.

"I was born here," he answered. "I have no family."

"What a pity!" Serena said with genuine concern. But Loyalty had glanced up and then dropped her eyes again and Steel was amused. Serena obviously was thinking of a family such as the Blakes. But to Loyalty, Matthew's reply meant that he was unmarried. He felt that he knew Loyalty Blake very well. He was quite sure he knew what she was thinking. She was smarting at his indifference and was plotting revenge.

The meal ended finally and Serena and Loyalty left the room. The men stood and Matthew watched Loyalty's pretty back. Her curls danced and her skirt rustled and he greatly admired the line tapering to her waist. He could sense her indignation, though she departed demurely; he believed, with a good deal of pleasure, that she would not drop the matter. Some way or other Loyalty Blake would make him pay for ignoring her.

Blake led the way to the library. The butler followed with coffee and a slender-necked decanter of Vanderlyn Madeira. Blake offered a chest of cigars and explained that the elder Austin was his legal adviser and his son was here at his invitation to hear their discussion. He began smoothly. He picked up the model of an extreme clipper and handed it to Steel.

Matthew stood with his back to the fire, holding the beautiful little ship in his hand, half-smiling, smoothing its glossy hull with a large finger.

"She's a beauty, all right," he said. Then he looked up. "But to me she'd be more beautiful after she came back from her first run, and had a few scars, maybe, scars that show she's seaworthy and disciplined and can take the storms and the heavy seas. Until a ship's been tried and knows her master she has only the beauty of a pretty virgin."

The men laughed. He handed the model back to Blake, dismissing it. He noticed that Austin had relaxed. He was looking at Steel in more friendly fashion now. Cass became more interested in Matthew Steel. Blake immediately moved into the business at hand.

"I've seen the ship, Steel, in Brighton's yards, owned by a Captain Brenner," he said bluntly. "She's all you say she is, according to the best advice I can get. I presume that is the one?" Matthew nodded, unsurprised. He waited. "I have also investigated your own abilities, through the men whose names you gave me this morning. They speak highly of you."

Still Matthew said nothing. Blake pushed a chair toward him and he sat down. Cass lounged in another chair in the shadows, listening. Blake sat easily, smoking, his face inscrutable, choosing his words carefully. Austin took a chair near the large desk, and now he fingered some papers lying beside a dispatch case on the desk's gleaming top.

"You've been away from New York much of this year?" Blake asked suddenly.

"Yes, sir. I was here about a week last spring and shipped out again."

"Then perhaps you are not aware that business has been very sluggish during the last six months. Politics—the Crimean War—" He waved his hand. "Partly reaction from the California gold rush, I suppose. Many factors. General unrest. All the riots the Know-Nothings are fomenting. I think we are in for a recession, perhaps one of long standing. If not an actual panic."

"That's possible," Matthew said, noncommittally.

"A year ago I'd have been inclined to gamble on your proposition."

Matthew leaned back in his chair. That meant that Blake was not so inclined now. Why, then, waste all this time? He had forgotten Loyalty now, forgotten his surroundings, and his mind began to work keenly, jumping ahead, marshaling his arguments. Perhaps he could still persuade the banker.

"There's as much money to be made this year as last, Mr. Blake," he said. "There are not the sensational profits on a San Francisco voyage that there were during '49 and '50, but they are still in need of cargoes—dry goods, hardware, food, boots—it's a growing town and it's a good and steady market for some time to come. The England-to-Australia run is busy and there's always a demand for Chinese silks."

Blake nodded thoughtfully. "That is right. But there is still the fact that trade is falling off, profits shrinking. Insurance rates are higher. Only last week a ship arrived from China and for the first time that I can remember a good clipper showed a loss on the voyage. Over-speculation. Then you take *The Challenge*— a disgraceful, infamous voyage!"

"Your pardon, sir, but I think they were both exceptions. The China vessel you mean—I know her; she was mishandled and the cargo badly chosen. As for *The Challenge*, she's a prime example of what happens when a good ship is supplied with a crew by a runner on South Street. They were a bad, mutinous lot, and I've seen unskilled and weak men who were just as dangerous to a ship's success as troublemakers. With my ship, sir, I intend to select my crew personally, each man for his job."

Blake looked at him sharply. "That's not been done on South Street for many a year—if ever. And good men are harder to find now than ever before."

"Nevertheless, I'll pick my own crew, sir. I know the men I want. They'll work for me."

Blake bit his lips, his eyes narrow and intent. The firelight shone on his fine, thoughtful face. "You would be taking a big chance, Steel, to antagonize those who supply crews. Perhaps you could manage it for one voyage—but what would happen on the next, if men are still more scarce? Young men have more opportunities now, railroading, inland shipping; they are going west to settle in greater numbers than ever before. Unless wages aboard ships are raised it will be increasingly difficult to get men to put to sea, for long voyages at any rate. And if wages are raised the profits are cut, and the margin of profit has shrunk enough without that."

"There will always be some men who will follow the sea, sir. And much depends on their treatment. Furthermore, the best seamen like to sail on a fast ship. They'll go to sea if they think they are going to make a record run, and if they get fair treatment, decent food and a good mate who treats them like human beings and not like cattle. A fast ship can get cargoes, sir, in any port, even in slow times. I've seen Yankee clippers take tea cargoes out of Chinese ports for England—because they are fast, while British ships wait at the docks for weeks on end, begging for charters for the London teas at half the rates. Yes, some ships do fail. Some are lost. But others are sensationally successful. Look at the records of the *Surprise*, the *Stag Hound*, the *Sovereign*. Fast ships, all of them, and well manned. The *Surprise* showed a $50,000 profit on one trip to San Francisco, Canton and London—fifty thousand above her cost and running expenses. Then the *Stag Hound*. Three years ago she made $80,000 in less than eleven months. I know her rate was $1.40 per cubic foot, sir, and it's seventy cents now—but even if the profits are halved, it's still a good venture. Risk, certainly, but they are well worth it, and they can be cut by proper selection of a crew, and the knowledge that you have a well-built ship. This ship is that, sir; once she's properly repaired I'll match her against any. We've barely touched trade with Japan yet, though the treaty is signed and the ports are open. If nothing else I can always bring a load of coolies back from Hongkong to San Francisco. And on this coast—well, England's crying for cotton and New York for rails."

Blake was nodding slowly. "That's right enough. We haven't ships enough to bring cotton here from the South to reload it for England. And the British ships, passenger and mail carriers, have cargo space on almost every sailing."

Matthew knew now where Blake was aiming. Tessa Dunn had been right. Blake was more interested right now in coastwise shipping of cotton than in financing a tramp trade. He knew Matthew's arguments were sound and his investment would be safe enough. But Blake wanted that ship himself. He had other uses for her, uses that would fit into his enterprises which were already established. Damn, he thought, fiercely. If Blake refuses my loan there's small chance of getting it from anyone else at this hour, probably no chance even if I had a week's grace. Blake's known to be liberal. There's no other who will take a chance that he refuses. Wait, he told himself. Don't say anything. Let him lay his cards on the table.

"There's cotton lying in the warehouses in the South now, waiting to be moved," Blake said, carefully flicking the ash from his cigar. "The Southern planters need the money badly." He looked up and smiled slightly. "In fact, I have financed a good many of them, and I can't get my money out till their crops are sold. Neither is it safe to buy until I have more means of shipping. Most of our coasting vessels are small. We need ships with greater capacity."

He looked directly at Matthew. "I can use that ship, Steel," he said. "I have interests here in firms supplying goods for the South. I have interest in the South and I would like to be in a position to develop those ties and markets still more. Products from the West will be funneled more and more through New York and thence to the southern states. To be brief—I can use that ship, and I can also use a good commander. I have no interest at this time in financing such a venture as you proposed this morning. This is not a time for gambling, but a time for sound investments, close at home, a time to try to stimulate business and trade here in New York. If you will change your plans a little, however, I think we can come to terms."

Matthew was very careful. He met the banker's look and kept the sick disappointment out of his voice. He had been too hopeful, he told himself. He found himself gritting his teeth and he leaned forward in his chair, clasping his hands between his knees. He saw what Blake had in mind. He wanted to control the triangular trade—west to north to south; and another triangle, south to north to England. He was, likely, already deep into it, with his finger in numerous pies, plantations of the South, factories of the North, railroads of the West, directly and indirectly, and each part of his industrial empire would benefit from the other.

"Yes, sir?" he said. He'd let the banker talk for a while.

"There is one lot of cotton I want very much to move, and move quickly. It's long-staple, sea-island cotton, and I can get it now at a price below the market, if I can move it at once. I've had samples. It will bring the highest price."

Yes, goddam it, Matthew said to himself. You'll buy that ship from Captain Brenner in Brighton's yards tomorrow, and send her down the coast. You'll make the cost of her in a couple of trips, by knowing where to buy and when. You finance the planters and you know when they need the money worst, just how long they can afford to hold their crops, and then you have a ship waiting to take it off their hands. When the price is lowest you call in their notes. And they think you are their benefactor, the man who lends them money to plant, the man who buys when they can afford to hold it no longer. You're a smart businessman, Thaddeus Blake, and you are honest, but you are also as hard as iron. You'll buy my ship with only a "Sorry, Steel," and a wave of your hand, if that, and if I won't go to work for you you'll forget, in a few days, that you ever saw me, that I ever told you of that ship in Brighton's yards, or of its merits. Goddam it, Thaddeus Blake, that's what you can do because you have the money and the power. You can walk in, and buy my ship at noon tomorrow, and you will ask me to command it!

"I understand you have had several offers, Steel, for you are well thought of on the waterfront and a good commander—and they are hard to find. I'll be frank with you. I'm in need of a young man who will stay with me. I believe you are qualified. I am prepared to make it attractive for you, a salary equivalent to the best you've been offered, and shares in the company I am forming to deal in cotton. You can build, more slowly perhaps, but much more surely, and I am certain you would have a great future. It is not as difficult to secure crews for coasting vessels, as you know. I am more interested in this project, at the moment, than any other. I have a great deal at stake. I am hoping that my son, Cass, will join me in this venture and find it interesting and profitable. It will be a business for young men, and it is, I may point out, an unusual opportunity."

Matthew nodded. "I can see that, sir," he said. He glanced at Cass; Cass was watching him with interest, curious to know his decision. Austin was carefully pleating and unpleating a piece of blank paper.

"Your plan, then, Mr. Blake, is to buy the ship, put her in shape to sail, and then use her only on the coast?"

"For the time being, yes. Perhaps later on, when times are propitious and we no longer need her for already established trade here, she could be sent on a longer voyage. At the moment I hold too much paper for the planters and I'm forced to liquidate it. The first trip would be to Charleston. Are you familiar with the cotton ports?"

"Charleston and Mobile, yes."

"The cotton I speak of is in Latham warehouse in Charleston, waiting shipment. If I had your agreement to command that ship I'd send word at once that the cotton is sold. How long do you think it would take to put that vessel in sailing condition, if the money were available?"

"Two weeks. Perhaps three. There is quite a bit of work to be done on her. If I were going to command her I'd want to oversee the work myself."

"Exactly." Blake waited.

He thinks he has made me a very handsome offer, Steel thought. I suppose he has. He is in the driver's seat, certainly. He can dictate terms. I can see his side of it. If I were in his place I'd probably do the same thing. He does not mention my option on the ship until noon tomorrow. If I say yes now he'll take up my option and get the ship at my figure—perhaps offer me a small profit on the deal. If I delay he'll pay through the nose for that ship when the bidding starts after noon tomorrow. I'll be damned if I'll be errand boy for Thaddeus Blake, or try to make a businessman out of his dandiprat son.

Matthew stood up. He glanced about the room, the rows of books, the comfortable chairs, the low fire. Yes, this was a comfortable and beautiful and luxurious home, but he did not feel at ease here now. He was an intruder who had been admitted for a little while because Thaddeus Blake could use him in one of his many undertakings. It was a fair proposition, and Blake was quite justified in presenting it. But it was not what Matthew wanted and he had an unholy desire to give Thaddeus Blake a run for his money.

"Thank you, sir, for your offer," he said quietly. "I'd like to think it over."

"Of course." The other men arose. Cass held out his hand, friendly and warm.

"I hope you decide to accept it," he drawled. "Since Father insists that I go to work, I'd like working with you." He laughed and Steel managed a smile as well. Austin, too, offered his hand.

"It's been a pleasure to meet you, Steel," he said.

"Thank you."

"I'll call a carriage." Blake reached for the bell pull.

"No, thank you." Steel was firm. "I think I'll walk. You see, I used to live in Washington Square. I know this district well. I'd rather like to see it again."

Austin raised his eyebrows. "In Washington Square?" he asked. "I don't seem to remember—"

"You wouldn't," Steel said bluntly. For some reason he wanted to make it all very clear. The muscle in his jaw hardened and his eyes were defiant. "I grew up in Washington Mews, the stable block. My mother was a servant in the Follett home, and they permitted me to stay with her—until she died."

His face was hard and expressionless when he turned again to Blake.

"Thanks again for your hospitality, sir. Please give my respects to your daughters. I'll let you know what I have decided tomorrow."

"Morning?" Blake asked. He knows I have that option till noon, Matthew thought. He's damned sure it is of no value to me, that I can't possibly raise the money elsewhere. He had set Austin back on his heels with his bluntness and Cass Blake also looked a little startled and a little amused. Cocky devil, Cass thought.

"No," Steel said evenly and he was pleased to see a flicker of annoyance on Thaddeus Blake's face. "Afternoon."

The butler was at the door to hand him his hat. The house was silent. The Blake sisters had apparently retired. The door closed quietly behind him. He went down the steps and out into the street. He glanced back at the house. A light on the second floor went out abruptly. He wondered if it were Loyalty's room. A little while ago he had felt very close to Loyalty Blake. It would have been very easy, very natural, to reach out for her, as though she belonged to him. But the few minutes he had felt at home in the Blake household had been false. He belonged on South Street, with women like Tessa Dunn.

He began to walk. He reached Washington Square and strode on, and memories mixed with his disappointment, bitterness with frustration.

He felt trapped. Blake was trying to force him to accept his offer. It was generous though, in all fairness. But his desire to own the ship was so great that the thought of her going into Blake's possession, and only loaned to him to sail, galled him bitterly.

He thought of the last time he had walked southward from Washington Square, and of the time on Houston Street and Mercer, when he had fought Mike Globinsky. That fight had been a turning point in his life. Mary Steel had warned him not to lose his temper, and never to give up. Her advice had helped him in many a battle. Mary Steel had not given up when his father was killed.

Mary Steel had iron beneath the velvet tenderness of her hands and voice.

Remembering, he tried to put the anger out of his mind now, anger that was befogging his judgment and wasting his time. He began to take stock of his resources and to try to figure some way to turn them to advantage. He had twenty thousand dollars of his own. He needed an equal amount to buy the ship and at least ten thousand more for her repairs. He had given Captain Brenner a thousand dollars for the option on the vessel and it would expire in about twelve hours.

Blake was so sure of him that he had not even offered to buy his option. That he did not consider young Matthew Steel a serious threat to anything that he, the banker, wanted, made Matthew burn. The banker was willing to play a waiting game. But if Steel did not get in touch with him before eleven o'clock tomorrow, he was willing to wager that the banker would relax enough to send a message to him. Blake would not want to bid for the ship on an open market, when he had a possibility of getting it at forty thousand dollars, by handing Matthew Steel a little profit on the side. The price on that ship might go to fifty, sixty thousand before it was sold.

He rolled it over and over in his mind. He could take in a partner, or several, but that would be defeating his purpose, tying his hands, because he would not have the controlling interest. All his life he had wanted to work for himself, free as Thaddeus Blake was free, to follow the dollars around the globe. He knew he could do it, once he had a ship, particularly that ship in Brighton's yards.

No, he wanted the ship for himself or not at all. If all else failed he could turn a few dollars by selling his precious option to someone else, and then he would have to wait again, for another opportunity to buy, and it might be years, if ever, before it came. Undoubtedly England, perhaps Russia, too, would be bidding for this beautiful ship. Their agents would grab his option in a hurry.

Matthew gripped his fists. He did not want that vessel to sail under a foreign flag. She was a Yankee clipper, one of the most beautiful things man had ever created, one neither the British nor any other nation had been able to equal or even to copy. She spelled speed, speed, speed, and grace and beauty and gallantry—she was made for Matthew Steel and it seemed to him she was already his; he could not bear to see her pass into other hands, and he would not, without a fight.

Thaddeus Blake would not have his ship. Nor would any other man snatch her from him now. There must be some way, if he could only think of it. Matthew Steel was wearing his fighting face as he strode toward South Street.

[5]

WHEN the dining-room doors were closed quietly behind the Blake sisters, Serena promptly turned toward the stairs. But Loyalty loitered in the hallway, undecided what she would do with the evening ahead of her. She disliked nights when there were no festivities. During the day she attended Miss Heather's Female Seminary, and weekday evenings she was supposed to devote to study, reading to improve her mind, or working on a bit of silk patchwork or cord embroidery.

Loyalty sighed. Serena would retire to her room and read sonnets —*Golden Grains from Life's Harvest Field*, or *The Falling Leaves of Autumn*, and be quite content as a young lady should be. Saints, Loyalty thought affectionately, watching her sister disappear around the curve at the head of the stairway, had no problems at all. But their lives were very dull. Even duller than hers.

It was unfair of her father to keep Henry Austin with him all evening. And Cass, less than three years older than she, was permitted to attend these business discussions, just because he was a man. It annoyed Loyalty very much. She thought business was interesting and political discussions were quite exciting. But the gentlemen never permitted them to become heated or controversial when there were ladies present. She was not allowed to ask questions, even on the rare occasions when the family dined alone. Her father and her teachers constantly reminded her there was nothing worse than a strong-minded female.

She went to the mirror and surveyed herself soberly. That Matthew Steel. He had acknowledged her presence and then he had ignored her. Completely ignored her! Loyalty turned her head slowly from one side to the other. She could not see anything exactly repulsive about her. At sixteen she was hardly faded, though sometimes she did feel much older than people gave her credit for. She put her hands on her hips and turned her body. She carried herself well, her shoulders were smooth, and this dress, this perfect love of a dress that she had chosen so carefully—who could resist it? But Matthew Steel had. It was very nicely cut, not too low but revealing in its lines, nevertheless. She touched the shoulders daintily. She was glad she did not have to use bust padding like some girls she knew, to give her a good line. She turned and looked over her shoulder into the mirror. She did not have to wear a *tournure* to give her hips a graceful curve, either, even when she did not wear crinolines; and these were the widest hoops she had ever had.

Of course, Matthew Steel was not of their circle. Nevertheless, his manners had been good, and he seemed well read and intelligent enough, and her father had treated him with considerable respect. Father wants something from him, Loyalty deduced sagely.

She heard a movement in the dining room and she fled quickly into the drawing room where she could see without being seen. She watched the men move down the hall to the library. Matthew Steel was taller and stronger than any of them. He was as handsome a man as she had ever seen, handsome and something else. She sought for a word to describe him. Exciting, yes; he was very *male*, she decided. She supposed he knew many women. Men like that always did, she thought unhappily.

She sat down before the fire. There were several books on a table beside her, Thackeray's *Pendennis,* Hawthorne's *The House of Seven Gables,* Dickens' *Bleak House* and Julia Kavanagh's *Women of Christianity.* There were a few magazines, *Harper's* and a *Godey's Lady's Book.* She picked up the latter, flicked the pages.

There was an article, "The Casket of the Year." Loyalty shuddered. She noted directions for making a chemisette—"Alternate puffs of muslin and insertion." There were illustrations of an Inside Spencer and an Outside Spencer, an over-blouse for small evening parties at home. She studied it; it was of dotted muslin, edged in needlework. Serena would like that. She read a receipt: "To Whiten the Hands. A wineglass full of eau de cologne, another of lemon juice. Scrape two cakes of brown Windsor soap and mix well." Loyalty looked at her hands. They were white and soft as cream. She put down the magazine.

She could go to the music room, but she had already practiced "Won't You Tell Me Why, Robin?" so many times she was sick of it and the other pieces cloyed as well. Mazurkas were better, but it was no fun when there was no young man leaning against the piano, watching her. She sighed again.

The wineglasses the men had used still stood on the mantelpiece. Loyalty rose. There was a drop or two of wine in each glass. She lifted her father's and rolled the wine over her tongue experimentally, and then Cass's, and then Henry's, and then, her eyes dancing, Matthew Steel's.

"A very fine Manzanilla sherry, sir," she mimicked. She giggled. She could not get Matthew Steel out of her mind. He had spoiled the only fun she had. Cass might drive very fast horses to very light gigs; he might go to the Astor House or the St. Denis or the Clarendon or Metropolitan—he could dance all night every night and drink and smoke, even chew tobacco if he wanted. He could go all over New York at will and was not limited to the few blocks in which young ladies of good family were permitted to go or have luncheon—properly chaperoned, of course. For her there were only the approved parties and balls, not frequent enough to suit her, an occasional box at the opera at the Academy of Music, and visits with the same group of friends. Everywhere she had a paid chaperone, an older female relative, or perhaps Mrs. Austin. Cass could travel or go to college or run for office, join his father in business, or take up any activity or profession he pleased. But Loyalty —what could she do? Few of the exciting things Cass was permitted, only the prescribed things that all her friends did, clothes and shopping and gossiping!

So she had discovered an exciting game and she played it constantly and it helped, a little, to make up for all the privileges Cass enjoyed which she could not. Cass could learn to compound a sherry cobbler, he could play billiards and gamble and drink champagne with pretty actresses. But Loyalty had just recently learned she could bring some spice to her own life by flicking her curling lashes in a certain way in the general direction of any male. She was sure to get an answering smile. It was a harmless game, she thought, and she gave no thought to what it might lead. It was fun; it was daring, because she could carry it on right under the eye of Serena or her father or a chaperone. At parties she was always surrounded by a crowd of men. She had been used to admiration all her life. But this was different; on a stroll, a carriage ride, a shopping expedition, she had tried it, and several times she had actually seen men take a quick, involuntary step in her direction, or halt in their tracks and turn to look at her again, quick interest written plainly on their faces. Giggling inwardly and quite delighted at the discovery of her new power, Loyalty thought it very funny and very exciting. It also infuriated Henry.

Now Matthew Steel had spoiled it. He was the first man, the very first one, who had failed to respond. When she had bowed to him she had smiled ever so slightly and peeked at him. His bold black eyes had swept over her from head to foot—very knowing, they had been! And there had been the faintest flicker of an appreciative grin, and then he had not looked at her again, but had made a remark about the wine, a man's remark, relegating her to the outer circle of women and children. Her anger arose again as she thought of it. It was even worse because Cass had noticed her discomfiture, and he would tease her about it later. She began to plan. She was going to make Matthew Steel pay for that, by hook or by crook. She would, in some way, captivate him completely. He would desire her, and then, when she was sure he was simply mad about her, she would turn her back on him coldly. The thought gave her immense satisfaction.

The butler passed down the hall again with coffee and glasses and he came back with an empty tray. What did men talk about after the ladies left them? Loyalty wondered. She had asked Cass, but he only grinned and would not tell her. Sometimes she had heard bursts of laughter and she imagined they were telling stories, risque stories, perhaps. Serena wouldn't tell her either, nor any of her chaperones. Loyalty had always determined that one day she would eavesdrop on the gentlemen after dinner and find out. How else was a girl to know?

She pursed her lips. The house was very quiet. Suddenly her eyes began to sparkle. She jumped up and went into the hall. It was deserted. She glanced up the stairs. There was no sign of Serena. She went to the dining-room door and could hear the servants clearing away the dishes. She dimpled and caught her lower lip in her small teeth and tiptoed down the hall to the library door. Her heart was beating fast. She looked back over her shoulder quickly, once, then she knelt and put her pretty eye to the keyhole. Her skirts billowed about her like the petals of a flower.

She had a good view of Matthew Steel. My life, he's handsome! she thought, with a little shrug of delight. He was standing with his back to the fire and he was very straight and tall. Her father was handing him a ship's model and he took it in his strong hands and looked it over. He gave it more notice than he had given her!

"She's a beauty, all right," Steel said. Loyalty liked his voice. A tingle of excitement went through her. "But to me she'd be more beautiful after she came back from her first run, and had a few scars, maybe, scars that show she's seaworthy and disciplined and can take the storms and the heavy seas. Until a ship's been tried and knows her master she has only the beauty of a pretty virgin."

Loyalty gasped and put her hand over her mouth. Behind her Serena's scandalized voice whispered:

"Loyalty Blake! Whatever are you doing?"

Loyalty scrambled to her feet. She ran to her sister and caught her hand and pulled her toward the stairs.

"Serena! Serena! He said—he said—"

"Loyalty Blake, have you lost your mind? Eavesdropping, of all things! Father would be furious if he knew! Whatever you heard—it serves you right! Of all the unmaidenly—"

Loyalty was running up the steps, seeking the sanctuary of her own room, still holding Serena's hand. She reached her room and threw herself down on the bed, bouncing in her excitement.

"Serena," she said, ignoring her sister's protests completely. She opened her mouth and closed it again, at a loss for words.

"Loyalty, what has come over you? What did he say, then?"

Loyalty swallowed. She clasped her hands in her lap and looked at her sister for a long moment.

"Oh, never mind," she said more slowly. "I guess you wouldn't understand."

A maid rapped discreetly and entered. "Shall I unlace you now, Miss Loyalty?" Loyalty nodded and arose and submitted herself to the maid's practiced hands. Serena stood hesitatingly for a minute and then she left, her face worried. Loyalty did not notice. Her eyes were stormy and she went through the motions of undressing quite automatically. She went over Matthew Steel's words again. They might almost have been directed at her, almost as if he knew she was listening! The men had laughed, with funny expressions on their faces, expressions they did not wear when ladies were present, as though they shared some secret. *Only* the beauty of a pretty virgin, he said!

A voluminous nightdress slid over Loyalty's head and for a minute she was lost in it, then she wiggled her hands through the sleeves and emerged. Beneath it she dropped her stays and chemise and stepped out of them. She sat down and the maid took the pins from her hair and began to brush it. Then the woman put away her clothing, picking up the numerous petticoats, the small satin undergarments, the slippers with the long satin laces, and then she left. Loyalty, sitting bolt upright in bed, her hands clasped in front of her, stared at the opposite wall.

"So that is what he thinks of me!" she said aloud. "So he has no use for pretty virgins! Only for experienced women. I'll bet he is the kind of man who even speaks to divorced women! That is why he ignored me, he thinks I am too inexperienced to bother with. That I am not exciting. Well!"

Her eyes snapped and her pretty mouth set in a straight, dangerous line. She turned and thumped her pillow viciously and jerked it behind her head. After a while she heard the door below close and through her open window footsteps on the walk below. She leaped out of bed and blew out her candles quickly and knelt in the window behind the curtain. The cool, fresh air blew in upon her. Matthew Steel was walking down the street. Neither Cass nor Henry ever walked when they could avoid it. But he was swinging along, powerful and fast beneath the street lights. All right, Matthew Steel, Loyalty said furiously. I'll show you. You just wait. I'll show you.

[6]

AT NIGHT upper Fifth Avenue was still, its people safe and withdrawn in their fortress homes, but the mad activity of the waterfront only increased with the coming of darkness.

Steel turned into the Cock and Bull. Tessa Dunn was singing and Steel leaned against the bar, pushed his hat on the back of his head, and watched her. He let his drink sit for a while, untasted, while he listened to Tessa. She saw him and smiled at him in the midst of her song. Tessa had been watching for him from her vantage point on the musicians' platform, and now, catching his eye, she let her own eyes move farther down the bar and back again. Matthew followed her glance. He turned then and picked up his glass and looked in the mirror behind the bar. Two men whom Tessa had indicated by her glance were deep in conversation several yards away and in the mirror Matthew could see their faces. He recognized one as Thilo Kalin, a Russian with whom he had made several voyages. It had been a year since he had last seen Thilo, and at that time the Russian had been a junior officer in the Russian Imperial Navy. But he was not in uniform now. Matthew remembered him as an exceptionally able seaman, an intelligent, adventurous man of good family, a friend of young Peter Segonov whose guest Steel had been in St. Petersburg. Thilo's broad, flat face was serious now and he was nodding in agreement to something his companion was saying. The second man, also a Russian, was older than Thilo and neatly dressed, and he gestured as he spoke.

Matthew turned his back to the mirror again and looked back at Tessa. She nodded slightly, and her husky, rich, haunting voice floated over the crowded room. Tessa was wearing a green dress, a tight sheath from shoulder to knees, and flaring in wide folds to her ankles. Her tall, slender figure swayed a little as she sang, and her gorgeous hair swept across her bare shoulders as she turned her head. Her eyes were half-closed, her lashes shining, and the flickering lights at her feet emphasized her high cheek bones and the slight hollows beneath. The dress was of cheap and shoddy material; the stones in the combs of her hair were of colored glass. But the faces upturned to her were avid, greedy, and when she finished her song and stepped down, men's hands reached for her. Tessa seemed always to sway just a little, barely out of their reach and delighted laughter followed her. As the music stopped the two Russians drew apart and glanced around the room quickly. Thilo put his hand on his companion's arm and said something shortly and left him. He had seen Matthew Steel and now he pushed his way through the crowd to him. Tessa changed her course and went to a table near the wall and sat down. She waited for food, but her eyes were upon Steel and she was praying.

Whatever Matthew Steel wants, Tessa was praying, let it come to him. Let me be of some help to him. She tried to tell from his face the results of the interview with Blake, but Matthew's face was closed and guarded. She knew that expression well. There was neither elation nor defeat there. She had studied Matthew's face so many times, she knew every expression, every line, every light. In her imagination she had run her fingers over that face a thousand times, over his brows, along the hard jaw line, across his lips. Now, as she watched, her heart was thumping so loudly that she was sure those about her must hear it. Matthew Steel always affected her so, whenever she saw him. She could feel his presence in a room the minute he entered. Sometimes, knowing he was in New York, not knowing at what moment she might look up and see him, on the street or entering the Cock and Bull, it was almost too much to bear. When she was singing and he appeared, her voice seemed to catch in her throat and she had to call on all her strength to keep from faltering. Tonight her heart had been singing, too, because she shared Matthew's secret. He had confided in her, told her where he was going, and she had a closer insight into Matthew Steel's secret dreams and ambitions than she had ever had before. All evening she had felt Matthew's hand on her arm where his fingers had gripped her. She had touched the place with her own fingers, liking to remember, thinking of his face, alive and eager with his plans, sharing them with her.

The two Russians had come into the Cock and Bull and asked for Steel more than two hours ago. Tessa had said he would probably be in later. She hoped and prayed that he would be. She was eager to know the outcome of his meeting with Blake, but, successful or no, she wanted to see Matthew Steel again. Sometime, she thought grimly, perhaps Matthew would really see her, too.

Tessa Dunn had been on the waterfront for seven years. She had been only thirteen when she was landed there, a survivor of a sea disaster that had taken the lives of both her parents. The ship on which the Dunn family had sailed from Ireland had burned at sea, and there had been tortured days in a lifeboat before the survivors had been picked up. Matthew Steel, at seventeen an ordinary seaman, had been aboard the rescue ship. To Tessa, numb with shock, terrified at the unfamiliar faces about her, the sight of Matthew Steel, young and strong and clean, had been reassuring and of the greatest comfort. He had talked to her quietly, seeming to know the right things to say and she had trusted him as she had not trusted—and with good reason—the older men.

Once ashore Matthew Steel had continued to shield her. He had found a woman who worked in the kitchen of a coffee house, who agreed to give Tessa shelter in exchange for her labors. Little by little Tessa's grief and fright had worn off, and she had begun to fit into the life of the waterfront. Her young adoration for Matthew Steel and her gratitude grew as she grew, and she lived only for his return to South Street. Tessa Dunn guarded her secret well, waiting and praying, and she guarded herself, too. Tessa's remoteness was not a pose; she evaded the hands of other men, not because, as some said, her price was too high, but because she was waiting for Matthew Steel. After the next voyage, she had told herself, each time he came and left—next time he comes—

But Steel had never seemed to consider her anything but the waif he had helped to pick up out of the sea. He had not recognized that she was a grown woman now, until, perhaps, today. There were times when Tessa Dunn hated South Street and all that went with it, the hungry eyes in the Cock and Bull as she sang, the problem of trying to clothe herself on the few dollars she could earn with her songs and her commissions on the drinks she could persuade the customers to buy. But South Street, and the Cock and Bull, was where Matthew Steel came when his voyages were over. The rotund Hite and the hawk-faced Morton were his friends and occasionally, during his absence, had news of him.

Thilo touched Matthew's shoulder and Matthew turned and the two clasped hands.

"It's good to see you, Thilo, and a surprise," Steel said. Thilo grinned widely. Matthew spoke in Russian and Thilo gripped his hand in appreciation.

"Matthew Steel, it has been more than a year. And I have been waiting for you more than a year tonight! You look well. Very prosperous." He raised his eyebrows and they both laughed.

"It has been a good year, Thilo. And you? I suppose you were in the Black Sea, giving hell to the British and French."

Thilo's face sobered. He shrugged. "Maybe we still will give them hell," he said darkly. "If we could just get our ships out to fight."

"They have you well bottled up, haven't they? And in your own ports. Too bad."

"The fight is not over yet," the Russian said, and there was no humor in his face now. "Some place we can talk?" he said abruptly. Matthew nodded. He set down his glass. He made his way through the room toward a door at the rear. Tessa Dunn sat quietly at her table, watching him go.

It was in this room that Matthew had fought matches as a boy, and it was here he had come the night his mother died. It was lighted dimly now and furnished with a few small tables and chairs and three men were engrossed in low conversation in one corner. Matthew looked them over. He knew what the lists and figures on the papers before them meant, and why they talked with their heads close together. One was a Spaniard, from a spanish banking house near the waterfront; one was Morton, half-owner of the Cock and Bull, and the other was captain of a ship Matthew had seen at the foot of Jones Lane. He had suspected the ship was a slaver. Now he was sure. There would be more than palm oil and ivory in the hold of that ship when she next left the African coast.

He indicated a table to Thilo and the two sat down. The Russian bent toward him and wasted no time nor words.

"Steel, you have an option on a ship in Brighton's yards—Captain Brenner's ship."

"Well?"

"I want to buy it."

"You, Thilo?" Matthew regarded the Russian thoughtfully. "But I've no wish to sell." He shoved back his chair and smiled. "If that is all—"

Thilo motioned with his hand and Matthew paused.

"I will pay you well. You paid a thousand dollars to Brenner for the privilege. I will give you two thousand."

Matthew laughed.

"Why do you suppose I gave a thousand for the option? I intend to buy the ship myself, Thilo. I've been wanting to become a shipowner for a long time, just waiting till the right vessel came along."

Thilo chewed his lip and frowned. "If not the option, then the ship. I'll buy her from you."

Matthew shook his head. "Ships like Brenner's are not up for sale at a decent price very often these days, Thilo. The British grab them all. The shipyards can't turn them out fast enough. And this one, I may say, is an exceptional vessel. Not three years old, better built than the hurry-up jobs some yards are turning out today. Well-designed. Fast. Exactly what I want."

"Every man has his price."

"That's a Russian axiom, isn't it?" Steel grinned. "No, I'm sorry, Thilo." He arose.

"Well, wait a bit, anyway. Let us have a drink together. For old times' sake?"

"Of course." He went to the door and signaled a waiter. "What'll it be for you, Thilo? Vodka?"

Thilo sighed. "Your whisky. I'm becoming fond of the stuff."

Matthew sat again and raised his glass. "The Emperor. Your health. Thilo, I thought you were in the navy."

"I was." Thilo shrugged, changed the subject. "Steel, what do you intend to do with your beautiful ship?"

"Cotton to Liverpool, probably, as a first trip, to try her out. Then perhaps Australia. I'd like to visit the ports of Japan. Coolies to San Francisco. Wherever I can pick up a good paying cargo." He watched the Russian narrowly. "Why do you not sail with me, Thilo? There's no first mate I'd rather have."

Thilo smiled. "I know a better way for you to make money, Steel. And as I remember you are one who is after money. I remember you would bet with Peter Segonov on the length of the pier or the height of a mast—and you usually won."

"Money is a very good thing to have."

Thilo leaned across the table and lowered his voice. "Why do you not sail under the Russian flag, Matthew Steel? Britain and France are hiring Americans to fight for them in their land armies. Why do you not make of your ship a Russian privateer? You could go to Alaska, get letters of marque, become a Russian citizen along with two-thirds of your crew, and there!" Thilo spread his hands wide. "There you have complied with international law!"

"Rather sketchily, I think. What then?"

"Prey on England's merchant shipping. Think of the prizes! One Australian gold ship and you are fixed for life. You can outsail any British ship. We who have sailed with you know that. They stand still as you pass them!"

Steel picked up the bottle and filled Thilo's glass. He was watching the Russian, trying to see behind his words. It was understandable why Russia would want such a ship as Brenner's for a privateer, and it was not surprising that Thilo, obviously an agent for his government, was attempting to press every possible ship into his country's service. But some half-buried instinct told Steel that there was more behind Thilo's suggestion than that. The Russian's face, like those of most Russians when they were trading, was inscrutable, but Thilo, by an occasional restless movement in his chair, revealed tension, eagerness. Steel probed mentally, trying to understand the thought processes of the man across the table from him. Thilo wanted this ship badly, he thought. He must find out how badly, and for what purpose. Was it for an immediate, specific purpose, or was it just part of Russia's over-all campaign to throw as many ships as possible against her enemies, in every possible capacity? Were Thilo's orders from his government blanket instructions to buy, man and send against Britain and France all the able ships he could secure? Or was he sent here to find one ship, one fast, stout vessel, to carry out one particular mission?

"There is only one thing wrong with that idea, Thilo," Steel said. He spoke slowly, watching the Russian. "I'm not a pirate. The war between Britain and France and Russia is not my fight. I've no desire to sink British or French ships. Nor Russians either, for that matter."

"You want to make money, don't you?"

Ah, now we are getting some place, Steel thought. He could almost see Thilo's quickened interest as he answered.

"Yes, as a matter of fact I am in need of money." He glanced away as though dismissing the subject. "But I've no desire to sail under a Russian flag. Once I were a Russian citizen, even as a privateer, my ship could be commandeered by your government, for whatever use the emperor wished. Isn't that right, Thilo?"

His eyes came back to the Russian suddenly and their glances interlocked. Then Thilo looked down into his glass.

"I was not thinking of that."

"The hell you weren't."

The Russian brooded, silent. Thilo had made a good try, Steel thought. It had been a clever move but Steel had not taken the bait. If a Russian determined to enter and the front door was barred, you could not blame him for trying the back entrance. Steel understood this kind of trading. He pushed back his chair.

"Well, Thilo, I'm sorry. There will be other ships available from time to time, I suppose. I don't blame you for wanting this ship. She has been abused, but she's a beauty. I wish you luck. I hope you find the vessel you want."

"Steel," Thilo said finally, leaning back in his chair. "I won't try to bargain with you. You can name your own figure."

Steel's query was answered. His heartbeat quickened but he took a cigar from his pocket, offered one to the Russian and leaned forward to the candle to light it. His movements were deliberate. If Thilo was determined to have this ship now at any cost, it was for an immediate and pressing purpose, as he had suspected.

"Ordinarily you'd argue about the price of a casket for your own mother," Steel said bluntly. "I'll be equally frank, Thilo. I will not sell that ship, nor the option. But, as I said, I do need money. I'm no pirate, but I am interested in doing business. I do not believe you want that ship solely for a privateer. I think you need her for one particular voyage, and at once. It could be—that you want to make a trip to St. Petersburg, perhaps—and you need a fast ship to run the British blockade."

Thilo made no answer. Steel knew that he was not free to reply but he believed he was on the right track.

"As I said," Steel continued slowly, "the Crimean War is not my fight. But I do believe I have a right to sail my own ship wherever I damn please. With a good crew—you among them, Thilo—and a good pilot, that ship can outrace any the British or French can send against her. In fact, I'm willing to make a side bet she can run the blockade to St. Petersburg. Of course, by international agreement I could not—knowingly—carry contraband cargo to a Russian port, so there would be no reason for me to try to evade the British."

Thilo's eyes met his and the Russian waited. Steel grinned. "Except, Thilo," he continued, "that delays turn profits to losses. I have heard the British of late have a nasty habit of stopping American ships, herding them into ports, and then taking their own good time about inspection and release, even if the cargo is found to contain no contraband and ship and crew are above suspicion. The British are very slow and deliberate about those things, as you know, though they are quite within the letter of the law.

As a result, it is making legitimate trips to Russian ports highly unprofitable, which, of course, is their purpose. I could not afford such a delay. Accordingly, on any voyage I would make to a Russian port, regardless of my crew, passengers or cargo, I would not permit my vessel to be stopped on the high seas by any British ship, steamer or hermaphrodite brig."

It was like a poker game, Steel thought. They had most of their cards on the table now. Thilo had turned his over, one by one, and Steel had matched them. The Russian's need for the ship; his willingness to pay any price. Steel's need for money; his determination to keep the ownership of the vessel; and now his willingness to run the British blockade—for a price. Slowly Thilo nodded.

"You are a very wise man, Matthew Steel," he said. "Of course, on your first voyage, you would wish to make a profit, and if your ship were forced into a British port for inspection it would be quite a financial blow to you." His white teeth gleamed in his dark face. "It would be much simpler, as you say, to avoid them altogether. I do not think they could stop you, if you did not wish to be stopped, Matthew Steel." He was thoughtful and silent for a long time. Matthew filled his glass and waited. "How much?" Thilo said.

"If I were unlucky and the British stopped me, and if, without my knowledge, there were contraband aboard, I would be in trouble perhaps with my own government. I would lose my ship and cargo, even if I escaped with a whole skin. If there were no contraband the delay itself would be enough to break me. I cannot stand a loss on even one voyage. You understand the risks are very great."

"I understand," Thilo nodded. "How much?"

Matthew studied the ceiling. How much could Thilo stand? How great was his need? Thilo was gripping his glass with his short, blunt fingers. Matthew was sure he had guessed correctly. There was some cargo—gold, guns or perhaps some Russians of importance now in this country who had to return to St. Petersburg. Steel studied his own chances. The odds were about even, he thought. He had not exaggerated. If he took Thilo's cargo, and it was contraband, and he was caught in the blockade, he was through. If he ran the blockade successfully he would have his vessel and a profit on the voyage. It depended on his skill, on his luck and his careful preparations, his crew, Thilo as a pilot, and the ship. With that ship he could run any goddam blockade, he thought, thinking of the vessel's clean, fast lines; he felt a surge of confidence. No one could catch him to question him.

He looked at the bargain from Thilo's viewpoint. There was no other shipowner in the port today who would take that risk. Because of his immediate need for the money, Matthew Steel would gamble. Thilo had confidence in his seamanship and Thilo, himself a master, likewise judged the ship. I'll make the stakes high, Steel decided. Here it goes—all or nothing.

"For one trip to St. Petersburg, cargo to be furnished by you—forty thousand dollars. In advance."

"Goddam, Matthew Steel!" Thilo put down his glass, aghast. "That is the price of the ship!"

Steel shrugged. His face was closed again, expressionless.

"It makes no difference to me, Thilo. The risk is great. And you will be able to get another ship, perhaps, within a few months. If you have no need for haste, then of course you are not interested in my offer. And on my part—I have another offer, from a New Yorker. I have been with him tonight. He will be delighted if I send him word in the morning that the ship is at his command. Perhaps you have heard of him. Thaddeus Blake."

Steel had turned over his last card and Thilo took a deep breath.

"You trade like a damn Russian, Matthew Steel," he said, half-grinning. "You drive a hard bargain. . . . Will you wait here for half an hour?"

"Yes, I'll wait half an hour. I'm in no hurry."

Tessa Dunn saw Thilo emerge from the inner room and his companion at the bar joined him and the two hurried to the street. She arose and went to the back room. Matthew Steel had resumed his seat at the table alone and he was turning his empty glass around and around in his fingers. The three men in the corner concluded their business and left. Tessa Dunn stood beside Matthew and he glanced up at her and smiled a little.

"Is it all right?" she asked.

She saw that his forehead was wet with perspiration and his face showed signs of the strain he had been under during the past hours.

Almost involuntarily her hand crept out to cover his, to stop the moving, restless fingers on the glass. At her touch he shoved back his chair and stood up and she was very close to him. He put his hands on her shoulders and looked into her face, but he was not seeing her, he was seeing only a comrade in arms, someone who was interested in what he was trying to do.

"Maybe it is, Tess," he said. "Maybe I've parlayed a thousand-dollar option into a forty-thousand-dollar ship. Maybe—"

Tessa's head was back and one of the combs set with its pathetic, cheap bits of colored glass slipped from her hair and shattered on the floor at her feet. At the same time the still mask of Tessa's face seemed to crumble, too, and her sullen lips were soft and trembling a little, her eyes were young and beseeching and vulnerable. Matthew bent his head, still not seeing her, and kissed her lips, almost absently, because she was there, because she was wishing him well. But Tessa's arms crept behind his neck and her body, in the thin, tight gown, was one great throbbing heartbeat and its curves fitted Matthew's own. His arms tightened about her and for a long instant Tessa was a part of him and exaltation shook her and left her weak. His hand tangled itself roughly in her hair and forced her head back till he could look into her face. Her fingers, gentle, yearning, touched his face, his lips.

"God, Tessa," he said. "You're—" He stopped and laughed shortly and then he let her go. He picked up the broken comb and held it in his hand and looked at it. "I'll buy you a new one," he said gently. The careful mask slid over her face again and she smiled, too.

[7]

In a room in the St. Nicholas Hotel, just as day was breaking, Matthew Steel received a letter of credit on a New York bank for forty thousand dollars. It was handed him by a Russian whose name he was yet to know, a man to whom Thilo Kalin had taken him. The speed with which the Russians moved amazed and puzzled Matthew. It had been his experience with them as traders that they were careful with money, and he was sure they would not part with this amount unless they were confident they were to receive the worth of every dollar.

He left the hotel in the freshness of the early morning to go to Mrs. Doughty's Boarding House. He would have a couple of hours for sleep. He was exhausted but exhilarated, and the heady wine of triumph lightened his steps. As he walked he mentally reviewed his interview with the Russians. They had been frank in expressing their need to charter his ship for this voyage. But Matthew felt that there was some missing factor, something he could not yet put his finger upon, that had influenced them.

He suspected that portion of the cargo which they would furnish was gold, or guns, or perhaps only the short, heavy-set, blond Russian with whom he had dealt. They had discussed the legitimate cargo politely and made no mention of contraband. Tariffs had been lowered on cotton and other needed goods to encourage United States shippers to trade with Russia, to grab the opportunity to snatch the Russian markets from Great Britain for all time. Matthew rolled this over in his mind. Was this Russian money in part a good-will offering to Yankee businessmen, in the hope that others, seeing Steel's profitable venture, would follow suit, and a steady stream of goods would flow from United States ports to Russia in American ships?

Well, there was nothing illegitimate in that, surely. Encouragement of trade between the two nations would be mutually profitable. Lowering of tariffs had been the first step. Perhaps he was the lucky instrument for the second. He wished he were sure. It would take a big load off his mind.

It was possible, he thought. Thilo Kalin's recommendation of him had undoubtedly helped to tip the scales in his favor. Thilo was an intelligent and well-educated Russian and his opinions were given thoughtful consideration by his superiors. Matthew guessed that Thilo was in a position of some importance to his government, but whether it was diplomatic, economic or military he could not tell. Perhaps it was a mixture of all three.

Throughout the hours of talk Matthew had been conscious of Thilo's eyes upon him, serious, intent, as though he was appraising his friend. But that friendship, Matthew was sure, as all of Thilo's friendships, would be secondary to his duty, to the mission to which his government had assigned him. Thilo was no less his friend for that. Matthew had long ago realized this particular facet of Russian character and had accepted it.

Matthew's steps slowed, keeping pace with his deliberate reasoning. God Almighty, he thought, even the wealthiest Russians do not throw their money around. He remembered Peter Segonov, midshipman and son of one of the oldest and wealthiest of St. Petersburg families. Peter loved gambling, but even he was cautious; he spent money lavishly to entertain his friends, to buy gifts—but he was careful also that he was not overcharged by the tradesmen with whom he dealt. Matthew remembered the naval captain, Lesovsky, a great military strategist, a man who would undoubtedly some day be one of Russia's greatest leaders; and the jovial Popov, whose ambition it was to command Russia's Pacific fleet, good men and good friends, all of them, but each with that hard, immovable core in him that, to Matthew, was characteristic of the Russian people —a core into which friendship did not penetrate. In some Russians this core was crusted with distrust and suspicion and it took a long time to break through it. Matthew had thought of it before, when small, revealing flashes of it had come to him in conversations with Peter Segonov, with Lesovsky, even with Popov, and with Thilo, tonight. Patriotism, idealism or discipline, whatever it was, it was there, if one probed deep enough, real and hard and not to be ignored.

He considered the possibility of treachery. Was this money a trick, to gain possession of his ship by some means he could not now foresee? He put that thought in the back of his mind, but he did not dismiss it entirely. He must examine it carefully, be prepared for any eventuality. He had worked alone and depended on his own strength and wits too long to trust anyone else to look out for his interests. It was up to him and him alone.

But he owned the ship. As soon as the banks were opened he would get the money and he would close the deal with Captain

Brenner. He had bested Thaddeus Blake and Blake had, inadvertently, been of benefit to him. The threat of his name had closed the deal with Thilo. He had made a good trade with the hard-bargaining Russians themselves, at least on the surface of it. There was work to be done, plenty of work, and he could not waste much time in sleep, only enough to keep his mind clear.

He breathed deep of the fresh, moist, morning air, and though problems pressed upon him he could not suppress a grin as he walked, and his eyes, despite the fatigue lines about them, were shining. He had the ship—yes, and he had ten thousand dollars more than he needed for the vessel and he knew what he intended to do with it.

As soon as the papers were signed and the ship became his, Matthew had business with a cotton broker. He intended to buy the cotton in the Latham warehouse in Charleston. There was no reason why he, instead of Thaddeus Blake, should not have the profit on that long-staple cotton on a Charleston wharf. He had explained to the Russians that he must have a trial run of his ship down the coast before he attemped the Atlantic crossing. He believed, once he owned the cotton, that he could sell it to the Russians, and transport it himself to St. Petersburg. The profit would pay his crew, give him a little margin above the ship itself.

He entered his room in Mrs. Doughty's Boarding House for Seamen and he did not notice the bareness of it. He hung his coat carefully over the back of a chair again, loosed his collar and sat down on the lumpy straw mattress and removed his boots. He held one in his hands, staring ahead of him, and his grin widened. New York to Charleston to Russia. That was unorthodox. That was deliberately reversing Thaddeus Blake's pet theory of the proper direction of triangular trade—south to north to European markets.

He tossed the boot on the floor and stretched his long body out on the bed, his hands beneath his head, his eyes on the flyspecked ceiling. Thaddeus Blake would be chagrined when he learned that the ship had slipped through his fingers. He'd be even more irritated when he learned that Steel had bought the Charleston cotton about which Blake himself had told him. Blake had been overconfident, sure that his power and his money could bend Steel to his will, and, as a result, incautious. There was a lesson in that for Matthew. He must remember not to grow careless, regardless of success.

Matthew tried to relax, but in spite of his victory over Thaddeus Blake and the singing, triumphant knowledge that the ship was his, he could not rest. There were the extensive repairs on his vessel to consider; there was the dangerous job of selecting his own crew, there was the British blockade. He must meet those problems one by one.

The British blockade. Suddenly Matthew sat up, wide awake, and the smile was gone from his face. The pieces of the Russian puzzle began to fall into place, assume a perfect pattern. He understood it now. Russians were happiest when they gambled on a sure thing, and they had paid out forty thousand dollars to him because, either way, *they couldn't lose!*

It was perfectly clear. If he were successful in running the blockade, the Russians had secured a needed cargo of goods, and they had strongly promoted the increase of trade with the United States and good-will with American merchants. Matthew knew it was their opinion, and perhaps rightly so, that Americans would go after anything that had enough money in it. If Steel returned to South Street with a fabulously profitable voyage behind him, the news would spread fast, and other ships would follow.

But if he were stopped by the British—what then? If the British suspected that Matthew Steel's ship carried contraband, and his vessel was challenged and his goods confiscated, then what happened to the Russian money?

Relations between the United States and Britain were already strained. It would mean that the United States could protest the confiscation of Matthew Steel's ship and defend the principle that the flag covers the goods. Russia would have an active ally in her war against England and France.

Slowly Matthew Steel nodded to himself. By God in heaven, that was it. He doubted if there would be any contraband cargo at all aboard his ship when he set his course for St. Petersburg. But the British might be led to think so, and if he were stopped, an international incident would be provoked—to the advantage of Russia.

No, the Russians had nothing to lose, whether he ran that blockade or not. They could sit back quietly now, sure their forty thousand dollars was well invested. The only one who could lose would be Matthew Steel. No wonder Thilo appraised him thoughtfully!

Matthew reached for his boots. He pulled them on and stood, hitching up his belt. The limp, gray lace curtains were blowing back from the windows in the morning breeze. Wagons were clattering along the street below and he could hear the day's activities beginning in the lumber yard across the street. No, the Russians couldn't lose. Once again they were betting on a sure thing. But there was only one possible way in which Matthew could win. He must run that British blockade. He must hand pick the finest crew South Street could provide, he must outfit his ship with the greatest care, and then he must show the British the speed of a Yankee clipper. Now that he knew what he faced he was not afraid. He accepted the challenge.

He was suddenly hungry and his weariness was gone. He had work to do and he was eager to begin. He reached for his coat. Thilo Kalin, he thought, was a smart man. You could not underestimate the Russian strategists. Well, Matthew Steel had no complaints. He had the money, he would have the ship. The job of protecting the vessel was up to him. There would be no help from anyone, including the Russians.

He tightened his cravat quickly in front of the mirror and noticed the black stubble on his chin. His thoughts went back to the night before, when he had dressed with such care to present himself to Thaddeus Blake. He thought of Loyalty and his face softened. She would be asleep still, at this hour, warm and rosy and sweet against snowy pillows. He had never seen a girl with face and figure so nearly perfect, he reflected. She was a spoiled little rogue, he thought, smiling to himself. He was a little amused to find that she had so intrigued him. For all her gentle upbringing, Loyalty Blake was no docile, passive little maid; she was a willful and spirited girl with a mind of her own, and she would be an exciting and stimulating companion. Yes, he would greatly relish another meeting with her. He tried to analyze her charm for him; vivid and gay, fresh and untouched, Loyalty Blake seemed all the youth and laughter and lighthearted mischief that he had missed as a boy. While Loyalty Blake had been learning how to enter a room, how to seat herself without allowing her crinolines to pop up in front, how to enter a carriage without displaying a pretty ankle, how to answer a compliment demurely, Matthew Steel had been fighting, slugging, dodging, planning to keep himself clothed and fed. She also symbolized all that he hoped for the future—security, wealth, position.

But better days were ahead. If his first voyage were successful—and by Heaven it would be!—Matthew would be a shipowner and a man to be respected. There was no reason then why he should not see Loyalty Blake again. The anticipation was pleasant, and as he started down the stairs the idea hardened swiftly into decision.

CHAPTER II

THADDEUS BLAKE SAT before his library fire, talking with Cass and Henry Austin. For once he was so absorbed in his subject that he paid no attention to Loyalty, sitting quietly in the shadows, and she was discreet enough not to draw attention to her presence. It had been four days since Matthew Steel had sat here, trying to persuade Thaddeus Blake to grant his loan. But the young seaman's presence could still be strongly felt.

Loyalty had seldom seen her father as affected as he was by the knowledge that Matthew Steel had secured the money elsewhere and had bought the ship without Thaddeus' help.

"I confess I was amazed when I received his note the next morning," Thaddeus was saying. "Polite and brief it was, but very positive. Thanked me for my courtesy, refused my offer, and that was the end of it. I sent Christensen, a clerk, to South Street at once, to find out what had happened, and to see if anything could be done, and another man to Brenner to bid on the ship."

"And it had already been sold," Cass said.

"Yes. I knew Steel was disappointed that I refused his loan, but I believed him intelligent enough to consider my counter-offer and recognize its merits. I misjudged him. I thought he had good sound business sense beneath his youthful enthusiasm."

Loyalty moved a little uneasily in her chair. She would like to ask questions but she was afraid she would be promptly banished if she did. Thaddeus deliberately flicked his cigar ash into the fire.

"I immediately took steps to find out who had financed him. Usually I can get such information in a matter of a few hours.

This took me three days." Thaddeus smiled a little wryly. "His letter of credit was signed by some common name—John Smith or something of the sort, which, of course, meant nothing. The funds in that account, I finally discovered, and no easy job it was—are from the Russian government."

"Ah!" Henry Austin started and Cass' face lighted with new interest. Thaddeus nodded.

"Yes," he admitted. "It is highly significant. I should not be in the least surprised if young Steel were to become a corsair. It would certainly not be out of character for him."

Loyalty gasped. Austin's glance rested upon her. Henry Austin was an intelligent and perceptive man, and Loyalty Blake's interest in the fortunes of Matthew Steel had not been lost upon him. That muscular, bronzed young seaman, big and vital and quietly self-assured, had greatly impressed Loyalty and now this aura of danger and adventure about him was adding fuel to the fire. Austin's pale brows drew together in a frown.

Cass, too, had heard Loyalty's quick indrawn breath, and his attention flicked from his sister to Austin and back to his father again.

"A corsair?" Cass said. "A privateer?"

"Yes. Russia's way of disturbing British trade. Insurance rates for the British have gone sky-high as the result of Russian privateers, and Russia intends to use them, apparently, to make a shambles of Britain's shipping. Of course—it is war. Britain, however, has withdrawn all privateers from the seas, in the hope that Russia will do the same. But Russia has no vessels for the British to prey upon, so they have nothing to lose by pursuing the practice. Our young dinner guest will perhaps become a privateer and feather his nest with loot from Australian gold ships, or Britain's merchant vessels! At least, that might explain why he secured forty thousand dollars from the Russian government."

Austin laughed shortly. "Perhaps he'll be caught before he does much damage," he said. Cass saw indignation and concern touch Loyalty's mobile face.

"Perhaps," the banker said. He was frowning intently into the fire. "What disturbs me is not what happens to him, nor to the

British, for that matter, but that so fine a ship should slip from my hands. Of course—that may not be his purpose. Perhaps he is taking a load of goods to Russia. With the lowered tariffs such a voyage would be profitable, providing the British do not halt him. Perhaps he thinks he can run the British blockade." The banker slapped the arm of his chair in sudden irritation. "It is something of the sort, I'll be bound! He's not content with a legitimate business proposition with reasonable profits. He wants ten times the usual returns, in exchange for a great risk, brash young devil that he is. I should have known it, and bought his option before he took it elsewhere."

Cass stretched lazily. "What's the penalty if he is caught?"

"Britain will not treat corsairs as prisoners of war, and exchange them for British captives, of that you may be certain," Blake said dryly. "If he tries privateering and is caught, as he eventually will be, of course, he'll be hanged."

The banker's tone indicated that he approved the penalty. Henry Austin watched Loyalty. She sank back in her chair and her face paled a little. Cass took pity upon her.

"But he may not be a privateer. If he intends only to run the blockade with a cargo for a Russian port—then he risks nothing but his ship?"

"If the British stop him, the delay will undoubtedly ruin him, as it has many a man." Thaddeus chewed on his cigar reflectively. "If he carried contraband his ship would be seized. He'd rot in some British prison until the end of the Crimean War, at any rate, and if he were ever freed, he'd be a pauper. I should not be surprised if he had agreed, for such a sum, to run contraband." Thaddeus arose and paced the width of the room swiftly, then came back to the fire. He passed his hand over the back of his head as he often did when in deep thought. "It is my duty to notify the State Department."

"The State Department, sir?" Austin asked quickly.

"It is said that our fleet was on its way to Japan and has been recalled to protect American shipping. An international incident could arise from all of this, if there is bungling. In any case, that ship should be watched. I would certainly like to know," the banker added slowly, "by what means he secured that money from Russia."

"Is the ship still at Brighton's yard?" Cass asked. "I'd like to see it. Suppose I make a call on Steel—to congratulate him, and wish him well?"

Blake sat down again wearily. "If you like. I presume there is no harm in it. You might attempt to find out what his cargo is and where he is heading on his first voyage. Not that he is apt to tell you. He can be very close-mouthed. Furthermore, he has already antagonized the waterfront. Christensen says he is determined to choose his own crew, as he told us. He is working on the ship himself, pushing the repairs as fast as possible, and he is heavily armed wherever he goes. The ship is supposed to be almost ready to sail. Steel is forced to guard against attempted sabotage, even while his ship is tied up in his home port. He is wading in trouble up to his neck. Non-conformist, on all counts. I should have guessed it and dealt with him accordingly."

"He's taking a great chance," Cass said after a minute. He could not keep a little admiration from his tone. Thaddeus nodded.

"If my guess is correct he's risking his life and every cent he possesses on a slim chance of owning that ship free and clear. It is a great gamble."

"Yes," Austin agreed. His face was slightly flushed. "While your proposition to him, sir, would have been as safe as any business venture could be. Steel is a fool."

The banker tossed his cigar into the fire and brought his eyes around to Austin's face. He stroked the back of his head again, frowning, thinking intently. Irritation and chagrin were not sufficient to fog the banker's judgment nor his fairness. He preferred caution, himself, longer, safer investments, careful trading and political maneuvering. But he had seen other men found fortunes by staking all they possessed on one magnificent move. Those men were not to be underrated. He smiled a little and shook his head slightly.

"No, Henry," he said softly. "Not if he wins."

[2]

LOYALTY sat, straight-backed and determined, on a small, stiff chair in the Blake drawing room, her gloved hands clasped in her lap, over her tiny enameled scent-box and her folded carriage parasol. From beneath the velvet brim of her bonnet she was regarding her brother and Henry Austin calmly.

Neither Cass nor Henry was calm. Cass paced back and forth restlessly and Austin stood stiff and disapproving, his back to the empty fireplace.

"You can't go, Loyalty, and that is the end of it!" Cass said furiously. Loyalty's gray eyes rested on him thoughtfully for an instant.

"Then I shall go alone."

Austin took a step toward her and his voice was firm.

"Loyalty, certainly you do not wish to be in any situation in which you might be subject to insult—or which would cause gossip?"

Loyalty tossed her head. Plainly the threat of gossip disturbed her not at all. Loyalty's eyes were steady and clear and she made a beautiful picture, Austin thought, regarding her with devotion and exasperation. Her cloak was of blue-gray velvet and the bonnet, held in place by a wide satin bow, was of the same color and material. It was decorously brimmed; a single scarlet rose of shimmering velvet nestled behind one ear, half against the bonnet, half against the shining black curls that escaped over her collar. It was knowingly placed, by a milliner with an eye for accent and innocent invitation. The tight basque of her jacket fitted her straight shoulders smoothly and hugged her small waist, neatly outlining the full, high, beautiful curve of her bosom. Loyalty's costume was rich and expensive and in the best of taste and fashion; but its soft and helpless femininity encased a stubbornness and determination that was slowly wearing down the defenses of the two men before her.

"Father will never permit it. Respectable girls do not appear on the waterfront," Cass argued.

"But they do," Loyalty protested. "Alice Merrill went, to a ship's launching."

"That was different, Loyalty," Austin explained patiently. "Alice went with her parents, and proper provision was made for her and all the ladies present. This is not a special event, like a launching, or even a ship's sailing. Cass and I are just driving to South Street on business. It might even be dangerous."

Loyalty arose. "Very well," she said. Her skirts swayed as she sailed toward the door. "It seems to me a very small thing to do for me, Henry, to take me on a drive with you. Of course, if you do not wish to please me—" She shrugged. "I am sure," she added, her voice sweet and injured, "that nothing could happen to me with Cass and you to protect me. But of course, if I must go without protection, then I must." She turned her back and crossed the hallway, but she walked more slowly when she was out of sight, listening to the voices behind her.

"Your father must be informed, Cass." Austin spoke first. Cass was silent. On the stairway Loyalty paused and dimpled. She had aided her brother too many times and the bond between her and Cass was too close. He would never betray her confidences. There was a silence behind her and Loyalty began very slowly to mount the stairs. From the hallway below Cass called sulkily.

"Loyalty." She stopped but did not turn her head. "Come on, then," he said grudgingly. "It's against my better judgment but—" He shrugged. "The carriage is waiting."

She turned and ran down the stairs, clasping Cass' arm and sparkling up at him in delight.

"I'll be no trouble, Cass, I promise!" Despite himself he grinned back at her. Laughing, she turned to Austin, willing to forgive his obstinacy, now that she had her way. This excursion to South Street was to be a real lark. She wanted nothing to spoil it. Austin shook his head slowly, not taking his eyes from her face, and raised her hand slowly to his lips. He was very serious, Loyalty thought. Too serious. She took his arm and the three left the house and were seated in the carriage. Austin's face was dark with displeasure.

She snuggled back against the cushions, and, after stealing a glance at him, and then at Cass, gave her complete attention to the coming meeting with Matthew Steel.

Her heart was pounding like a bass drum and she wondered that Henry and Cass could not hear it. It was true that Austin could sense her excitment, for her color was high and her eyes were sparkling, and Austin did not like it. The last thing in the world he wanted was for Loyalty to meet Matthew Steel again. It might be just another adventure for the girl; but Steel, though he had appeared unaware of her beauty when he had first met her, was not blind. Austin believed the man as unscrupulous as he was daring, and Loyalty, young and sheltered as she had been, was no match for a man like Steel. She was innocently playing with fire and Austin was well aware of it. However, if she must meet Steel, it would be better for Austin to be present. He had contemplated a pleasant year of correct and conventional courtship of Loyalty Blake. This Captain Steel was an unexpected interruption. Austin was uneasy as the carriage turned toward South Street.

Cass, too, was thoughtful. Close as he was to Loyalty, sensing his sister's every emotion, he had felt an intense attraction between her and Matthew Steel. It was a good thing the man was sailing almost at once. He was certainly no serious threat to Austin, Cass thought, this soldier of fortune who admitted he preferred sophisticated women to pretty girls; but at the same time, Cass, though not usually discreet, felt instinctively it was unwise to take Loyalty to South Street. At any rate, it was going to be an interesting meeting, Cass decided.

Loyalty had never been this far down Broadway before, never below the Astor House. She craned her neck, trying not to be too obvious, trying to mask her eagerness with adult dignity. The carriage turned on Fulton Street. She was delighted they were going directly to the waterfront, and then along the strand toward the repair yard near Corlear's Hook. It was not the most direct route, but it gave them an opportunity to view the waterfront. Loyalty bent forward, forgetting herself completely as they turned into the street of ships.

It seemed to her there were a thousand drays, heavily loaded and drawn by heavy horses, and they stopped the progress of the carriage again and again. There was a peculiar smell in the air, not only the pungent animal odor, but the moldy, fishy odor of tide-flats and the East River, and her nostrils quivered, not liking it. But the carriage passed almost directly beneath the bowsprits of giant ships, and she caught her breath at the size and the number and the nearness of them. Their bare spars towered high into the sky, thick and sharp and endless, strong and powerful.

They passed a shipyard and Loyalty caught a glimpse of scaffoldings and heard the sound of hammers and mallets and men's shouts. There were odd crowded shops and great warehouses, and within only a few minutes, it seemed to her, the carriage came to a stop. She wished she had time to prepare herself a little more, before she faced Matthew Steel again. This was his world, he was at home here, in this welter of busy, laboring men and great weights and ropes and ships, and it was terrifying and fascinating all at once.

But she peeked out and upward curiously and saw for the first time Matthew Steel's ship. Its clean, sharp lines, spelling grace and speed, were evident even to her, in contrast to the heavier, weathered vessels she had passed. The ship's hull was newly painted, a gleaming jet black, and above that she wore a band of dashing scarlet. The name, whatever name she wore under Captain Brenner's command, had been erased, and she had no figurehead. But the ship looked huge and beautiful, sparkling and proud. It seemed to Loyalty the vessel had already taken on some of the dashing confidence of her new owner. No wonder Matthew Steel had yearned to possess such a craft!

Austin and Cass had alighted from the carriage, and were staring at the ship, but a man blocked their path. He was a tall, spare man, with a thin face and irregular features, and his eyes were small and sharp. Loyalty could not hear what they were saying, but the man was armed and she gathered that he was a guard. He turned his head once and spat tobacco juice, and then he motioned to someone she could not see. Cass came back to the carriage.

"The fellow has sent our names to Captain Steel." He grinned. "Are you sorry you came?"

Loyalty did not answer. Over Cass' shoulder she saw Matthew

Steel. He was wearing a faded pair of dungarees and a bright red shirt. The shirt was open at the throat and the sleeves were rolled up. His arms and neck were as brown as his face. There was a battered officer's cap on the back of his head, a slight concession to his rank. As he approached he wiped his face swiftly on his sleeve and his forehead wrinkled as he looked at his visitors. The sun was in his eyes, and Loyalty realized that he did not yet see her. It gave her a moment's advantage and she was grateful. In his belt were both a pistol and a knife and he wore them with the ease of practice. His manner did not appear to be hurried or tense, nor was his face drawn with excitement as she might have expected it to be. He did not look as though he was much impressed with the danger of becoming a privateer, she thought. He looked happy and at ease, and when he saw her his black eyes did not sweep over her and dismiss her as they had before. Instead they fastened on her, ignoring Cass and Henry, and a grin twisted his lips and his teeth flashed. Loyalty swallowed. Despite herself she could not prevent an answering smile. She thought it would be very easy to laugh with Matthew Steel. He bowed, and she forgot that she had never seen anyone but servants or workmen wear dungarees; he might have worn the velvet and satin of a cavalier. She laughed outright and returned his greeting. She was no longer afraid of the waterfront, for all its noise and confusion.

He turned to greet Austin and Cass, holding out his hand in easy friendliness. His voice was as deep as she remembered it and she gripped her hands very hard, trying not to show her excitement. A dimple appeared in her cheek and Matthew fastened his eyes upon it.

"It's a great honor," Matthew was saying. "You came to see my ship? I should be delighted to show her to you."

"We came to congratulate you," Austin answered. He was trying hard to keep his voice even. "She's very beautiful."

Matthew nodded. Then his eyes left Loyalty and swept over his ship. There was pride and fondness in his face.

"She's a fine ship. She's stout and strong and fast."

"You are almost ready to sail?"

"Only a few days more." He turned back to Loyalty. "Would

you care to come aboard? She's been freshly painted inside, but I think the paint is dry by now. I'd be proud."

He offered his hand and Loyalty put her own into it without hesitation. His hand was strong and warm and it steadied her as she stepped from the carriage. The guard stood back, watching, and Loyalty thought she saw a quick look pass from him to Steel. They moved toward the ship. Loyalty clutched her scent-box and parasol, maneuvered her skirts as gracefully as possible as they went aboard. As she stepped on the deck she caught her breath; a host of men were working on the rigging, some were aloft, unconcerned at the height and danger, and others were holystoning the deck to a spotless, gleaming white. The brasswork shone and sparkled, and over all was the odor of fresh paint, of new lumber, of new ropes, and the close-reefed sails were snowy white. Clean and sparkling and new and beautiful, Loyalty felt the power of the graceful ship beneath her and she stared about her with pure delight.

Austin was at her side, occasionally placing himself between her and the workmen who glanced up at the party, curious, unself-conscious. Now and then their tour was interrupted by a sailor who approached Captain Steel respectfully, waiting to ask a question and receive orders. Loyalty glanced into the forecastle, the galley and then the main cabin and she touched gleaming wood panels, and stood on the bridge and ran her hands about the great wheel, listening, entranced, while Matthew explained to her the ship's instruments, named for her the binnacle and compass, pointed out the great ship's bell. At last he took them to his own cabin, and Loyalty sank into the Captain's chair at his table, trying to veil her curiosity, trying not to let her eyes rove about the small but comfortable quarters, eying Matthew Steel's few personal possessions. A new uniform, brushed and pressed, hung on a wall. Maps and charts and writing materials littered the table. There was no sign of any feminine occupancy, Loyalty noted shrewdly, no picture, no momento for the Captain to take with him on his first voyage. Loyalty hardly listened to the conversation of the men. She was lost in a world of which she had never dreamed, and then she remembered suddenly what her father had said. Was Matthew Steel really going to take this beautiful ship to sea, to raid and plunder British and French ships? Would he, and those men she had watched at their work, actually fight and steal and kill? Was he going to run the British blockade, race British ships for his fortune and his life? If that were his sole purpose—then confidence welled up in her heart. With this ship, Captain Steel could win any race!

They were ready to leave the ship. They had taken enough of the Captain's time, Austin said smoothly. Matthew preceded them, guarding Loyalty with his own body from any new paint or unfinished carpentry. He leaped lightly down the small ladder to the deck below and held up his arms to her. Hesitantly she put her hands upon his shoulders and he lifted her quickly to the deck without effort. She turned her head to hide her face beneath the bonnet. She had remembered that she had intended to repay Matthew Steel for his treatment of her the first time they met. She had enjoyed the excursion so much and he had been so courteous she had almost forgotten her real purpose in coming. It was almost too late. They had left the ship now and neared the carriage.

"What will you name the ship?" she asked.

"That's my biggest problem," Matthew answered. Well, she thought, if his biggest problem is the naming of his ship, then he cannot be facing such dangers as my father suggested. She glanced at him a little speculatively, her lashes lowered, and noted again the weapons at his belt. "Perhaps you could suggest a fitting name, Miss Blake?"

She had a feeling that he was laughing at her, indulgently, as at an amusing child. She had been very close to him when he lifted her to the deck. His bold eyes had hardly left her since she came aboard the ship, for all his gallantry. She took her place in the carriage with dignity, settled her skirts. She turned her stormy gray eyes directly upon him. Matthew Steel could sail away, to wherever he was going, but he would not forget her!

"You might call her the *Pretty Virgin!*" she said swiftly.

There, she thought. I'm not as stupid or as young as you suppose. She was gratified that he started slightly and then he laughed. Too late she realized that now he would know that she had been so unladylike as to eavesdrop upon him. She blushed crimson, but Matthew Steel was not disturbed.

He bowed, a trifle mockingly and though his reply was polite she felt uneasily that his words were double-edged.

"I might take your suggestion. However, I must give it a little thought. The *Pretty Virgin* would be a fitting name, ma'am, if she were always to lie safely at a snug New York dock. But this ship will be with me in all kinds of weather and my entire future depends upon her. I must be sure she has a worthy name."

Loyalty heard Austin mutter beneath his breath. He was on the opposite side of the carriage, his foot upon the step, and she turned to look at him and was startled to see that he was white and frowning. For the first time Loyalty felt a little twinge of fear. What had she done? What had happened? She glanced back at Matthew and she saw the smile fade from Steel's face as he and Austin looked at one another, and Matthew's mouth hardened, all humor faded from it. Matthew moved back to permit Cass to be seated, and Loyalty was silent, glad to be shielded by her brother.

"Why rename her, Captain?" Cass asked. "What did Brenner call her?"

"Under Brenner she was the *Sea Rover*. Nothing wrong with the name, except that it's associated with the coolie trade—and I want no part of that. I don't mean the legitimate business of transporting Chinese miners from Hongkong to California. Brenner wanted to make a fortune quickly, and he took coolies from Swatow to Peru and sold them to speculators. Some Portuguese and South Americans pay well for coolies and Brenner could pick them up in Swatow for a song, from gamblers holding them for debts. But slaving is a bad business. Brenner's last load mutinied and set fire to the ship, and many of them suffocated, for he was carrying too big a load. I want all traces of slaving removed from my vessel. I've torn out the sleeping shelves and repaired all damage done by the fire and mutineers, and I want no reminder of that kind of cargo. I'd never take a ship named the *Sea Rover* into a Chinese port. I've friends among the Chinese. They are good people."

Steel had seemed to forget Loyalty's presence, and Austin's face was grim. Didn't Steel know that such talk was distressing to a girl? She was staring at the ship with new eyes now, horrified, unable to believe that the beautiful vessel had been used for such inhuman purposes. What a monster Captain Brenner must have been! No wonder Captain Steel would rename the ship, erase every reminder of her infamous past. And if he would do that, surely he would not disgrace this lovely vessel by putting her to another illegitimate use—privateering. Loyalty was puzzled and confused. He was a contradictory and complex man, different from any she had ever known. Now his attention was brought back to her and his voice was gentle, as though to soften for her the terrifying picture he had just painted.

"We seamen are a superstitious lot, Miss Blake. That is why we take seriously such things as the name of our ship and her figurehead, for they must bring us good fortune. I must decide soon. Cromwell, the carver, near Market Slip, is waiting for my order, and we've discussed many ideas, but none yet seems to fit." He bowed, stepped back from the carriage. "It was nice of you to come. Please pay me another visit when my ship is in port. My respects to your sister and your father."

Loyalty inclined her head and said nothing. Austin bowed stiffly. The carriage, at a word from Cass, moved ahead and prepared to turn in a wide arc to take them back the way they had come. As the carriage swung around Loyalty saw Matthew Steel again. He was standing with his hands on his hips, his hat pushed back, looking after them. A girl had approached and she was only a few steps away, and Matthew had not yet seen her. The guard did not stop her, but smiled and permitted her to pass. The late afternoon sunlight caught in the girl's hair and seemed imprisoned there, for it glimmered and shone like polished copper. She was a tall girl and she moved smoothly and gracefully. Cass and Austin saw her, too, and Cass leaned forward for a better view. The girl turned her face toward Matthew, a pale face with a smiling mouth. She went up to him and slipped her arm through his and Matthew looked down at her, undisturbed, as though he were quite used to having her at his side, and then he glanced back at the carriage again. Loyalty was glad when they had passed and were out of sight.

"Who the devil—" Cass began. Cass and Austin exchanged glances and Cass was silent. When Austin spoke he did not refer to the woman who had taken her place so confidently at Matthew Steel's side, nor did he state the obvious fact—that it had been a great mistake for Loyalty to insist upon accompanying them to South Street. He spoke casually of other things until the carriage stopped once again before the Blake house, and Loyalty was grateful for his courtesy. Henry Austin was a gentleman, she thought, and it was, at this moment, a great comfort. Austin himself thought he could afford to relax now. The meeting was over and Loyalty, Austin thought, had seen Matthew Steel for the last time. She had also seen the red-haired girl for herself. His spirits lifted.

Loyalty climbed the stairs to her room and slowly took off her bonnet and put down her parasol. She was trembling and she felt weak inside. She wondered about the red-haired girl and what she meant to Matthew Steel. Was he in real danger, as the weapons he wore indicated? Her cheeks burned as she thought of her own remark to Captain Steel—how childish it seemed now, how petty and silly a flirtation with a man like Captain Steel!

She sat down before her mirror and began to arrange her hair absent-mindedly, and then, for the first time, she missed her scent-box. She tried to convince herself she had left it in the carriage, but she knew she had not. She had placed it on the table in Captain Steel's quarters, and when she had left she had gathered up her parasol and gloves and overlooked the tiny box. She wondered if Captain Steel would return it to her—and if he did, would he send her a message? Perhaps not. Perhaps only the red-haired girl interested him. The thought disturbed Loyalty very much.

Cass was forced to report to his father that Captain Steel had given him no information whatsoever about his sailing date or his destination or his cargo. Cass watched the shipping notices, and Loyalty surreptitiously read them, too. It was three days after their visit to the ship that the bomb burst in the Blake household.

Under Marine Intelligence, Arrivals and Departures, Vessels Arrived, Vessels Cleared, Vessels Up, appeared a dignified notice that startled and puzzled Loyalty. It was, moreover, a stunning blow to Thaddeus Blake, and a stinging challenge to Henry Austin.

It stated, in careful block letters that the *Loyalty,* Matthew Steel, captain, would depart at seven o'clock the following morning for Charleston, carrying a cargo of hardware and drygoods. The Captain would not be responsible for any debts contracted by his crew.

[3]

THE conference in Thaddeus Blake's library had gone on for several hours. Loyalty, in her room, was wild with curiosity to know what was occurring in the room below. Now and then she tiptoed to the upper hall and looked over the banister, and she could hear voices rising and falling behind the closed library door. Once a servant had entered the library with a tray, and Loyalty had heard her father's voice, louder than usual and much agitated.

"And have my daughter's name in the public prints? Heaven forbid!" Thaddeus had shouted. The door had closed and Loyalty had winced and gone to Serena. Her older sister blamed herself for the entire affair. She had been derelict in her duty as chaperone to permit Loyalty to go with Cass and Henry to the waterfront. Thaddeus had assured Serena the fault was not hers; that even this rash escapade of Loyalty's might have been without untoward incident if Captain Matthew Steel had not happened to be a scoundrel, and if he, Thaddeus, had not so misjudged the man as to invite him into the Blake household in the first place. It was, Thaddeus had told Serena and Loyalty, a most unfortunate, appalling occurrence, but it was men's business to handle it. The only thing the Blake sisters could do was to treat the entire affair and any inquiries about it with dignified silence. And they might, he added as an afterthought, pray that Captain Steel's ship was not featured in any infamous ventures that would bring ill repute to his vessel and which might reflect on Loyalty Blake.

Loyalty herself wondered just what Matthew Steel meant by the gesture; did he think *Loyalty* synonymous with *Pretty Virgin*, and was this his way of accepting her suggestion? Had he done it just to plague her, or as a final jibe against Thaddeus Blake, or was it really a tribute to her? She was not at all sure whether to be angry, humiliated or flattered. If the ship was to become a corsair, she did not, of course, wish it to bear her name. But when she thought of Captain Steel, and the way he had looked when he told her the name must bring him good fortune—then she felt it a high honor and the thought sent tingles of pleasure through her. He loved his ship. Her name was important to him and he had chosen what he thought a fitting one. But Thaddeus apparently considered it a brazen piece of business that he could not tolerate, and he had called into the discussion not only Cass and Henry Austin, but his attorney, the elder Austin, as well; Christensen, his faithful clerk and assistant; and two strangers whom Loyalty had never met.

Now Loyalty waited in her room. She had prepared for bed but she wrapped herself in a dressing gown and sat down to wait, leaving her door open a crack. It was late when voices below told her the guests were leaving, and then after a while she heard Cass come up the stairs. Her father was still below. Loyalty slipped to the door and whispered urgently.

"Cass!"

He hesitated, and then he came into her room and closed the door behind him.

"Cass, what happened?"

"Hush. Father is furious. Henry Austin wanted to call Steel out."

"Fight a duel? Why—that's unlawful, and anyway, why?"

"He can't, of course, but he'd like to run a sword through him. . . . Mr. Austin said there was no legal way to make Steel change the name of his ship without causing a lot of talk and probably stories in the newspapers, and Father thinks that would be worse than to let the matter lie. After all—not many people know Steel has met you, and the word Loyalty need not necessarily be a girl's name—so, they've decided to ignore the whole matter for the time being—unless, of course, Steel gets into worse trouble. Then Father will take steps."

"Who were the other men, besides Christensen?"

"Ned Carrigan, a cotton speculator." Cass laughed softly. "Steel bought that cotton in the Latham warehouse that father told him about."

"Oh, Cass, that's—"

"Well, Father would have bought his ship if he could have got to it first. It's legitimate enough, but it hasn't endeared him to Father. The other man was Graham White, of the State Department. It seems everyone thinks Steel is going to run contraband to Russia. But no one is sure. There are plenty of rumors along South Street, Christensen says. Steel had published notice he's going to Charleston, and that's right enough, for he's going down to pick up that cotton, and I think he wants a trial run of his ship. But he's also carrying a ship's carpenter and sailmakers aboard; ordinarily the coasting vessels do not carry such a crew; all their work is done in port. It looks as though he is planning a longer voyage. He has a superb crew. They say he hand-picked most of his men, and others, hearing about it, volunteered to join him. He hasn't hired a one through the usual channels, and his men are sleeping aboard, under heavy guard."

"Cass, what is wrong with that? That sounds very brave to me."

"It is. It's a system that shipowners have been trying to break for years, but without success. Father has often said it's an evil custom. These runners, or land sharks, whatever you wish to call them, get the seamen drunk or drugged; then they throw them aboard, and naturally such a crew, sick and beaten and in debt and virtually kidnaped, aren't loyal and are hard to handle and that accounts for much of the brutality aboard the ships. It's hard to maintain discipline and work a ship with such men. But it seems it is a powerful system and Steel has antagonized some bad characters on the waterfront by defying it. They swear to kill him." Cass chuckled. "It is funny, really—the worst scum of the waterfront are after him, and so is Father, most respected financier in New York!"

"But Cass—why Father? I know he's furious at losing the ship, and I suppose buying the cotton makes him angry, but do not such things often happen in business? Hasn't Father done the same sort of thing to others?"

"It's not only that." Cass hesitated. Then he sat down on the edge of her bed and looked up at her. "Your honor is at stake. It's the figurehead."

"The figurehead?"

"Yes. That's why Henry wanted to call him out." Cass grinned. "They say it is the most beautiful figurehead ever to be seen on South Street, and it is attracting as much attention as the ship itself."

"But what is it—a ship with my name?"

"It's a woman, my dear. A pure white, very graceful and very —well—attractive young woman, very scantily clothed."

Loyalty gasped.

"They say," Cass continued, "that it is a very appropiate figurehead for Matthew Steel's ship. He's very popular with women."

"My life!"

Cass stood and yawned. "That's what comes of your flirtations, my girl. And so Father is out to ruin him. He says he'll black ball him in New York if it's the last thing he ever does. That's all. I'm going to bed." He looked up and down the hall quickly and slipped out. Loyalty dropped her dressing gown and lay down, but not to sleep. If there were only more time, she thought, she would send a message to Captain Steel. He had said a name and figurehead must bring him luck; this name and this figurehead certainly would do exactly the opposite. Perhaps, if he knew that, he might change it before it was too late.

She tossed and slept and awakened again. It was not every girl who had a beautiful ship named for her, she thought, defiantly. If only she were quite sure that Captain Steel would do nothing to disgrace the name—she sat up in bed and then she got up and knelt by the window. Once before she had knelt here and seen Matthew Steel swinging off down the street. If only she had an opportunity to know him better. She felt growing within her an increasing certainty that he was an honorable man, and the more she thought about it the more strongly she believed it. If the ship were named for her, that gave her a certain responsibility, did it not? No harm must come to him through her father, or her suitor, Henry Austin, because he had chosen to name his ship for her.

She wished that she could see the ship once more, and the figurehead, and know for herself exactly what it was. Then she believed she could understand exactly what Matthew Steel's intention had been. The newspaper notice had said the ship was sailing from Burling Slip, at Pier 21. At seven o'clock.

Early morning sounds began to come to Loyalty through her open window. She dressed quietly, and she put on a long, gray cloak, to make herself as inconspicuous as possible. She left her room silently, slipped down the back stairs and out the servants' entrance and called a boy on his way to the stables. She waited in the entranceway until Bennett appeared at the alley entrance and then she ran to his carriage.

"Pier 21, Bennett, and hurry."

She crowded close in a corner of the carriage, paying no further attention to the driver. Bennett's big, bloated face was doubtful and serious, but he did not question her. There was little traffic until they were far downtown, but it thickened as they neared the waterfront. Finally the carriage slowed.

"Wait for me, Bennett," she commanded. "Right here. Please don't move from here, so I can find you easily." She was frightened but she was also determined. There was a crowd milling about the pier, and over their heads Loyalty could see the ship. There it was, the beautiful black and white and scarlet vessel—and there was the name, flashing in great gilt letters—*Loyalty*. And there was the figurehead.

Why, there is nothing disgraceful about it, she thought; it's beautiful and gallant, the flowing lines, the proud carriage. It was sensuous, yes, and young, but so artfully carved it seemed the only possible figurehead that would properly fit that proud ship. Loyalty stared at it, her face flushing, wondering. Does it look like me? Is that the way he sees me? She heard a shrill cackle and looked down to see the old beggar clutching his violin. He was sitting on his small stool, as if he were on his usual street corner, and his dog crowded close beside him. His old, wrinkled face twisted and worked, his dim eyes watering. He looked up at her and gestured, delighted to talk to anyone, friend or stranger.

"I've known Matt Steel since he was a boy, and now he's owner of that fine ship! Pray for good winds for the lad!"

Loyalty glanced beyond the beggar. A massive, bull-necked man with an ugly, coarse-featured face, which she felt instinctively covered an ugly soul, hunched his thick shoulders against the early morning breeze and muttered. He was staring at the ship, swearing, and now he whirled to the beggar.

"Shut your slobbering mouth, Old Dan! I pray he burns in hell and his bastard crew with him! If he gets his just deserts his first voyage'll be his last!" A stream of profanity poured from his lips and Loyalty recoiled, repelled by the hate and fury in his face. The man plunged into the crowd and was lost. She looked down at Old Dan and her lips felt stiff as she spoke.

"Who was that man?"

Old Dan spat tobacco juice in the direction the man had taken.

"That's Jimmy From Town," he croaked. "Jimmy Burns—a crimp—only he didn't supply Captain Steel's crew! Matthew took his bucko mate from aboard a slaver, and took the rest out of the Cherry Street boarding houses right under the nose of Jimmy From Town! That one'll never collect a commission on Captain Steel's men." Old Dan chuckled in great glee, his shoulders shaking "Swore to run a knife through Matt Steel, or fire his ship, but he'd not the chance!"

Loyalty stood on tiptoe, craning her neck. Right at the water's edge, staring up at the ship, stood the red-haired girl. She had her hands hidden in the pockets of her coat, and her head was bare. She seemed unaware of the crowds pushing her from both sides. Sometimes people spoke to her and she answered them without taking her eyes from the ship.

"The figurehead," an eager voice said behind Loyalty. "I came to see the figurehead."

A man laughed coarsely. Beside her a sailor spoke, to no one in particular:

"She's built to stand up under sail. A good thing, too, with Matthew Steel in command!"

"Steel will let a sail blow away before he'll take it in," another volunteered. "I sailed with him once, when he was first officer. She'll break all records, that one."

A well-dressed merchant spoke meaningly: "Outrun the British, do you think?" There was a spurt of laughter and no answer.

The sailor raised his head, studied the sky. "A strong westerly breeze and an ebb tide . . . a good start." There was a note of envy in his voice.

Suddenly, over the mumble of the crowd came music, and this time it was the slow, rising chorus of men's voices, young and powerful voices, and then one lone voice, the strongest and deepest of all. Loyalty recognized it as the crowd quieted to listen and she strained to see the singer.

"The Captain's leadin' the chantey himself!" The word went through the crowd like a breeze.

"By the livin' God—" Old Dan spoke reverently.

A fat woman, whose arms strained at the seams of her coat, dabbed at her eyes with her sleeve. A servant girl patted the woman's big shoulder.

"He'll come back, Mrs. Doughty," she said comfortingly.

"Of course he'll come back, Lexie," the woman said sharply. "But there's somethin' about a ship's sailin' . . ."

Apparently Captain Steel had no fear of problems of discipline aboard his ship. He could forget his position long enough to tell South Street good-by as he had on many a voyage. Loyalty could not see him, but she could hear him, and now she knew why this crowd was here to see Matthew Steel's ship sail on this early morning. Except for Jimmy From Town and his cohorts, these people were his friends; they knew Captain Steel was going into danger. They had followed his fight from his childhood, to this supreme moment, and they were here to wish him well. There was gaiety and assurance and bravado and courage in the voice of Captain Steel, and Loyalty was not surprised to feel the crowd grow still.

"If the wind served fair he'd not be using towboats; he'd take her into stream himself!" It was Old Dan, the beggar again. But another man had moved to the beggar's side, a short, round man with a moon face, and he shook his head vigorously.

"You don't know Matthew Steel very well, to say that, Old Dan," the man said. "Matthew isn't one to make empty gestures. He'd take her out without towboats if there was something to be gained by it, but not as a flourish. He'd not endanger his ship to put on a good show—unless there was some purpose to it. He's not one to avoid danger if necessary, but he has good judgment, that boy, and he doesn't give a damn what anyone thinks of him." He turned to a companion. "You mind, Morton, when he was a kid, he'd not fight for fun, but only for money? And then how he put his heart into it!"

"You're right, Hite. Matthew Steel is no exhibitionist. . . . There she goes."

There was a slap of ropes, a crash of the gangplank, a sudden cheer. The towboats whistled and puffed busily and inch by inch the beautiful clipper began to ease away from South Street. Loyalty caught her breath. And then that lone voice again, alternating with the deep fierce chorus of a score or more voices:

"*Sally Brown she's a bright mulatto*," Matthew Steel's baritone rose.

"*Wa-ay, roll and go!*" his men answered him.

The ship had parted from the land and soon Matthew Steel would swing her head to sea; she would pass Governor's Island and outside the Narrows the snowy white sails would be spread, and they would carry him and the *Loyalty* down the channel and out by Sandy Hook. Into danger, perhaps, but somehow Loyalty Blake knew that it would not be dishonorable, and if it were to be a race she already knew the outcome. Her chin came up, though her throat felt full of tears. She was proud the ship bore her name and she resolved that he should be glad of his choice, even though she must become a buffer between her Father and Austin and Captain Steel. She was proud of the figurehead, the beautiful companion that would be with Matthew Steel on all his voyages. Her heart was singing, too, that haunting, lilting, rowdy song of the sea. As she hurried back to the carriage again she was humming the tune, and she did not notice the worried face of the bumbling old coachman.

She leaned out for one more look at the ship. Matthew Steel's friends and enemies were drifting away now, headed for the coffee houses, to discuss and speculate and wager on the outcome of his voyage. But the red-haired girl still stood, staring after the ship, and she was still standing there when Loyalty's carriage moved away.

Tessa Dunn watched the vessel until it was out of sight and then she turned and began to walk slowly down South Street. She was very tired, her face was pale and remote, but inwardly she was in a tumult. Matthew Steel had sailed away, but he would come back. Tessa was certain of that. However, when he docked again he would not be the same man she had known. He would come to the Cock and Bull, not only as an old friend who made the gin palace his headquarters, but as a sea captain and a hero, and crowds of admirers would be at his heels. For sentiment's sake he might call on Mrs. Doughty, but he would not occupy his old room at her boarding house. His position would be too important for that. He would go uptown, to one of the big hotels; he would be sought after by the city's merchants and traders and financiers; and he would be invited to the homes of the city's leaders and introduced to their daughters and wives. He'd be feted and dined and fawned over, and he would be farther removed from Tessa then than he was when there were thousands of sea miles between them.

That is, Tessa considered, her narrow eyes hard and glittering, he would be beyond her reach if she stood still while Captain Steel flashed ahead into power and glory.

She climbed the stairs to the drab little room which was her home. She closed the door behind her and lighted a candle, for the light was dim, even in daytime. She placed the candle on the bureau and looked at herself in the mirror. She took off her cloak and tossed it on the bed, and then she pulled the combs from her hair and let the glittering mass of it fall free about her shoulders. She put her hands on her waist, turning her slender body, measuring herself impersonally.

"My hair will help," she said aloud. She wrapped the gleaming rope of it swiftly around one arm, fastened it in a roll on her neck. "I'm too thin." But the proper clothing would help that. She smiled slowly. There was little mirth in Tessa's smile. She danced a few steps and nodded. She danced very well indeed, with an inborn sense of rhythm, and she could learn new steps and figures quickly. Her voice was good, low and haunting and unusual, and with a little training—

She began to plan carefully. There were teachers and agents, for the better establishments uptown. She must begin to work, to observe, to study and to cultivate those persons who could help her on her way. She ran her hands down her sides and then she laughed shortly and the sound seemed to hang suspended in the silent room. She had thought she could win Matthew Steel, bind him to her, by her very faithfulness, waiting for him and being near when he had time to notice her, by making herself a part of the waterfront he loved. But that was not the way to the heart of a man like Captain Steel. He would value nothing for which he did not have to fight.

She had seen Loyalty Blake in the carriage the day she had come to visit Matthew's ship. She knew why Matthew had named his vessel the *Loyalty*. The girl's beauty and her expensive dress had not been lost upon Tessa Dunn, and, watching Matthew Steel, a cold, icy ring had begun to form around her heart, a ring of fear and fury. That was when the determination had begun to crystallize inside her. Tessa Dunn, like Matthew Steel, was not one to give up without a fight. And she had many things in her favor. She took stock of them methodically.

First, she knew Matthew Steel and his background. She talked his language. She was his kind of woman. She loved him with all the intensity of a warm-blooded Irish girl starved for devotion. And Tessa Dunn would fight, using fair means or foul, for what she wanted. It made no difference to Tessa if Matthew Steel were privateer, contraband-runner, or slaver; she loved him. Loyalty Blake now—child that she was, indulged and spoiled and soft, no doubt, would not look at Matthew Steel unless he were respectable and successful and secure, Tessa thought, and her sullen lips curled at the thought. What could Loyalty Blake give Matthew Steel? What did she know of love and passion and sacrifice and fighting side by side with a man like Steel, through successes and failures, praise and slander? But Tessa knew. And as far as Tessa was concerned there were no rules to be followed; she would fight, tooth and nail, for the one she loved.

[4]

THERE were no passengers aboard the *Loyalty* save Thilo when she left Charleston harbor. The hold was crammed full of Charleston cotton, and the ship was well supplied for a longer voyage. Matthew Steel had been too busy with the thousands of decisions and details, last-minute preparations and repairs, to give much time to his own intimate thoughts. It was only when he was at sea again, beginning the trans-Atlantic run, that he allowed himself the luxury of remembering Loyalty Blake.

He had selected the name of his ship on a sudden impulse. He had thought of it as he stood watching the Blake carriage move away, and he had a last quick glimpse of Loyalty's lovely, serious face. He had said to himself "Loyalty," a little wonderingly, thinking that the name fitted the girl well. And suddenly it had come to him—*Loyalty,* for the name of his ship. He had looked after the carriage, thoughtfully, and then he had looked at his ship. Tessa Dunn had come to him and taken his arm and he had hardly noticed her, so engrossed was he in his thoughts.

But the more he thought of it the more he believed it right—the only possible name for his ship. The colors of it alone seemed to him to express Loyalty Blake, the jet black, the snowy white, the dash of scarlet; black hair, white skin, red lips—clean, startling contrasts—that was Loyalty Blake. He had thought of her first as a fascinating and beautiful girl not yet grown up—and then, in the instant he lifted her down the ladder something had changed. Her eyes had met his, shyly, questioningly, and her perfume, the touch of the soft velvet of her dress, the small waist beneath his hands, the warmth of her cheek as it came near to him, had made her very real, very much a woman and a most desirable woman at that. He had felt the girl's intense magnetism, and, he thought, she had felt some new emotion, too, for she averted her face quickly. Then, in the carriage, she had flashed at him that remark about the "pretty virgin," and he knew then that she was not unconscious of him, nor had she been since they first had met.

A friendship, he thought, or love, if it came to that, between a man and a woman, was built from so many little things. One small incident, one minute, piled upon another, like the hair-fine strands of a rope, until all together, interwoven, they grew into a strong bond. Because he was a man of the sea, and would not be near to Loyalty Blake day after day, he must make every minute count, every meeting a stronger, bigger strand in that final bond between them.

Henry Austin fully intended to make Loyalty his wife; of that Matthew was certain. Austin was possessive and jealous, and, by the standards of his world and the Blakes', it was a perfect match. He would be a thoughtful suitor; his courtship would neglect nothing, none of the small attentions which impress a girl; he had already had months and years of close association with her and her family, he had the advantage of a common background. Austin had everything in his favor.

But Loyalty Blake was only sixteen. It was unlikely, even though many girls married at that age, that she would wed before she was eighteen, at the earliest. Loyalty, despite her father's wishes, would undoubtedly make up her own mind about when and to whom she was married. She knew very well that marriage would circumscribe her activities even more than her sex and social position did now. If Matthew guessed rightly, and he felt he understood Loyalty Blake very well, she would be in no hurry to become Mrs. Henry Austin.

Meanwhile, if he were to strengthen their friendship, he had to take whatever means were at his disposal. He considered it carefully for twenty-four hours. Did he want to strengthen their friendship? Did he want to keep himself in Loyalty's thoughts? He laughed at himself at the certainty of his answer. He had never been quite so convinced of anything in his life.

What better gesture could he make, then, than naming his ship for her? What stronger link could there be between them—and what more appropriate name for the vessel itself?

He had described the figurehead he wanted to Cromwell and the wood carver had nodded his head and smiled and his eyes lighted with quick understanding and approval. His skillful fingers had fashioned the figurehead quickly and with genius, and the fame of it swept the street quickly. It proved, Matthew thought, that his decision was right. *Loyalty* was the proper name for his ship, the figurehead was the only one the ship could logically bear. It would bring him luck.

Tessa Dunn had been with him when he found Loyalty's tiny scent-box. He had picked it up and turned it in his hands, liking the tiny daintiness of it, feeling, as he did, that it, too, was an omen; he knew he should send it back to her, with a polite and formal note, but, thinking that, he shook his head. It was another strand, another link in the bond that he wanted to build between them. She was like no one else in the world, he thought. Gaiety and color and sweetness and michief. And beneath it a genuine steadfast integrity that a man could depend upon—no weakness, no compromise. These were new emotions for Matthew Steel and he did not wish to reveal them. But Loyalty Blake crowded his thoughts; she stood beside him at the wheel at night; he saw her in the shadows on the deck, in the occasional unexpected rainbow in the vessel's wake.

The strain of the voyage was telling on Matthew Steel, and as he sat at night over his log he found himself listening, tensely, all his senses overly keen, for any change in the force or direction of the wind, waiting, feeling with every nerve, any new motion or sound of the ship. There was no snugging down for the night under reduced sail for Matthew Steel; his ship sped on, and he logged the miles, praying for continued good winds. Thilo watched him, a smile now and then cracking his broad face, and sometimes he shook his head, thinking that the speed of the ship was due more to Captain Steel than to her hull and rigging.

During the day Matthew kept a glass glued to his eye, and now and then he sighted a sail. He watched for the flags of Britain and France. Once he passed a bark, with a Hamburg flag, going the same way, and each saluted and once he overtook a ship flying the stars and stripes. The other vessel was laying-to, and Matthew signaled for her number and was answered, and then he raced onward. The crew knew they were setting a record, and there was little talk in the forecastle, as the men grabbed every precious spare moment for rest, anxious to keep up with their sleepless commander. They sailed through squalls and fair weather, there were wild nights when only scraps of stars were visible, and then, as they passed the halfway mark, Captain Steel's work and vigilance increased.

He was outwardly more calm than before, but he was constantly alert. He watched most carefully of all for a thread of smoke on the horizon, or the flash of a sail no larger than a flag.

Twice they sighted British ships; one was hove-to, riding out a gale, and she disappeared quickly in the *Loyalty's* foaming wake; the other Matthew sighted at sundown and at morning she was gone. There was much other traffic, a Spanish ship and a Portuguese vessel, merchant ships and whalers.

But there was ahead of them the narrow passage into the Baltic sea, and there would be a ring of British ships closely guarding the traffic in and out of that entrance. Matthew had studied and figured carefully. Ships that did not want to be stopped—neutral vessels with contraband, Russian ships attempting to slip through the blockade, privateers, would make an effort to go through that passage at night. British blockaders. then, would patrol in an arc in the area through which incoming vessels would pass before dark. That was the danger zone and he was approaching it.

His only chance to avoid being halted was speed. If he could stay outside the area heavily guarded by the British blockaders until darkness fell; if he could slip past them by night and into comparative safety before dawn, by sailing faster than the British might imagine a ship could sail, he had a chance. But he must have the winds and the tides and darkness with him—and luck.

He saw the thread of smoke he feared just before sundown. She was a British war steamer, a lone patrol, and she was angling across his course. Thilo Kalin saw her, too.

She carried two ten-foot-long guns, forty-two-pounders, Matthew reckoned, fore and aft. Two forty-two-pound mortars and some smaller pieces, and as she swung around he saw that she had two broadside sixty-eight-pounders as well. Matthew's eyes slid to Thilo, standing silent beside him. Thilo was waiting—waiting for him to change his course, wondering how long it would be now before he would admit he could not run the blockade, before he would surrender to the British demand which was sure to come. Matthew could sense Thilo's tension, and his crew's quick response to his commands, the silence aboard the *Loyalty,* the attitudes of his men told him better than words that all of them were waiting —waiting sickly to witness his failure.

Matthew watched the sky and his compass and calculated the time before darkness. If only he could delay until darkness fell, if he could out-maneuver the man-of-war and then make a dash for it—he squinted at his watch. He could turn tail and throw the ship off his trail and lose himself in the thickening dusk. The man-of-war could not keep the *Loyalty* in sight if Matthew chose to make a race of it. . . . But if he did so, he'd have no chance of making his way through the passage this night; moreover, if he fled now and back-tracked another night the British would be in wait for him, and his chances of success would be halved. No, if he were to succeed at all he must keep straight on his course; he must not be detoured or delayed.

The ships were nearing, coming to the point on the triangle where they would meet. The first flash of canvas which Captain Steel had sighted had become a heavy cloud of sail, standing for the *Loyalty,* and through the glass he could distinguish many men aboard her. The Union Jack went up, and the Loyalty, at Matthew's crisp order, responded with the Stars and Stripes.

There would be no boarding party from the British vessel in these heavy seas. But there would undoubtedly be an order to proceed into a British port for inspection. And if he ignored the order, that ship was mighty well prepared to enforce her demand with shot. But the British vessel was awkward and slow compared to the fleet *Loyalty,* and darkness was coming. He had to play for time.

The British ship asked for his number and Matthew was not quick to respond. The *Loyalty* was gaining speed, preparing to run before the wind and put distance between her and the man-of-war. After a little while Matthew sent his number. The mate barked sharp orders to the waiting crew and the men were poised, ready for Matthew's order to change her course, to carry out the inevitable British command.

The British acknowledged Matthew's message, but now, despite the efforts of the man-of-war to come abeam, the distance was widening between the two ships. Matthew watched the barometer, he listened to the wind whistling in the rigging, and felt the motion of his ship, and he knew that the gods of the storms were aiding him. Before the next signal could go out from the British ship, which would, as a matter of course, ask him where he was from and bound, Matthew countered with a query of his own for longitude, and the British politely replied.

Captain Steel laughed aloud. Just a little more time—just a little more—was all he needed. The mates were grinning, too, and his crew took its cue from its officers. The steward and the cook had taken their places on deck, watching the British ship, sensing a race, and they were laughing and the cook slapped his thigh in delight. They knew now that Captain Steel would not bow meekly to the will of the British. Captain Steel was going to defy them. It would take shot—plenty of shot—to halt him or change the *Loyalty's* course, and respect for their captain's daring touched every man aboard.

There was a flurry aboard the British ship and Matthew knew that it was coming now, the order to proceed to a British port. But his deliberateness had gained precious time for him, and darkness was closing in fast and the wind had risen slowly and sullenly to roar and a shriek. But Matthew Steel did not take in sail and still he kept to his course. The *Loyalty* could take the gale and streak along before it, elusive and as hard to wound or capture as a shadow. Swiftly he sent the Stars and Stripes flying again, signaling that his conversation was at an end and he drew farther away from the British ship. The sails were strained full and tight; the deck slanted like a house roof, and Matthew waited, braced for a shot.

The man-of-war was frankly in pursuit and the order came, flashing at them abruptly across the waves; for the moment Matthew ignored it. There was no chance now for the British ship to come alongside, not with the *Loyalty* set for a race, but her guns could reach Steel's ship. Matthew watched, and he saw the guns trained full upon the *Loyalty*. Again he played for time, fumbling his signals, widening the distance, praying for quick darkness. Thilo waited, a passive bystander.

If Matthew guessed correctly there was some uncertainty and disbelief on the British ship. A heavily armed vessel such as that was not used to having her orders ignored, particularly by an unarmed merchant ship. It would take them a little while to decide, for firing on the Stars and Stripes was no small matter. Matthew trained his glass on the man-of-war, and his lips drew back from his teeth as he waited, almost holding his breath. If the *Loyalty* were seriously crippled, he'd have no choice but to yield. His ship would be hauled ingloriously into a British port and it would lie there through endless inquiries, and in the quarrels of nations his own future would be submerged. That would suit Thilo well. The price the Russians had paid him was not too much for a pawn that would be the instrument for securing the armed support of the United States against Great Britain.

There was movement on the British ship—unmistakable preparations to fire. Matthew snapped an order and his crew responded with the speed and smoothness which he had drilled into them for just such a moment as this. The *Loyalty* answered sweetly, swiftly; she swerved, like a great gull, her masts dipping, seeming almost to touch the water, and the first shot from the British guns thundered past her, harmlessly, and the ship righted itself again.

It was seamanship such as Thilo Kalin had never seen. Matthew Steel handled his great ship as though she were a toy, knowing exactly how much strain she could stand, feeling the wind currents and pressure on his own body and translating them instinctively into power and direction for his ship. The *Loyalty* moved like a dancer, lightly, daintily, evading, confusing her pursuer. Only once did a shot jar her; and at last the darkness Matthew awaited folded protectively about her, and she sped on, straight and true, toward her goal.

But the darkness and the high winds that had saved the *Loyalty* from the man-of-war were themselves a threat to the vessel. When at last the *Loyalty* came up to the long pier of St. Petersburg, her captain was at the helm. A three-days' growth of beard darkened his chin and his eyes were deeply smudged with fatigue. The ship's foretopsail was gone; the leeward staterooms showed watermarks and part of the lee rail was missing. The beautiful figurehead was polished by mountainous waves and a deep, raw crease, where a shell had struck and glanced off, marked the smooth deck. There was not a man aboard who was not nursing bruises and cuts and hands raw with rope burns; but the *Loyalty's log* showed no delay by British or French ships, nor any encounter with them. The most sensational entry showed that in one memorable twenty-four hours the *Loyalty* had sailed almost four hundred miles. Captain Steel had written the figures slowly, his fingers cramped and stiff, but they were plain and clear for all to see and that record alone was something to talk about for years to come.

Thilo Kalin was silent, alternately watching the pier and watching the work of the ship. He heard Matthew Steel's voice arise again in song and heard his exhausted men respond. The waiting crowds ashore did not understand the words of Matthew Steel's chantey, but the condition of the gallant ship itself, the Stars and Stripes flying proudly, told a clear story. They listened to the Captain's voice as he bade his crew:

"*Oh, the times are hard and the wages low.*"

And the crew responded, their voices hoarse but even: "*Leave her, Johnny, leave her.*"

"*And now ashore away we'll go,*" Matthew informed them.

"*It's time for us to leave her!*" his men roared in answer.

Only when the gangplank slammed to the wharf did Matthew Steel turn to Thilo. His bloodshot eyes, smarting from salt spray and fatigue, rested on the Russian and Thilo met his look squarely. Slowly Thilo held out his hand and Steel took it, and the Captain's cracked and swollen lips parted in the semblance of a grin.

"Well, Thilo?"

Thilo's other hand came down on Matthew's shoulder in a warm, affectionate grip. The welcoming cheers of the crowd ashore washed over them. A group of officials were coming aboard, and above them the protective Stars and Stripes flew in the cold, sharp Russian wind.

"You win, Matthew Steel," Thilo said slowly.

"What you mean, Thilo, is that I win—too," Matthew answered deliberately. "You could not have lost." His black eyes held the

Russian's. "Even—" he hesitated deliberately—"if the British had been so indiscreet as to fire upon us."

Thilo started. "But they—" he began swiftly and then he stopped and nodded, comprehending. "I see," he said, finally. "If the Captain of the *Loyalty* sees fit to make no official protest—then the incident did not occur." For a minute there was silence and Matthew could almost see the Russian making a mental survey. No record of a British attack in the *Loyalty's* log; no statement from any of Matthew's carefully selected officers; no evidence, after that one wound of the *Loyalty* was repaired; Matthew had agreed to run the blockade and he had fulfilled his bargain. It was to his advantage to let the incident be forgotten—and the *Loyalty* would then be free to go her way.

"I am glad this is the way it is, Matthew Steel," Thilo said at last. He shook his head wonderingly and took a deep breath. "By God, in seamanship, in navigation, I have never seen your equal. You are a genius, Captain." Then a flicker of amusement crossed his broad face, his delight and high spirits overcame him. "Else it is true that fortune favors fools!"

His grin broke into a slow chuckle and the chuckle to a laugh. Matthew joined him and in an instant the two men were roaring together. The Russian and the American understood one another very well.

The port officials were puzzled as they approached politely, to see the commander of the *Loyalty* and Thilo Kalin laughing together. The leader of the group held out his hand as Captain Steel turned to him and spoke in careful English.

"Welcome to St. Petersburg," he said formally.

Matthew Steel took the man's hand. "*Spasibo*—thank you," he responded quickly. Surprise and pleasure lighted the man's face.

"He speaks our language," he said approvingly to the group behind him.

Thilo Kalin spoke swiftly. "Indeed he does, gentlemen," he said. "Indeed he does."

[5]

THE story of Matthew Steel's voyage, the beauty of his ship, and the excellence of his crew lost nothing in the telling and retelling in the taverns, offices and drawing rooms of St. Petersburg. Ladies and gentlemen of rank, government representatives, naval officers and merchant seamen visited, inspected and admired the *Loyalty*. Matthew Steel had his first taste of the pleasures for which he had long labored and dreamed, the respect and recognition that come to a successful shipowner and daring commander. The warmth of the Russians' welcome was genuine. Their pleasure at the sight of the American flag was heartwarming, and Captain Steel was followed by crowds wherever he went. He was toasted long and heavily in vodka and he was considered by the Russians one of themselves, for his knowledge of their language endeared him to them.

The dark green of Russian naval uniforms was everywhere in evidence, for many a navy officer was moodily sweating out the war at the Kronstadt base, chafing because he could not get his ship out of the harbor to fight. Peter Segonov was one of them. He wore on his cuff the one broad and two narrow stripes of a lieutenant, and at his waist a short dirk in place of a sword. He was aboard the *Loyalty* a few hours after she docked, for the fame of the ship and her commander traveled as fast as the wind.

It was at the Segonov house where Peter triumphantly took him that Matthew Steel again met Captain Lesovsky of the Russian Imperial Navy, and it was after his conversation with Lesovsky that Matthew noted thoughtfully in his journal that Russia had already lost the Crimean War. "But that will not be the end of it," Matthew wrote. "It appears to me that Russia is stopped—this time—in her drive to reach the Mediterranean. But I believe that Russia will make other attempts for control of the Dardanelles. Naval officers (Lesovsky, Segonov and many others) are agreed that until they control that seaway they will be crippled as a sea power. If not this time, then the next, or the next, they will reach their objective, for that is the Russian nature, determined and with an almost Oriental patience and persistence. It is inevitable that the British will win this war, and it is likely that not a Russian warship, arsenal or naval base will remain in the Black Sea. The British lifeline of trade through the Mediterranean to India will hold and Britain will forever defend that line; she will fight to her last man to prevent Russia from winning a foothold in the Mediterranean. But Russia will never be satisfied until she does. Russian officers claim it their moral right to control the Dardanelles, so their Black Sea fleet will be able to sail into the Mediterranean in time of war; and that they may seal the Black Sea so an enemy fleet cannot enter and strike at Russian ports. It will ever be a bone of contention between Russia and Britain, and, until that problem is solved, I doubt the two countries will ever be truly at peace. It is fortunate for both the United States and Russia that no such barrier to their genuine and lasting friendship exists."

Captain Steel accepted the Segonovs' invitation to be their guest during his stay in St. Petersburg. The big, complicated, happy household was almost home to him, and in its shelter he could rest and learn and relax his instinctive vigilance. He started his crew on the repairs of his ship, and swiftly the *Loyalty* was polished and scraped, inspected and painted; the homeward voyage would not be easy in early winter. But the ship was his now, and though he wished to avoid it if he could, he could afford the delay of a British inspection when he was headed westward. He arranged for a cargo of linseed and hemp, spirits and furs, and he firmly turned a deaf ear to the suggestions of Thilo and other Russians that he turn privateer, or that he attempt again to run the British blockade. It was evident to him that the efforts of his one vessel would in no way affect the outcome of the war. He had already demonstrated his friendship, which the Russians took also to be a demonstration of the friendship of the United States—and such, in fact, was the case; and, as he explained again to Thilo and Peter, the Crimean War was not his fight.

"I have my ship. That was all I wanted. Some day, perhaps, there can be peaceful and profitable trade again between my country and yours, without the present risks. Then I'll be back. In the meantime," he grinned, "fight your own war."

It was the kind of realistic talk that Peter and Thilo understood.

In the Segonov household Matthew Steel also found another release. The tension and weariness of the voyage gradually faded from his healthy young body in the warmth of the Russian friendships; but he found himself for the first time in compelling need of someone to whom he could talk of his most personal thoughts. For a man as reserved as he had been it was a new sensation to Captain Steel, but then, he thought, things had been moving fast for Matthew Steel and many things had changed for him and within him in the past few months. He believed with all the superstition of his Irish mother's forebears and those of a seaman, as well, that Loyalty Blake and her name had brought him good fortune. And he could not forget her. If he had named his vessel for her to keep himself in her thoughts, it had also accomplished the purpose of helping to keep her foremost in his. He was not one to talk of his personal affairs to another man. But to Madame Segonova, wrinkled and tiny and sharp and merry, the grandmother of the household and the matriarch, he could speak.

On Matthew's last evening, after the long and informal dinner, Madame Segonova summoned him to her. She spread her black silk skirts carefully about her, bent forward stiffly from the waist —her heavy corsets would not permit her to relax, even had she wished—and rapped his knuckles lightly with her fan. Her sensitive, kindly, crumpled old face showed only the faintest shadow of the beauty that had once been hers; but Madame Nathalia Segonova had certainly not forgotten her youth.

"And have you, then, Matthew Steel, no wife or sweetheart? You never speak of a girl."

"You are very direct, Madame. There is no use to try to evade you," Matthew smiled. He settled himself at her side.

"Smoke if you wish. I have no objection to good tobacco," Madame ordered. "Now," she said comfortably, "you shall tell me."

"I've no wife, Madame. No sweetheart."

Madame Segonova darted a quick, bird-like look at him. "What is the matter with you, then?" she asked. "A mistress, surely? A man like you should have a mistress."

Matthew laughed. "You are more of a realist than many women, Madame."

Madame sniffed. "Love—ah, a man should have that. To balance all the other things, the loneliness and conflict and the harsh things a man must do to be a success. As beauty balances ugliness." She bent toward him confidingly. "Furthermore," she whispered wickedly, "I love a little scandal, Captain Steel."

"Then I shall tell you. No, I have not a mistress. There is a woman, a red-haired woman—"

He stopped. He had thought only fleetingly of Tessa Dunn until now. He was confused and it showed upon his face. He looked at his hands, clasped between his knees, and frowned. Somehow, in times like these, when there was music and laughter, when he'd drunk plenty of wine, he felt as though he were back on South Street again, fresh from a long voyage, starved for a girl's companionship—and then he thought of Tessa, her slow, sultry smile, her cat-grace; then she was not just Tessa Dunn, she was all women.

"She's—I've known her since she was a child. She's of my class."

"And you desire her. She is a good companion. But not a wife." Madame nodded. "Yes. And now—the other one?"

Matthew raised his eyebrows. "How did you know there was another?"

"There is?"

He smiled. "Yes, I guess there is, Madam Segonova. She is much in my thoughts. I do not know her well. I've seen her only twice. But she is very beautiful, Madame, the most beautiful girl you have ever seen. When she grows up a little—what a woman she will be! Her name is Loyalty. I named my ship for her."

Madame Segonova sat very still. Captain Steel, the young, tough American whom all St. Petersburg loved and honored, had forgotten for the moment where he was. He was talking almost to himself and there was a look on his face that had never been there before. After a minute he straightened and brought his eyes back to her face and his smile was almost boyish.

"But I think she is already betrothed, and to a man of her father's choice. They do not arrange marriages of convenience in America, of course, but naturally the family's approval carries some weight. She has been much cherished. And after all, Madame—how could

I court her, if I would—when I am busy bringing Thilo Kalin to Russia?"

Madame smiled and fluttered her fan busily.

"I, being an old woman, and experienced—" she bent toward him, her fan hiding her mouth, her old eyes dancing merrily above it. "And nice experiences they were, too, Matthew Steel! I shall help you. A gift for this girl, this Loyalty. Eh?"

"Yes, Madame. A gift. I'd like to take her many gifts, but of course I cannot. There is one thing, though, I have been thinking about. Could Madame help me to select a box—a scent-box, a very small one? You see, I have her own, she left it aboard my ship. I should like to replace it."

Madame Segonova chuckled. Then she stiffened with a sudden inspiration, and her voice was like a girl's as she answered.

"Of course! Matthew Steel, my mother was lady-in-waiting to the Empress," Madame crossed herself swiftly. "I have a box that the Empress gave to her. I shall give it to you, for your Loyalty!"

"But Madame, I cannot take your treasures. And after all, as I told you, I hardly know this girl. She is, really, nothing to me. But if Madame would give me the benefit of her faultless taste and help me to select a gift from a shopkeeper—"

Madame clapped her hands for a servant and then she gave him a meaning, sidelong look.

"Of course she is nothing to you," she said briskly. "But consider it a gesture from my country to you and your ship. Your coming has raised our spirits. We owe something to the *Loyalty* and her captain." A servant was at her elbow and in an instant Madame had a tiny box in her bleached, knotty, small hand. Its filigree was jewel encrusted and it was lined with old velvet.

"She will wish to fill it with her own perfume—a vial, a paste jar," Madame said wisely. She held it to her nose and sniffed. "You may assure her that if a scent is there it is of a long-dead Empress or her lady-in-waiting. That, Matthew Steel—" she rapped his arm with her fan—"is important to a girl. Remember that."

"But I cannot take it, Madame."

Madame took his hand and laid the box within it and then she clapped her hands again. "It is time for me to retire, Matthew

Steel, and I will perhaps not see you again. I am a very old woman. . . ." Matthew stood and steadied her as she painfully raised herself from her chair. "Oh, yes, and the other one," Madame Segonova said thoughtfully. "Furs for her, perhaps?" Her eyes sparkled. "Furs, of course!" she patted his arm intimately. "There should be two women in every man's life, Matthew Steel—a wife and a mistress. Some are fortunate enough to find both in the same woman, and some, unhappily, are not." She sighed. "Perhaps you will be one of the lucky ones . . . yes, perhaps you will. . . . I wish you were to remain with us. Ah, well, we cannot have everything. God sends corn and the devil mars the sack! May Heaven bless you, Matthew, and grant you good winds."

Loyalty Blake was dressing for a Christmas ball when her maid brought her a parcel that had just been taken in at the door. It was addressed in a strong, unfamiliar hand, but Loyalty knew, even before she removed the wrappings, from whom it came.

She dismissed her maid and sat down to open it and her fingers were trembling. She lifted the delicate, velvet-lined box from its coverings and held it in her hands and the suspense of the last months lifted from her. The tiny box was a priceless, age-old bit of Russian artistry. Loyalty had no need to read the Marine Intelligence columns to know that Matthew Steel's dangerous voyage had been a success.

The gift contained no card. It was a very valuable gift, and a young lady did not accept such a present from any man except her husband. But to return it to Matthew Steel would reveal that she knew where she had left her own scent-box, and it would show that she took for granted that he had sent this one to her. He was quite capable, she thought, in sheer, wicked perversity, of politely declaring she was mistaken, that the gift was not from him at all, and so, of course, he could not take it back, and then where would she be? She laughed, thinking of it. No man in the world was so capable of humiliating her as Matthew Steel!

She should, her conscience told her, report the gift to her father, or at least to Serena. But she had pledged herself to try to heal the breach between her father and Matthew Steel—not to add fuel to the fire of Thaddeus' indignation at the Captain. Loyalty was fundamentally forthright and she disliked secretiveness. She had been silent about her brother's escapades because she dearly loved both Cass and her father and hated dissension between them. But in some way her connection with Matthew Steel seemed too intimate, too complex a thing to discuss or attempt to explain to others. It was new to her, this relationship, the feeling that she knew him very well and understood his very thoughts—and she wanted to protect it. Conventions, somehow, did not seem to apply to Matthew Steel. He appeared to make his own rules, and the proprieties she had been taught so carefully dissolved like mist before his amused and mocking grin.

Loyalty looked at the little box, turning it over and over slowly, marveling at the delicate workmanship, the beauty of the jewels, loving it as she did all beautiful things. A man capable of so charming, though bold, a gesture, must have much good about him, she thought. By omitting his card he had automatically blocked the return of the gift. Captain Steel was a very clever man, a very thoughtful one.

And he was back in New York, safe; not dead or imprisoned or disgraced or impoverished. Perhaps, she thought hopefully, Father will change his mind now, no longer be determined to ruin him if he can. If only they would be friends, if only Captain Steel could call on her, as other friends did, if only she could see him again.

The thought thrilled her and she promptly backed away from it. It was odd, to want so much to see a man, and still to be afraid; for she felt that something, anything, might happen, if she were in Captain Steel's presence often or long. Theirs could never be a passive friendship.

She put the beautiful little box safely away, but she did not forget it, or its donor, for a moment as she gave herself over to the enjoyment of the evening. She threw herself into the delight of music and dancing and laughter and the pretty speeches of her partners. Loyalty had never been so beautiful, so vivacious, so sparkling, her friends said fondly. And with typical feminine logic, which no man could be expected to understand, Loyalty was kinder and more charming to Henry Austin than she had ever been.

[6]

IT HAD been a hard voyage. There was not the stimulus of chalking up a new record with the *Loyalty* nor the heady excitement of racing the British ships. They had slipped out of the Baltic under cover of a heavy fog, feeling their way, inch by inch, depending on the leadsman to keep them off the rocks. The cold had settled down upon them and winter storms had struck them in full fury. Ropes and yards were sheathed with ice, and men suffered from frostbite and bitter cold; sometimes the motion of the ship was so great it seemed they were racing, yet the men knew she was being raised and lowered like a giant elevator, with all the monotony of a metronome, and was making no headway at all, at the mercy of the winds. There was the work of the ship, the hauling of ropes that bit into raw hands, the chopping of ice, scraping, cleaning, fighting the elements and the darkness that came all too early in the short, gray days. The sea was like pewter, depressing and threatening at its best, and at its worst, not far from home, while the men pitted their brawn against the season and the storms; it had taken one man in sacrifice. That was when the spirit of the men had been tried, and when the weaker of them broke.

The *Loyalty* had canted in the howling, tearing wind; most of the men were retching with seasickness and some were unable to leave their berths and were coughing deep and spitting blood. It took men strong in body and courage to go aloft; the decks were awash and the spars describing a wide arc over the sea, the men clinging to them at right angles to towering, reaching, hungry waves.

It was then that one man lost his hold. It happened quickly. One minute he was there, clinging monkey-like in the ice-coated rigging, and the next he was falling and the sea swallowed him, so small, so very small, in that great grinding, roaring, pushing sea. No boat could have been lowered, though they had carefully been kept free of binding ice. The worst of all was his scream as he fell. It cut through the shrieking, whining, pounding, creaking, bubbling, sucking of the sea and the ship and went deep inside every man who heard it, never to be forgotten. Only once his head bobbed, a tiny, helpless speck in that tremendous, furious liquid lead of the sea, and then it was gone and a life was gone. Every man aboard felt *it could have been me, it almost was me,* and the shock of it, even to men accustomed to tragedy, shook them all. Such accidents happened just often enough to prove to them that if they followed the sea long enough it would claim each of them; so what did they have to lose?

The shock, the fear, the weariness, above all the sound of the lost man's last despairing, terror-stricken cry as he fell, and the wind-hounded ship swept on, the awful feeling of forced desertion of a perishing fellow-human—these had burned deep into the souls of even the most hardened men aboard. Matthew Steel knew it well, and he could understand why they sought some means, however foul, to forget.

I want to get ashore, they were thinking, the words pounding like a drum in their brains. Even the dullest, most inarticulate of them could put those thoughts into words, for it was a fundamental urge of land creatures. *I want to get drunk, roaring, helpless drunk, I want music, I want a real bed in a real room, not shared with a half-hundred other men. I want to feel land beneath my feet, see houses and stores and smell land smells. I want to get off this God-damned stinking ship. I want a woman, soft and alive in my arms. I want to hear a woman's laugh, and if it takes my wages, and my wages for the next voyage, and the next, what does it matter? Let Jimmy From Town come aboard—what the hell! If we can forget for just a little while—what have we got to lose? We're homeless, we're lost, we're sea-tramps, with the taste of salt in our mouths; stir-crazy, for the ship and sea have been prison and jailer.*

The growing tension in the crew had reached its peak forty-eight hours before they sighted Sandy Hook. The mates spoke of it uneasily. The men were watching for small boats bringing Jimmy From Town and others of his kind, South Street crimps with liquor and promises. The sailor's high resolves to stay out of the clutches of the waterfront sharks had dissolved in their desire for rum and release.

Matthew was not without pity for the men, but he would not change his decision not to allow the crimps aboard. He was convinced it was good business policy. He could not save weak men from their own excesses, and his contempt for weakness was such that he did not care to try; but he could refuse to support a vicious practice that victimized his men by playing upon their needs and their appetites.

Accordingly, as they neared port, Matthew mentally measured his men. He looked at his ship, punished by the storms and the cold and the long voyage. It was hard to jeopardize her further now, for a principle. He stood at the rail, watching for the coming of the small boats, and he frowned in thought. If all ship masters defied the custom it could be broken, seamen would be freed from the grip of men like Jimmy Burns and be better for it. Neither he nor any other master could break the system alone—unless a successful example might start a chain reaction and encourage others to follow suit. It would be easier, now, to let the crimps come aboard, as they did on every vessel entering the harbor, let them grab the sailors and their possessions, if the men were fools enough to permit it; and then he could bring his precious ship safely into port and save himself trouble and danger. Perhaps he was a fool to defy the old custom alone. But Matthew Steel's face hardened at the thought and his hand clenched and unclenched on the rail.

"I'm not going to knuckle down to any crimp or any other man who tries to ruin me," Matthew muttered to himself. He was well aware that there were uneasy, secret conversations going on among his crew and he guessed the men were preparing to ask him—perhaps even to demand—that he permit the crimps aboard. He determined to move quickly, and forestall their request. He signaled his officers to tell the men to gather.

The promise of action, he thought, knowing his men—a battle with the crimps—would break the tension. The majority of his men had followed him faithfully throughout the voyage and he believed direct action would keep them with him now. Their animosity was not against him; it was against the sea and its loneliness and dangers.

He had to shout above the roar of the waves, but his voice carried. When the tugboat fleet surrounded them he proposed to select his tugs and pilot quickly and signal the police boat to come alongside. He would tell the officers of the law no crimp would be permitted to board the *Loyalty*. If any tried it, they did so at their own risk.

There was a rumble among the men, indecision, a few protests, and there were a few dark faces, sullen and mutinous. But the leaders in his crew rallied behind their captain. Matthew passed the word along that he would sign up anyone who wished for the ship's next voyage, but his men would speak for themselves—not through Jimmy Burns or any other landsman. In preparation for the fight ahead, Captain Steel ordered a round of drinks for every man aboard. Only a few failed to join in the cheer which followed, and Matthew's quick eye singled them out. To his mate Captain Steel quietly gave the order: "If any man makes trouble or attempts to help Jimmy Burns or any of his followers, club him under."

The puffing small boats surrounded the ship. Matthew signaled the police boat and shouted his warning. The ship's ladder was lowered for the pilot and officials to come aboard.

Jimmy From Town held a consultation with his men. Lining the rail of the *Loyalty* was a row of hostile faces; some of the men were chewing tobacco, and they spat over the side, expressionless, their eyes narrowed against the wind. Some held belaying pins in their fists. Jimmy, used to hostility on the part of officers, but expecting his usual welcome from thirsty, weary seamen, watched for a sign aboard the ship that would mean cooperation for him and his followers.

The South Street mobsters had fortified themselves well with rum. They talked fiercely, arguing that an example must be made of Matthew Steel's ship. Once aboard the ship, Jimmy declared, and the sailors, now obviously controlled by Matthew Steel, would turn against their Captain and support the time-honored custom of the crimps' right to board incoming vessels. All sailors hated their officers. Jimmy's mob surged close to the ship and leaped for the ladder.

Matthew Steel shouted a warning but the men came on. The

Captain's fist smashed full in the face of the first man to put his head over the side. He loosed his hold and fell, taking others with him, and shouting men below caught them and pulled them back into the boats. The faces aboard the *Loyalty* were alert now and grinning, and the men were wild to fight. A couple of skirmishes broke out on deck and were quickly subdued. There was no doubt that Jimmy's men would have a bloody battle on their hands if any number of them succeeded in boarding the ship.

The small boats withdrew a little and the police boat hovered carefully on the outskirts, observing. Then Jimmy's men broke and attempted to stop the tugs engaged by Steel from fastening lines to the *Loyalty*. It was an uneven struggle and Matthew watched only for an instant. The officers of the law were going to take no part in it, that was evident. Captain Steel called for volunteers and a number of his men sprang to action. Small boats were launched and the men were over the side, swarming eagerly to the aid of the tugboats.

The battle did not last long. Jimmy Burns signaled a retreat, promising revenge. Matthew leaned on the rail, watching calmly, examining each man who came back up the ladder, sure that only his own men came aboard.

A strange face, contorted with fury and drink, appeared over the side, and Matthew moved quickly. He grabbed the fellow by the coat and yanked him aboard. Then he picked him up bodily and tossed him over the side. The fellow floundered in the icy water until he was pulled aboard a small boat. The *Loyalty* began to move again, the tugs, with Steel's men standing guard, getting under way.

Jimmy From Town saw his man tossed overboard and he knelt in his boat slowly. He was well concealed. He took a pistol from a holster beneath his coat and now he aimed it carefully and deliberately and pulled the trigger. He had the satisfaction of seeing Captain Steel stagger back from the rail.

Like a flock of ducks the small boats scattered. A fight was one thing, but murder was another. Honest, old-time tugboat-operators who wanted no part of Jimmy From Town headed toward home, torn between their desire to tell the story of the fight and to deny their presence there. If Captain Steel was dead it would be better to have been a long way distant from the scene.

But the story traveled like a crackling flame along a fuse. It spread out over the waterfront and deep into the city. Because it was Christmas and the people were in a holiday mood, they flocked to the pier assigned to the *Loyalty*. They waded through ankle-deep slush, curious, concerned, excited, to watch the ship dock. Already the *Loyalty* was becoming a legendary ship, a fabled one, and stories about her would be told and retold wherever searfaring men gathered. There was about the ship the dash and color of a heroine, and as she moved slowly and surely to the pier, the ice that sheathed her glittering and dripping in the mid-day sunshine, she was of breathtaking beauty. Those ashore had not had the privilege of seeing the *Loyalty* with her acre of snowy canvas set, flashing along lightly, faster than the wind; but even with the tugs furnishing her power at journey's end she was a triumphant and graceful queen of the seas and no other ship on the waterfront could compare to her.

The crowd watched her and held its breath. Men stood ready to toss out the lines to fasten her snug to the dock. The people ashore strained for a sight of the ship's master, and tried to tell from the expressions of the crew whether tragedy had come aboard, and, as they drew nearer, the question was answered. Steel's men, many bearing signs of a fight, were grinning widely. The first mate, confident and arrogant, stood with his hands on his hips, in high good humor. His voice boomed out over the ship and shore: "Give us a song, men!"

But the mob on the wharf heard only the first line. When Captain Steel's familiar voice arose: "*Oh, the times are hard and the wages low,*" and the crew's low rumble began "*Leave her, Johnny—*" the people of the waterfront burst into a roar. They had welcomed back many a sailing master from a hazardous voyage, but never had South Street witnessed before such a reception as it gave to Captain Steel of the *Loyalty*.

When Matthew appeared, erect and well-groomed, but with the right sleeve of his heavy coat hanging empty, and raised his one good arm in greeting, the crowd went wild. Police officers shoved their way through to make a path for Captain Steel, and Matthew waited, watching. His throat felt tight. He had dreamed of this, since boyhood, longed for it, labored and sweated and fought and schemed for it. But never, in all his wildest imaginings, had he anticipated such a welcome as this. Later he would try to analyze it; now it was enough just to savor it and taste it slowly. It was not given to many men to taste such triumph, nor to have it as sweet as he had dreamed it would be. Matthew's eyes swept the crowd and came to rest on Jimmy From Town. His brutal, big-featured face was full of hate. As Matthew watched he turned and disappeared. Jimmy had not given up the battle. His vendetta had just begun. And Captain Steel knew it very well.

[7]

TESSA DUNN had never sung so well. In the two months she had been at the House of Lords she had become a favorite, but tonight her husky, low voice had a new, live quality; her rare smile came oftener and seemed to have in it genuine friendliness. Already Tessa had been taught some stage tricks and she was carefully, if theatrically, dressed to make the most of her own peculiar charm. Patrons at the House of Lords came for the pleasure of watching Tessa; that her voice was also pleasing, her off-color songs, which she had brought with her from the waterfront, amusing and daring, was only an added attraction.

The House of Lords was elaborate and clean, glittering with mirrors, polished rails and many lights, and decorated with paintings in heavy frames and statuary generally believed to be genteel works of art. The customers also were of a different stamp from those who had come to the battle-scarred, fly-specked Cock and Bull. These men were business and professional men, young men-about-town, wealthy sons of wealthy fathers, spending time and money in search of amusement. Entertainers at the House of Lords were not well paid; the manager explained that the privilege of appearing there and meeting men with fat pocketbooks more than made up for meager salaries; moreover, threatrical agents frequented the place. Tessa had found this to be true. She also knew that her own growing popularity was of value to the establishment, and she looked forward to the day when she could demand—and get—more money for her services. Then she would be ready to move on, a step higher, in her professional career.

As she had done so often in the Cock and Bull, tonight she sang with her eyes on the entrance. Matthew Steel was in port, and sooner or later he would come to find her. She pictured his surprise when he inquired for her at the Cock and Bull, and found she had moved on to the larger gin palace uptown. She knew that Matthew's time was no longer his own, and that he was surrounded at all times by a crowd of men seeking favors or business or information, or only basking in the light of a celebrity. She had made certain that Matthew Steel's wound was not serious, that his trip was a success, but she had not attempted to see him. This time, she thought, she would work differently. Matthew Steel must come to her.

Cass Blake leaned on the bar, watching her, forgetting the glass in his hand. When she had first appeared at the House of Lords, unheralded, a tall, pale girl with flaming hair and a husky voice, a little stiff, very remote, Cass had seen her and recognized her at once as the girl who had joined Matthew Steel in the shadow of his ship at Brighton's yard. He had watched her work, watched her rapid improvement, and he had made it a point to meet her. It had been a pleasant meeting, and Cass, at first attracted by curiosity, was fascinated with the girl herself.

On Tessa's part, once she discovered who Cass Blake was, she was glad to continue the association, for her interest in Loyalty Blake was the avid interest of a jealous and intense woman in a rival. Furthermore, Cass, with his easy manners, his sense of humor, put her at ease. It was Cass who suggested a theatrical agent to guide her progress, and Cass whose gifts helped to pay the fees.

It was quite fitting, Tessa thought cynically, that a Blake should aid her, since it was a Blake who was the greatest threat to her happiness. She had no qualms in taking all she could get from Cass, with no repayment except her companionship, and at the same time she sought information from him which might be of aid to Matthew Steel. Her efforts had not been unsuccessful, for Cass was neither reserved nor subtle.

Cass Blake, of all those watching Tessa on this night, suspected why the girl had bloomed, why her beauty had suddenly and startlingly emerged. He wished that Tessa's excitement was because of him. Cass Blake felt the first twinges of jealousy as he watched Tessa, and he knew that his attraction to the actress was growing and deepening to intense infatuation. It was a peculiar coincidence, he thought, that Matthew Steel could so influence the lives of the family of Thaddeus Blake. Cass wanted only to see Matthew and Tessa together. He knew Tessa's feeling for Matthew all too well; but he was likewise interested in Matthew Steel's attitude toward Tessa Dunn.

Tonight Tessa was certain he would come. Every song was for him, and she felt that he must feel the strong pull of her own desire, and at any moment the door would open and he would stand there, and their eyes would meet again. The suspense was almost too much to be borne. She was not sorry that Cass was present. She hoped that he would tell his sister that Tessa Dunn was Matthew Steel's woman, make her believe that no other had any small part of his heart.

Tessa had watched the door open and close so many times, watched men enter, bundled against the cold, snowflakes white on the shoulders of their dark coats, scanned their faces eagerly, hoping for Matthew Steel, that when he did appear she could not at first believe it. She stared at him and then her voice caught and faltered for a second. She smiled, her even, strong white teeth flashing, and her song went on, but her eyes did not leave him. Several turned to see to whom Tessa Dunn was singing and a whisper went over the room. Cass Blake followed her glance.

Matthew stopped inside the entrance and slowly removed his coat, releasing his left arm first and then carefully freeing the right. He was smiling, and admiration and surprise were mirrored in his face, and as he walked toward the bar, to see the singer better, Cass saw the interest and pleasure shining in his eyes. Cass looked back at Tessa and to him her devotion was plain and naked. Tessa Dunn had never before sung from her heart, and never before had her face and eyes glowed with such life and happiness. She was singing to Matthew and there might have been no other person in the room or in all the world.

When she was finished she acknowledged the roaring applause with a smile and then she came down the steps at the end of the platform, ignoring the calls and exclamations of the men she passed. She came, as she had always come at the Cock and Bull, publicly to greet him. Tessa held out her hands and Matthew took them, saying nothing, just shaking his head in disbelief, and Tessa threw back her head and laughed. Cass had never heard her laugh like that before. Matthew's arm encircled her and drew her toward the bar, and in an instant, still silent, he had put a glass of sparkling champagne into her hand. Its color blended into the color of her dress and her imitation jewels and her hair, and many stared in appreciation at the picture she made. Matthew raised his glass, and Tessa's clinked against it.

"My God, Tess," Matthew said. "What's happened to you?"

Cass Blake put his glass down on the polished bar, harder than was necessary and swung toward the door. Tessa did not even look up as he passed.

"What's happened to you, Matthew?" she countered. "Your trip was successful, of course." He nodded. "But you had to get in a fight even before you docked."

"A brush with Jimmy From Town."

"You were not seriously injured, then?"

"No. A flesh wound. It jarred me a little. But tell me of you, Tess. You're a new person. You're beautiful. You look prosperous. Things have been going well for you?"

Tessa nodded. "Yes. I decided it was time for a change. It has been surprisingly easy, so far."

"No wonder. You're wonderful, Tess. I can't believe it—in three months, or less, you've been transformed."

He continued to stare and Tessa laughed again. She had never been so happy. Hours later they sat at a table, still talking. Matthew had told her of his voyage and she of the work and study she had been doing. She watched the expressions on his face, absorbed, drinking in every word, enjoying each moment.

"There are a lot of things I can't understand, Tessa, a lot of complications I did not foresee," Matthew was saying. "For instance, one of the first visitors to the ship when I docked was a man named Graham White, a representative of the State Department. I know they often send representatives to talk to men who have traveled abroad, but it was new to me. He asked me to write a detailed report of anything I thought might be interesting or new to the State Department—how the British treated my ship, my observations in St. Petersburg, the attitude of the Russian people toward us. He wanted it immediately. I've kept notes—they helped me to clarify things in my own mind. So I wrote him a report, told him I had sighted and exchanged greetings with a number of English ships, but had not been halted on the voyage, and gave him my observations on the progress of the Crimean War. He also asked for a copy of the manifest of the goods I delivered to St. Petersburg and those I brought back. I think he suspected contraband. If there was contraband aboard, Thilo Kalin put it there. I'll never know for sure, nor do I want to know."

Matthew took out a cigar. "He asked me a good many questions about the Russian naval officers I knew, what their attitude was toward us, and the like. From all I could see it was very friendly—but it is hard to explain the Russian attitude to people who do not known them intimately. Their suspicions cloud everything. Anyway, I sent the report to Mr. White for what it is worth. He's a fine man. He impressed me greatly. Serious and very intelligent."

He leaned over the candle to light the cigar and Tessa's eyes followed him.

"But Tess, since I got back—in two days on South Street, I've run into some odd things."

"What do you mean, Matthew?"

"My ship had a wonderful reception. Of course the crowd was mostly workers—people you and I have known for years. It was a warm feeling, and there have been many callers at the ship, everyone from a board of inquiry about the trouble with Jimmy

Burns, and port officials, down to Old Dan. But I am in a hurry to ship out again. I am running on too small a margin, though I have the ship. I can't afford to stay in port long. And I'm having trouble lining up a cargo."

Tessa frowned. "But why, Matthew? I should think after the *Loyalty's* record—"

Matthew blew smoke rings slowly and thoughtfully. "There's something wrong and I cannot quite put my finger on it. It is true that business is very sluggish. Thaddeus Blake prophesied that three months ago. And businessmen expect it to get worse before it gets better. I think they are in for a real recession in New York, if not a panic. In that case, it is no place for me."

Tessa's face sobered. "You mean, then, you'll leave soon?"

"I'll have to, Tessa. I can't afford to have my ship tied up for lack of cargoes. I've seen it happen to too many skippers. A number of clippers that I thought would be here have been chartered by the British and French to transport troops into the Black Sea. Yet the shipyards are still active, turning out more vessels than ever. Trade inland has increased and the West is absorbing a lot of goods that would normally have been exported. The slavery problem has everyone in a state of unrest. I found much dissatisfaction in Charleston when I was there. But in spite of all that, there is something else. Jimmy Burns has no influence, I'm sure, on the merchants of the city. He can turn the scum of the waterfront against me and make it hard for me to get crews, certainly, or he could sabotage my ship or run a knife in my back. But he could not prevent me from getting cargoes, well insured. I missed one shipment yesterday, by being an hour too late, or so they told me. I missed another this morning, and this afternoon another firm would not even take my bid. Those were all San Francisco cargoes and that was what I wanted. The real worth of my ship will be proven on a long voyage; the *Loyalty* does not have as great an advantage over steamers on short runs. She's built for distance. But I did not get those consignments, and I believe it is because of a personal prejudice against Matthew Steel."

"What will you do then?"

"I can get small lots to the Clyde. I'm going to take them and get out of here as fast as I can. I have enough money to fill out the load with goods I will buy myself and resell. I have to carry up to capacity to make anything, with the crew I must support. When I build up enough capital so I can buy entire ship-load lots and transport and sell them myself, then I'll be independent, for money talks in any language and can overcome many prejudices. But why, in my home port, Tessa, was I not given even a chance to bid on the San Francisco cargoes? I know my reputation was good when I left here—Blake told me so himself. It was good enough so he wanted to hire me to work for him."

Tessa's eyes narrowed. "Matthew, Thaddeus Blake is very angry at you. Did you know that?"

"I expected he'd be a little annoyed. What do you mean?"

"It is more than that. He was furious that you named your ship for his precious daughter. He was afraid of a scandal. He was also angry that you bought that cotton in Charleston."

"How do you know that, Tess?"

"Cass Blake comes here. I see him often. He talks a lot, especially after he's had a drink or two. He said his father considered trying to restrain you legally from using that name on your ship. Cass said he is afraid his daughter's name will be in the newspapers, if you should get into trouble. He thinks the figurehead is an insult. Do you suppose his influence . . ."

Matthew leaned back in his chair, frowning, and rubbed his chin. He thought back over the interviews of the last two days. What was the common denominator—what had influenced all three men to turn him down so abruptly? He had been treated courteously until he had given his name and the name of his vessel. Then the coldness had been very apparent and very puzzling.

"So he intends to break me if he can," he said finally. "Tessa, I believe you have the answer." For a long time he was silent, and Tessa watched him, her heart aching. "He's a powerful man. He's made his money by being ruthless and I guess that is the way it is done."

Suddenly he laughed shortly. He picked up a wineglass and drank and then he pushed back his chair. "I guess that answers it, Tessa. It confirms what I already believed—that I'd better get out of New York, and in a hurry. I'll come back only when I have enough money to defy Thaddeus Blake. I think Blake himself is in for a bad time if the panic hits. He's a clever man, but the big ones are bound to be hard hit. That's where I, at least, have the advantage, being foot-loose. I can go where business is, and right now I believe it is any place but New York. Liverpool to Australia is busy and the British need ships. Blake's prejudices and influence won't extend that far."

Tessa's heart sank. "Maybe that isn't it at all, Matthew," she said hesitantly. "Perhaps it is just bad luck, just at first. In a few weeks it may be different."

Matthew shook his head. "My success depends on guessing right and guessing quickly—before I get caught. I'm going to make a fast trip to the Clyde and go on from there. Thanks for talking to me, Tess. Things are always clearer after talking with you." He brought his attention back to her and smiled. The smile made Tessa's eyes smart suddenly. She could not speak around the lump in her throat. He reached across the table and covered her hand with his own.

"If I were going to be around a while, Tess," he said softly. Tessa's eyes were soft with tears and she caught her lip in her teeth. "If I were going to be here I'd like to see you often, very often. You're the best friend I ever had. I'm glad things are going well with you. I'm proud of you. You'll be famous by the time I see you again." He grinned at her. "With a trail of broken hearts in your wake."

"How long do you think it will be, before you come back, Matthew?" Tessa whispered.

"That I can't say. I want money, a lot of it. I want it badly. I want to be able to come back here and whip Thaddeus Blake on his own ground, if he wants to fight. I have to do it."

Tessa thought wildly. If she asked him to take her with him, what would he say? She opened her lips to speak, but the words stuck in her throat. At least, she thought, now that he knows that Blake is his enemy, he will not think so kindly, perhaps, of the Blake daughter.

"When will you go, Matthew?"

"A few days, at most. I'll see you before I sail." He stood and looked down at her and she managed finally to get to her feet. "Tessa, do you need anything? Have you enough money, for lessons, for clothes, for things you need?"

Tessa nodded. "I have enough, Matthew, but thank you just the same," she said huskily. What a fool you are, Tess, she thought. Why not take money from the one man in the world you love? You'd take it quickly enough from anyone else. From Cass Blake, for instance.

"I'll write you, Tessa. To what address?"

"To the Cock and Bull. I'll be moving on soon, I hope, but Hite and Morton will know where I am. They've been kind."

"I'm glad of that. When I know where I'm bound, Tess, I'll let you know. Let me know of your progress, and if ever you need anything, will you?"

Tessa nodded. He smiled at her again and was gone. She stood watching him go and then she quietly left the room and went backstage. She did not cry. Her loneliness was too deep for that. I'll have to wait, she said to herself, wait and work. She gripped her fists till her nails bit into the palms. Women always had to wait, she thought bitterly.

Matthew Steel walked back to the *Loyalty*. He spoke to the guard and went aboard. There were several letters and notes on his table but he pushed them aside. The bullet wound was aching and his head was aching, too, and he was very tired. He reviewed again and again the interviews and considered Tessa's solution of the puzzle. The more he thought of it, the more he believed her right.

If that were the case he would certainly not be welcome in the Blake household. He could not make a call on Loyalty, not now, not until he was able to defy Thaddeus Blake. Nor would he gain anything by it, even if he saw her. She'd likely been forbidden to receive him. He was glad he had sent the scent-box on Christmas Day, with no card. Loyalty would know from whom it came. He would send others, from time to time, to remind her. He would keep himself in her thoughts, though he was far away. She was still only a child. When he came back she would be a woman, old enough to know her own mind. Meantime he also could consider. Just how far would he want to go with a friendship with Loyalty Blake?

He had believed the girl and the name of the ship brought him luck. He shook his head slowly. Not on South Street. Blake and Burns, as opposite as the poles, were his enemies. South Street was in for a depression that would ruin many men. The answer was clear. He'd get out and get out quickly, for sometimes a retreat was necessary to gather one's resources for the final battle. When he returned he'd have money to do business in spite of Thaddeus Blake.

He thought again of Tessa and affection for her warmed him. Her improvement had startled and pleased him. It would be easy to become involved with Tessa Dunn now, but it would not do—not when he was leaving again so soon. He'd be wise to keep their friendship on the old basis, keep himself free from entanglements. Three days ashore—and already he was restless and eager to go to sea again. He wanted to feel the clean wind in his face, look out over the shifting waters, look up at the swelling sails of the *Loyalty;* there was a great beauty in the unlimited space of the ocean, he thought, a freedom, and aboard his ship he felt unfettered and removed from the petty, mean little things of the earth, a sensation, he thought, which must be akin to flying. If a man had a home, something, someone to come back to, then it would be different, but he had nothing, nothing but a goal to work for. At first that goal had been to secure his ship. He had secured that. But it was not the end. It was only the beginning.

He drew a map toward him and began to chart his course toward Scotland and the Clyde. There was a steamer leaving soon for the same ports. His face relaxed and he smiled to himself, absorbed again in his plans. Perhaps he could get a sizable bet with the captain of that steamer on the time of their runs.

CHAPTER III

IT WAS the fall of 1857 before Matthew Steel saw South Street again. He had money in his pocket but he had not come by it easily. He had a cargo which he owned outright and he had dependable information on the needs of San Franciscans, which he intended, as his next venture, to fill. He planned to touch at South Street only briefly, pick up a carefully selected cargo and passengers, if possible, for California, and then to the Orient. He knew the China seas well; he had learned fast sailing there as a common seaman, and he owed his skill with a knife to skirmishes in the opium trade of the late 1840's. He wanted to visit Japanese ports; and Amur and Sakhalin Islands, in the possession of Russia, had not yet been tapped, though Matthew had been informed by Popov, of the Russian fleet, that he believed secret agreements opened them to American ships.

Sometimes it seemed to Matthew that he took two steps forward and one step back, in order to make any progress at all, for not all his ventures were successful. Upkeep on his ship was tremendous, and often he was forced to cut freight rates to compete and to keep his ship moving at all, and some of his trips netted only operating expenses and no profit. But he was glad of his youth and his strength; in his business, endurance seemed more important than years of experience. He froze out competitors ruthlessly, he fought against time, he studied the operations of his crew so he could cut down the number of men required to work his ship, he spent long hours working out new and cheaper methods of stowing and unloading cargo. Time enough, once he were established, to become a kid-glove gentleman trader. Now he slugged it out with his rivals and no holds were barred in his fight for business and profits.

He was making certain though not too rapid headway and he could look forward to adding another ship to his holdings, and after that, another. Occasionally now ships were available as one owner after another gave up the battle against slowing trade and costly insurance and high operating expenses. With money in his pocket Matthew Steel could take advantage of the failure of others. He intended to buy another vessel on the Pacific Coast and another in Australia. With three ships in operation, the proper men to handle them—and he had trained his men well— he believed he would be strong enough to stand any impact, whether it be a world depression in trade or a personal feud with a financier like Thaddeus Blake.

The *Loyalty* needed a complete overhauling. Despite the skilled crew which he had kept almost intact, not all repairs could be made at sea, and he had pushed the beautiful ship almost to the limit of her endurance. His routine never varied at sea, and the vessel made a glittering, immaculate appearance in each port. The careful inspection, the monotonous working at the pumps, had paid dividends, for his cargoes had been in perfect condition and the reputation he had gained had aided him in securing others. But the needs of his ship were a good excuse to go back to South Street.

Loyalty Blake would be mature at eighteen, and Matthew was curious to see her. He took considerable pleasure in knowing he could return now, successful and with a promising future ahead, despite Thaddeus Blake, and Blake himself had no doubt suffered some reverses. The prospect gave him intense pleasure and he had allowed himself little time for pleasures. There had been much loneliness, much self-discipline, for the Captain of the *Loyalty*, for Matthew Steel kept his sights high and looked far ahead. Effort and denial now—and the great rewards would come later. He would not be satisfied with compromises or small returns. An empire, a great fortune, respect and power; a home like Thaddeus Blake's, impregnable and a symbol of success—he would have them, regardless of the cost to himself or any other.

Despite the fact that he had schooled himself to reserve, he felt a rush of excitement as he neared New York harbor. To Loyalty Blake he had sent a tiny jade box from China; a bit of porcelain from Constantinople, a mosaic from Italy. He had no direct word of her, though Tessa's letters often mentioned Cass. Tessa had mentioned no wedding in the Blake family. It was more likely, Matthew thought, that Loyalty had become a follower of Mrs. Bloomer, or an advocate of Women's Rights. But Henry Austin would be well established in his profession now and ready to marry. The thought disturbed Matthew more than he liked to admit.

Tessa herself had made surprising progress. She had been on tour, a circuit of theaters throughout Boston, Philadelphia, Washington and into the South. She had sent him some press notices of her performances and he was pleased to see that Tessa was little short of sensational.

Matthew also had some business to settle with Jimmy From Town. Captain Steel did not forget a grudge.

Jimmy did not meet the *Loyalty* in Sandy Hook waters. Others of his calling made the attempt, but when they were refused they left without protest. Slowly the ship moved toward South Street, and Matthew, watching the familiar landmarks, felt again the joy and excitement of coming home. It was good to see the canal boats again and the small sloops that traded on the Sound; there was more smoke than he remembered having seen on the waterfront before, more steamers and steam-driven tugs, and the ferries from Fulton and Catharine and Wall to Brooklyn seemed more numerous. There was a clipper anchored off Battery Park, and the familiar cluster of fishing smacks discharging their smelly, scaly cargoes at Fulton Market. There seemed a greater number of foreign flags, making New York appear more like an international trading settlement than ever. The docks were crowded, some with two or three ships lying abreast or tandem fashion.

Yet there was less activity. Idle men stood about on the strand, longshoremen waiting for work, crew men, waiting for the ships to go out again, unemployed men from the quiet shipyards. There were plenty of idlers on hand to greet the *Loyalty* when she edged into her berth.

But there was no rest for the master of the *Loyalty*. For the first twenty-four hours he could not leave his ship. Among his first callers, along with warehouse operators, brokers, port and customs officials, was Graham White.

"Before you go ashore, Captain Steel," Mr. White told him, "The State Department seeks your report. I might say that your last one received much attention, and I have orders to request a similar one at your earliest opportunity. All of us are seeking all the information we can possibly gather on world affairs these days. We need your help, sir, and you'll be doing your country a great service by giving it your prompt and complete attention."

Matthew explained the shortness of his stay, the many duties awaiting him. It seemed to him an imposition on his limited time in port. But the State Department aide was firm.

"It is your patriotic duty, Captain Steel," he insisted.

"Patriotic duty!" Matthew said impatiently. "My God, man, I've a duty to the ninety men of my crew, too. They have to be paid off. I have to get this cargo unloaded and sold and buy another. I've repairs to my ship to arrange for—and one other chore that is of more value to the merchant marine than my observations on foreign affairs. That is a detailed report to a man in your Depot of Charts and Instruments. Fellow named Maury. Do you know him?

White smiled. "Indeed I do."

"I'm only one of hundreds of ship captains sending him data, but I would not refuse him. If he completes his charts on winds and weathers and ocean currents, what a magnificent help it will be to sailors! I'm more interested in that work, Mr. White, begging your pardon, than foreign affairs."

"I can understand that, Captain. You've spent much of your life at sea, and in other countries?"

"Yes. Probably more time than in this country. At least, since I was twelve years old."

"Then perhaps you cannot understand how important it is to us here at home to know more of politics, economics, war, personalities, around the globe. Of course, we have observers, diplomats, consular corps, in all the world capitals—but ofttimes we have gained more valuable information from just such men as you, those who deal with the people and not the governments of other nations. Surely, Captain Steel, you will not deprive your country of any information which might aid her."

"It's a matter of time, Mr. White. I haven't been in New York in more than two years. I'm sailing within a week. And anyway, I doubt that I have much to contribute. One man's observations surely can't be of much value. My own conclusions may be inaccurate and do more harm than good."

Graham White stood up. He was a tall man, with a gentle, grave face, but he was quietly persistent.

"One man's observations may be of small value, Captain Steel. But—like the reports to Maury, in the aggregate they sometimes give us perfect patterns, help us also to chart a course. Captain Steel, if you have no time to write reports, would you, then, be kind enough to attend a discussion if I can arrange it, with some men interested in foreign affairs? In shipping, navigation laws, tariffs, mail subsidies, and the like? I assure you your time would not be wasted."

Matthew fingered a pen impatiently and then nodded shortly. "I'll do that. Let me know the time and place."

"I'll send you word." Mr. White held out his hand. Matthew arose and gripped it firmly. He went on with his work, dispatching messengers for appointments with people he wished to see. Once he had taken care of all the necessary business of his ship, what little time was left would be his own. He would call on Loyalty Blake, ask her to drive with him, perhaps.

He was careful to watch for any signs of Thaddeus Blake's influence. But since he did not depend upon consignments, and purchased goods outright, he found none. He found it also easy to fill the vacancies in his crew. For the first time in several years there were plenty of men eager to go to sea, eager for any work that would provide them with food to eat and a place to sleep. Breadlines had formed in front of all the missions, men told him, and suffering in the poorer sections was acute.

When finally Matthew went ashore he was careful to keep his eyes open for Jimmy From Town. He was warned that Jimmy had vowed revenge, and had no intention of permitting Matthew Steel or his ship to sail again. Old Dan himself had risked Jimmy's disapproval by limping to the ship to warn Captain Steel personally of the crimp's threats. Matthew put a heavy guard about the *Loyalty,* himself supervised her removal to the repair yards, and waited. Jimmy would come to him. It was not necessary for Matthew to seek Jimmy.

Matthew had arrived in New York on Monday and it was late Friday afternoon before he arranged to meet Tessa Dunn. Tessa had replied to his note that she would meet him at the Cock and Bull. Waiting for her he leaned against the bar, talking to Hite.

"It'll be a hard winter," Hite said, "after the panic. Nine hundred businesses have failed this year in New York alone." He moved a towel slowly across the bar. "There's some that haven't lost, though. Slave trade. More active than I've ever seen it." He leaned toward Matthew and lowered his voice. "Plenty of men putting money into it now, only venture that pays, they say. Even some rich women are investing, though they don't know, or else pretend not to know that they're in the slave traffic. Dealers tell them they can guarantee them fifty, a hundred per cent profit, if they just lend them a little money—to import blackbirds—and so they outfit another slave ship. They get their money all right, so why ask where it comes from? With folks losing their fortunes all around them, they figure it is good business. And all the time politicians are arguing slavery, newspapers are arguing, Southerners and Westerners are arguing with the North—we're in for real trouble before it's settled. You heard that 'Free soil, free men, free speech, Fremont' all over New York last year—but don't think all New York is abolitionist. Hell, no!" Hite laughed. "I'll bet if the truth were known more New Yorkers than Southerners depend on slavery for a living."

"What's happening to shipping?"

"Slowing down. British steamers are getting more and more of it—what there is of it. Railroads take a lot of stuff inland. If we had mail subsidies some of our men would develop steamship lines, too. But can they get it? South and West won't have it. Say mail subsidies to ship lines would be using national funds to aid New York."

"Why not give the South a subsidized line too? They are entitled to it, if it is from national funds, same as New York."

Hite looked at Matthew pityingly. "You'd better not talk like that on South Street, Matthew," he said. "Give the South anything?" he snorted. "Let her become independent of New York and Boston and Philadelphia?" He laughed. "What would become of South Street then? It'd no longer be the 'gateway to America,' and this panic would be a permanent thing. New York would be ruined. Western goods are going into the South a little now, directly, without going through New York. They say there'll be more of it, and that's brought about some of the troubles here already. Take away the Southern markets, and New York business is sunk. No, you'll never find New Yorkers permitting that. Makes 'em mad any time a British or French ship goes into Charleston or Mobile or New Orleans. Robbing New Yorkers of their birthright, so they say. Abolitionists just make things worse, stirring up the South. You figure it out, Matthew. I can't."

Matthew turned, his back to the bar, and stared thoughtfully out at the street. South Street had certainly changed, he thought, and was due for more changes. This growing sectional controversy was building up to a peak. Biggest danger of all, he thought, was the fact that now the British had won the Crimean War they were in a position to swing their ships back into international trade, and would fight to regain the mastery of the merchant marine which they had temporarily lost to the United States and its clippers. The British had never been able to match the Yankee clippers; but they were making great strides in improvements of their steamers. If America were engaged in internal quarrels that would affect its shipping, then those quarrels directly affected Captain Steel. He thought of Graham White again, wishing he had given the man a little more time. He had been exhausted and harassed with a thousand jobs to be done, and he had been abrupt. He'd attend White's meeting with more pleasure and more interest, now, than Mr. White would suspect. Matthew Steel felt no responsibility for his government, nor to it. So far as he could see, it had never done much for him. But political or economical trends that affected his business were something he should know more about.

A messenger entered the Cock and Bull and spoke to a waiter, who indicated Matthew with a nod of his head.

"Captain Steel?" the man asked.

"Yes?" Matthew answered, not changing his position.

"A message for you, sir, from Mr. Graham White." The man handed him an envelope and waited. Matthew broke the seal and read the few lines on the sheet of paper.

He shoved his cap on the back of his head and his forehead furrowed. Despite himself a grin played around the corners of his mouth.

"Will you tell Mr. White that I will be there—with pleasure," he told the man politely. The messenger nodded and left. Matthew turned back to the bar and pushed his glass toward Hite. "Fill it up once more, Hite," he said. He spread the paper out on the bar and read it again. "Well, I'll be damned," he said softly.

Mr. White, the note said, requested the pleasure of Captain Steel's presence at eight o'clock at a conference at the home of Mr. Thaddeus Blake.

[2]

Tessa Dunn alighted from her carriage and stepped across the walk to the door of the Cock and Bull. She hesitated just a minute, her hand on the door. The soft blue plumes of her hat curled about the glittering masses of her hair, and her cheeks still bore faint traces of the stage make-up she had worn at her afternoon's performance. The glittering stones at her neck were real, and the stuff of her gown was of the finest. She carried a carriage parasol, elaborately trimmed, and she wore a cluster of small pink roses at her waist. Tessa had made her all-of-one-color costumes her trade mark, depending on her magnificent hair for the startling, theatrical accent. The soft blue she had chosen today was especially kind to her, and she raised her chin as she caught a glimpse of herself in the small pane of glass in the door.

Tessa had learned to make an entrance. Her long, easy stride had not changed, every movement still seemed liquid and smooth; but, actress though she was, she found it hard now to mask her eagerness at meeting Matthew Steel. She saw him at once and for an instant she was disappointed, for he was leaning on the bar reading a letter, not watching for her. Hite saw her over Steel's head and spoke and Matthew looked up, put the paper inside his coat and came to greet her.

He looked very fit, a little older, perhaps, more mature, quieter, a little harder. His eyes were as bold as ever and he had the same slow grin. Tessa studied him as he bent over her hand, raising it to his lips. Her gloved fingers tightened around his.

"What did I tell you?" he said. "So you are the toast of New York. Not married yet, Tess?"

She shook her head. "Why should I marry?" she asked calmly. She took his arm and moved toward a table. She turned to nod and smile at Hite and other of her old friends. Hite himself came with champagne for them. He was proud that Tessa Dunn and Captain Steel chose the Cock and Bull for a rendezvous. It was good to think the two had some sentiment left. His round red face was beaming as he popped the cork and poured the wine. The two raised their glasses and the rims clinked.

Matthew's glance traveled over Tessa. "Tell me of yourself, Tess. You like your work, of course."

Tessa shrugged. "It's been profitable."

"That's obvious."

"And you, Matthew? You were very wise to leave New York. We've been hard hit. All the coast has been in the doldrums, but particularly the North. The South seems to have survived the panic better."

Matthew hardly heard her. She was a beautiful woman, he thought, appreciatively, and he was absorbed, watching her. He did not notice two men making their way between the tables toward them. One of the men appeared to be drunk. As he reached Steel's table he stumbled, striking Tessa, and her wine spilled and splashed over her dress. Matthew jumped to his feet and grabbed the man by the arm.

Tessa was standing, her back to the wall, the wine making a dark stain down the front of her gown. Matthew jerked the man erect and started to hustle him toward the door. About them chairs scraped as men and girls arose to their feet.

Whether it was a movement he caught from the tail of his eye, or a sound behind him, or some sixth sense that warned him of danger, Matthew did not know; but even before Tessa's scream rang out he had started to duck, to crouch and to turn. He loosed his hold on the drunken man and whirled on the ball of his foot even as Tessa cried.

"Behind you, Matthew!"

Jimmy Burns' knife had been aimed at the small of Matthew's back. As Matthew pivoted he grabbed for Jimmy's wrist, but he missed by a fraction of an inch and the blade buried itself deep in his palm. Jimmy From Town tried to free the weapon but he could not and he stepped back. In one lightning-like movement, Matthew jerked the knife free and flung it, and it clattered and spun and slid to Tessa's feet.

A hundred fights in crowded quarters aboard ships and on waterfronts the world over had prepared Matthew for just such a battle as this. He did not delay what he knew he had to do. He lowered his arms and waited a split second, inviting a charge. It came.

Jimmy's fist, like a sledge with all the man's great weight behind it, smashed toward Matthew's unprotected chin, but Matthew's chin was not there. His head moved just far enough and the blow passed harmlessly and the fingers of Matthew's good right hand fastened about Jimmy's wrist like a vise; at the same time Matthew's lithe body turned, his back to Jimmy; Jimmy's arm, straight and stiff, was over Matthew's shoulder. Jimmy's hand was palm up.

Tessa's eyes were wide with horror. She watched the blood streaming from Matthew's helpless hand, making dark blobs upon the floor. He can't fight Jimmy with one hand, she told herself, hypnotized, sick, unable to drag her eyes away. The crowd was a silent, tight, circular wall about the two men; Hite had run from behind the bar, a bottle in his hand, and now he stood, his mouth open, his eyes protruding. Morton, pushing his way to Hite's side, a gun in his hand, stopped, frozen, and the drunken decoy whom Matthew had released stood motionless, staring.

The straining men turned and Tessa could see Matthew's face. A lock of black hair was over his forehead and his face was glistening with sweat. Tessa saw the muscle of his jaw knot, and then, with one sure, swift movement he brought his left arm, with its bleeding hand, over Jimmy's outstretched forearm. In the silent room there was a sickening, crunching sound, like a man's heavy heel on seashells, and then there was Jimmy's scream.

It had been only a matter of seconds. Matthew released Jimmy and the man slumped to his knees, writhing, clutching frantically at the helpless, twisted grotesque right arm that Matthew Steel had broken. Jimmy's barrel chest was heaving as he twisted in agony. His thick blunt fingers curled helplessly, loosely.

The room was no longer silent. Jimmy's henchmen who had been planted in the crowd were rushing for the door. They wanted none of the punishment that Captain Steel had given Jimmy Burns. They'd heard that sound before and they knew that Jimmy would carry a twisted arm for life.

"Steel broke his arm, at the elbow. I saw him do it. I heard it break. It was like—it was like—did you see it? It was all over in a minute. He just turned and got Jimmy's arm over his shoulder like this, and came down on it with his right forearm, like this—"

Matthew Steel stood, his arms at his sides, his head lowered, looking at Jimmy. He waited a minute, breathing deep, and then he glanced around the room for Jimmy's drunken aide. The man had disappeared. Matthew ran his good hand over his wet face, and then he raised his left and looked at it, as though he realized for the first time that he had been hurt.

Tessa forced herself to move. She picked up the tablecloth and tore a strip from it and then she went to Matthew and began to bandage his hand. He looked at it impersonally at though it did not belong to him.

Three police officers were shoving their way through the noisy crowd and Morton was giving them an account of the fight. Hite motioned to some waiters and they ran forward and began cleaning up the mess. Tessa tightened the bandage, but the blood seeped through and she shook her head.

"It won't do," she said. She thought her voice sounded as if it came from a great distance. Matthew took the strip of cloth away from her and shoved a chair toward her.

"Sit down," he said. "I'm sorry, Tessa, damned sorry. This won't do your career any good, will it?"

"I've sent for a doctor," Hite said. "God, Matthew, I'm sorry it happened here. I thought the bastard would lay for you in the dark some place. Clever of him, at that. Thought he'd catch you off guard, and he had enough of his boys here to make plenty of confusion for the police. You took care of the rat quick, Matthew. By Jesus, was that fast! You should have killed him."

"I'll take you home in a few minutes, Tessa," Matthew was saying. Tessa raised her head and managed a shaky smile. "Say, Tess, you've seen fights before." He was chiding her gently, trying to ease her tension.

"He—he almost got you, Matthew," she whispered.

They were leading Jimmy Burns away now but Tessa kept her eyes away. A doctor entered and when the hand was dressed Matthew called for a carriage. Tessa could see that the crowd inside the tavern had overflowed through the open doors to the street. Someone was pushing his way through.

Old Dan, the beggar, squirmed and shoved his way to the table. "There's a carriage ready, Matthew," he said, in his high treble. "I saw Jimmy Burns. I saw them take him out. You broke his arm, didn't you? Didn't you?"

"Thanks, Dan," Matthew said. "Come, Tess."

Old Dan limped alongside them as they left the tavern. The mob parted for them. Tessa sank gratefully into the carriage and closed her eyes.

"I'll take you home first, Tessa," Matthew repeated. "Then I'll go back to the ship and clean up a bit. I'm due at Thaddeus Blake's at eight o'clock."

Tessa straightened. "To the Irving House, then," she said. Matthew spoke to the driver. He recognized the fat back, the creased, red neck of Bennett.

"Yes, Captain Steel," the old coachman said. He glanced over his shoulder, his rheumy eyes accusing, his mouth pursed with disapproval.

"The Irving House," Matthew said again. "A good, respectable place. Would you rather I'd not see you in, Tessa?"

"Of course not. I have a suite of rooms. You will come with me and we shall have our champagne after all. Yes, it is a respectable place. And look at me—wine all over me! Oh, Matthew, I guess I'll never be a lady. But what matter?"

Matthew held up his bandaged hand and laughed shortly. "Nor I a gentleman. I'm to go to the Blakes' by request of the State Department. Every time I want to make a good impression, Tessa, something happens."

Tessa laughed and put her arm through his. Her heart lightened. He was not going to the Blakes' to call on Loyalty. He had been summoned there. She indicated a side entrance to the hotel and Bennett, staring straight ahead, stood at attention as they alighted.

"Wait for me, Bennett," Matthew said. "I'll be only a few minutes." The coachman nodded stiffly. Matthew and Tessa disappeared into the hotel.

Tessa fitted her key into the lock and opened the door to her suite and turned up the gas flame on the wall beside her. She turned to speak to Matthew and suddenly froze in her tracks. Matthew too, stopped, and then he stepped ahead of her. The beautiful room had been ransacked. Tessa's magnificent costumes had been dragged from the wardrobe adjoining and lay torn and ripped and slashed on the floor; Matthew motioned Tessa to stay at the door. He stepped over the ruined dresses and moved carefully toward the bedroom beyond, listening. He turned up a light, opened closet doors. In a minute he was back.

"There's no one here. They worked fast." Tessa went into her bedroom, surveyed the damage. Drawers were emptied, the contents smashed and scattered.

"My jewels are in the safe downstairs. It seems they were not robbing—only destroying things." Tessa swallowed back her tears.

"Tess, it's because of me. It's not safe for you here." Matthew was thinking fast. "Listen, dear." Tessa looked up quickly. "We'll report this, of course. The publicity won't help you. But it is too late now. Tonight you'll spend aboard the *Loyalty*. There's a heavy guard there and that is one place Jimmy's men won't dare to come. This, I think, was just intended as a warning."

Tessa's face lighted, and her wide smile broke over her face. "Of course," she said. She came close to Matthew and put her hands on his chest. "Matthew—Matthew, I've always wanted to go to San Francisco! Take me with you! I wouldn't be safe here now, and with you I would be. Please, Matthew!"

Matthew laughed. "You're crazy, Tessa. Your career—all you've worked for—we'll straighten this out."

"But I can continue my work in San Francisco as well. New York is dull now. And after this—dangerous. I shall become the toast of the Barbary Coast! I shall go. If not with you, then on the next ship. But let me go aboard the *Loyalty*, please, Matthew! After all," she laughed up at him, "it is your fault—all this." She indicated her ruined possessions with one sweep of her arm. "You wouldn't desert me now?"

Matthew studied her eager face. "You'd better think it over, Tessa. I'll take you to the ship now, for the night. Gather together what you need—whatever is left," he said, glancing about the room again. "Then if you want to go—of course you may. And this—I'll make it up to you. I'm sorry to bring you bad luck, Tessa."

"I do want to go. Oh, Matthew, I never wanted anything so much!" Tessa clasped her hands and danced a few steps. She picked up a few bits of her costumes, tossed them on a chair, unconcerned. "I'm glad, I'm glad it happened! I'll be just a minute, Matthew!"

Matthew placed the small case Tessa gave him in the back of the carriage.

"To my ship, in Brighton's yards, Bennett," he said. The driver stared at him and then at Tessa meaningly and made no comment. He climbed to the box and Tessa grinned at his broad back. She put her arm through Matthew's again and he smiled at her excitement.

"I'll take you aboard," he said, when they arrived at the ship. "Bennett, I'll need you again. Wait."

Matthew returned to the carriage alone. He had changed his clothes and was drawing a glove over the bandage on his hand. He put his foot on the carriage step. "To the Blake residence, Bennett," he said, over his shoulder.

Bennett stood stiffly. He made no move to mount the box. "No, Matthew Steel, I will not drive you," he said.

"What the devil is the matter with you, man?" Matthew said in exasperation. He turned back to stare at the driver.

"My carriage is for hire, Matthew Steel, and I'll go a long way for a fare," Bennett said firmly. "But I'll not take you straight from that red-haired harlot to the presence of a decent young woman like Miss Loyalty Blake. You, in a tavern brawl over a woman! I heard about it—the whole city will hear of it by tomorrow. You bring her to your ship, her with her carpet bag, means to stay, I take it, brazen hussy! And then you ask me to drive you to the Blakes'. Matthew Steel, you was a bad 'un from the beginning. The Blakes are quality. You never knew the difference as a lad, and you don't know it now. But there is a difference, Matthew Steel, and I'll not be one to aid you in getting out of your class. You belong below stairs and you'd ought to know it. You're not fit to tie the laces of Miss Loyalty's slippers! Why don't you stay away from her, lady that she is, and leave her to her own kind? Trouble, trouble, that's all you'll ever bring to her, Matt Steel!"

Matthew listened to the vitriolic rush of words, stunned.

"Wait a minute, Bennett," he said finally. "What makes you think I'm going to the Blakes' to see Miss Loyalty? As a matter of fact I'm going because I'm summoned there."

"A likely story," Bennett was bristling with outrage. "And what would Mr. Blake want of you, Matthew Steel? Own your ship, that you do, and by foul means rather than fair, I'll warrant you! Don't I know how you named your ship for Miss Loyalty, and upset the family for fair by doing it? A brazen bit of business, and the nerve of you, a stable boy! Wasn't I the one to bring Miss Loyalty to the pier the day you sailed, so she could see the ship and that devilish figurehead for herself? Slipped out in early morning, she did—and it is your fault, encouraging such unmaidenly acts! She's a lady, and if it weren't for you she'd never have chanced it! Scared me to death, she did, and I tried to shield her and took her home as quietly as possible, so none would be the wiser. Not going to see Miss Loyalty—hah! I'm surprised you don't ask her to meet you in secret some place, behind a hedge, like a servant girl!"

Matthew raised his fist and then he dropped it helplessly to his side.

"Why, you—" he began through clenched teeth.

"Yes, I know all you would say, Matthew Steel. It's a blessing your poor mother didn't live to see the way you've turned out. I heard about you. I made it my business to find out. Fightin' on the waterfront as a boy, run away you did, and went to sea. Gambling and fighting and brawling, and now with that actress for a mistress, on your ship, and you show no shame! Don't think you can keep it secret—she's known too well! You've no heart in you, Matthew Steel, so you've no heart to break. But I'm a-warning you, stay away from Miss Loyalty. There's good men and decent men as wants to marry her and keep her safe. Don't go meddling with that."

Matthew advanced a step and Bennett fell back but he would not be silenced.

"I know I'm a poor one, Matthew," Bennett continued. His face was purple in his excitement and fury. "You look at me and you think I'm no one to be talking of quality, because I took to the bottle and lost my position. Maybe I'm a sot, Matt Steel, but I can still have respect for quality when I see it. When I drive Miss Loyalty it is like the old days, when there was them as was proud to have Bennett on the box. She appreciates skill and good form, Miss Loyalty does, and all the genteel things that go with it —she's a lady, that's what. Catch her running around with a man that's blood and muss from being in a grogshop fist fight! And her with champagne on the front of her gown! Catch her entering a hotel with a man, and coming out with him, too, bold as you please, with her portmanteau! Not in a thousand years! Well, you'll not get inside the Blake house, Matthew Steel, rakehell that you are, and good enough for you. I'd not drive you, even to the back entrance. You'll walk there, for all of me!"

[3]

THE Italian opera season had just begun and Loyalty Blake, on her way to the Opera House, drew her scarlet cloak about her shoulders and drank deep of the cool, autumn evening air. She was glad the parching summer was over; the fresh, crisp, fall days held promise of excitement, stimulating after the heavy heat of the dull, depressing summer. Almost anything could happen, Loyalty thought, on a night like this.

Opposite her in the carriage sat Serena and her escort, James Thurlow, and beside her was Henry Austin. They had dined at the home of Alice Merrill, and they would meet Alice and others of her party again at the Opera House. It was good to be alive and young in New York, Loyalty thought. with a long evening of music and laughter ahead of her.

She smiled at her sister. Serena had bloomed under the attentions of James Thurlow this past year. At twenty-four Serena was almost an old maid. Any other girl would be considered so. But Serena, beautiful and gentle and beloved, seemed only to grow more charming with every birthday. James Thurlow, a good-looking, established young man of good family, whose mercantile business had struggled successfully through the panic, had recently discovered Serena. If it were not, Loyalty thought, with a rush of affection, for the responsibilities Serena had shouldered long ago, she would be married now, with a home and children of her own.

Loyalty's conscience pricked her as she watched her sister, saw her smile up at Thurlow, her face appealing and sweet beneath the soft, light sweep of her hair. Serena was so good. Serena was entitled to all the happiness there was. It was not right that she should hesitate to take it, when it came her way, because she was waiting for her impulsive sister to make up her mind about her own marriage.

Loyalty was swept up in the crowd at the Opera House and she tried to join in the light chatter. But she was glad when they were finally seated and the lights were turned low. When the music began she leaned back and relaxed and let it wash over her, the lusty, heady, rich music of Verdi; it caught her up and made her blood race and for a while she was lost in it. It matched her mood and she let it carry and engulf her.

Henry had draped her ruby-red cloak over the back of her chair, and he sat silently watching her. She was eager and entranced, a motionless statue in her white gown. Her necklace was of deep red stones and her lips and cheeks were red. When the music was over she sighed with regret because it was ended. She had been too far removed from her surroundings to come back quickly and easily. Her eyes were dreamy and she was hardly aware when they parted from the others in the group. They were to meet at the Blake's house, Serena said, for a late supper. Loyalty was in the Austin carriage then, alone with Henry, and she was quiet, exhausted by the intensity of the emotions the music had produced.

The memory of the music, the quiet, expectant night, the close intimacy of the carriage enveloped Loyalty and when Austin's arms went around her the man's own desire reached her, too. Loyalty hesitated and Austin took her hesitancy for consent. His lips brushed her cheek and then they found her own; he had never kissed her like that before, fierce and demanding, as though he would never let her go, seeking her response. Loyalty was shaken and confused, attracted and repulsed at once, bewildered at her own surrender, surprised at the intensity of her own emotion, new and strange and terrifying. She drew back, trying to regain her composure, but Henry's arms still imprisoned her.

"I've waited a long time, Loyalty. You will marry me, soon?"

Loyalty put her hands to her flaming face. Austin laughed, a short, exultant laugh and he took her hands away and kissed her again. Loyalty felt tears of exasperation pressing at her eyelids.

She could not seem to find the words to say, to express her own feelings to Austin, nor could she explain them to herself. She felt that she was slipping, sliding down a dark road, being pushed along by her family and friends and circumstances, urged and hurried along by Henry against her own volition. She was not ready, she was not ready, she told herself.

"It will be a beautiful marriage, Loyalty," Austin was saying. "I love you so very much."

"Henry—I—"

"Everyone will be pleased, Loyalty."

"Yes," Loyalty said. "I know." She was silent as the carriage drew up to their door. Serena and James Thurlow were ahead of them, just mounting the steps, and the Merrill carriage drew up behind them. The party moved into the house, laughing and talking and Loyalty hoped no one noticed her confusion. Austin was smoothly correct, as usual, but Loyalty saw Serena looking at her with anxious, loving eyes.

"I wonder if Cass is home," Loyalty said. "Perhaps he is with father." She wanted a minute to compose herself and she turned toward the library. "Excuse me just a minute, please." Henry whirled but already she had her hand on the door and she flung it open. "Father, is Cass—"

There were several men in the room and the air was heavy with cigar smoke. A tray of empty brandy glasses sat on the desk. The room was very quiet as Loyalty spoke, but Loyalty did not notice. She was standing face to face with Matthew Steel.

For several hours Matthew had been sitting in the Blake library and his hand was giving him considerable pain. The bandage now felt too tight, cutting into the swelling, throbbing flesh, and the ache was a bone ache, constant and inescapable, and it ran to the tips of his fingers and up to his elbow. He had found himself moving restlessly in his chair, finding it hard to keep his mind on the conversation, and so finally he had stood, his back to the fire, gripping his aching wrist behind his back with the fingers of the other hand. His face was drawn and weary.

When he had reached the Blake house, the defiance and fury that Bennett's tirade had produced in him still smoldered within him. Thaddeus Blake had met him with courtesy and nothing more and had presented him to his other guests quickly and immediately the discussions were under way. Thaddeus made it quite clear that this was purely a business meeting, and Matthew knew that only the importance of the gentlemen who had requested it would have persuaded Blake to have Matthew Steel in his house again. Blake's clerk and confidant, Christensen, had been seated behind the large desk, a pad of paper and pens before him, and he had scratched busily taking notes throughout the entire evening. He might as well have been preparing a dossier on a criminal, Matthew thought angrily. Graham White, quiet and observant, led the discussions; there were many questions interposed by a tall, spare man, dignified and distinguished, who had been introduced to Matthew as the Massachusetts statesman, Charles Sumner, and by John Hobart, a colorless, dry, small Philadelphia merchant and politician. Thaddeus himself, older, grayer, his skin lighter, showing traces of the translucency that would come with age, had contented himself with a few comments. The talk had ranged over many topics and many countries. Yes, Matthew had replied to Mr. Sumner; the British had attempted to charter his ship to transport troops to India to help quell the Sepoy Mutiny. No, he had not been interested in such a charter. His opinion of the feeling between Russia and Britain? Well, some Russian naval officers felt that Russia and Britain were natural enemies, for their national interests conflicted at so many points. Russia resented Britain's influence on the continent. Russia believed in her right to defend her borders, and to govern any area that she thought was a soft spot through which an enemy might strike her. Russia was crippled as a sea power for many years to come, as a result of the Crimean defeat. This attitude might or might not reflect the opinion of the government or the people—which were not always the same, Matthew added.

Matthew found that Sumner was watching him keenly, asking him questions which could only be based on his previous written report to Graham White. They had paid particular attention to that report, Matthew gathered, and he congratulated himself secretly that the events of the past two years had borne out his observations and conclusions. They discussed steam and sail and mail subsidies, and Matthew said it was a pity the United States was not making progress as rapidly as the British in developing steamships. The British could never compete with America in building and designing sailing vessels; but, jealous of the clippers which were queens of the seas, the British were forging ahead, now, in the improvement of steam-driven ships.

That Matthew Steel, a clipper captain, believed that some day steam would supplant sail was almost heresy, Mr. Sumner observed, smiling.

Matthew felt that the discussions had been quite complete and it was on that remark that he had risen and taken his place before the fire, wondering how soon he might take his leave. There had been no other sounds in the great house; Loyalty, he was certain, was not there. He might have known she would not be. Thaddeus would have taken care of that. Thinking of it, his face hardened. He was good enough to call to Blake's home, as a favor to these esteemed gentlemen whose good will Thaddeus valued. He was not, however, a social equal, to be presented to the Blake daughters. Resentment rose in him again and he stood stiffly, clutching his aching hand, waiting for the older men to be through with their questions.

Then he had caught the sound of the outer door opening and young voices and laughter in the hallway. He had braced himself, listening, his eyes on the doorway. The door had opened and Loyalty Blake stood there, facing him.

She's a little taller, Matthew thought, more breathtakingly beautiful than she was before. Her wide white skirts filled the doorway, tapered upward to her tiny waist; then the stiff brocade curved upward, cupping her breasts, swept on into long, tight sleeves that left her shoulders and throat bare. Over her arms she carried the scarlet cloak and her rippling black hair glistened in the light from the hallway behind her. Black and white and scarlet, he thought, the most exciting, most beautiful, most vivid colors in the world. Loyalty stood quite still, poised, her eyes, wide and direct, upon him. She didn't know I was here, Matthew thought; they did not tell her.

The other men arose as Loyalty appeared and finally she glanced around at them, silently. Serena was beside her, her hand on her arm, protecting and quick. Serena spoke swiftly, her voice easy and gracious. "Forgive us, please, Father," she said. "Loyalty did not know you had guests. Good evening, Mr. Sumner—what a pleasure to see you again! And Mr. Hobart." She bowed also to Mr. White and Christensen, and then, a little stiffly, to Matthew. "Mr. White . . . Mr. Christensen . . . Captain Steel."

Loyalty inclined her head toward her father's guests and there was a murmur of courtly greetings. She moved away from the doorway and Thaddeus motioned for the others of her party to enter and be presented. Henry Austin went to Loyalty's side and took her cloak from her arm. He nodded coldly to Captain Steel. The other girls fluttered and chattered and the older men relaxed a little, smiling at the pretty array. But Matthew Steel stood silent, apart, his eyes on Loyalty.

The color was rising in Loyalty's cheeks and her eyes grew stormy. Suddenly she was angry at Henry Austin, furiously angry, at her father, even at Serena. Serena and Henry as well as her father had known Matthew Steel was to be in this house tonight and they had not told her. No wonder Henry had attempted to exact a promise from her. No wonder Serena had given him the opportunity and had arranged to have the entire party return home with them to an after-theater supper. The plan had been for Matthew Steel to come and go, be hustled out of this house, without encountering Loyalty Blake. The presence of Mr. Sumner and Mr. Hobart meant that the meeting was of some importance. For only under such pressure would Thaddeus have had Matthew Steel here at all.

I'll never know now, for sure, if he would have come to see me if he had not been summoned, Loyalty thought. She was surprised that it did not matter. The important thing was that he was here, in the same room, and that, while he had not spoken a word to her, it seemed to her that he was holding out his arms to her. Alice Merrill was watching Captain Steel with undisguised interest.

Thaddeus Blake had taken great pains to conceal the fact that Matthew Steel's ship was named for his daughter. As far as Loyalty knew, only a handful of people were aware of the fact. But it would be a spicy bit of gossip for Alice Merrill and her party, and it would travel like wildfire throughout the city if it were once revealed.

Directly behind Matthew, on the mantelpiece, sat the little ship's model which he had once held in his hands. Loyalty realized Matthew was in almost the exact position he had been in when she had peeked at him through the keyhole. She felt Serena's hand on her arm again. Serena and Austin and her father were trying, skillfully, to ease her from the room.

Loyalty's head came up and she took a deep breath. She had never before dared to defy her father or question his judgment. But now she walked directly across the room to Matthew Steel. She came very close to him and looked up into his face and smiled, a sweet, understanding smile, as though they were entirely alone. She reached up on the mantelpiece and ran one slim finger down the hull of the little ship.

"And how does the *Loyalty* perform, Captain Steel?" she asked clearly.

She was so near, Matthew could catch the faint perfume she used. He noted the fine texture of her skin; his eyes, straight and fearless, traveled over her face, the perfect hairline, the sweep of her eyelashes, her lips. The magnetism that had drawn him to Loyalty Blake the first time he had seen her, that had kept her so strongly in his thoughts, was still there, but magnified in this instant a thousand times. She had deliberately aligned herself with him, for all to see.

"She has proven my estimate of her," Matthew said slowly. His voice was not loud but it could be heard by everyone in the quiet room. "She has perfect balance. . . ." Loyalty was smiling, too, her eyes dancing. How good it was to be near to Matthew Steel again, to hear his voice! He was a reckless man, she told herself, and her heart raced at his audacity, which so perfectly matched her own. "She relaxes completely to the winds and lets them carry her swiftly on her course," Matthew continued. "She fights with me to resist the storms. And she is still the most beautiful ship I have ever seen."

Alice Merrill gasped and the little sound was loud in the silent room. Graham White regarded Captain Steel and Loyalty thoughtfully and then he glanced at Thaddeus Blake. Thaddeus was frowning and his face was white and he opened his lips to speak, but Henry Austin was before him.

Austin's voice was acid, cutting, and there was no mistaking his meaning. It slashed between Loyalty and Matthew like a knife blade.

"And who will take over the *Loyalty* when you are done with her—or when you add another and newer ship to your fleet?"

Loyalty stood perfectly still but her hand gripped the skirt of her gown convulsively. Matthew Steel turned slowly to Austin and his bold black eyes met Austin's unwaveringly. He answered without haste and his words were a promise.

"The *Loyalty* will know no other master," he said. "Not only because I love my ship—but no one else can handle her." It seemed to Loyalty that he had come a step nearer to her, but he had not moved. "She's very temperamental," he said. "Variable as Cape Horn weather. But with a captain who knows her strength as well as her weaknesses—and they are very few—none can best her. She has never failed me. Neither shall I desert her."

The tension in the room had increased till it resembled an approaching thunderstorm. Matthew Steel felt it and it did not disturb him. It was his turn, now. With Loyalty beside him, the hostility of the rest meant nothing. As long as Loyalty had faith in him, there was no limit to his strength. She is as much a part of me as my right arm, he thought, and she knows it and has accepted it.

Matthew turned to Thaddeus and bowed. "I am glad to have met your guests, Mr. Blake. If I can be of service at any time, please call upon me. I hope to meet you again, Mr. Sumner. Mr. White, my gratitude for making it possible. Mr. Hobart. Mr. Christensen."

One by one the men bowed. "You sail Sunday, Captain Steel?" White asked.

"Yes. But I will be back." Matthew turned to Serena. "Good night, Miss Blake." He included Austin and the rest in one careless gesture of his head. Then he faced Loyalty again and she gave him her hand. He raised it to his lips.

"My ship is well named, Loyalty," he said quietly.

Without another word he left the room. Henry Austin strode into the hall after him and Loyalty followed. The servant was waiting at the door with Matthew's hat and gloves, and as Matthew reached for them Loyalty noticed the bandage and discolored left hand. Involuntarily her hand went out toward him. Matthew covered the hand with his hat.

"Just a minute, Steel," Austin said. His voice was low and tight with anger.

"Yes, Austin?"

"You may be interested to know that Loyalty and I are to be married. We became engaged tonight."

Matthew looked beyond him at Loyalty. He searched her face and one of his eyebrows went up, quizzically and then he grinned. His eyes were laughing, too, but he bowed to Austin again, politely.

"Congratulations," he said, and was gone.

[4]

THE master of the *Loyalty* pushed his ship to the very limit. He waited till the last split second to take in a sail, and the ship flashed southward, one thousand, two thousand, three thousand miles, as though she, or her captain, were demon-driven. The sea-gulls that followed the ship from New York harbor were left behind, and small whales and dolphins played about the ship. Autumn gave way to summer and within three weeks the *Loyalty* had streaked across the Equator, running finely with the southeast trades. Then the warm winds came from the north and Tessa Dunn, standing at the rail, watched the flying fish, gauzy wings flashing, and she strained her eyes toward the west, trying to see the coast of Brazil.

Tessa thought Matthew's crew well trained and his first officer, a squat, thick, powerful Frenchman named Jules Descase, handled the men well. Jules kept up a constant stream of profanity in French and English, at the ship and at his men, but Tessa knew that he would have been the first to resent any outside criticism. He worshipped the ship. His ape-like face, his beady black eyes, revealed his admiration and pleasure when his crew accomplished a task in perfect time. When the *Loyalty* in the lovely tranquility of tropic seas sailed along as smoothly as a toy ship on a millpond, Jules bragged that a child could steer her. And he was never happier than when they sighted and overtook another vessel on the same course.

Because much of her life had been spent on the waterfront, the sea and ships were a part of Tessa, and she gloried in the beauty of the *Loyalty*. This voyage could have been an enchanted voyage, a dream come true; for long, lazy golden days filed by, and Tessa had nothing to do but enjoy them. But Tessa was not happy, nor was the voyage the adventure she had dreamed.

Each day she lounged among her pillows on the deck, watching the work of the ship and the changing cloud patterns and the sea itself, listening, watching, for Matthew Steel. At first she was puzzled, and told herself she must be patient—there was work to be done, and Matthew would come to her in his own good time, and she comforted herself with happy anticipation. Perhaps, she thought, he was purposely avoiding her to shield her from gossip. But Matthew had never been one to be concerned about public opinion, and even if he were he could easily make opportunities to see her privately. Matthew Steel was a man who did exactly what he wanted to do.

Tessa was glad she was an actress. She had to call upon her talent and training to keep up a pleasant, polite front to the other passengers. Actually she felt restless, irritable; small things annoyed her out of all proportion to their importance. The rhythmic creaking of the ship began to wear on her nerves, and even the gentle motion of it was no longer soothing. At night she found her body tense, her hands gripping the sides of her berth, her whole being listening for the sound of Matthew's footsteps outside her door. And when at last she fell into uneasy sleep, dark and terrifying and nebulous dreams tormented her, and she awakened no less weary than when she had gone to bed.

The days seemed endless. Loneliness bore down upon her like a heavy weight. The small stateroom seemed too confining. She wanted to push the walls back with her hands, to give herself more space—space in which she could pace and prowl in her restlessness. She began to think with foreboding of the inevitable storms they would encounter off the Horn. With Matthew Steel they would be adventure, wild, exhilarating, dangerous, wonderful—violent as passion; alone they would be terrifying, something only to be endured.

But it was not the storms that frightened her most, for Tessa was no physical coward. It was the fear that Matthew Steel would not come to her at all, and it seemed to her that was something she could not bear. Her dreams of becoming indispensable to Matthew Steel, once she was aboard his ship with him, had begun to give way to sick doubt. And the loneliness and unhappiness combined to make Tessa ill, to shake her usual composure, to make the little noises of the ship seem a din to her tortured nerves, to magnify a slight wind to hurricane force.

Tonight Tessa lay in her berth, closing her eyes tight against tears. She would will herself to sleep and perhaps tomorrow—but how many nights had she comforted herself with that thin hope—perhaps tomorrow? She turned on her face and buried her head in the pillows. Her hair felt hot and heavy against her neck and she pushed it away impatiently. It was not her imagination that the ship pitched and rolled more heavily tonight, or that the wind howled stronger than it had for many days. She raised her head and listened and then she forced herself to lie down again and she tried consciously to relax her body, inch by inch, the fingers, the wrists, the arms— She pretended she was in the wings of a stage, soon to go behind the footlights, and she breathed deeply and slowly, gathering her defenses against stagefright. After a while the little device was successful and exhausted sleep crept over her.

She wakened slowly and heavily, her body wet with sweat. Dull and heavy pain started at the back of her neck and felt around her head with cruel, clamping fingers. She sat up and wiped her face and pulled herself back to consciousness, knowing that she must awaken completely to throw off the lingering horror of an already-forgotten nightmare. The ship pitched and she was flung to the edge of her berth and she reached out her hands to catch herself and fear and loneliness stabbed her again.

I can't stand it, she whispered. I can't stand it alone. Unreasoning panic drove her to her feet and she reached for her dressing gown and wrapped herself in it, her fingers shaking, fumbling with the fastenings. I can't be alone any more. I've got to see someone, talk to someone—Matthew—Matthew. The wind was howling and pounding and there was the jerking, creaking, complaining of the ship and the hiss and clash, the thud and roar of the beating waves.

Tessa put her clenched fist hard against her teeth to smother the hysterical screams that rose in her throat. Her knees were shaking and they would hardly support her and she clutched the doorknob, pushing frantically. The door would not open and she threw her weight against it and still it held and she slipped to the floor, whimpering a little. She buried her face in her hands, her fingers tightening in the hair at her temples, and she fought for control. Shakily she pulled herself erect again and braced herself against the movement of the ship. For just a moment the storm seemed to pause, the ship stood still, poised, and then it plunged again, down, down, dropping beneath her, and the sickening descent seemed to shake her and she could not stop trembling. Again she tried the door, tugging, bruising her hands, tearing her fingernails. The latch gave way and for an instant she paused in the open doorway, panting, facing the blackness of the passageway, feeling the cold gust of air sweeping down it, grateful for it, despite its chill. She stumbled into the passageway, and turned blindly to her right, feeling her way, thinking only to reach the deck where she might feel herself one with the storm, get a feeling of space and freedom, give herself over to the violence of the sea and wind, and leave behind her in the little stateroom all the fears and longings that had hounded her.

The ship paused again, motionless, on a crest, and seemed to hold its breath before the sickening plunge. Tessa saw a light coming toward her and she gathered her strength and ran, stumbling, toward it.

Matthew Steel saw her in the flickering light of the lantern as she ran and he caught her in his arms as she fell. His coat was dripping wet, but Tessa clung to it, her slender body shaking, her breath coming in long, broken gasps.

"Tessa, Tessa!" Matthew Steel's arms were strong about her and his familiar voice reached her through the torturing racket of the ship and storm. He pushed open the door of his cabin and, with one arm still about her, he hung the lantern. Then he swept her up in his arms and laid her on his bed. He ripped off his wet coat and flung it aside. He was beside her, holding her tight, her trembling body straining against his, her hands clutching his shirt, her face buried in his shoulder.

Quietly, strongly, Matthew held her, and gradually her sobs quieted. At each motion of the ship her body stiffened and she clung to him more frantically. His hand smoothed her hair and he spoke to her softly, his lips close to her ear.

"It's all right, Tessa," he said, his voice steady, reassuring. "It's quite all right. There's no danger, Tess. The ship is sound, and we'll be out of this soon, perhaps in only an hour or so. It is not as bad as it was. The ship has been through much worse storms than this, Tess. Don't be frightened. You are not alone, Tess. It's all right."

Gradually his words got through to her and she relaxed, limp in his arms. It seemed to her that even as he talked the storm did die, and the wind lessened, the motion of the ship was less violent. She moved now only as Matthew moved, his hard, strong body taking the motion of the ship as though he were a part of it. There was nothing to fear. Matthew was here and she was in his arms.

"I awakened—and I thought it was a nightmare—and it wasn't. I had to get out," she said brokenly. "I had to find you—Matthew—"

"I know," Matthew said. He smoothed her hair and his lips moved softly over her forehead and down her cheek. "I know, Tessa. But it's all right now. It's all right. Don't be afraid, ever, any more."

Her body seemed drained of strength and she rested against him, feeling at first only his protection and safety after terror.

Then, gradually, life came back and she was conscious that his face was hard and cold and fresh from the wind and rain. Beneath her cheek she could feel his heart beat and she moved her head a little against his chest in a sensuous, yearning movement, straining to be still nearer to him. Her hand moved, trembling a little, almost unbelieving, almost afraid, down his cheek, down his arm, caressing, possessive, and then she raised her face and brushed his lips with her own, barely touching, tempting, inviting. Her eyes closed against the shifting lantern light and a yearning, intense as hunger, raced through her veins like an overpowering drug and possessed her utterly. Her forehead smarted where his rough chin had rubbed it; the feel of the hard muscles of his arms was like a tangible thing clinging to the palms of her hands and she gloried in these evidences of his nearness. For an instant he was motionless and then he raised his face, away from her lips, and his strong fingers closed firmly about her wrists. Tessa waited and then Matthew slowly, still gently, drew her arms from him and Tessa, unbelieving, opened her eyes to stare at his face. He smiled a little and his dark eyes, direct and understanding, rested on her. Tessa drew back uncertain at the change in him, and fright flicked its fingers in her face and left its mark.

"You're all right now, Tess." Matthew spoke matter-of-factly. He released her hands and slid her from his arms. He stood and went to the chart table and straightened some papers and weighted them with a heavy book. The book dropped upon them with a little thud. "You aren't the first to become hysterical during one of these storms," he went on, casually. "Even men who have sailed for years sometimes have an attack of nerves after a few hours of this. But there's nothing to be worried about. Not now."

"Matthew—" Tessa's lips were stiff and she could not raise her voice above a whisper. He glanced at her and then his eyes turned away again.

"If you like I'll ask one of the other women passengers to stay with you," he said evenly. "I don't blame you for not wanting to be alone. Would you like that?"

There was silence broken only by the creak of the ship and the wail of the wind. Then Tessa spoke aloud. "No," she said flatly.

She stood, drawing her dressing gown around her. She was suddenly cold, bone-cold, and she clamped her teeth tight to keep them from chattering and Matthew saw her face harden with the effort. "No," she repeated. Her face with its slightly hollowed cheeks, heavy-lidded eyes and sullen mouth, was white and without beauty, pinched and drawn with strain and gathering rage. "I wanted," she said clearly, rather loudly, using her voice as a whip with which to flay him, "to stay here. With you."

The ship lurched and automatically Matthew braced himself for the motion, but Tessa stumbled and threw out her hand to catch herself. He reached for her, steadying her, his arm around her waist, and at his touch Tessa's momentary defiance melted, running from her. Again she was against him and sobs began to come and she was helpless against them.

"Don't, Tess," he said. "Don't. Listen to me. I'm the Captain of this ship. I'm responsible for the welfare of my passengers." He smoothed her hair, then held her away from him, forcing her to meet his eyes. He was trying to make her smile, she knew, and obediently her lips twisted, ever so little. "Tess, you're the best friend I ever had. I have—a deep affection for you, Tess. I admire your courage and your ambition. I remember you as I first saw you—a tragic, terrified little girl. You were that little girl again tonight—and I want to help you now, as I tried to help you then. I was scared, too, when I was a kid. You're my friend, Tess, can't you understand that? And I can't let you stay here now, Tess, because—"

Tessa leaned against his arm, worshiping the strength of it, and with a great effort the words came huskily from her throat. She spoke recklessly, not sparing herself, determined to wrench the truth from him. "Don't lie about it, Matthew. You don't love me, and you never will. That is what you are trying to avoid saying, isn't it?"

"It's like this," he said finally. "You couldn't stay with me tonight, Tess—you couldn't give yourself without giving your heart, too. And Tess—" he stopped and then, looking straight at her, he delivered the final blow. "There couldn't be anything more. Not for me."

Tessa's body went lax. She dropped her hands and stepped back, free of him, and her shoulders sagged and she had the shameful look of the defeated. Matthew took a deep breath. "I'm sorry, Tess," he said, after a while. "But that's the way it is."

Tess's lip curled suddenly and her head raised a little. "Don't you pity me, Matthew Steel." Her breath began to come unevenly and Matthew recognized growing anger. She backed toward the door. "Matthew Steel" she said fiercely, "I hate. . . ." She choked on the word. She reached behind her and her clutching fingers closed upon the doorknob. But even as she spoke she was watching him, yearning, thinking: *he won't let me go. Not really. He won't really let me go.*

He made no move toward her. *But he will let me go, he's waiting for me to go,* Tessa thought in growing panic, appalled at the truth of it. *He's telling me to get out, that is what he is doing—as gently, as kindly as he can—but telling me I'm unwanted.* "Oh!" The one word, heavy with fury and overwhelming shame was torn from her and she flung open the door and was gone.

She reached her own stateroom and closed the door behind her and leaned against it, breathing heavily. Only a little while ago she had fled from the confinement of this small cubicle but now she welcomed its privacy. She turned her head frantically from side to side, looking for something, something she could not define, trying to shake off the growing certainty of a horrible fact she did not want to recognize. But she could not escape it. She threw herself into her chair and buried her face in her hands. Matthew did not love her. He would never love her. And tonight he had told her so in the clearest, cruelest manner man could devise. A woman forcibly possessed could not reach these depths of shame, Tessa thought wildly; for even one thus ravished would know that she was desired. Is there any loneliness greater than that of an unloved woman, she thought? Any shame greater than that of a woman refused? She jerked spasmodically, sobbing, and after a long time, exhausted, dulled, partially cleansed, she relaxed, breathing deeply, evenly, not thinking any more, and perhaps she even slept.

She did not know when she awoke but with awakening she began to sort her thoughts from her emotions. The bitter knowledge that she meant nothing to Matthew Steel twisted inside her, jagged and painful. She would have to get used to living with that pain, she told herself; she would have to pick up the scraps of her pride and rebuild, salvaging what she could. Shakily she pulled herself upright and bathed her face and then she started to brush her hair with long sweeps of her arm. She turned to the mirror and was surprised that the night had left so few ravaging signs. Her eyes had been washed clear by tears and they were shadowed, which did not detract from her beauty. Her trembling mouth was soft; her hair still burned against the white of her neck. She stared at her reflection and she saw a beautiful woman denied and indignation began to rise within her and stiffen her. Her teeth clenched. Indignation swelled to anger and anger dried her eyes and gave her strength.

She dressed carefully and then she put her stateroom in order. She sat down with her hands clasped in front of her, trying to control herself, trying to make sensible plans. Rage and resentment at the man who had hurt her shook her deeply. Bitterness made ugly lines on her face and still she sat, her hands gripped, waiting till her mind returned to normalcy again and she could think coherently, without the racking passions that had possessed her.

She went back over the events of the night, deliberately. It was like exposing a deep wound before treatment was applied. In the midst of the storm, she had been terrified and hysterical here in this room.

Then she had found Matthew Steel. Her thoughts tiptoed up to him reluctantly and retreated, but she forced herself to go on. So deep had been her longing that she had offered herself to him and been refused. That was the one shameful fact she could never escape. Why had she failed? The intimacy of the ship—their common backgrounds—her own love—the appeal which other men had assured her she possessed—why were they not enough for Matthew Steel? There was only one answer. It was Loyalty Blake.

All her fury, seeking an object on which to center, concentrated on Loyalty. Tessa grasped the table top and her long fingernails bit into it. Hating Loyalty brought her some small relief, explained her failure. For her own satisfaction she would some day confirm that suspicion.

She stood up with a great effort and raised her head. She sought her mirror again for confidence and she was proud of the woman who looked back at her. She would not hide, nor cringe, nor avert her eyes in shame and despair and defeat. Not Tessa Dunn.

She smoothed her dress down over her hips. "Well, Tessa," she said to herself in the mirror, her voice smooth and normal. "What have you left?" She gave herself one last reassuring smile and went back to her bed and lay upon it. She was physically exhausted but her mind, at last, was clear. "At least you have Matthew to thank for your career."

Except for Matthew she would never have left the Cock and Bull and dared the offices of theatrical agents and applied herself to study, nor would she have achieved her present success. She began to remember nostalgically the moments when she was behind the footlights, when applause swept about her and sent her blood racing; and the hours in her dressing room, when she ripped open notes from admirers, and lifted great bunches of flowers from their wrappings. It had been pleasant to sweep into a cafe or hotel dining room on the arm of Cass Blake, lazy, sweet, devoted Cass!—and to know that heads were turning to watch her. It had given her the greatest pleasure she had yet known to feel between her fingers the money she had earned and to know she could spend it as she chose. How many women would sacrifice their homes, their pompous, respectable husbands, for such independence and acclaim? Desire for that life came back to Tessa, stronger than it had ever been. As soon as she set foot on the Barbary Coast she would begin her campaign. She'd outshine them all, all the glittering golden girls of San Francisco, the gayest city of them all. She had been a fool to consider sacrificing that life for one man. It would, she tried to convince herself, have been a poor exchange!

Complete resignation and comfort did not come to Tessa all at once, nor to stay. Night after night as the ship sailed southward, Tessa fought her loneliness and hurt pride and grief. But she was winning the battle, and with surprising rapidity. She did not seek Matthew Steel; she knew there was nothing more that she could do.

Matthew, driving himself and his ship relentlessly, cut through Le Maire Strait, separating Staten Island from Tierra Del Fuego. His daring saved him a hundred miles or more of hard sailing, and he fought his way through and then he pitted his strength and his skill against the huge cold seas of the Horn. The *Loyalty* was swept far south and still farther east as she attempted to round Cape Horn, and still Matthew fought and gradually he brought the ship westward and again north and once again he was safely free of the tempests of the Horn. The ship was caught in the northeast trades then, and another season was left behind, and they went on into spring and then into summer.

When the days were warm again Tessa went back to sitting in her favorite place on the deck, half dozing in the sun. In a little while now they would sight the Farallon Islands. Jules Descase was already driving his men relentlessly to polish and repair and clean the ship, preparing to enter port. When the *Loyalty* entered the Golden Gate, the hundred days from New York to San Francisco by clipper ship would be over.

To Tessa, drowsing in the sun, it seemed much more than a hundred days. She wondered, idly, if it were right for human beings to travel so far and so fast, ignoring the usual plodding march of the seasons. Down the east coast the ship had sailed through autumn and winter, spring and summer, with a brazen contempt for time and now, going north along the west coast, she was again running through a year's changes in only a few weeks. Perhaps she really had lived two years in those hundred days aboard ship, Tessa decided. At any rate, the first bitter agony of her disappointment was gone, her plans for the future made and it seemed that the nightmare night of the first storm had been a long time ago. The healing of her heartbreak was aided by the speed of the ship, the defiance of time and space and the complete disregard for the calendar and the sun.

Matthew stood beside Tessa for a full minute before she was aware of him. She turned her head then, her attention caught by his shadow, and looked up at him and smiled. He sat down beside her.

"It won't be much longer, Tessa," Matthew said finally. Tessa shook her head. His nearness brought a lump to her throat and she could feel her high resolves crumbling. She knew, frantically, that she was going to plead, shamelessly, again. She set her teeth against the words that pressed against them. She wanted to reach out and touch him, but she gripped her hands tightly and waited. Matthew watched her, trying to look behind the set mask of her face. He had believed that she had moved from shame and remorse to anger, and that the anger had burned itself down to resentment, and then that, too, had begun to fade and a cool resignation take its place; and then, in the last days, her old, natural, self-confidence had begun to return. He had waited, giving her time to regain her self-control, before he talked to her.

"Tessa," he said gently, "I have not told you before—but I am sorry." Tessa sat very still for an instant. A tiny vestige of hope tugged at her and she could not prevent herself from making one last frantic grasp at it. But she saw only pity in his face. Her voice was husky as she answered.

"You have—you have simply no feeling for me at all?"

"I am fond of you, Tessa. I will always be."

"And that is all?"

He did not answer. Rebellion and the old pain washed over Tessa again. *It's not fair,* she cried inwardly. *I can't stop loving him—any more than I can stop the eternal motion of the sea. But you can help what you do about it, Tess,* she told herself, stubbornly. And in that moment Tessa at last forced herself to give up her dreams. She had planned the complete revelation of her own devotion would bind them together and that Matthew, indebted, at journey's end, would marry her. *You gambled and you lost, Tess,* she admitted, silently, bitterly.

"All right, Matthew," Tessa said, after a long while. She looked out over the water and it seemed to her suddenly bleak and cold despite the sun. There was only one thing more she wanted to know. It would answer the big question of why she had failed; it would explain why her devotion had not been enough. "It's Loyalty Blake, isn't it?"

Matthew stood up. He walked to the rail and leaned against it. Tessa's complete capitulation and acceptance of the situation relieved him, even though he had both expected and hoped for it. Knowing Tessa as he did he had not believed that she would brood over-long. He had believed also that, left to herself, she would, once her rage had died, find other consolation. In her work at first, and then, undoubtedly, in another man. She would find satisfaction also in material possessions, of that he was sure. To someone who had always known luxury, money might bring little comfort. To Tessa, remembering the poverty of her childhood, it would be salve to her wounds.

But Tessa's mention of Loyalty Blake was like a sudden and unexpected knife thrust. For weeks he had been unable even to speak her name without a quickening of his heart. Tessa's presence aboard his ship had, paradoxically, only deepened his love for Loyalty, strengthened his conviction that she was the one woman in all the world for him. There were in Loyalty spiritual depths that it would take a man a lifetime to know. With Tessa, close association would bring nothing new. Loyalty would inspire a man to seek new heights; she would confidently expect him to be a bigger man than he was. In that way Loyalty was like Mary Steel and perhaps that was the reason, unconsciously, why he was so drawn to her. She had an innate nobility, a fineness, deeper and truer than a man possessed, and it would urge him on above his own level of moral growth. Perhaps behind all progress was just such a woman, Matthew thought, a woman whose will and sense of justice and love of beauty and desire for better things forced some man to greater accomplishments. A man needed to look up to the woman he loved, to worship her as being made of finer and purer clay than he. A woman like Tessa was too nearly like himself; to marry her would be to halt at the exact limit of his own abilities. It would be a leveling off—a compromise. It would take no effort to live up to Tessa. It would take every ounce of his strength and ability and courage all the rest of his life to live up to Loyalty Blake and her clear-eyed, innocent trust in him. He only hoped and prayed that he was man enough to do it.

He turned back to Tessa and the conviction in his voice sent a sick chill through her. "Yes, Tessa," he said. "It's Loyalty Blake."

"And what makes you think she'll have you? You are hardly well matched!"

Matthew kept his voice even. "We are perfectly matched, Tessa."

Tessa rose and faced him. All the viciousness she had sought to bury was in her voice. "Marry her, then! And what a disappointment that will be! A pretty fragile figurine on a mantel-piece is nice to look at—but not very exciting to live with! Loyalty Blake is a lady, and ladies, they tell me, have many inhibitions. You are hardly the type for a meek and submissive partner, Matthew Steel."

"You are wrong again, Tessa. There is nothing meek and submissive about Loyalty."

Tessa snorted. "Hah!" Never, she thought, would she be able to accept the thought of Loyalty sharing her life with Matthew Steel. Jealousy, intense and overpowering, took possession of her tongue. She sought for words that would stab and hurt and force him to lash out at her in return. If he would strike her, she thought wildly, it would be better.

"Marriage means not only all your days together—but your nights. Perhaps she would be a model wife in the daytime, Matthew, but at night—"

Matthew raised his hand as if to strike her and automatically she drew back a step. He dropped his hand to his side but his words were a harsher blow.

"Loyalty is the kind of woman who would laugh with a man—on their wedding night."

He turned on his heel and was gone. Tessa grasped the rail with both hands, steadying herself, rage and frustration shaking her. That was the end of it. She had heard it now, from Matthew Steel himself. Desire, love, protection, the respectability of marriage, and that other precious intangible something which Tessa had sought and not found—respect, devotion, worship, what was its name? All of the things Tessa had wanted from Matthew Steel were wrapped up in his words about Loyalty. He spoke as if he knew Loyalty very well; he dreamed of her, longed for her, with an intensity and depth that Tessa would never reach. Matthew Steel had always got what he wanted. He would have Loyalty, too.

God, she thought, I was an awful fool, to think for an instant he might offer to marry me. It never entered his head. Matthew Steel never sacrificed anything for anyone else—only for himself and his own fierce ambitions. He's made of iron and stone, Matthew Steel is, and he'd not let me or anyone else stand in his way. He'd break me—with as little regret as he broke Jimmy Burns' arm. It's Steel and his dreams, first and foremost, and to the devil with the rest of us. Maybe I am not the only woman who has broken her heart trying to influence this man, beating against that rock-like determination of his. Can Loyalty Blake, or any other flesh and blood woman, break him down? Will he ever know what it is to want something he cannot have, and know that no matter what he does he cannot get it? Will he ever give up anything of his own to bring happiness to another? Will he ever, in all his lifetime, know humility? I know what he is, and I love him, and I hate him, too, for what he has done to me, and to any other who would attempt to alter his course. I'd be better off to be free of him, forever and ever free of him!

Tessa had a few days yet to climb back up to the resignation she had achieved before her talk with Matthew, and this time the road was easier and swifter. She knew her bitterness and jealousy had made a bad display. If she had been gallant and comradely she could, at least, have kept their old friendship. But her scars had been too deep and too new. Perhaps Matthew would realize that and not hold it against her. At least Matthew, always contemptuous of weakness, had paid her the compliment of being brutally honest with her.

The ship shone in perfect cleanliness and polish and repair, the brasswork sparkling in the sun that rose from the land before them, when the *Loyalty* at last entered the Golden Gate. Tessa watched breathlessly as the ship entered the harbor, welcoming the sight of land so close, the rolling brown hills, the wisps of smoke from the city ahead. She was glad the voyage was over, and, searching inwardly, she was glad, also, that she had made it. One chapter of her life was finished, but a new one was beginning. She felt suddenly free of fears and responsibilities and old loyalties. San Francisco and new triumphs were before her and she was eager and hungry again for applause and the stimulation of music and lights and an audience. She needed them to restore her shaken faith in herself. It was good, she thought, to have another chance.

She turned reluctantly and went to her stateroom and gathered her belongings together. She would leave the ship soon, and she would never set foot on this or any other vessel again. They were to come to dock at Long Wharf, the pilot had said. Tessa was already trying to visualize the San Francisco streets in her mind. She must be careful to make no mistakes. Her entrance into the city must get her off to a fine start. For the first time she thought longingly of her beautiful, ruined clothes, back in the Irving House in New York. She must replenish her wardrobe and elaborately, at the first opportunity. She would go direct to the Parker House in Portsmouth Square, and it would become her headquarters, and she would go on from there.

She hurried again to the deck. A dark, well-dressed man with a neat mustache was talking to Matthew Steel and he turned to regard her with interest. He had come aboard with the pilot, and Tessa had heard him speak with a clipped, British accent.

Tessa paused and Matthew turned to her and bowed formally.

"May I present Mr. Thomas Hinigan, reporter for the *Alta California*—Miss Tessa Dunn," Matthew said. Tessa offered her hand.

Matthew Steel quietly moved away. When he looked back Hinigan, a British writer who had come to San Francisco by way of Sydney, was completely engrossed in conversation with the New York actress. Tessa had forgotten Captain Steel completely, and so, apparently, had the reporter. Tessa stood tall and regal and beautiful, her eyes half-closed, her voice low and husky, giving her first careful interview to a member of the San Francisco press.

[5]

MATTHEW checked the last item on the ten-foot long manifest of the *Loyalty* and regarded it with satisfaction. His profit on the New York to San Francisco voyage was greater than he had hoped. He considered his next move.

His ship had been tied up at Long Wharf for three weeks and

he allowed himself only another week in port. He had examined not only the California papers, but all the foreign publications that came into the city as well. After a careful survey and much talk with businessmen and other seafarers, he judged that his best bet was a cargo of grain for Australia, grain and California lumber for the Oriental ports into which ships put for repairs. There was always a demand for great, stout masts from the forests of California.

That left him with the profit from his last voyage, free and clear, to invest. Idle money was of little value. With shipping definitely in the doldrums, was it possible for him to choose paying cargoes and paying runs for more than one ship? A steam sloop, the *Messenger,* now in San Francisco bay, was for sale. Matthew had inspected the vessel carefully and he believed the price was right. He had trained Jules Descase carefully and the man was capable of commanding the *Messenger* and would follow directions to the letter. Matthew stood and stretched, frowning in thought. Most men were retrenching, afraid of the future. Political unrest and sectional strife in the United States were increasing and there were threats of secession and division of the Union. No one knew what such a move would do to trade. New York businessmen favored the South, urging peaceful solution of the South's grievances, even if it meant peaceful separation—anything to hold the Southern markets.

Nevertheless, there would always be some shipping, and San Francisco could support a number of ships. Isolated from the Eastern sources of supply as she was, facing the Pacific, San Francisco would always be a great port and the city's leaders were forward-thinking men, bent on making it a great maritime center. A Matthew Steel ship based here, with his reputation for fair play and safe cargoes, was bound to be a good investment.

Matthew looked at his watch. It was ten o'clock and he had not yet dined. He had determined to come to some decision tonight regarding his next move. The sensible thing to do, he told himself, was to buy the *Messenger,* and to set sail at once for Australia.

He reached for his coat. It was not easy to head out into the Pacific, when all his desire was centered on New York City, a hundred days away. It might be a year or more before he would get back there, if he went into this new venture. Yet reason told him he could not sail his great ship and her crew halfway around the globe with an empty hold, and no prospects of securing cargoes at the end of his journey, simply because the *Loyalty's* master desired a gray-eyed, black-haired girl in New York. Sentiment must play no part in a man's business decisions.

Matthew closed his door behind him and left his ship and strode up the pier. From the Mississippi House, a bar presided over by Pablo de la Maza, a resort famed for its knife fights and the cooking of one Antonio Gonzales, came sounds of revelry. A number of Matthew's men had left the ship and had gone as far as the Mississippi House the first night of their arrival, and Matthew believed that many of them were there still.

San Francisco at night was garish and rowdy and noisy and unapologetic. Despite its size it was still raw and new, but there was about it a light-hearted bravado that fascinated him. Perhaps it was because the people who had come to San Francisco were the adventurous ones, the hot-blooded, foot-loose gold-seekers, gamblers and dreamers, and they lived in a more rarified atmosphere than the people of the older Eastern cities. San Francisco was still growing; there had been many major changes and improvements since his last visit and some order and feeling of permanence had been brought out of the mad chaos of the early days of the gold rush. Nevertheless, there was still a carnival spirit, a holiday feeling in the air, particularly at night, when the city's five hundred saloons and dance halls were jammed with pleasure-seekers. The heavy fogs that rolled in through the Golden Gate, the winds that came from the Pacific, were more stimulating than wine; people walked faster, slept less, drank more, gambled more heavily, laughed and danced and worked and hurried faster, than in any other place.

Matthew hired a hack and headed uptown. Most of his business had been done in the El Dorado or the gambling rooms of the Parker House, or in the United States Restaurant next door. There he would find the brokers and merchants, shipowners and financiers with whom he would deal. His business could be concluded rapidly now that he had made up his mind.

Late that night Matthew lounged against a bar in a crowded,

brightly lighted saloon, and listened to Tessa Dunn. Her performance was now professionally smooth, her voice well placed. Against the background of beruffled dancing girls Tessa stood out like a jewel in a dark mounting. Her songs were wicked and boisterous and they brought whistles and shouts, and then they were sad and plaintive and the crowd went wild. When the music stopped and the crowd clamored for more and Tessa sang again and then she shook her head, laughing, and refused another encore. She swept from the stage, her head high, her eyes shining, warmed by her success.

Matthew made his way through the mob to a side entrance and bribed his way backstage. Tessa was making slow progress through the people gathered in the wings. She saw him and raised her eyebrows and then sauntered over to him carelessly and he watched her come, her glittering dress shimmering with the movements of her body.

"Hello, Matthew Steel."

Matthew grinned at her in admiration. "You're quite a girl, Tessa," he said. She laughed aloud. "Will you stay in San Francisco long?"

Tessa shrugged. "I like it here. But I suppose I'll go back to New York eventually. However, I'll go overland. I'll never go around the Horn again for anyone—not even you, Matthew."

He laughed. "No sailor's life for you, eh?"

"No. I don't envy you. You make your money the hard way. When do you sail?"

"Within a few days. I've bought another ship. The *Messenger*."

For an instant Tessa looked like the girl she used to be. She put her hand on his arm impulsively.

"That's good, Matthew," she said sincerely. "Another ship with your house flag. . . ." She took a deep breath. "I'm glad. You'll be off to Australia, then?"

"Yes." Matthew took her hand and laid a folded paper in it. "There are a couple of lots here in San Francisco, Tess. I got them several years ago—won them at faro, or monte, I forget which. I want you to have them. They should be worth something by now."

Tessa's long fingers closed about the paper. Only a few weeks ago she would have accepted nothing from Matthew Steel. But now she smiled and pleasure lighted her face. San Francisco real estate meant money, and money meant independence. What did it matter where it came from?

"Thanks," she said. Despite himself Matthew grinned. No, he had no need to worry about Tessa. He had believed applause and money would console her, and he had been right.

"Good-by, Tess."

For an instant his hand closed over hers, warm and strong. She could feel her control breaking and she spoke swiftly.

"Good luck, Captain Steel," she said steadily.

"I was hoping you'd say that," he answered. Behind Tessa the music clashed. Instantly her body tensed and her eyes began to shine.

"That's my number. Good-by Matthew." She raised her face, brushed his lips with her own and was gone, to the stage, behind the footlights. Matthew made his way out of the wings and back to the bar again. She was singing as only Tessa Dunn could sing, and she was feasting on the pleasure of her audience. Matthew went on through the crowded room and the door closed behind him and he turned back toward Long Wharf.

Tessa's kiss burned on his lips and her song followed him but he did not look back. He raised his head to scan the sky. The wind was high and the sea would be rough outside the Heads. The far reaches of the Pacific would be very lonely after the gaiety of San Francisco. He walked on doggedly, passing music-filled and light-flooded resorts, till at last he came again to the waterfront. Lights and laughter, he thought; mermaids to lure a seafarer off his course. He raised his head and his footsteps were measured and sure as drum beats as he went on, toward his ship. The wind had swept away the night mists and the sky was very clear.

Matthew Steel, the stable boy, son of an Irish immigrant, owned two great ocean-going ships. He must remember that. And there, almost near enough to reach up and touch them, were the stars to steer them by.

CHAPTER IV

LOYALTY BLAKE SAT in an easy chair in her sister's room, her slippered feet on an ottoman before her, a stack of newspapers in her lap. Alice Merrill was stretched comfortably on a lounge, enjoying the freedom from her tight stays which she had removed for an hour before dressing again for dinner. Serena sat before her embroidery frame, putting the last exquisite stitches into a large sampler before her.

"Newspapers," Alice said lazily. "Why ever do you read them, Loyalty? Nothing but stories of secession and how Mrs. Lincoln is a teetotaller. So tiresome!"

Loyalty smiled and picked up the *Tribune*. "Father never brings the *Tribune* home," she said. "And he is very careful not to be seen reading it in his office—or he'd be taken for an abolitionist. But I," she added calmly, "like it, and so I have to send a servant for it."

"Father and Loyalty discuss politics by the hour," Serena said indulgently. "And sometimes even argue! All about compromise and abolition, the Kansas question and the Republican Party. I confess I understand none of it. Before Mr. Lincoln's inauguration they prophesied riots and rebellions and attempts to assassinate the new president—and then all that excitement died down. Loyalty seems to be an abolitionist and Father talks about property rights! So much ado about nothing."

Loyalty was absorbed in her paper. She sat up suddenly and her eyes brightened with interest. "Here it is—the 'infamous' sheets republished from that Atlanta paper." Her eyes swept down the lists of New York business firms. "My life! Forty firms are listed as abolitionist and forty-seven as 'constitutional.' Father," she said disapprovingly, "is constitutional."

She sank back in her chair again, frowning a little. "Father was so concerned," she explained. "Since the panic he had depended on Southern trade more than on the West, and so he is for compromise, or peaceful separation. He even leans favorably to the suggestion that New York become a free city and separate herself from the states; I disagree." Her pretty lips straightened. "I think the Union must be preserved at all costs, and I think slavery of any human being a disgrace to our nation."

"I declare, Loyalty, you talk as though you understood what it was all about," Alice yawned. "Surely you don't question a man's judgment about these things? Is it finished, Serena?"

Serena's face flushed a little as she removed the sampler from its frame.

"Yes. And now I shall start its mate." She held up the sampler for the girls to see.

"It's beautiful, Serena," Alice said, reaching for it. She smoothed it out carefully and read the embroidered scroll respectfully. "'Requirements of the Wife. A wife's desire shall be to her husband. She shall be subject unto him. Wives submit yourselves unto your own husbands as unto the Lord. Let the wife render unto her husband due benevolence.' Well, Serena, it's lovely! But you do not need such a reminder to be a good wife to James Thurlow."

Serena laughed, embarrassed. Loyalty reached for the new sampler her sister was measuring against the frame. "No, of course she doesn't, Alice. But if she displays that one then she can display this one—and it will be a tactful reminder for James! Read it, Serena."

"'A man shall leave father and mother and cleave unto his wife.'"

"That, of course, is taken for granted," Alice said, putting her hands beneath her head and looking thoughtfully at the ceiling. "If it were any but you, Serena, I'd be intensely jealous of your new house. When I am Mrs. William Hastings I shall be poor as a church mouse and William and I will live in a cottage and I will be fortunate to have one servant! Read on."

" 'If a husband provide not for his own wife and children he is worse than an infidel.' "

"That is a pretty strong statement," said Loyalty, her eyes dancing. Serena glanced at her warningly.

"If you poke fun, Loyalty, I'll not read more."

"Go on, darling. I'm not laughing. I'm approving."

Her sister's soft voice continued. " 'A man shall cheer up his wife.' " The girls nodded in approval. " 'It is a wicked act that a man should gain the heart of a woman and then forsake his wife.' "

"Very charming, Serena, and what an immense amount of work you put into them."

"I've finished all the linens and my trousseau is ready. I thought these would be a pretty addition." Serena frowned prettily as she fitted the material into her frame. Then she raised her head. "Wasn't that a carriage?"

"It is time for Father to be home," Loyalty said. She left her chair and went to the window, smiling at her sister's happiness. Serena had never looked so lovely, her sister thought, as she did bending over her embroidery frame, dreaming and planning the home she would share with James Thurlow.

Alice slid from the lounge and reluctantly reached for her stays. "There was a carriage," Loyalty said, "but it has gone on. Someone left a message, perhaps." She wandered into the hall and turned toward her own room. A maid met her at the head of the stairs. "What is it, Rosa?"

"A note from your father, Miss Loyalty, and one for Miss Serena from Mr. Thurlow."

Loyalty took the two envelopes and ripped open the one addressed to her. She stood motionless for an instant and then she ran back to Serena's room.

"Serena. Alice."

"Loyalty, what is it?"

"A message from Father." Loyalty cleared her tight throat. "It's —the Rebels have fired upon Fort Sumter. They have demanded the surrender of the Fort. Father says they expect momentarily a proclamation from the President calling for volunteers." She glanced down at the innocent, day-old newspapers beside the chair. "But everyone said it could not be," she said, unbelieving. "Everyone said it would not come to war."

"War?" Alice sat down quickly. "War between the states? Loyalty, are you sure?"

Loyalty handed the other envelope to Serena silently. Her sister glanced at the handwriting and tore it open quickly. Serena took a deep breath and then she turned her face away.

"James will not be with us until late this evening," she said evenly. "There is a meeting which he must attend, having to do with raising money for the Union forces." She caught her lip in her small teeth and she did not look at Loyalty or Alice. Loyalty sat, stunned, still disbelieving, her thoughts racing, tumbling over one another, incoherently, trying to grasp the real meaning of her father's message.

"Of course, I've heard the gentlemen talking of it, but I never dreamed—" Alice began stupidly. Her face was white. "Will William—will Cass and James—do you suppose they will go?"

Her question hung in mid-air, unanswered. After a little Serena picked up the embroidery frame and slowly and stiffly she carried it to a closet and put it carefully away. Loyalty watched her, her eyes wide, and then she arose and went back to her own room. Her throat was tight and tears pressed hot behind her eyelids.

She had discussed with her father the possibility of a rebellion many times. Thaddeus, his health failing since the panic, had leaned more heavily upon Loyalty than she had ever dreamed he might. When he found her interest in public affairs genuine he had at first bowed to it and then fostered it, and he had gradually instructed her and directed her reading and discussion. The comradeship that had grown between them as a result was a precious thing to them both.

It was, moreover, unexpected. There had been a day when Loyalty felt that she and her father could never be friends again. But that had been almost two years ago, when she had told him firmly and quietly that she would not marry Henry Austin, and that she would wait for the return of Matthew Steel. His cold fury and intense disappointment had beat about her head. He had been ruthless in his denunciation of Captain Steel, and in his efforts to influence her had gone so far as to mention to his daughter the name of Tessa Dunn. Loyalty had listened silently at first, and then, shaken but defiant, she had deliberately walked from the room, permitting her back and her silence to state that she would hear no more. She felt, for the first time in her life, completely alone, but she had convictions behind her. She learned the truth of the knife fight in which Matthew had engaged, and she remembered Jimmy Burns' evil face, and Old Dan's report to her of Jimmy's threats against Captain Steel. And Tessa Dunn—deliberately Loyalty closed her mind against that other girl who shared some part of Matthew's life. But his love, she told herself passionately, was for her.

Her decision had alienated her to some extent from Cass, whose dislike of Captain Steel had crystallized into unreasoning hatred; and it had severed the valued old friendship between the Austin family and her own. Her father had been cold and reserved for many weeks and then, gradually, his disappointment and his anger had seemed to temper to something like respect for her own firmness. He had begun to treat her more as an equal and as an adult, and their companionship had grown and bloomed, and Loyalty, eager to atone for the hurt she had brought her father, made every effort to strengthen the new bond between them. But her decision had delayed Serena's wedding. Only recently had Serena been persuaded to go ahead with her plans, for Loyalty's demeanor, for many months now, had been above reproach. Thaddeus and Serena's older women relatives, after consultation, felt that Loyalty, now twenty-two, was capable of taking over the reins of the household which Serena had handled so capably so long. They likewise believed that Loyalty would, in all likelihood, never marry; it was a pity, they said, that she should make so tragic, though romantic, a decision. They doubted if Captain Steel would ever return to claim her, or that he would make a suitable husband if he did. The story of Loyalty's romantic attachment to the colorful young shipowner was much whispered about in social circles; it lent to her a charm which younger girls envied.

But the month of April, 1861, had been a happy month for Serena, and for James Thurlow. Loyalty, pleased at her sister's happiness, had felt longingly that perhaps it would all come right at last. Serena's long, heart-breaking delay in her own marriage plans had been hardest of all for Loyalty to witness, her sister's silent acceptance of the delay the only threat to Loyalty's decision.

Loyalty stood at her window now, gripping her hands tightly. Below her, carriages were arriving, messages were being passed in at the door, and friends were coming to discuss the news that had fallen like a thunderbolt on New York and all the nation. She must go down, presently, to talk to them. What would it mean to them all? Thaddeus had been one of those to urge caution in dealing with the South. But now that the cleavage had come, that the flag had actually been fired upon, Loyalty knew what her father's reaction would be. Thaddeus, like every other Northern patriot, would immediately forget his own financial interests, submerge his own problems in that of his country, and he would throw all his weight behind the Union cause. The shot at Fort Sumter was a call to arms for every loyal man, woman and child in the Union.

She wished that she could forget the look on Serena's face when she read James' note and put her sampler away. Serena had not looked at her sister. Loyalty knew that Serena was thinking that because of her sister's wild, stubborn infatuation for Captain Steel, she had delayed her marriage too long. Perhaps there would never be a need for the trousseau now, nor would the samplers ever be displayed in a home of Serena's own.

But for me, Loyalty told herself, pressing the damp palms of her hands together, Serena and James would have had these last two years together. James will go to war, and Cass will go, and Henry, and Alice's William Hastings. Her heart twisted, thinking of her brother, her friends, her sister's sweetheart, and she felt that already she could hear the sound of marching feet and the roll of drums. She leaned her head against the window pane and its coolness was comforting. *Matthew Steel, where are you?* she whispered. *I need you so much. Will you, too, be going to war? Will the*

Loyalty become a fighting ship? Fear shook her, and she turned away, eager for activity and companionship. Perhaps, she told herself reasonably, it will all be over in a few weeks. Surely the Rebels would not hold out for long. She began to dress swiftly. But she wished she did not have to see her sister's still, reproachful face again tonight.

[2]

THE peaks on the coast range of California were just in view when the Aberdeen Clipper Barque *Charlotte Andrews*, heading out of San Francisco for the gold fields of Otago, New Zealand, spoke to the *Loyalty*. Matthew Steel, hungry for the sight of land after weeks at sea, starved for news, sent his flag flying in answer to the *Charlotte Andrews'* signal. He was grateful for the smooth seas that permitted the Barque to come alongside, but when at last the ships parted company and the *Loyalty* headed on toward the Golden Gate, Matthew's face was serious and the excitement of his men was evident in the rush of talk and activity from one end of the vessel to the other.

The Rebellion was on, and it was expected that the Rebels would use privateers to capture or destroy the shipping of the Northern forces—in fact, by pre-arrangement, they might even now be at sea and ready to strike. The Stars and Stripes were small protection now. All ships must be warned, and Matthew thought of Jules Descase and the *Messenger*, following him within a fortnight, and the third ship he had recently added to his fleet, the *Comet*. The *Comet* was a stout vessel and Matthew had intended putting her on the long, hard San Francisco to Shanghai run.

But this news changed his plans. It was a time for a man to keep his head and make careful moves. The *Loyalty* had poked her aristocratic bow into remote harbors on the Russian islands of Amur and Sakhalin and Matthew had fortunately met Russian naval men there, including an old acquaintance, Captain Scripliff, master of H.I.M. Russian steam corvette *Novick*. The two had celebrated together on vodka and the Russian's favorite American drink, a mixture of ale and gin, and Scripliff had told Matthew of the new Polish uprising and the growing unfriendliness between Russia and France and Russia and England. There would be a European war again, Scripliff had declared, before another year was out, unless some miracle of power politics prevented it.

Scripliff painted the governments of both Great Britain and France darkly and he declared France had designs on Mexico and only awaited her chance to make a mockery of the Monroe Doctrine. The internal squabbles of the European powers were of little interest to Matthew, for, like the poor, he believed they would be always present; but he was interested in their effect on trade.

Matthew, taking stock of his assets, could total now a half-million dollars in ships, in valuable fur and silk cargoes, and in cash, to his own credit. It was a brilliant accomplishment, and enough to give him a feeling of security. He had felt he could afford to relax a little, move a little more slowly, now that he was so firmly established. Only strokes of business genius, and lucky gambling, could have amassed so great a fortune so fast and he was proud of it. Now, however, standing beside the pilot and discussing the news as they entered magnificent San Francisco Bay, Matthew's thoughts leaped ahead and he began to rearrange his future.

War, in the United States or abroad, meant increased shipping. Governments would charter or buy ships and more ships, and pay quickly and dearly for needed cargoes. The South particularly would be in need of ships. The reasons for the Rebellion and its probable final outcome were not entirely clear to Captain Steel, and in that he was not alone, for thousands of Americans were confused. Matthew felt there was something to be said on both sides. The North's economic strangle hold on the South was bound, sooner or later, to produce convulsive attempts toward freedom. Extension of slavery was bound to be opposed by the North, not necessarily from humanitarian motives, but because, in new states and territories, numerous free farmers and their families would offer far greater markets than a few slaveholding land-owners.

But, as in all contests, Matthew thought, unless you were actually an active contestant, the thing to do was to pick the winner, and then place your bets accordingly. Clever men enlarged their fortunes during a war. Not a half-million, but ten million dollars could belong to Matthew Steel, if he took advantage of this opportunity.

He could best choose the winner when he was nearer the scene of conflict—in New York. San Francisco was only a seething hotbed of rumors and arguments, charges and counter charges, fear and unrest, threats and apprehension. A man had to seek his own unbiased information at the source.

He stayed in San Francisco only long enough to discharge his passengers and a small part of his cargo. He left word for the *Comet* and *Messenger* to tie up on their arrival and await his orders. Then the *Loyalty* again put to sea.

She sailed with a skeleton crew and a watch alert for prowling Rebel cruisers. Matthew felt a twinge of uneasiness as he left the Golden Gate behind him. A lone, bold privateer could take that unprotected harbor, for not even a Union gunboat was there to defend it. "The only protection San Francisco has is the fog," uneasy residents grumbled. San Diego was likewise vulnerable to attack, and Southern sympathizers, including Brigham Young's fifty thousand followers, were talking openly and loudly.

He would not leave the *Comet* and *Messenger* and their valuable silk and tea cargoes in San Francisco's wide open port for long. He must dock at South Street as soon as it was humanly possible and arrange to deploy his ships in the most strategic spots to gain the most from zooming freight rates. This was an opportunity that would come only once in many lifetimes, a chance to become one of America's wealthiest men. He was very fortunate indeed, he congratulated himself, to enter into this period of conflict with the outright ownership of three stout and magnificent ships, and plenty of capital with which to gamble.

And for once, Matthew thought, as the *Loyalty* beat her way southward again and braced herself for another battle with her old enemy, Cape Horn, luck rode with him. For this time opportunity beckoned from New York city, the one place where his heart longed to be. The strongest winds could not carry him fast enough. Regardless of war between the states, or Rebel privateers,

Matthew Steel was headed, at last, toward his love. Loyalty, as brilliant as sunlight, as real as the winds that drove his ship, as exciting as music, as necessary to him as food and drink—it was only a matter of days, now, till she would be where she belonged—in his arms. It was unthinkable that she might not be waiting for him.

[3]

THE heady music of the regimental bands invaded Loyalty's blood and paced her heartbeats. Tense excitement held the capital in its grip and Loyalty and Alice, watching the troops march over Long Bridge and Chain Bridge, toward Centreville and Fairfax County Courthouse, were enveloped by it. For weeks Washington had been packed with troops and now, confident and lighthearted, they were leaving on the first stage of the march toward Richmond—the drive that was to end the three-months'-old war. The brilliant sun glistened on the beautiful, clear colors of the flags and was caught in the vicious polish of bayonets and on the trappings of cavalry horses and the gold braid and vivid sashes of officers.

But to Loyalty, elation and pride in the display of Federal might was tainted with fear. The clatter of artillery and munition wagons, the few frail, two-wheeled ambulances doubling as supply carts, the pounding of hoofs and rattle and clanking of harness, the unforgettable, even tread of thousands of marching feet as the troops moved toward the front, seemed to her a forewarning of the greater din of battle ahead—the sinister, low, prebattle growl in the throat of the war monster soon to be released. And even as she waved to Cass and William Hastings and other friends her heart sank. Together they were an army, a military machine for destruction. But singly they were individuals—not killers; just boys she knew in new, unwrinkled uniforms, who set their caps at a jaunty angle and tossed compliments over their shoulders to the pretty girls along the line of march.

Like thousands of other wives, sisters and sweethearts, Alice, a recent bride, and Loyalty had come from New York to the capital to attend the balls and reviews for the volunteers stationed there. The battle of Manassas or Bull Run would be the first engagement for the new troops, and, the people declared proudly, undoubtedly the last—for they'd make short work of the Rebels!

After the men were gone, the two girls waited the entire week in Washington, eagerly devouring every dispatch from the advancing troops. The weather suddenly turned mercilessly hot, and even though the men were proceeding by easy stages, Loyalty knew they would begin to find the rigors of the march distasteful. Out in the Virginia countryside they were beyond the cheers of civilians; they were no longer being pelted by flowers and flattered with kisses blown from pretty fingertips; it was not unlikely, Loyalty thought, that despite their bravado, fear padded softly beside the inexperienced, almost untrained men. There were rumors that due to poor planning food supplies were slow to reach them and the men were quick with complaints; and, once the soldiers were gone and the music of the bands faded into the distance, there were disturbing hints that the men were not as well prepared to fight as they were to parade. All night wagons rumbled across the bridges, following the Army, and dispatch riders followed one another importantly back to the capital, calling for more supplies, bringing little news.

Some of the younger officers left the troops at night and galloped back to the capital for a gay evening, boasting a bit, enjoying the adulation the people heaped upon them and Loyalty's apprehension grew. She knew these men as gallant dancing partners, friends of Cass and Henry, commissioned, she suspected, because of their proud names, their political influence, their money. Many of them, her heart told her sickly, were not fitted to lead other men; they were, moreover, too confident. Immediately she was ashamed for her lack of faith in them and told herself the Rebels were a raw army, too. But she knew that the Rebels were on the defensive, which gave them an initial advantage; that Southern leadership was actually superior, for many of the nation's finest officers had elected to go with their states.

And the South was united. They knew what they were fighting

for. They were fired with fury and righteousness and had a singleness of purpose. The Northern men were confused. If Loyalty asked a Union volunteer why he was in the Army he parried the question or answered with a laugh and a toast—*We are in the Army because there is a Rebellion, ma'am, haven't you heard? The President called for volunteers and so we are going to teach the Rebels a lesson. On to Richmond! Be ready to help me celebrate when we return, ma'am. Come out the turnpike to meet us when we come marching home. . . . I'll bring you Beauregard's sword, Loyalty—*

To them it was a lark, an exciting holiday, a Fourth of July celebration, with firecrackers and popguns, a costume ball, a make-believe war—

Henry Austin had been an exception. He had sought Loyalty out and advised her seriously to return to New York. She had been grateful to him and she was glad there were some intelligent, thoughtful officers like Henry in the Union Army. They needed more like him—men who were going into this first major battle of the war with a clear knowledge of the hazards. But Loyalty had not taken his advice. Alice would stay in Washington until the battle was over and William's enlistment was up, and then she and William would go home together. Loyalty must stay with her, Alice declared. And Loyalty, too, wanted to be as near as possible to Cass.

She knew, almost as if she were watching his face, what Cass already was enduring. He would be impatient first, at the heat and weariness, for Cass had never been one to tolerate discomfort with good grace. And if Cass were wounded, how would he stand pain? Like every soldier he thought that death or wounds could not possibly come to him; but with Cass, this feeling of security was even more pronounced. His own good fortune, his father's money, his refusal to accept responsibility, had saved him from the disappointments that most boys took for granted. Loving him, but knowing his weaknesses as well as his virtues, Loyalty thought Cass might need someone near to him when he came back —someone who would understand and not condemn. No, she told Henry; she would stay in Washington till the Battle of Bull

Run was won, and they could go back then to their stable, well-ordered lives, the war over.

Alice grew taut as the days wore on. She laughed too quickly and too shrilly. She read the early bulletins, her eyes too bright, her lips working as she tasted every word. Those first dispatches were comforting. The Federals had much the advantage in preliminary skirmishes. Anyone who said otherwise was a propagandist for the Rebels and not to be believed. The capital was wildly jubilant and at week's end pre-victory celebrations had already begun and at night the Washington streets were crowded with drunken celebrants.

Loyalty watched Alice anxiously, fearing hysteria. Alice's wedding had been one of the first war weddings and the few weeks of marriage had been charged with the bitter knowledge of this parting to come. Loyalty suspected that Alice was now in the first weeks of pregnancy and she was more gentle and considerate of her friend.

Hundreds of civilians were preparing to pour out the Warrenton Turnpike on Sunday morning. That day's battle would be the decisive one, they said. Many hoped to witness the battle itself. They wanted to see Rebel prisoners being marched back to Washington, to see other Rebels running before advancing Federal troops. There was a ridge, they declared excitedly, overlooking the battle site, on which carriages could stand and from which the occupants could watch the fight through field glasses. Others did not hope to see the fighting, but they wanted to be among the first to welcome the returning heroes. But Alice and Loyalty, who had joined the mad scramble to hire a carriage, were drawn by secret foreboding. Alice wanted only to be as near as possible to her soldier husband, to know that the battle was over and the nightmare of the past week was done.

The blazing sun climbed high and dust curled and settled sluggishly as they rolled out into the Virginia countryside. Loyalty fanned herself and settled the skirts of her white muslin dress more comfortably. Alice sat stiffly erect, but as the day grew older she began to droop a little and weariness drew parentheses about her mouth.

There was a hamper in the carriage but at noonday the girls

could not eat. They drank a little water and pushed the food aside. Their carriage halted now and then and they leaned out, eager for news from an occasional dusty horseman coming toward them. The dust seemed drier and it rose in choking waves at the tiniest touch of a wheel or a hoof; an elaborate carriage was halted in the shade of a tree and Loyalty noticed within it a giggling party of girls and men. They were holding wineglasses in their hands and their laughter was shrill. The girls had too many bright-colored ribbons on their hats and Loyalty had the dismayed feeling that this was no place for a proper girl to be; she felt as though she had stumbled into a disreputable place, unescorted, and she wished heartily that she had not listened to Alice and had remained sensibly in their rooms at the Willard.

At last the sun began to lower but the humid, sticky air seemed heavier, hotter than it had been at noon. The line of vehicles moved more slowly and after a while, as it drew nearer to the battlefield, it barely crept along. For a little while Alice drowsed, overcome by heat and exhaustion, and Loyalty sat quietly, watching, glad that Alice, white and pathetic, might have a few moments of partial forgetfulness.

She wondered if the carriages that had preceded theirs were lined up on the ridge, if the people were watching the battle, as Romans watched gladiators at their bloody festivals. Despite the heat her own hands were cold and now and then her teeth chattered with nervousness. There was in the atmosphere of heavy heat and dirt of the road, rutted by the Army that had passed, the constant gunfire, an almost drunken spirit of revelry and intense excitement, a note of approaching storm, of impending disaster. *It's because death is so near to us,* Loyalty thought; *it is like waiting for an execution.*

Reports from the battlefield reached them from time to time and trickled down the line behind them, toward Washington. In mid-afternoon the accounts were jubilant; laughing, delighted men leaned from their saddles to speak to Loyalty. "The Federals are winning—what did we tell you? You can't beat our boys! On to Richmond! It won't be long now, girls. . . . We'll hang Jeff Davis!"

In mid-afternoon they began to meet returning foot soldiers, slogging along, leering, insolent, half-defiant, and behind them came wagons piled high with packs and equipment, carelessly stowed. Loyalty recognized them as men from the Eighth New York and the Fourth Pennsylvania. One man slowed as he neared her carriage and as the line of vehicles halted he came and leaned against the wheel. He eyed Loyalty and jerked his head toward the hamper.

"Anything to drink, ma'am?" he asked boldly. Mutely Loyalty reached for the water bottle and handed it to him. He tipped it up and drank, not taking his eyes from her, and her face colored. Ahead of them there was a roar and a crack like a great thunderclap and Loyalty waited until the gunfire died before she spoke.

"Are you deserting?" she asked sharply.

He took his time about replying and then he grinned unpleasantly. "No, ma'am," he said with mock politeness. He put down the water bottle, his lips and chin wet. "Our three months' enlistment was up yesterday morning, so—" he shrugged. "We just put down our guns and started home. We had enough soldierin' . . ." He swayed toward Loyalty and she caught the heavy odor of liquor on his breath and she saw dirt thick in the creases of his face. "We didn't see no use of fightin'—not when there's Washington and some pretty girls . . . ." His eyes traveled over her and he grinned again and tipped his head a little to one side. "You'd suit me fine, ma'am."

Alice gasped and Loyalty's voice was hard and quiet. "Get out," she ordered. The man allowed himself time for a long appraisal of her and then he decided to obey.

"He is a deserter, just the same," Loyalty said furiously. "Even if his period of enlistment is up—to put down his gun the day before the battle and start home!" Her fists clenched and her eyes flashed with indignation and insult. She determined to put the incident out of her mind and she drew back into the carriage and arranged her parasol to protect them from the eyes of the returning volunteers.

In late afternoon Alice drowsed again. Her face was greenish white and Loyalty coaxed her to rest while she could. "You want to be fresh and pretty when William comes," she told her. There was a momentary lull in the firing and Loyalty listened breathlessly. Could it be over? And then the boom and crack of guns began again, heavier than ever. For a little while there were few riders with dispatches, and then suddenly there was a great spurt of them, but they no longer stopped leisurely to talk. They flashed back, on their way to Washington, and their faces were serious. Was something wrong? people asked one another, leaning from their carriages. Occasionally a vehicle drew out from the line and turned back toward the city, the occupants, not yet alarmed, only weary of waiting, their taste for the excursion burned out in the heat and dust of the long day.

Like a soft breeze first, the rumors came. The Rebels had slowed the Federals' advance. No matter—the Federals would regain their position. The breeze very swiftly grew to a wind; the Rebels had stopped the Union forces. They had taken the offensive—they were beating the Federals back! And the wind of rumor grew and swelled to roaring storm-force and it wiped the triumph from the faces of the men and women, left them incredulous, shocked. Impossible, they said, but their voices lacked conviction, and the report was confirmed, again and again, in a dozen different voices, hammering at them, forcing them to believe.

The long stream of traffic came to a complete stop. Almost imperceptibly at first the change came over the excursionists. And then the serpentine of vehicles began to break, here, there and everywhere, as the sight-seers, stunned, horrified, realized suddenly that they themselves were in peril, and carriages began to turn hurriedly, unskillfully, to head back toward Washington.

The Federal line had broken, the Army was in wild flight, the Grand Army of the Republic had stampeded, men were deserting, heading back for the river, running from the Rebels! Clear the turnpike, get back over the bridge before it is overloaded and breaks down, get away from the Rebels, clear the roadway before the Army, crazed with defeat, pours down upon it! Get back to the city, barricade your doors, pray for fresh troops to protect Washington from the victory-mad Rebels!

The people were no excitement-seekers now, nor a welcoming

committee for returning heroes. They were refugees with fear in their faces, running from danger at their backs. The voices rose to shouts and courtesy and rules of the road were forgotten as people shoved and teams tangled and the drivers fought for positions. The dust was a thick, smoke-like blanket and Loyalty, standing in the carriage gazed fascinated, at the weird, unreal shapes through the shifting, choking dun blanket, horrified at the violent metamorphosis that had come so plainly and swiftly over the people about her.

But she was not altogether surprised. It had been the fear of this, a premonition, perhaps, that had compelled her to come with Alice. If we had delayed this morning, one part of her mind said, matter-of-factly, we would be nearer to the bridge now; instead we are perilously close to the battlefield and there are hundreds of vehicles between us and Washington. . . . The boy driver turned a frightened face to her.

"Shall we turn back, ma'am?"

Alice raised her head and stared at Loyalty dully. She was drugged with sleep and the turmoil about her had not yet touched her.

"They say, Alice, it is a defeat," Loyalty said steadily. "They say we must go back across the river, quickly. They say our men will be coming—retreating—and we must clear the way. Do you understand?"

Alice was on her feet, straining her eyes, trying to see down the turnpike before them. As she watched an Army wagon appeared, forcing its way, pushing the civilian carriages back, recklessly swerving, crowding horsemen into the ditch. The wagon slowed, waiting for the road before them to clear and the driver shouted: "Make way, make way!" and added a string of epithets at civilians whose carriages choked the turnpike.

"Is it true—is it a defeat?" Alice called to him and the soldier driving the Army wagon turned toward them. His face was black with dirt and sweat and he was grimacing in anger at having his path blocked. He stood, holding fast to the reins to steady his plunging horses, and then he jerked his head toward the rear of the wagon.

"Look at that!" he yelled. "Hell, yes, it's defeat!" His whip cracked and the wagon passed them and Loyalty and Alice, standing motionless and appalled, saw the wagon's contents. It was filled with injured men, their wounds open, unbandaged or tied about with ragged, bloody strips torn from uniforms. Alice's screams cut through the racket and Loyalty pulled her back, into the seat.

"Yes, turn back," Loyalty ordered. The boy was only too glad to try. He made an effort to turn the carriage but Alice's fingernails dug into Loyalty's arm.

"We can't turn back! I won't let you! I must wait—I must find William!" Loyalty looked at her and then at the driver. The boy's face blanched and his Adam's apple moved up and down his throat in agitation. He had been eager enough to drive them out on the sun-dappled turnpike this morning; he had congratulated himself that he was to be paid, all too handsomely, while he was enjoying the spectacle himself. Now he had no thought of money. He was stiff with fear and he wanted only to run.

Loyalty pleaded with Alice. They could do no good by remaining here, Loyalty declared sensibly. They were only adding to the confusion and the longer they delayed the more difficult it would be for them to get back to Washington. The returning carriages already moved only at snail's pace, hampered by snarled traffic ahead, and if it became worse they might not be able to move at all. As they sat, the first of the retreating soldiers came, half-running, half-shuffling through the dust on both sides of the road. They had thrown away their guns and their haversacks. Men who had started out in carriages early in the morning were also coming back on foot, disheveled and exhausted. They had been caught in the fierce onrush of Rebel troops and were lucky to have escaped at all; not all of them were so fortunate, they said grimly. They brought harrowing tales of the battle and the casualties and the debacle of Bull Run. More wagons and a flimsy, inadequate, jolting ambulance passed them, demanding the right-of-way, and as darkness crept over them the walking wounded began to come, staggering, supported by other men or tramping doggedly, heads bent, breath coming hard and noisily. Alice huddled in a corner of the carriage, sobbing, protesting wildly that she would not turn back.

Finally Loyalty stepped down from the carriage. Here and there torches appeared, dotting the turnpike like a long line of jack-o'-lanterns, as far as she could see, and the rumble and roar of voices and hoofs and feet and carriages, caissons and wagons and carts were muted thunder steadily increasing with the waning light. Alice was actually ill, shocked by the defeat, nauseated by the wounded, terrified with fear for William. There would be small chance of finding William Hastings, unless he soon passed this way, and they could not sit here in the carriage all night, squarely in the path of the advancing Rebels, watching this awful stream of defeated and maimed and injured men. Loyalty spoke quietly to the boy driver and gratefully he took up the reins again. And at last he had the vehicle facing back toward the river. Loyalty's foot was on the step then and Alice's shaking, clutching hands were reaching for her when someone bumped against her in the semi-darkness.

Loyalty felt the rough scratch of a sleeve on her bare arm and a man doubled up at her feet. He made no sound, he just crumpled, silently, and a flickering torch shed its light on his face for just an instant. A part of his face was gone and Loyalty's heart came up in her throat. Loyalty knelt and raised the man's head carefully. He was still breathing and she reached quickly into the carriage for the water bottle and held it to his lips. The blood on his face had caked and dried and only a little fresh blood was oozing from the wound now. The water spilled over his face and his lips worked a little and she could feel his muscles tense as conciousness came back. "Thank you, ma'am," he said. His voice seemed to come from far away and Loyalty felt a wave of sickness pass over her and she blinked to clear it away. *Thank you, ma'am!* It was almost more than she could bear. She reached again to the hamper on the floor of the carriage and whipped out a towel and carefully, gently, bound it about the man's face.

"Help me, Alice," she said crisply. "Stop crying at once, and help me." Alice did not move. Loyalty's eyes were dangerous. "Alice, you fool! Help me lift this man into the carriage!" Stiffly Alice scrambled to obey. The horses were pawing and the boy, his eyes bulging, tried to hold them steady, and behind them coarse voices cursed and yelled: "Make way—move on!" The girls struggled, slid the man into the carriage, on the floor, unable to lift him to the seat. "Steady him, Alice," Loyalty ordered, and she straightened and wiped her hands on her skirt. "All right," she nodded to the boy. "Go on. Take them back across the river—to the nearest hospital—any place where he can be helped. Hurry! He hasn't long!"

"Loyalty," Alice cried. "What are you going to do? You can't stay here!"

"Take this man to a hospital," Loyalty repeated clearly. "I'm better able to walk than he." Sharply she slapped Alice's wrist, shoving her hands away from her. "Suppose," she said steadily, "Alice, suppose he were William?"

Alice's hands dropped and Loyalty heard her sob again, but she made no further protest. The boy flicked the horses and they plunged forward and with more skill than she would have believed he possessed he managed to work the vehicle through the thick traffic and make rapid progress.

For a few moments Loyalty stood still. She must keep out of the way, she thought carefully, not interfere with the movement of any vehicles or of any of the wounded. She had no fear for herself. Even in war, she thought innocently, civilians are not molested, and even the Rebels would not harm a lady. She stepped back quickly to avoid a careening sutler's cart and then she had to run a few steps farther to get out of the way of a stray Army mule, trotting determinedly, nostrils distended, fright driving it. There was a piece of rope dangling from its halter, and Loyalty saw a soldier grab for it. After a little tussle he stopped the animal and he pulled himself to its back.

The soldiers passing her now were not men of the Eighth New York and the Fourth Pennsylvania, whose terms of enlistment were up before the battle. These men had seen the actual fighting, they were the very troops on which victory had depended. They were coming in increasing numbers, but they did not look like the men Loyalty had seen marching confidently out of the capital the week before. These were beaten men, shamed men, defeated, frightened, disgusted men. Pity for them and for all the North swept over Loyalty.

The heat and the confusion and the horror of the defeat and retreat, the glassy, set faces of the people who passed her, unseeing, intent only on their own safety, gave Loyalty a feeling of unreality; surely it can't be true, she thought. This isn't real! She began to walk slowly, watching the soldiers, searching for Cass. He was somewhere in this bedlam, this nightmare, else he was lying injured or dead in a trampled, bullet gouged cornfield. She stumbled now and then over the debris left by the fleeing Army—a tar bucket that rolled and tumbled and disappeared in the weeds at the roadside, a discarded haversack, an empty canteen, an Army belt buckle. The moon came up, pale at first, its brightness increasing as the night aged.

Sometimes the men ran a little, seeming spurred on by some new fear, and Loyalty heard the shouted, panicky warning: "The Rebel cavalry is coming!" But the Rebel cavalry failed to appear out of the ghostly semi-darkness, and then the men slowed again, tramping automatically, as though all feeling were gone from them.

Loyalty stopped finally, exhausted, conscious of dry dust in her shoes, inside her stockings, curling around her toes. There was dust in her nostrils, too, and a smell of powder, and thirst was nagging at her. She ran her tongue over her dry lips. Here and there she heard a man call for water, saw men drain canteens and throw them away, and saw others stop to snatch them up, and fling them aside in fury when they found them empty. Water, here on this dust-choked road, was more precious than molten gold, and the eagerness in the men's faces as they reached for the canteens was naked and primitive. Loyalty wiped her face with her moist hands and closed her eyes and again the feeling of unreality possessed her. But she could not close her ears, she could not shut out the noise of the retreat.

She felt a movement at her feet and she opened her eyes with a great effort and looked down. At first she saw only a spark of light, and with a start she realized it was a firefly; fireflies—the beautiful little signal-lights that dotted all Maryland and Virginia on hot summer nights—how odd that they should he here, in the midst of war; how perfectly silly, she thought. Then she saw a man dragging himself from the roadway, crawling slowly on hands and knees, into the shelter of an abandoned caisson, out of reach of hurrying boots, flying hoofs, relentless wheels, and she heard him sigh as he let himself rest against the earth. She saw his fingers fumbling in the moonlight, reaching for the canteen lying on his chest and she was about to bend to help him when another hand crept out. It closed about the canteen, eagerly, snatching it from beneath the weak, groping fingers. Loyalty turned her head slowly; another soldier sat, his back against the opposite side of the caisson, his face lost in the shadow, and she heard him panting as he raised the canteen and drank noisily. The wounded man moaned a little, his searching fingers still fumbling a little in the moonlight, and then he was still.

Loyalty dropped to her knees and felt for the prone man's wrist. There was no pulse. His mouth was slack and his hand dropped as she released it. She raised her condemning eyes to the man who had stolen the canteen; he still held it, and his eyes were upon her, dull and uncomprehending. His face was blackened by smoke, and water from the canteen glistened on his chin. His left arm hung limp and there were bits of straw clinging to his shirt. For a long time Loyalty stared at him, mute, across the body of the man who died there, beneath the caisson.

"Cass," she whispered finally and it seemed to her the word was torn, painfully, from her throat. Cass nodded a little, his whole upper body moving with the gesture, as though his neck were stiff and he could not bend it. "You're hurt," she said hoarsely, after a long silence. Again he nodded and his lips twisted and his white teeth were grotesque in his blackened face.

"The sonsabitches got me in the shoulder and there's a minie ball in my leg," he said. His voice was husky, strained. He began to curse softly, steadily and Loyalty drew back and again her eyes slid to the body of the man beside her.

"Cass!" she said again, and the sharp, shocked protest stopped Cass' voice. Loyalty got up, her knees shaking, and walked around the caisson and knelt beside her brother. Her fingers touched his shoulder and Cass winced and drew away from her.

"Leave it alone," he said sharply. "God in heaven—it hurts!" He tried to raise the canteen again and his hand shook and the water spilled down the front of him. Loyalty dragged her eyes away. She touched his leg, experimentally and he jerked away from her. "I wish this was whisky," he said, with a sloppy gesture with the canteen. "Damn minie ball," he went on, thickly. His head lolled back, against the caisson, and suddenly he laughed. It started down inside him somewhere and came out harsh, unnatural—"That recruiting officer, God damn his soul to hell! He said we'd never have to bivouac. . . . He said we'd never have to fight. . . . He said we'd come to Washington and guard the capital and dance and get drunk. . . . God damn his soul to . . ."

Loyalty straightened. She had to get Cass out of here, to some place where he could be treated, where his wounds could be examined, where he could rest. He was delirious, drunk with shock and suffering, weak from loss of blood. She must remember he was delirious, he did not know what he was saying, nor what he had done. She looked about her desperately for help, but the figures on the roadway rushed on, like figures on an endless belt, with no end and no beginning, a constant stream, leaving her on its edge. Cass was talking again and she looked down at him, fascinated, trying to forget that she had seen him take the canteen from the dying man. He didn't know what he was doing, she kept telling herself, over and over. . . . Cass wouldn't do a think like that, knowing.

"Lying there in that stinking cornfield—me, Cass Blake, lying there on my face, with dirt in my mouth and a ball in my shoulder—and there were mosquitoes, too. Did you know that? Mosquitoes, thousands of them, to drive a man mad. And then I got up and started to run—to hell with the war, I said—to hell with it. I started to run and the bastards got me again, in the leg. It spun me around and knocked me down." The words came fierce and tight from between his clenched teeth and bitterness made every word an oath. "Finally I got a gun—I got a gun—but I couldn't remember." Again he laughed. "Handle—cartridge! That's what they said." His voice rose a little, mimicking, sarcastic. "Charge—cartridge! Draw—rammer! Ram—cartridge! That's what they told us, damn drill sergeant. Twenty-six of them, twenty-six commands and motions, for a single shot with a Springfield musket. Practice, they said—not that you'll ever need to fight! Cast—about! Ready—aim—and I couldn't remember. I tore open cartridges with my teeth and the taste of them, the taste of them—"

Again he raised the canteen and filled his mouth with water and spat it out, sloppily. "I used their God damn musket for a crutch and I got to the road, and nobody would help me. You can walk, they said—you can walk, me with a minie ball in my leg, God damn them. I got across Cub Run before the bridge broke down—just before. Lot of men out there, between Bull Run and Cub Run, can't get out, either, not till the Reg'lars bring them. . . ." His leg jerked, a sudden reflex action. "And then I fell out there—right out there—" He raised his hand with the canteen in a wide, awkward wave and his voice was indignant, insulted. "I cut my knee, bad. It was a spur, a rowel from some son of a—some son of a—"

His chin dropped and his voice trailed off and he began to weep. He was sobbing like a weak woman now, his shoulders shaking, his breath coming unevenly; but Loyalty could not cry. There was a little gust of wind, and a few drops of rain fell upon her and she raised her face to it. If only it could wash me clean, she thought, me and Cass—if only it could wash out all of this, this horrible night, the sight of Cass' snatching hand on the canteen—

Cass was quiet again and she wondered if he had lost consciousness, but he was staring at her. His face looked thin and drawn and unnatural. "I guess you don't know what it is to be thirsty—crazy-thirsty," he said clearly, half-defiant, half-apologetic. So he did know what he had done! "I guess you don't know you could kill a man, even, for water. I guess you don't know there's nothing worse than being thirsty, and that cartridge taste in your mouth—"

Loyalty gritted her teeth and she ran forward. Her white dress caught the moonlight and a driver of an Army wagon saw her and his eyes bulged. Speechlessly he pulled up his team and he reached over the side to her, but Loyalty shook her head. "My brother," she called. "He's badly wounded. Please, please take him with you!"

The soldier stared at her and then at Cass in the shadow of

the caisson. He jumped down, quickly, and handed the reins to Loyalty and she clung to them. The man picked Cass up bodily, swiftly, and placed him in the wagon and Loyalty heard moans and smothered curses from the men already there. "What about the other one?" the soldier said, jerking his head. Loyalty's eyes flicked toward the body.

"He's dead," she said softly. She accepted the soldier's hand and she climbed up beside him on the wagon. She glanced back over her shoulder once and she saw Cass' face, among all the other tortured faces of the wounded, and she was glad his eyes were closed.

The rain, starting slowly, grew to a downpour and the road churned into a sticky river of mud. The first pallid light of the cloudy morning came as the wagon plowed toward the Potomac. More vehicles lay abandoned beside the roadway, their wheels mired hub-deep, and men dragged their boots from the sucking ooze with each strength-sapping step.

Loyalty pulled a soldier's blue coat about her but it was little protection against the slanting sabers of rain. With each jolt of the wagon her own body ached, knowing the pain of the suffering men. At last they came into Alexandria, gray and bleak in the early morning, and Loyalty saw dozens of other conveyances lined up ahead of them. A young officer, his face powder-blackened, his eyes bloodshot with fatigue, was giving orders to the drivers and as they came opposite him he squinted at them through the rain. Water raced in the gutters, water dripped from the eaves of the buildings, but here and there lights showed in the windows and Loyalty looked at them hungrily.

"First house on your right," the officer was saying. "Unload there." The driver saluted and the exhausted officer looked at Loyalty. "Caught on the Pike, ma'am?" he asked politely. Loyalty nodded. "Sorry we can't send you across the river but Long Bridge is jammed and we fear it's weakening. Hospitals are full anyway. We'll move these men on to Washington as quickly as possible—but it may be a day or so." He motioned them on, turned to the next. The tired horses strained again to start the wagon moving, and when they came to the house indicated they stopped gratefully, their heads lowered, their bodies sagging.

"Don't make no difference to me," the driver said stoically. "Don't make no difference. Reckon if Radford's cavalry was after us they'd a overtaken us by now. Reckon Beauregard's got plenty of casualties too, ma'am." He was trying to reassure her and perhaps himself, and Loyalty smiled at him gratefully and climbed unaided over the wheel.

"I'm not afraid," she said stoutly. Her slippers sank into the mud and she moved quickly to the uncovered porch. The few furnishings had been cleared from the cottage and dumped hastily in the small yard and the rain was painting them all one drab color. Loyalty glanced inside. On the bare floor, wounded men were lying, packed tightly, side by side, shoulders touching. She hesitated and glanced down the street. There were many houses like this which had been commandeered as makeshift receiving hospitals and wagons were still unloading men before them. She stepped over the pool of water on the worn doorsill. A large, middle-aged woman kneeling beside a man glanced up at her. "They all want water first," she said briefly. Loyalty dropped the wet coat on the floor and picked up a canteen.

[4]

IN THE two days and two nights after the battle, Loyalty felt as if she had aged a thousand years. The impact of war had not stunned her; it had sharpened every sense she possessed, increased her capacity for feeling and her capacity for self-control a hundredfold. She had found reserves within herself, physical and mental, which she did not know she possessed. Such suffering of bodies and souls as she had witnessed left her no room for fear for herself. These men had been through trial by fire; in the crucible of war many of them had become ashes, but a few had hardened and been tempered to the strength of sword steel. She could tell the ones who would come through this and be better men. She could tell the ones who had been broken and ruined by it. Except Cass.

She could not judge Cass. She could not look behind the white, set, tortured face of her own brother and know how the ordeal had affected him. He only stared at her with his button-bright eyes, sometimes, she thought, accusing, hating her, for seeing him as he was now; sometimes with amazement. But whenever she looked toward the shadowed corner in which he lay she met his eyes.

She had helped to cut the minie ball from his leg and she had bound the wounds tightly with strips of her own petticoat. She had examined the wound in his shoulder. She tried to talk to him, to find if he had other wounds they had not discovered, but Cass only shook his head. It was shock, she thought; Cass was no more prepared for this carnage than I.

She had to get him out of here and home and nurse him back to health and find out what had happened to his spirit, to the inner Cass. That was more important than the wounds on his body. He was too silent, too patient. Surely scars of bitterness and shame would sometime heal.

But thousands of men were more seriously injured than Cass and the authorities who were trying to bring some order out of the bloody chaos were moving them, as rapidly as possible, to hospitals and good care. Cass, more lightly wounded, would be one of the last to go, if she waited for the Army to move him. It was up to Loyalty to take him, to get him out of here, to find out the actual extent of his injuries.

She was so weary that her movements were uncertain, lacking coordination. Sometimes when she reached for a cup she misjudged the distance and her hand went past it and she had to exercise her will to bring her hand back to grasp it firmly, to fill it, to keep from spilling water upon the clothing of the men she tried to tend. Her arms ached as she lowered their heads back to the folded coats which she had made into pillows. Her knees shook as she pulled herself upright again, and she stumbled a little and had to reach for the wall to support herself as she made her way from one man to another. But she had tried to keep her mind clear, to figure out how she could get Cass to safety and good care. Already she was making plans still further ahead. Once Cass was at home she would come back. She would work in the Army hospitals or wherever they needed her. She could not turn her back to it now that she had seen it. No sane woman could. No fatigue, no nausea from the horrible sights and sounds and smells, no hunger, no aching limbs and throbbing head of an overworked nurse could be as bad as the things these men had endured. Particularly defeated men.

It made her stomach crawl to hear them, talking in their sleep and in their delirium, living over the battle again. It was uncanny to hear the babbling of sick and tired and feverish minds, still seeing, even in sleep, horror pictures of the battlefield. Was there no sane person left in the world? Was she herself, losing her mind under the impact of war? She passed her hands over her face, fumbled in her hair for a comb and fastened it again, tight, not caring how it looked, anxious only to get the curls out of her way, away from her wet forehead. She leaned against the wall, watching the morning light come in through the narrow windows, listening to the drip, drip of the rain from the eaves, listening to the mumbling and the shuffling of the bodies of the sleeping men, the snores and grunts and moans and rattling gasps. This is the War Between the States, she thought. The States are not so many units—the States, the Union, is One—one man, like any one of these soldiers here, one unit, one body. *And the Rebels are trying to tear it apart!*

The states are a man, one man, upon a medieval torture rack. And his body has been stretched to the breaking point and left there, straining. And in the spreading joints, the groins, the armpits, the pain is the worst. And there the sores form and swell and the skin tightens crimson, for the body fights its rending. And one of the sores has festered, now, and broken, at Manassas, and the evil-smelling pus, yellow, contaminated, vile, bubbled and spread over the Virginia countryside, the quiet and neutral countryside, unsuspecting and sun-baked. And these men were touched by it and they will never be truly pure again. And women, like me, touched by it, will never again be unscarred. Pus, from the sore of a tortured, breaking body, God's creation, meant to be whole. . . . Acid of war.

She began to tremble and she closed her eyes, overcome by the wave of compassion that swept over her, for herself and all her countrymen, knowing what they faced. Each of us is so small, she thought, so very small, in all the whole great picture of war. Our pain is so personal, our bodies so important to each of us, and yet each of us is so small a unit in the whole great struggle. If only everyone could see, as I have seen it here, after Manassas, she thought, her thoughts a pleading cry. They would try to stop it, then; they'd try to keep the Union whole, to stop tearing and maiming our nation, draining it of its life and strength. It was so clear to her, like a revelation, and she knew, in that moment, the fire of a zealot, a person who sees the truth, complete and sharp and clear, in one blinding flash, and is convinced, and wants only to show it to others, too.

I swear, she whispered, in dedication, that I will do all I can to stop this thing. Do not let me forget this house here in Alexandria. Passion welled up in her, her throat ached with all the tears she had not shed, all the bitter, blinding knowledge of the heartaches still to come. But heartaches did not matter, nor physical pain, nor even death—if the Union was saved. Her fists gripped spasmodically; what could one woman do, to make the rest see and understand—make them understand it was not only the suffering of these men, the awful crimes against their bodies and their spirits, but the suffering and salvation of the straining Union itself? Only to save the greater, glorious body of the nation should men—and women—know the torture and degradation of war.

A man called her. "Ma'am," he said. "Ma'am." Her eyes hunted among the men to find the one who summoned her, and she saw him, staring at her, pleading. She went to him quickly and knelt, and he smiled apologetically, and again it was almost more than she could bear. "My leg's swollen so, ma'am, the bandage cuts it like a knife," he said, explaining. "If you could loosen it just a bit —I'm sorry—ma'am—"

Loyalty's hands worked quickly and the man closed his eyes and gritted his teeth and then he turned his face toward her again in thanks. His eyes closed, the smile of gratitude still on his lips. *Excuse me for dying, ma'am,* it seemed to say. She glanced away, at the doorway, and back at the still figure at her feet.

I guess my mind is tired, too, she said to herself. My mind is playing me tricks and I cannot govern it any more, no more than I can my hands. My hands shake, and when I try to pick up something, this coat, for instance, my fingers do not grip it and it slides from me. I am imagining things. Cass' eyes are upon me, and someone is entering, someone is standing in the door, a tall, straight, unwounded man, a man who walks lightly, a man with strength and confidence in his step. He looks like Matthew Steel.

She almost laughed, at the ridiculous things one could imagine when one was exhausted and suffering from shock. She managed to bend and pull the cloak over the soldier's set face, the face with the smile of thanks upon it, and she managed to rise again, thinking she must go quietly to call the men at the door once more, to remove another body before his mates awakened. She turned to the entrance and still the tall man stood there and she put her hands out, as though to push the illusion away. Then she began to walk toward him, and she remembered to walk slowly, carefully, so she would not stagger, and fall.

He would disappear, of course, as she approached him; his features would settle into an unfamiliar pattern—they would not be those of Matthew Steel at all. She glanced uncertainly over her shoulder, and she saw that Cass' eyes had left her at last, and were upon the doorway, and he had raised himself on his elbow. Why, Cass sees him too, she thought; how silly we both are, having hallucinations.

Her steps wavered and she stopped. "Please ask the men on the porch to come in. A man has died. His body must be removed." She spoke very quietly, in a half whisper, forming each word carefully with her lips, like a child learning to mouth a new language. The man in the doorway moved, came toward her, and she watched his face, dully. His eyes were fastened upon her and she had never seen that look on a man's face before. He was beside her, his arms were about her, his face was very close and still he looked like Matthew Steel.

"You must ask the men on the porch to come," she repeated stupidly.

"Yes, Loyalty. Yes. I'll ask them," he said.

Matthew caught her as she fell.

THE train was hot and dirty and jam-packed with wounded men and their anxious relatives, with soldiers on leave, with three-month volunteers who had enough fighting and were going home, with women refugees from the capital. Loyalty sat stiff and straight on the hard seat, concentrating on keeping her heavy eyes open and her chin up, with proper dignity.

If it had not been for Matthew Steel sitting opposite her, seeming quite comfortable and completely oblivious of the heat and dirt and flies and the jolting, jerking, crawling pace of the train, Loyalty would have put her head down and wept. When she had been at Alexandria, working with the wounded, she had been too busy to think of herself. Now reaction had set in, and it was the little things that were driving her mad. Yet Matthew Steel, lounging, relaxed, talking quietly of the most inconsequential subjects, impersonal and apparently ignorant of her distress, so infuriated her that she would have died rather than shed a tear.

Cass half-sat, half-lay on the two seats they had arranged for him, trying to find a comfortable position. His wounded leg was outstretched and stiff, and his shoulder did not permit him to lean back for support. He was moody and sullen, but he did not complain. He moved restlessly much of the time, and that made Loyalty restless, too.

Cass had searched for a musket to use as crutch when at last they were ready to leave the house at Alexandria. His own gun was gone long ago, but a soldier lying near him had grinned at him, his homely Irish face cracking wide open, it seemed, with the effort, and had thrust a weapon at him.

"Take it, boy," the soldier had said. "It's a little souvenir of Bull Run. I took it off'n a damn Rebel at Sudley Spring. Others was fighting over the big guns, and they changed hands three or four times there—but this Reb and I, we was fightin' over this one. Take it, boy, might as well do a Yankee some good."

Cass had taken it gratefully, but later, in the railway car, he had looked at it with distaste. A Rebel gun. He told Matthew where he had got it, and Matthew picked it up and turned it over in his strong, sure hands.

On the butt plate was some engraving, and Matthew read the words slowly: "*Deo Duce Vincimus*"—"We conquer with God, our Leader." Then he ran his finger over the lock plate and read "N. P. Pond, London, England." After that he sat silent for a long time thinking, staring at the weapon.

"British guns," Cass said, his lips curling in a sneer. "Confederates can fight forever—and will—as long as the British keep them supplied with guns like that." Matthew had nodded slowly, and even after he put the gun down again and leaned back in his seat his face dark with thought. Loyalty watched him and suddenly fear made her shiver. What did she actually know about Matthew Steel? She had put her blind faith in him. He had come to her when she needed him, as though drawn by her great need. But what was he thinking behind that dark mask of his face?

Sitting next her brother, Loyalty began to sense his trouble and her heart ached with pity for him. Cass had said little about his part in the battle. Shame was written all over him. He was trying to bear the pain of his wounds and his weakness as bravely as possible now, but disgrace had left its mark upon him. He would not look straight at Matthew Steel, he would not meet Loyalty's eyes. Cass' suffering, with his wounds demonstrating clearly that he had been running away from the enemy when he received them, was more than wounds of the flesh. He had lost all self-respect. That Matthew Steel had come for them, and that he was now in Steel's debt only increased his torment. If he had been half a man, Cass was saying to himself, he'd have told Steel to go to hell, to leave him alone, that he was a soldier and wanted no mollycoddling from a civilian or a girl, that he would take his chances with his comrades. But he did not refuse Steel's help. He was too glad to get out of Alexandria, out of Washington, back to the comforts and safety of home.

It had not helped any, either, to discover that his sister was made of stronger stuff than he. Pitying him, she would not condemn him. But Loyalty herself had not given way to fear. Under fire, Loyalty would have stayed and fought, till death or capture, or until an officer ordered retreat. Loyalty had courage and strength which her brother lacked, and in a way he hated her for it. He had watched her in Alexandria, in admiration and amazement; he had watched her change from a sheltered girl to a crusader with multiplied strength. It had shaken Cass deeply. It only exaggerated his own weakness.

He dreaded meeting his father. He dreaded Serena's tears. He dreaded most of all the stupid people who would greet him as a wounded hero. He wished he had been killed, back there near Stone Bridge—only he was afraid to die, too. He was plumbing depths of misery he had never known existed, and to make it worse, Matthew Steel's knowing black eyes seemed to read his very soul. If Loyalty were not with them, Cass thought, Steel would make no attempt to hide his contempt. He probably would not even have reached out a hand to help him. He'd have turned on his heel and left him to suffer or to die—as not being worth saving. And there would have been justice in it.

The train crawled on. In Baltimore Matthew managed to get some newspapers and he read the incomplete lists of casualties at Bull Run—nearly three thousand Federals killed, wounded or missing. The battle was reported piecemeal and the part of each officer was discussed, explained, apologized for; Matthew read slowly, trying to put the pieces together, trying to catch up on the events that had happened while he was en route from San Francisco. It appeared to him that the South had been comparatively well prepared even before they fired upon Fort Sumter. Southerners apparently had been in control of nearly every fort from Pennsylvania to Key West at the start of the conflict. They likewise had taken over arsenals, custom houses, mints, post offices, revenue cutters and sub treasuries all through the South—millions of dollars' worth of government property. They had cleverly stripped the North of its resources, they had been fully organized, united, armed and likely had some assurance of the support of France and England before the first shot was fired.

Matthew read the reports and he looked at the British gun beside Cass. Pond, a London contractor, was already supplying the South. Matthew remembered what Captain Scripliff of the Russian Navy had told him of Britain and France, several months ago. If France had designs on Mexico, perhaps even on the Louisiana territory; if it was true that Great Britain also was turning covetous eyes on America—if the North was as divided as the papers indicated, with secessionists, abolitionists, pacifists, all pulling and hauling at the administration, the outlook for a Northern victory was dark indeed.

The small, scattered, crippled Navy of the United States could not halt the British if they intended to supply the South with arms and supplies. At least, not for many months, not until ships could be bought, built and manned; the Army of the North was no fit opponent for that of the South—yet. Matthew leaned back in his seat, lost in thought. It was going to be a long conflict, not an insurrection to be quelled quickly with a few smashing blows. The President had proclaimed a blockade of the Southern ports, but so far it was only a paper blockade, which the British, at least, ignored.

It was not as easy as he had thought it might be to pick the winner in this fight. Right now, the South had the great advantage. For the North to win, for the Union to be preserved—except by compromise—would require a long, hard campaign, with much suffering and denial. Matthew was not sure the North was prepared for it.

If the South were winner, where did that leave Matthew Steel? His eyes strayed back to the Pond rifle again. There was money to be made immediately in supplying the South with materials of war. But a man must be careful to be on the side of the final victor as well.

The Union also would offer high prices for ships. If they were to make any gesture toward enforcing the blockade they would need hundreds of ships. Each ship taken into the navy as a fighting vessel meant there would be one less on South Street to carry on what foreign trade remained. Freight rates would go up. Risks would be correspondingly heavy. Many a shipowner would immediately transfer his vessels to foreign flags, to escape Rebel privateers that would undoubtedly prey on Northern shipping. Each one who deserted would further deplete the merchant marine, and there would be more cargoes for those remaining.

Yes, Matthew thought, it was a great opportunity for a man to make a fortune.

But it was not easy, now, sitting so close to Loyalty, to think of war. Her little face was gray with fatigue; though her shoulders were straight, her gloved hands clasped in her lap, he knew that she was near the breaking point. She had been through an ordeal that would have turned many men into shivering idiots. Admiration and love for her poured over him in a warm stream and he had to check himself to keep from reaching out and gathering her into his arms. To see her suffer was the worst thing that had ever happened to him. The involuntary trembling of her lips, the polite attention she strained to give to each casual remark, the proud set of her pretty head with its ridiculous, stiff, little flower-encircled hat, the damp curls escaping and touching her white cheek, sent stabs of pain through him. He wanted to protect her from such horrors as she had undergone, he wanted to keep her safe and well and rested and at peace, laughing and gay and unworried; that so delicate and perfect a thing should have witnessed violence and seen the aftermath of battle, that she should have been in that stinking, crowded house in Alexandria, surrounded by dirty, suffering, cursing soldiers angered him. He would not soon forget the fear he had known when he had discovered Loyalty was in Washington, caught in the retreat. He had bribed and threatened his way from New York to the capital, and his relief when he found her was so intense it had shaken him to the very depth. That she had come through danger and panic unscathed had heightened his respect for her and his love grew within him. He remembered how she had been when he first had seen her, a dainty and gifted coquette, charming and untouched, mischievous and perfect, altogether delightful to tease, to laugh with and flirt with. The courage and strength that existed in that small, exquisite body amazed him.

But he must not let her crumple now, not until this tedious journey was over and she was safely within the walls of the Blake home. He was grateful to Thaddeus Blake for providing such a home to shelter Loyalty. Once he had taken her there and she could turn over the care of Cass to other competent hands, then she could find blessed relief in tears. She was entitled to that. But not now. She would never forgive him, proud little patrician that she was, if he saw her, here, on a public train, give way to emotion. He must help her to keep up this pretense of polite small talk, not permit a single personal note to enter their conversation, not exhibit any sympathy which might soften her. So he continued, watching his words and his expressions carefully, knowing that she was cool and, in her inner agitation, probably angry at him for his seeming cold-heartedness; proud of her gallantry, worshiping her, secretly feasting his eyes on every line of her beautiful, tired face and the young, desirable curves of her figure. What a girl she was, Matthew said to himself. And she belonged to him. He was as certain of that as he was of day and night. He thought of Henry Austin. In his search for Loyalty he had found Austin in a hospital, feverish and sick and seriously wounded—but not too sick to fasten pain-dulled eyes on Matthew Steel and tell him: "If you harm Loyalty Blake, Matthew Steel, in any way—I'll kill you, so help me God." So Austin still loved her. He could not blame the man for that. But—hurt Loyalty? Matthew would protect her with his last ounce of strength and skill. Life without Loyalty Blake would be life without music or color—gray and heavy and plodding.

Cass was a weakling, Matthew thought. It was no surprise that he had so disgracefully acquitted himself at the first taste of gunfire. If this was the stuff of which the Union Army was made, the Rebels would have a glorious campaign. Matthew was contemptuous of weakness as he was admiring of strength. Regardless of the rights and wrongs of a fight, once a man was in it and had taken sides, he should give it the best that was in him. Any man who ran and was wounded in the back deserved his wounds and the disgrace that went with them. For Loyalty's sake he tried to conceal his disgust with Cass, but he knew that Cass could feel it, not in what he said or in the tone of his voice, but in the things he failed to say, the comfort and admiration he failed to give.

At long last the train crept into New York. For miles Loyalty had sat in silence, drawing on all her endurance to stand the last hours of the journey. She managed to stand on stiffened limbs and to gather a few of her boxes together, when it was finally time to leave the train. Matthew protected her from the jostling crowds, and at last she was on the platform and Cass was beside her, with Captain Steel supporting him. Cass' face was ghastly and he staggered and Matthew caught him and lifted him bodily into the carriage. It was good to see the familiar Blake carriage again. The feel of the soft, clean cushions with their well-known smell of luxury and richness, the wonderful comfort of them after the hard seats in the train, the knowledge that she was nearly home, were almost too much for Loyalty. She felt weak tears pressing behind her eyes, but she fought them down and prepared herself for meeting Serena and her father.

The doctor was waiting. Loyalty saw his old, kindly face with relief and gratitude. Her father was confined to his bed, the doctor told her, else Thaddeus himself would have been seeking her and Cass in the capital. His failing health had been aggravated by the news of the disaster at Bull Run. Serena, shocked at the sight of Cass, shaking with nervous excitement, put her arms about Loyalty and began at once to sob. To her own surprise Loyalty pushed her away. There was no time—yet—for tears.

There was much to be done. Thaddeus called for Loyalty and she braced herself and went to him. He was white against his pillows, but he was improved, Dr. Plant said, and he would get up again. Loyalty reassured him about Cass. She said merely that she had waited in Washington until her brother could be moved, and she had helped out in one of the receiving hospitals, and Captain Steel had kindly aided them. Thaddeus, his eyes seeing more than she knew, let her go.

Loyalty stopped at Cass' door, and then she had to turn away. She had reached the final limit of endurance for this day. Captain Steel was helping Dr. Plant, and again Loyalty said a prayer of thanks for his presence. Serena stood in the hallway, wringing her hands. Dr. Plant was removing the filthy bandages from Cass' leg, and sweat stood out in big beads on Cass' forehead and trickled down his face. The hideous, oozing wound looked and smelled gangrenous and Dr. Plant clucked in dismay. He directed Steel to hold the limb steady; but it was more the stony expression on Captain Steel's face than the strength of the hand on his knee, that kept Cass Blake still while the wound was cleansed. Loyalty, sick and reeling, made her way to her own room and closed the door behind her.

After a while Matthew went into the hallway, rolling down his sleeves as he walked. Serena came to Matthew quietly and stood looking up at him, mutely expressing her gratitude.

"You'd better go to bed, Serena," Matthew said gently. Serena shook her head.

"I can't, Matthew," she said. "I can't leave Loyalty. Dr. Plant gave her a sleeping draught, but she cries out in her sleep. She cannot rest. I am afraid she will be very ill. It wrings my heart."

Matthew did not answer. He fastened his cuff and the silence in the upper hallway was heavy. He could hear Cass' heavy breathing in the room behind him. Cass would sleep for a long time now, from exhaustion alone. Thaddeus' room was quiet. But from the room at his left, Loyalty's room, came a moan that went straight to his heart.

Matthew strode across the hall and opened Loyalty's door. The room was lighted with a single candle at the bedside; a maid sat silently beside the bed, her thin, wizened old face twisted with worry.

Loyalty seemed very small in the big white bed; her hair was loose about her shoulders and it gleamed and shone in the candlelight, jet black against the white pillows and the high-necked, ruffled nightgown. Her small hand, emerging from the ruffled sleeve, plucked at the sheet which covered her, and she tossed restlessly, tortured, finding no relief in sleep. She opened her eyes slightly but they were dull and unseeing and then she cried out again and the cry ended in a sob. Awake, Loyalty could control her cries at the memories of the things she had seen. Half-drugged, half-asleep, she was prey to them.

The maid moved aside. Serena and Matthew stared down at the girl in the huge bed. Shadows flickered in the corners of the spacious room and the night was silent. Matthew Steel gently tucked the white blanket about Loyalty and he ran his arm beneath her shoulders and raised her. Her eyes opened and she lay limp and helpless in his arms, dizzy and sick, her feverish, cracked lips working a little, tears spilling at last down her cheeks. Matthew gathered her up and, with her in his arms, sat down in the chair beside the bed, holding her as gently as if she were a tiny child. She lay against his chest, her head on his shoulder, her hand clutching the front of his shirt.

Matthew's chin dropped to her shining, precious head. She was so small, so soft, so infinitely dear. His love should draw from her the poison of war, should bring her comfort. He wanted passionately to give her his strength, his comfort and his protection, to bring her peace. Serena stood hesitant, watching him, and after a while he remembered her and he raised his head and smiled at her briefly. She started to speak but he shook his head warningly. After a little Serena moved around the bed and sat down in an easy chair in the shadows and leaned her head back, grateful for the quiet, feeling Matthew Steel's strong presence. No harm would ever come to Loyalty, Serena thought, from Matthew Steel. And some way it did not seem strange at all, Serena thought hazily, what with the war and everything, and Cass lying wounded, that Matthew should be here in Loyalty's room, holding her in his arms throughout the night. In a little while Serena slept, too.

[6]

"I THOUGHT—I thought—you—" Loyalty whispered.

"Be quiet, my darling, and rest."

"There was so much horror—so much suffering—"

"I know."

"Why must such dreadful things be, Matthew?"

"I don't know, Loyalty. But believe me it is balanced, always, by happiness. For someone. Somewhere."

"Then good will come from all this?"

"It must. Some time. Sometimes it takes a long time."

"It must be very great good, Matthew, to justify all of it. So ugly—"

"Don't think of it, darling. Just rest."

"Matthew, you've seen horror before. I never have."

"I know. And it must not touch you, ever again." His arms tightened.

"I must take my share. We must each take our share."

"I will take your share, Loyalty. I am strong enough to take it for us both."

Her hair smelled sweet and the fineness of it amazed him. It was like the finest, lightest silk, despite its waving, shining look of weight. It was not heavy at all, and when he raised it on his hand it was so soft and delicate it was a marvel to him. Her skin was so smooth, it seemed to him his finger was too coarse to touch her cheek. He had known her forever, and yet everything about her was new, her breath on his chin, her soft weight against him, the smallness of her wrists. The tenseness had drained from her body now and she was resting in his arms, content to be there, wanting nothing more. He watched the candlelight on her face, loving her as had never loved any other living thing. Her eyelashes were tiny black fans on her cheeks, her neck, above the virginal white ruffle of her gown, was white and smooth with youth. He pushed the black curls away from it with tender fingers, worshiping its innocence.

"I can't remember," Loyalty spoke again, suddenly, in a whisper. "I can't remember, in all my life, seeing beauty, Matthew—to balance such ugliness—"

Matthew smiled. He had all the beauty of the universe here in his arms, he thought. He leaned his head back on the chair, looking up at the shadows on the high ceiling. Even through the folds of the snowy blanket he could feel the slender lines of Loyalty's body, and yet he was content only to cradle her in his arms. Her presence in the same room was satisfying, to be where he could watch her, hear her voice, was almost enough; to hold her, closely, to feel her confidence in him, to know that he had quieted her fears and brought her some rest, gave him the deepest, richest satisfaction he had ever known.

"No beauty, Loyalty?" Matthew's deep voice was very soft, for her ear alone. On the shadowy ceiling he sought for pictures—pictures of beautiful things to describe to her. Beauty—he had not thought much about beauty, until now, when he had a need for it, to give to Loyalty. He wished he had been more observant, hunted out and remembered more beauty—for Loyalty. He couldn't fail her now. What beauty had he seen in the harsh life he had lived? He began haltingly, searching his memory.

"I wish you could see my ship—in full sail. She's beautiful. The sea is beautiful, too, even in a storm it is magnificent. And it is clean, and the wind is always fresh, with a taste of salt. There is no dust on a ship, Loyalty, did you know that?"

She raised her eyes, questioning, interested, like a child. "I never thought of that. Tell me of the sea, Matthew. What is it like?"

"The colors of the sea are beautiful and varied. You can tell a lot about it by the colors." These words, these kinds of thoughts come hard, he said to himself, but he had to speak them, for Loyalty. "Down off the coast of South America—or any coast, for that matter, near a great river mouth, the water is a different color than it is far out at sea. It reflects the sky, blue sometimes, or an angry gray. The sea is temperamental and she wants you to know that she is the boss. The sea is always changing, it is never twice the same. . . . Ships are beautiful, Loyalty, coming toward you, graceful as birds, growing larger as they come nearer, skimming along over the water; sometimes they are even funny, the heavy, awkward ones, plowing through the water like fat, puffing old women—"

Loyalty laughed. The sound made his heart leap and he dropped his chin to her hair again. "Tell me more," she commanded.

"There is so much to tell." The words came easier now and he could think of many things, beautiful things, to tell her. "I have some old-timers in my crew. They believe in mermaids, and sea-smoke and phantom ships. They think they can foretell disaster in the way the waves break against the ship, and they swear they see spectres in the fog. . . . It is beautiful to watch a good crew work, all in unison, their arms moving as if they all belonged to one man, and all the while singing. Chanteys are beautiful music, Loyalty.

Men who turn to steamships will never know the beauty of sea chanteys on a clipper ship. . . . It is a pity."

Loyalty's eyelids drooped and her hand on his shirt front loosened a little. He could feel sleep creeping over all her body and she did not resist it now, she welcomed it gratefully. He watched her face, saw a tiny smile about her lips, happiness crowding out sorrow and grief as it must always do for Loyalty Blake. He leaned his head back again, and his voice went on, softly, evenly. Perhaps it would penetrate the sleep curtain and guide her dreams, drive out the nightmare demons that had tortured her.

"And there are other beautiful things—flying fish in the tropics are beautiful. And Mother Carey's chickens, with their tiny web feet. Dolphins are beautiful, green-backed with yellow tails and blue fins. Some of them are banded with green and the oldtimers say they change color when they get excited. An albatross is beautiful, magnificent with its tremendous power. Its breast is like white satin and its wings like black velvet. . . . Sunsets off the Horn are beautiful, too, all the colors of the rainbow in the sky and sea and the distant hills ashore. . . . Sometimes winds carry moths and butterflies far out to sea, and it is beautiful to see a great butterfly, delicately and finely marked, on the clean deck, miles away from land. It is a link, some way, a beautiful and delicate link, with the rest of the world. There is beauty in the sky at night, when stars hang so low they seem tangled in the masts. There is a different kind of beauty to every port in every nation with the little boats nestling close to the piers, and the piers themselves in long rows, ragged little fringe to the land. Every harbor is home to a sailing man. You take a port like Charleston, for instance—it seems like it's out of a fairy tale, with the Forts guarding it, like great castles, warning invaders . . ."

His voice stopped and he glanced quickly at Loyalty. She was sleeping and his last words had not reached her and for that he was grateful. He, too, had forgotten the war in the magic of Loyalty's nearness and his complete submergence in her. He had forgotten the first shots had been fired in Charleston Harbor on Fort Sumter, on one of those guardians of the port.

The war. What was he going to do about it? Business, profits, money—he would think of them tomorrow. He could not, now, think of anything but the sleeping girl in his arms. He sat very still, not to disturb her, his eyes on her face, worshiping her, thankful that she had found safety here. She was very soundly sleeping now and after a long time he forced himself to stand and to lay her quietly in her bed. She did not stir. He straightened her arms as he would a child's, and she did not awaken. He smoothed her hair back from her damp forehead and bent and kissed her. He sat again, watching, to be sure that dreams would not again disturb her and the night lightened and morning tiptoed in and defeated the candlelight. Finally Matthew arose and snuffed out the candle and he bent once more and touched Loyalty's hand with his lips, and then he left the room, silently, and let himself out of the still and sleeping house.

[7]

MATTHEW STEEL sat at a table in the familiar back room of the Cock and Bull, talking quietly to Hite and Morton. The owners of the tavern had given him a royal welcome; indeed, no man could ask for a more heart-warming reception than South Street had given Captain Steel. His progress along the street each day was slow, for he was stopped again and again by men who wanted to shake his hand and welcome him home. Old Dan, the fiddling beggar, was always waiting for him, with a blessing and a bit of gossip of interest or value, to be exchanged for the coins that Matthew dropped, clinking, into the old fellow's cup. Big Wayne, Mrs. Doughty, Patrick Draddy and businessmen higher on the scale, brokers and financiers, shipbuilders and designers and outfitters, all were quick to stop and clasp his hand. It was good, and Matthew Steel, for all his reserve, relished it as much as any man.

Only Bennett, the aging, obese coachman, refused to greet him. Whenever they met, Bennett's eyes slid away. It reminded Matthew of himself as a little boy when Bennett, who shouted at him all day long in Washington Mews, pretended not to know him when he met him outside the stable block.

South Street had changed and Matthew was attempting to find out what lay beneath the change. The waterfront was in a frenzy of activity, of extravagant spending, of peak employment. There were no idlers on the wharves now; thousands of men labored in the shipyards, building or converting ships of all shapes and sizes into fighting craft, and the speed with which the ships slid down the ways was nothing short of miraculous. There was money on South Street and new excitement in the air. In the coffee houses men talked long and earnestly and parted with purpose in their faces; there seemed little leisure for anyone, and excitement, by day and by night, had reached a high pitch. Men pored over newspapers, arguments flared, there were more uniforms in evidence, and traffic was thicker than ever.

Hite placed his glass upon the table with a thump to emphasize his words.

"I tell you, Matthew, regardless of what the papers would have you believe—New York is endangered. So is every other Union port. Here's why."

He wiped his lips with the back of his hand and fixed Matthew's eyes with his own.

"When the war started the Navy consisted of thirty-five vessels. Only eighteen of them were available—that is, laid up at the different yards. There were eight that could be used immediately, and only four of those were steamers. But some say there was only one really efficient ship on the Northern coast when the war began. That's how well the South was prepared. They arranged all that before Fort Sumter. No navy at all, you might say, for the North."

"The North knew war was coming. Why didn't they prepare?"

Morton shrugged. "Any preparations, the navy men said, would have been considered a threat by the South. It would have been a warlike act to call in our ships and put them in fighting trim." The corners of his mouth turned down sourly.

"And the Navy has a job on its hands," Hite continued, his voice heavy with concern. "First, the government proclaims a blockade. They say the Navy must patrol thirty-six hundred miles of coastline and throw an unbreakable ring of ships around the Confederacy to prevent foreign ships from bringing in supplies and war materials. They say only if the South is completely cut off from all foreign sources of supply can the Army whip the Rebels on the land. Why, it's an almost impossible job! From Norfolk to Florida there are a thousand inlets which small vessels can enter. You could close all the main ports of the South and still the Confederates could get enough ships in and out of their territory to supply their Army with war materials for a decade. Men tell us they believe shore signals already are operating to help blockade-runners. Those Southern pilots know that coastline. They can slip in and out as easy as not—and the Navy can't stop it."

"Government men have had a lot of meetings with shipbuilders," Morton commented. "Some of them who have never been to sea and don't know the coast estimate they can make a tight blockade of the whole thirty-six hundred miles of coast with sixty ships."

All three men laughed outright. Matthew raised his glass and drank and tipped back in his chair.

"Sixty ships?" he said. "It would take six hundred."

Hite and Morton agreed. "Well, it's not only the blockade," Morton added. "They also say the Navy must keep the Potomac open. They say the Confederates have some iron-clads ready to fight if they can get them out to sea, and they'll turn privateer and sink Northern shipping."

"There'll be plenty of Northern ships sunk, Matthew. With practically no protection from the Navy, it's every man for himself."

Matthew nodded. "Yes." He turned his glass slowly, staring into it, and then, without raising his head, he glanced at Hite and Morton and grinned. "That ought to make freight rates go up, eh?"

The men chuckled. "Yes, rates will go up. Too bad you won't be able to take advantage of the rise," Hite said easily.

Matthew looked back at his glass. Morton stared at him and then exchanged an uneasy glance with Hite.

"But, as I say," Hite continued, after a moment's silence, "the port itself is in danger. New York hasn't any protection at all, except small harbor defenses, and can expect no protection from the Navy, with the work it has to do. Every port in the North is vulnerable to attack by a Rebel raider. That's one reason why the waterfront is knocking itself out to build ships. It's for the port's own protection as well as to strengthen the blockade and win the war."

"Hite," Matthew said slowly, "you don't mean to tell me everyone on the waterfront is loyal to the Union cause?"

Again Hite and Morton exchanged glances. "No," Hite said frankly. "You will find plenty who aren't. There are many who put their pocketbooks first, and there will be blockade runners carrying Northern goods as well as those carrying supplies from England and France. The city is shot with Southern sympathizers and war profiteers. Damn them!"

"If the Navy fails," Matthew said suddenly, "the finest Army in the world can't break the Rebellion."

"We admit that," Morton said drily. He took a cigar from his pocket and chewed on it reflectively. "That's another reason the shipyards are so damned busy. We need hundreds of ships—little gun-boats, able to enter the inland waters. And side-wheelers, that don't have to make a wide turn under fire. Fast steamers to chase privateers. Transports and supply ships and ships big enough to return the fire of shore batteries. You see—the Navy has one other job, too. They are to cooperate with the Army in recapturing the forts of the Southern coast and on the lower Mississippi. A good number of these shipyard workers have boys in the Army, Matthew. They're trying to see that the Rebels don't get English guns."

"There's plenty of work cut out for any skilled seaman, Matthew," Hite leaned across the table and his coarse, lined face was intensely serious. "Any man who can sail his own ship or train others—God knows we need them. And we need ships. The outcome of the war, as well as the safety of the ports, depend upon it. You've got three ships, haven't you?"

Matthew nodded. He pushed himself away from the table and his chair scraped the bare floor noisily. He put both hands on the table as he stood. They were strong hands, clean and young, and Morton stared at them broodingly. They were the kind of hands the Union needed, with power behind them.

"Yes, I've got three ships, Hite," Matthew said. "But don't think for a minute that because you men have gone soft and are full of sentiment about the good old Union, that I am going to give them up to the Navy, even for a price." He hitched up his trousers a little, in the old gesture that Hite and Morton knew well. He had used that gesture as a boy, before he went into a fight. "Hite, you and Morton know well what I've gone through to get what I have. I've no intention of losing it now, war or no war. This is my chance to double—triple what I have, and give me security for the rest of my life. I'm not afraid of Confederate privateers. Steam or sail—I can outrun any of them. That is—if I decide to outrun them. If there's more money to be made running the blockade, maybe I'll try my luck at that, too. I've not taken any sides in this fight, not yet. There's something to be said on both sides."

The partners arose together and their faces were grim.

"A man can't be neutral in this fight, Matthew. Call us sentimental if you like—but it isn't sentiment when it's your own survival. If the Union loses, New York loses, too, and South Street."

Matthew raised his eyebrows. "All right. You look out for your interests and I'll look out for mine. I've no patience with all this talk about patriotism. Seems to me those Rebels believe they are as patriotic as the Federals. It's all in the way you look at it. And what is this fight all about, anyway? States' rights? Slavery? Lincoln has said time and again he won't disturb the institution of slavery in the states where it is now established. The tariff? Landed aristocrats against workers? Industrial North against agricultural South? My God, man, so far no man I've talked to has been able to tell me just what it is all about. I'm not even sure if it *is* a war! I can't find out if it is a real, honest-to-God war, or if it is a Rebellion. That makes a difference, you know. If the Union government had simply closed the Southern ports they would have stamped the fight as a rebellion. But the government proclaimed a blockade. You know what that does? It implies recognition of the Confederacy as a belligerent nation—instead of treating the Rebels as revolutionaries. The blockade announces to foreign countries that the South is an independent and lawful belligerent, engaged in lawful war. That's an invitation to England and France to deal with the Confederates. It does exactly what the Rebels want—recognizes them as an independent nation. What a great help that will be to them in getting the active support of France and England!"

"You seem to know a hell of a lot about France and England. Do you think they will recognize the Confederacy?"

Matthew spread his hands. "How would I know? If they do, and if they go in with the Rebels, there will be no more United States—not as we have known it. England and France have plenty to gain by backing the South. Territory, perhaps; Southern markets. The break-up of this country and so a lessening of its strength. It would seem quite possible."

He lifted his glass and drained it and turned away. Then he spoke over his shoulder. "I may know more in a month or so. I'm going to England. There are plenty of passengers clamoring for passage, and I've a load of Western wheat. It will be a good paying cargo."

Hite walked around the table and took his arm. "Matthew," he said, almost gently, "we were hoping, Morton and I—all South Street was hoping— you'd be in this fight. You're a good fighter, boy, and you've got ships, and God knows we need them. And if you come in, others will follow. You always did attract a following. There's been some odd and evil deals here in this room of the Cock and Bull, Matthew—but this isn't one of them. We're going down the line for the Union. After this trip to England—is there a chance you'll—"

Matthew looked down at him and took a deep breath and his chin firmed. "Hite, I feel about this fight like I did about the Crimean War. I told Thilo Kalin then—and I tell you now—this just isn't my fight. What I'm trying to do is to pick the winner. I want to be on that side."

Morton took Matthew's other arm. "Listen, Matthew—I wish you'd think it over a little more. You think you've got nothing to lose—if you guess the outcome right. But I don't think you quite understand. Of course there are plenty on South Street—in all the North, for that matter, who aren't for the Union. But there are enough, and there will be more, and they are the people who matter.

So that a man who won't fight, who holds out his ships when they are needed so much, is going to find it pretty rough." Matthew started to speak but Morton raised his hand. "Not only that. The *Loyalty* is a fine ship—on long voyages—none can deny that. But she's a wooden ship, man, and she's got real competition in the new steamers. They are maneuverable, Matthew, fast, and they don't depend on the wind alone. Even if you offered the *Loyalty* to the Navy, she'd be used as a transport or a supply ship or something of the sort. She's outmoded, when it comes to fighting craft, whether it is trading with England and risking privateers, or running the blockade and risking Union ships; you're in plenty of danger. You stand to lose everything."

The men watched Matthew's face, but the set of his chin was stubborn. "This is a politician's war, Morton," Matthew said. "It's not my fight. From the way it looks now, the North has a slim chance. Maybe it would be a noble gesture on my part—but what would I get out of it? No, thanks. I've been poor. I saw my mother work herself to death. I don't intend to be poor ever again. As for what South Street, or New York, or the world thinks of me—who the devil cares? Men have tried to break me before. As long as a man has money he needn't be afraid of anything or anybody. He can do damn near anything he pleases. But a poor man —he's the fellow who has to be careful."

"You are making a big mistake, Matthew."

Matthew turned to Hite. "Well, now," he said easily, "you wouldn't be offering the Cock and Bull to the government to help win the war, would you?"

Hite straightened, his round, battered little face like a serious monkey's. He faced Matthew squarely and seemed to grow in stature.

"I'm a tavern keeper, Matthew, and a bum, you might say. But I'd give the Cock and Bull and everything else I've got to help save the Union. And there's a lot of other folks who feel the same way."

Matthew stared at him for a long moment and then his glance traveled to Morton. Morton's long, sharp face was dark and set as he met Matthew's eyes. These two men have been the best friends

I ever had, Matthew thought. Hard-bitten and rough, maybe, but they've been true friends to me. What is it that has touched them and turned them into Union patriots? Has this same fever touched the rest of the waterfront? They can no longer think clearly, he thought, almost pitying them. They've got martial music in their brains and a flag before their eyes. Poor devils—they are old, too; old people are apt to grow soft, even to grow religious. Matthew put a hand on the shoulder of each of the men and tightened his grip. Then he left without further speech.

But as the door closed behind him he heard Morton speak one word. He was to hear it often in the weeks to come.

"Mercenary," Morton said, and his tone made the word a curse.

[8]

LOYALTY sat before her dressing table, a note in her hand. The mirror proved that her excitement was reflected in her face, in her flushed cheeks and her sparkling eyes, and in the lips she could not prevent from smiling. She read the note for the hundredth time, and then she laid it down with a happy sigh.

The note was in Matthew's clear handwriting, and it announced that he would call upon her at eight o'clock. He did not ask her permission. He simply stated that he would be there. Loyalty's eyes strayed to it again and she laughed aloud, and for a minute she looked like the sixteen-year-old she had been when she first met Matthew Steel. What would happen, she thought wickedly, if she were not at home when he called? Matthew would undoubtedly seek her out, wherever she was, and she did not think she would like to face his wrath when he found her.

Loyalty had been working very hard in the days since her return from Washington, and now she bent toward the mirror anxiously, wondering if weariness showed in her face. She had dressed carefully in a gown of blue-green, the color of deep water, which suited her well. It was fun to dress up, Loyalty thought, woman-like, to prepare in proper fashion to meet one's lover. It would make up, to some extent, for her dreadful appearance in Alexandria and on the train and in a subsequent meeting with Matthew Steel.

Matthew had called formally at the Blake house the day after their return from Washington and had been received by Serena. He had inquired politely for the health of Loyalty, Cass and Mr. Blake, and not by word or manner had he indicated that there had been anything unconventional about the night preceding. Serena had been highly gratified. Loyalty, still confined to her room, had not seen him. The next day he had sent flowers, with his card but with no message.

Loyalty looked forward to her next meeting with him half-shyly, thinking it would be awkward for her to see him for the first time since the night she had slept in his arms. She had blushed when she remembered that night, but the memory made her heart sing. It had been so natural, so good, to be close to him. She had felt safe and at home, as though that were where she belonged, and she had needed him then and he had understood. It was odd how very certain she was of her love for him. Remembering Matthew's arms about her, his rich voice in the quiet night, reassuring, comforting, his tenderness and complete understanding, Loyalty was sure that no finer man lived. Few had pierced the hard exterior that was Captain Steel's protection, but Loyalty had pierced it and found gold beneath.

But her next meeting with him had been quite by accident—at least it appeared to be quite by accident. Loyalty wasn't sure. She had forced herself to get up from her bed and to dress and to attend the rally sponsored by the Union Defense Committee in Union Square. To lie in bed longer, even though weariness and lethargy weighed upon her, seemed wicked self-indulgence, when there was so much to be done. The rally had been no social occasion and Loyalty had not felt festive as she prepared for it. She had dressed in the first gown that came to her hand, a cool, old tarlatan, which had never been particularly becoming. And she had gone with Serena and had seated herself on a camp stool near to the platform and given her attention to the ringing speeches and to the response of the great crowd that had gathered to hear them. She was proud of her city's brave reaction to the staggering defeat at Bull Run; leaders called now for volunteers—not for three months, but for two years; and for contributions for mattresses and beds for Army hospitals, for ambulances and equipment for men to fight a long war. The response was enthusiastic and grimly determined, and Loyalty felt her spirits rise a little.

Then she had glanced up to see Matthew Steel, standing quietly not six feet from her, his eyes on the platform. It was pure coincidence, she told herself, that she should see him here, but encountering him without warning was something of a shock. Was it always to be like that, she wondered? Why was it that the sight of Matthew Steel, and of him alone, of all the people in the world, started her blood to racing? He had been paying polite attention to the speakers, but some way she knew that he had seen her, that he had perhaps, been watching her for quite a little while. Bless me, she had thought with a sigh, must he always have the advantage?

How would he act when he spoke to her? Now that the excitement and unnatural strain of the battle and their flight were over, would he embarrass her by recalling the intimacy of that one night? Would he be overly familiar—and what would she do or say if he were? After all, she had thought, and laughter had bubbled up within her and she had lowered her eyes to conceal it, she had willingly spent a night in his arms! No lady, Loyalty thought primly, would have permitted such a thing under any circumstances. What could he think of her?

Curiosity had overcome caution and Loyalty had glanced at him again out of the corner of her eye. This time he had turned casually and bowed and she had inclined her head also and then, forcibly, she had brought her attention back to the platform. But she had not heard the words of the speaker and she had wanted very much to turn again toward Matthew Steel.

Finally the orations had ended and the music and applause died and Loyalty had arisen. She had carefully kept her eyes averted but she had known that Matthew was beside her even before his voice had asked politely: "May I drive you home?"

Remembering now, Loyalty laughed again. She had been in an agony of embarrassment, she, Loyalty, who had been so carefully schooled at Miss Heather's Female Seminary in the proper conduct of young ladies! Seated beside him, she had been tongue-tied, unable to protest when the carriage turned the opposite way—toward Madison Square. She had seen heads turn and she could almost hear the whispers that had followed her as she drove off with Matthew Steel.

But he had been very considerate, very gentle and she had gradually relaxed. He had no intention of embarrassing her by reminding her of her unconventional behavior—and his. But she knew also that Matthew Steel had not forgotten. There was something in his eyes and voice that was warmer, less bold. There was no need to chatter constantly, as she did with other men. He seemed content just to be beside her.

He had not made the drive long. He knew it was the first time she had ventured out since her return home. She had rested against that knowledge, feeling again that she need never be on the defensive with him. He had mentioned changes in the city since he had been a boy here. She was delighted with his flashes of humor and pleased to find it so easy to laugh with him, and again the feeling of belonging with Matthew Steel had streamed through her.

Standing finally in the Blake hallway, she had tried to thank him but the words seemed hard to say. She had put her hand in his and he had looked at it, white and small in his own, and then he had pressed it to his lips and for a minute his eyes had lingered on her lips. She had been almost frightened; then he had smiled and said quietly "Good night, Loyalty. Sleep well," and he was gone. And she had not been sure whether she was sorry or grateful that he had not followed his first impulse.

It was good to remember every second of her meetings with Matthew, Loyalty thought. They were like little jewels to take from a box and run through her fingers, to enjoy their beauty again and again. She had waited a long time for him, and it was good now to know their romance was everything she had dreamed it might be. It was an unconventional and stormy one, she thought, smiling, and tonight's meeting she was sure would be the decisive one, and the loveliest of all. Matthew was too direct a man to carry on a long courtship, or even a long engagement. He had been considerate enough not to rush her while she was still suffering from shock; he had given her a little time to get her balance and to know his love for her, and perhaps he, too, savored these days that were preliminaries to the culmination of their love. He had told her, without words, in a hundred different ways; there was nothing tentative, nothing experimental, about Matthew's attitude toward her. He loved her—and tonight he would ask her to marry him.

Loyalty took out a scent-box and touched the tiny sponge within it and then drew her fingers across her hair and down her throat. . . . I want to be lovely for you, Matthew, she whispered to herself in the mirror. . . . I want every moment to be precious and perfect. I wonder if it is always like this, if every romance is so heady, so blissfully satisfying, if every girl hangs on to the moments so greedily—or is it the war that seems to make it so much more urgent, so much more necessary to cling to all the seconds together?

She was humming a little tune as she fastened a fragile butterfly bow, the color of her gown, into her curls, and turned her head from side to side to study the effect. The hands of the little clock had never moved so slowly. I've never been so happy, she thought, despite the war. . . .

She picked up the note again. Had Matthew been preparing to go to war? Just what had been occupying him during these last weeks when he was not with her? Their talk had been kept light, for the most part—they had so many years to catch up! They had talked of his travels, of their tastes, all the little things, skirting more serious subjects.

After all, she knew very little about him—except that she loved him, and he loved her. Long ago her father had stated flatly that Matthew Steel was a rake and a scoundrel, and Cass had agreed, and so had Henry Austin. She knew that was not true. But his political beliefs—his views on the war?

She was ashamed of herself for the momentary doubt that had wormed its way into her happiness. She put down the note and picked up her hairbrush again and gave her hair one last final pat. She wished he would come. The time was short enough before Matthew would go to war.

For of course he would go. The thought kept nagging at her. Families and friends had been ripped apart by conflicting opinions about the War Between the States. But such a thing could not possibly happen to her and Matthew Steel, not now, when finally they were together. Matthew had sought information from Cass. . . . She remembered his face, thoughtful and remote, when he had looked at the Rebel gun Cass carried with him. Matthew had, she must admit, not committed himself, given her no reason to think that he was a Northern patriot.

Except for the fact that he had been born in New York there was no particular reason why he should be a Federal supporter, she reasoned. Her mind was working fast and clearly now, methodically sorting the facts. He had no love for New York, for he had a bitter childhood there—except his affection for South Street. He had spoken warmly of Charleston. He was as much at home in a dozen different countries, a hundred different ports, no doubt; he was, in fact, almost an expatriate, and neither his mother nor his father had been American citizens. Only the accident of his birth made him an American.

Nor was his money, like her father's, at stake. Nor did Matthew have deep roots in American soil, for he had no family ties, no family tradition here. Moreover, he had been far removed from the events which led up to war, he had not been exposed to the inflamed propaganda which had sent Cass and others like him into uniform. There was, truly, no reason why Matthew Steel should become a member of the United States fighting forces.

The sparkle had gone from Loyalty's face when she arose and went to her window to watch for Matthew. I love him, she said to herself, passionately; I love him, regardless of what he believes, just as I love Cass, despite his weakness. But what can I do? The Union comes first, it must come first. I cannot expect others to give their lives, and not be willing to make sacrifices myself. At Alexandria I made a pledge to fight with everything I have, in every way a woman can fight, to preserve the Union. I must not forget that pledge. It is more important than any individual, bigger than any one of us, and it justifies death, it justifies denial.

Surely I am borrowing trouble, she thought hopefully. Perhaps Matthew does understand and is as loyal to the Union as I. I shall wait until I know. *But if he does not?* reason asked her. She shook her head, trying to free it of such dangerous thoughts. Then I must make him see, she thought, suddenly sure.

She had defied her father, in the past, and won, but not without a struggle. She turned back to the mirror again and smoothed her skirts. She was a slight girl, a tiny creature to lock wills with Matthew Steel, the man the waterfront pointed out as the toughest, most stubborn fighter of them all. And emotion was on Matthew's side, in case it came to a battle of wills. For she loved him and every fiber of her being reached out to him. She wanted to avoid the issue, to turn her back on the war and everything pertaining to it, and take her happiness while she could. It would be bitter hard to fight that great desire of hers, her need for him, as well as to resist his.

If only I can reach him, show him what I learned at Alexandria, how big, how important, how very true it is, she thought; if only he can feel what I feel so deeply, then there will be no wall, no possible barrier, between us. Her chin came up. Perhaps that was her part in the war. That was her challenge, and she would meet it. Unlike Cass, Loyalty would not run away from a battle.

She heard a carriage below her window. She turned and went to meet Matthew Steel.

[9]

MATTHEW stood in the Blake hallway, watching Loyalty descend the stairway. He was smiling up at her in sheer pleasure and the gaslight fell softly on his face. It was a clean, hard young face and the smile it wore was almost boyish now and his eyes were shining with admiration. Loyalty noticed the way his hair sprang crisp and black from his forehead, the strength of his neck, the stubborn chin. He came to the foot of the stairs and stood waiting, one hand on the newel post. He was quite at ease, quite sure of himself, and she wondered if she, or anyone, was a match for him. Matthew is not a man who can be crossed, she thought swiftly. He is a man who wants his own way and will have it. And if his way is not my way—

She caught her breath. His smile broadened and she saw horizontal lines on his forehead as he raised his eyebrows in that quizzical, half-challenging, half-laughing way he had. His eyes traveled over her quite brazenly and he liked what he saw. He nodded approvingly. She answered his grin and Matthew stared openly at the lovely dimple in her cheek and then he held out both hands. Quite naturally she put her own into them and she found her hands on his shoulders and he lifted her lightly down the last steps and into his arms.

Once before he had lifted her so, on his ship; his audacity had angered Henry and both shocked and pleased her. Then he had released her instantly—but not now.

Matthew put one finger beneath her chin and tipped her face up to the light. He studied it long and carefully. Loyalty felt her own eyes blurring, for his nearness, his dearness, swept over her again and she wanted only to stay here always, in his arms, to keep this moment safe and untouched. She saw the smile fade from his face and when he spoke his voice was a little husky and she knew he felt the magic of the moment, too.

"You're quite all right, Loyalty?"

So he had that secret fear, too, that in even a short separation something might happen to her; or that something might happen to change that which they had discovered between them.

"Quite all right, Matthew."

His arms hardened about her, as though he intended never to let her go. Suddenly he buried his face in her hair, drinking deep of its softness and its perfume and she could feel the steady beat of his heart and the warmth and strength of his hard body tight against her own. Loyalty's eyes closed. Thank you, God, she whispered, thank you for sending him, for giving me this moment. Her arms went up and she lifted her face. Matthew uttered a low exclamation, which might, too, have been a prayer, and it seemed to Loyalty that one flame swept through them and welded them together as their lips met.

The big clock struck eight, slowly, and still Matthew held her. She drew back and her cheek was tight against his own and she was shaken and she was content and she was half-smiling, though her eyes were misted. After a long minute Matthew released her and she saw that his face had flushed a little. She marveled that a man's hands could be so strong and so gentle, all at once. Fire and tenderness were in Matthew's face, desire and devotion in his voice.

"I've waited a long time, Loyalty," he said.

She nodded. "Yes. It has been—very long, Matthew."

"I love you very much. You do know that, don't you?"

Again she nodded. He waited and then spoke her name, questioningly.

"Loyalty?"

"Yes, Matthew." She stumbled a little over the words. "I do love you. I do—with all my heart, forever and ever."

It went so very deep it stirred her all up inside, she thought, so she could not stand it, this love of theirs, unless it were leavened by laughter. She drew away again until her lips barely touched his, and then she murmured. "I—guess you sort of suspected it—didn't you?"

His laugh was deep and exultant and she loved it, too. The armor was gone from him now and he was very close to her, close and open to hurt, she thought. Her heart ached and she pressed both her hands tight against her breast. She wanted to keep him laughing, keep him happy, keep him close; there had not been enough laughter in his life, and that alone was another bond between them. Loving him as she did, how could she give him up, into danger? Worse than that, how could she use her influence to persuade him to go into war? Her hands flew out and tightened themselves on his coat, clinging to him half frantically, and Matthew, quick to catch her every mood, looked at her anxiously.

"Loyalty—what—"

There was a sound of a latchkey in the door and Loyalty raised her head and stepped back.

"Come into the library, Matthew," she said, and managed a smile. "That will be Father and Cass coming home." Quickly she moved around him and led the way to the library door. Matthew followed. At the doorway they paused, for the outer door had opened and Thaddeus and Cass entered.

"Good evening, Captain Steel."

Matthew bowed. "Good evening, Mr. Blake. Good evening, Cass."

Cass replied with a silent nod. He was pale and thin and his eyes shifted from Matthew and Loyalty and fixed themselves on the floor. All his old swagger, all his old dash and charming audacity, were gone. There was a hang-dog look about him and his face seemed pinched. He limped slightly. He stood quietly, waiting, contributing nothing, half-apologetic. He was a wrecked and beaten man, and Matthew glanced back at Thaddeus with sudden understanding and pity for the father.

Thaddeus himself had aged; always immaculate, now his skin seemed as dry and white as paper, and tightly drawn over the bones of his face. His hair was almost snow white; but his eyes were as clear and keen as they had ever been and Matthew had forgotten that Thaddeus was almost as tall as himself. Deliberately he laid his hat, gloves and stick on the hall table and held out his hand to Matthew and then he gestured toward the library door. They entered and Cass followed hesitantly as though he had no will of his own and waited only to be told what to do.

"I've been looking forward to meeting you again, Captain Steel," Thaddeus said pleasantly. "We are greatly in your debt. We are grateful for your aid to my son and daughter."

Matthew shook his head. "It was a privilege, sir, what small aid I gave them. I deserve no thanks."

"I think otherwise." Thaddeus smiled slightly and offered a chair. His glance went to Loyalty and back to Matthew. Quietly Loyalty seated herself but Matthew still stood. He stood with his back to the empty fireplace and the little ship's model was behind him on the mantelpiece. Loyalty smiled. He had stood in just that place when she had peeked at him through the keyhole of this room; he had stood just there when he had told her, and her family and their friends, that he would come back to her. And he was going to speak to Thaddeus now. She knew it was coming and she put out her hand as though to stop him. There was so much to say first, so much to be settled between them. She had not meant it to be like this. But Matthew, in his usual forthright style, could see no need to wait. She had said she loved him. He had made known his intention to marry her. In Matthew's opinion there was no need for further delay. Loyalty's hand dropped in her lap and she leaned back in her chair. After all, perhaps it was better like this, sharp and swift and clean.

"Mr. Blake," Matthew said bluntly, "I would like your permission to marry your daughter."

Thaddeus' eyebrows raised a fraction of an inch.

"You are asking my permission, Captain Steel?" he asked, polite surprise in his voice. "Or are you just announcing to me the fact that you intend to marry her?"

"I intend to marry her, sir, if she will have me. We would be happy to have your approval."

Thaddeus nodded. "You are, I take it, fully able to support her?"

He knows to the last dime how much money I have, Matthew thought. He looked at Loyalty. She was blushing furiously and he realized that his bluntness had embarrassed her. Loyalty was not used to men's abruptness. He glanced at Cass but the boy's face was hidden in the shadows.

"Yes, sir," he answered Thaddeus. "I'd be glad to have you investigate my finances." The men's glances crossed like swords.

"Captain Steel," Thaddeus said slowly, "in the past we have not always seen eye to eye. That, however, is of little consequence. I trust my daughter's judgment. Loyalty has proven to me in these past few years that she is a young lady of intelligence and discernment. I may say that Loyalty and I have not always agreed, either. She has, for instance, been your loyal champion for many years." He smiled and glanced at Loyalty proudly. "But I am convinced that she is capable of making her decisions regarding her own future. Captain Steel, if you fulfill my daughter's requirements in a husband, then I shall not stand in your way. Naturally I shall always consider myself my daughter's protector, and I shall guard her interests in any way possible. But her choice of husband, now that she is adult, is up to her, and I shall not cross her."

A little warning note was struck in Matthew's consciousness; that isn't quite like Thaddeus Blake, to relinquish the reins so easily, Matthew thought, and he looked at the banker narrowly. He's not being quite as frank as he appears. He glanced at Loyalty and saw that the blood had left her face and she was white and strained and her hands were gripped tightly together in her lap. She was looking at Matthew almost pleadingly, but her lips were closed. Matthew bowed a little stiffly.

"Thank you, sir. I am sure your confidence in your daughter is not misplaced."

"I am certain it is not. This is a difficult time for young people," Thaddeus replied thoughtfully. "Wars, I think, are always hardest on the younger men and women."

Loyalty's eyes came up to meet Matthew's. Now is the time, she thought. In a few minutes I will know. She felt that her father had planned this quite deliberately; either he knew more than he revealed about Matthew Steel and was going to permit her to discover it for herself and make her own decision, or he was seeking information now, treading carefully. He was too wise a man to cross swords with his daughter again. He was taking an oblique approach. He is putting it squarely up to me, she said silently, so I will have no one to reproach but myself.

"It makes it difficult, of course, to make plans for the future," Thaddeus went on. "I understand your ship is back in its old place in Brighton's, being cut down and pierced for guns."

Loyalty leaned forward, her face alight. "Really, Matthew? You didn't tell me! Or is it a secret? Is the *Loyalty* to become a fighting ship? Matthew—have you joined the service, too?"

Matthew stared at her, puzzled at her eagerness. What had the ship and its conversion to do with Loyalty Blake? In a flash it came to him—Thaddeus' apparent agreement, Loyalty's obvious concern. The excitement and happiness of the few moments with Loyalty drained from him slowly and caution took their place.

"The ship is being cut down, yes," he said slowly. "But I have not sold nor given her to the government. I'm preparing her to protect herself at sea. There are privateers afloat, and it is only a sensible precaution."

Thaddeus' face froze. "Perhaps you have not yet been approached. You have been here such a short time," he suggested politely. "The Union is in desperate need of ships. It was my information that an offer was to be made to you for the *Loyalty* and your other vessels—"

Loyalty's face was white and stricken. Matthew was in no haste to reply. There was no doubt of his answer. He would tell her the exact truth, of course. He had never learned to lie and he had no intention of starting now. But he hated to bring that look to her face. His lips straightened but he spoke quite clearly.

"Yes, I did have such an offer. I refused it."

"Matthew," Loyalty's voice was hardly more than a whisper. "What do you intend to do?"

"I intended, Loyalty, to continue my regular business. Cargoes must still be transported, war or no war."

"Foreign trade is of little importance right now, Captain Steel, when the nation is in peril." Thaddeus' voice was dry and sharp. "And there are other vessels, unfitted for Navy service, to transport essential goods. Your ships, I understand, could be pressed into immediate service, with only a minimum of preparation. And I also understand a commission was offered you—a man of your skill—" Thaddeus paused. "It would seem to me a great honor, Captain Steel, and a great privilege, to be in a position to aid your country at a time like this, regardless of how much you might have to give up in the way of war profits. If I were a young man—"

In the shadows Cass Blake moved a little and Thaddeus' voice stopped and he set his teeth firmly against other words that he would say.

"It has been my observation, Captain Steel," Thaddeus went on, "that money has always been your paramount interest. I take it you are more interested now, despite your considerable success, to acquire still more wealth, instead of aiding your country. Withholding your help at a crucial moment like this is nothing short of—"

Again Thaddeus stopped and stood up, fighting for control. Captain Steel had infuriated him in the past, but the man's colossal impudence in proposing to his daughter under these circumstances was just too much. "Are you a Rebel sympathizer, sir?"

Matthew shook his head. No, Mr. Blake. I have taken no sides. I have no reason to fight the South. I have friends there. I bear them no grudge. Neither have I any reason to fight the North. Mr. Blake, to fight, and fight well, a man must have a reason, whether it is in a personal scrap or in a war. A man must have something to gain, or he must hate, or he must fight in self-defense, or for something he believes to be right."

Thaddeus interrupted swiftly. "I'd have more respect for you, Captain Steel, if you were a Secessionist. Southerners fighting for the Confederacy believe themselves to be right, even though they are not. They have the courage of their convictions behind them and are fighting for them. Misled they may be—but they are not standing on the sidelines, making money from the blood of other men—afraid to fight!"

Matthew opened his lips and closed them again. He could gain nothing by argument with Thaddeus Blake and he would not permit himself to be goaded into rash statements. He turned to Loyalty and at the same moment Thaddeus turned to his daughter. "Loyalty," Thaddeus said, "I have told Captain Steel I trust your judgment—a statement that few men are privileged to make about their daughters. That fact still stands. If you still wish to marry this man, I shall not stand in your way. If you refuse him, I must forbid him the house."

Father thinks I am going to fail and shame him, as Cass has done, Loyalty thought. She shook her head slightly and turned to Matthew, her face imploring.

"I'm sorry, Loyalty," Matthew said, and all the light was gone from him and there was no trace of laughter now. The armor had slipped back over his face again and it was there between them and she feared she could not break it again. "I did not think politics would enter into our plans. Loyalty, does it matter to you?"

His voice was gentle and it tore at Loyalty's heart. It would be so easy to say no, it does not matter, nothing matters, she thought; just those words and Matthew's face would light again and we could be together, for always. She heard a movement near the door and she knew that Cass had stood, too. Her father was waiting and Cass was waiting and Matthew was waiting. Cass loathes himself, Loyalty thought sickly; he must not loathe me, too.

"It does matter to me, Matthew," she said clearly.

Out of the corner of her eye she caught the triumph in Thaddeus' face. Matthew stood motionless for an instant and then he came toward her and his hands tightened on her shoulders. He paid no attention to Thaddeus and Cass. This was between him and Loyalty.

"Just a few minutes ago, Loyalty, you told me you loved me."

"Yes. I do love you, Matthew. I always will, all the days of my life."

"Then you will marry me—despite this—despite the war?"

"No."

His fingers dug into her shoulders. "Loyalty, I've loved you and wanted you and worked and waited for you. What I have is yours. I've wanted to make money—for you, to insure your future, your security. Loyalty, you don't know what it is to live in poverty. I do. It's an ugly life. But—I want you, above everything else on earth. If I give my ships to the government and join the service—will you marry me?"

Loyalty's eyes filled. He would do that—for her! No woman had ever been more completely loved and it shook her deeply. Thaddeus withdrew a step or two. His daughter could feel him waiting, almost see his smile of satisfaction. Every instinct within Loyalty drew her toward Matthew Steel. Then, again there was that slight, restless movement from Cass in the shadows.

Loyalty shook her head. "No, Matthew," she said again. "I do not want you to do that—for me."

"What!" The exclamation came from Thaddeus. Matthew dropped his hands, disbelief written on his face.

"I don't know if I can make you understand," she said, speaking slowly, searching for the proper words. "But I will try. You see—at Alexandria I saw what war means. It is carnage and suffering, death and pain. It is horror, pure horror, worse than anything I ever dreamed could be on this earth or the next. Men kill, they kill the husbands and sweethearts of other women, like me; they take the lives of fathers and sons, and where they can't kill they cripple, maim, blind, disfigure, destroy, with every fiendish method known to man. It takes something big, something tremendously big, infinite and right and good to justify it.

"The love of one woman would not justify it. If you joined the Navy, Matthew, simply because you love me and I wished it, every time you killed it would be murder. Every time you drew a sword, fired a gun, sank a ship, you'd be guilty of the worst crimes against your fellow men and against yourself—you'd be breaking every law known to God or man."

Every word she spoke was like a lash with a thin wand across the face of Matthew Steel. The silence in the room was heavy and ominous and Loyalty saw the color drain from Matthew's face, leaving it white and stricken. I have to do it, she told herself, I have to do it! She hesitated, praying inwardly for strength, and then she went on, knowing what she was doing, knowing that she was deliberately trampling on the delicate and beautiful thing that had grown between them.

"Nor would you be of value to the Navy, Matthew," she continued. "Not until you understand what it is you are fighting for. It takes something more than men and gun and bullets to win a war. People have to feel it, deep down inside them. Matthew, it will come to you, too, the need to preserve the Union. I hope and pray that it will. Until it does—no, Matthew, I cannot marry you, for we are too far, too terribly far, apart."

Her last words were a whisper, for they were hard to say. Her eyes stayed upon him, full of suffering, appealing, proclaiming her love for him, begging understanding.

Thaddeus cleared his throat. It had been in Loyalty's power with one word to put Matthew Steel in his country's service. Instead she had talked of ideals and patriotism, which really did not matter. The important thing was to get men and ships with all possible speed and put them under the direction of the War Department. But he held his tongue. After all, there might be a germ of truth in what she said—certainly the low morale of the troops at Bull Run had been mainly responsible for defeat. He began to look at Loyalty in a new light. With some men, her impassioned plea might be effective; but with Matthew Steel it was like pounding against a stone wall.

Matthew bit his lip and there was anger and hurt in his eyes. He did not speak to Thaddeus or Cass. He simply turned and strode toward the door. Loyalty wanted to run after him, to plead with him further, but she would not. I must be strong now, she kept telling herself, I must not weaken now. I must keep on praying and trying and hoping, and some way, somehow, he will understand. My happiness is so little to give, when men give their lives. I must give him time to think, and perhaps it will come to him as it did to me, and then what a fighter for the Union he will be! I must hang on to that.

She heard the door close behind her. Matthew Steel was gone. For a minute the room was silent and then Thaddeus Blake spoke. "Well," he said, "A man's true colors—"

Loyalty whirled upon him. "Yes," she blazed at him. "A man's true colors will out. Matthew will show his true colors before this war is over. It is there, I tell you! You've never been able to see it, you've never seen any good in him, any good at all, and you've tried to force him, tried to beat him, always! But you will see, everyone will see! He is honest enough not to pretend to be something he is not. It takes courage to declare your beliefs, particularly if they are different from those about you! Yet you called him a coward. But you cannot influence Matthew Steel by threats and slurs and name-calling. He will do as he thinks right, regardless of any of us. And I love him, and I admire him, and I always will!"

Her voice broke on a sob. She started for the door but her back was still straight. She had forgotten Cass but as she neared him he put his hand out to stop her. She was startled to see that he was smiling at her, the comforting old Cass smile that she loved. He put his arm around her shoulders and bent and kissed her cheek and then he let her go.

For a minute their eyes met and gratitude flooded over Loyalty. Cass' eyes held complete understanding and there was pride in them, too, when he looked at her. Cass, of all people, knew what she was trying to do.

BLIND anger carried Matthew Steel out of the Blake house and back toward the waterfront. He wanted to fight someone, to crush something with his bare hands, to release his fury and his hurt. Instead he walked swiftly, with long, even steps, straight toward South Street, at first making no attempt to control his wrath, waiting only for the first flash of anger to subside.

Loyalty, Loyalty, he said, over and over to himself, as if in repeating her name he could understand the thing that had hit him, as if it would bring him back, close to her, in complete understanding. He saw her face again, earnest, beseeching—My God, he thought suddenly, it wasn't just words she was saying, she's no shallow coquette any more. She really believed what she said. He tried to remember her exact words, found himself floundering, and he rubbed his hand across his face, trying to remember, but his memory held only one thing—Loyalty was lost to him. She had refused to marry him.

Damn it, he thought, why don't women stay out of men's business, keep out of war and politics? I love you, Matthew, she said. But I won't marry you! Like telling a man she loved him but she wouldn't marry him till he joined her church; then when he offered to join her church she said no, that wasn't enough—not until he believed the doctrines he vowed to uphold. Oh, hell, he said aloud, in disgust.

This damned war, how can it reach into my life and dictate *my* future, take Loyalty away from me? This war is getting too damned personal, he thought. In our home, just the two of us, there would never have been a cloud between us.

But Thaddeus had been glad; Matthew was sure there had been pleasure on his clean, thin old face, pleasure because his opinion of Steel, never a high one, had proven correct. Well, what was wrong with him, Matthew Steel, anyway? That Loyalty would refuse him, and Hite and Morton would regard him darkly? Because he didn't run out and grab a gun and start shooting Rebels, some of whom were good men, whom he had known in the past as friends? Because he wanted to keep and increase the fortune he had earned by sweat and suffering and denial? It was easy for Loyalty and for Thaddeus to talk of ideals; they had never been in want. To save the Union, Loyalty said. Hah! Matthew had been a victim of class distinction and prejudice in this same New York where Loyalty had seen only luxury and ease. What was fair or just about that? What was democratic about a government that permitted an immigrant girl like Mary Steel to give her last ounce of strength working for the wealthy? And the slavery question—if the war boiled down to a simple issue, such as freeing the slaves, then a man could see some sense to it. But the slaves were not free and no one expected them to be, except the few fanatics who went around singing *John Brown's Body.*

There was a gulf between people like the Blakes and people like Matthew Steel, and it seemed that despite his wealth he could never bridge it. He had refused to believe there was any difference that money could not overcome, but apparently there was. This issue of war. And yet, on South Street, tavern-keepers like Hite and Morton were aligning themselves on the side of men like Thaddeus. It didn't make sense. The whole damned city was a checkerboard of prejudice and conflicting opinions, and he was caught right in the middle of it.

Matthew turned automatically into the Cock and Bull. I wish Tessa were here, he thought fiercely. There are other women besides Loyalty Blake, he thought, in his hurt and bitterness. A girl was singing, but she did not compare to Tessa. He could send for Tessa and she would come at once. When he had put into San Francisco briefly, he had sought her, but Tessa had been in Sacramento with a theater troupe. He had left a message for her and some money, though all reports said she had been doing very well. He had forgotten her then, in his eagerness to get to Loyalty Blake.

Now he wanted her. He was hungry for her lush, flaming-haired, brazen beauty. Tessa, Matthew thought, with grim satisfaction, would love him even if he hung on a gibbet as a common thief, or was shot for holding crooked cards. When Tessa loved a man she took him as he was. She did not try to make him over, into something he was not. She did not tempt a man into wanting her so badly he could not sleep nor eat for thinking of her, and then withhold herself until she forced him to her will. Tessa offered herself generously, and asked little enough in return.

Some remnant of an old memory tugged at him. Was it not he, Matthew, who had left Tessa for that very reason? Had he not thought: to take Tessa means to compromise, to stop at this level, never to go farther? Had he not thought that striving to meet Loyalty's standards would give a man a purpose to living? Maybe he'd had an exalted opinion of Loyalty Blake. But that's not true, he argued with himself; I love her. I still want her—Jesus God, how I want her! Tessa wouldn't help, she wouldn't ease this hurt at all. He turned to the bar, turned his back on the singer.

His shoulder brushed the man next to him. The man was a Cuban and his face was dark and his features thick. Matthew glanced at him, unseeing, but the fellow put his hand on Matthew's arm and grinned.

"You're Captain Steel, aren't you?" he said.

Steel nodded. He glanced impatiently down the bar at Hite, who was taking his time about bringing him his drink. Hite had never been quite so slow before.

"I'm Fernando, captain of the *Annie B.*"

Steel nodded shortly again and then brought his attention to the man. The *Annie B.* was a slaver, as everyone well knew, a fast ship and an infamous one.

"The war must have put you out of business," Steel said bluntly. Hite was standing before them, looking at Fernando.

"What'll it be, Fernando—gin and bitters?" he asked. He did not look at Matthew. He knew Matthew's usual drink.

"Whisky," Fernando said. He chuckled. "Hite must have his little joke. . . . I hear your ship is being armed."

"Yes."

"Too bad the North hasn't passed a privateering act yet. If they do, anybody can go after the Rebel raiders and capture themselves a prize or two—eh?" He nudged Matthew in the ribs playfully and Matthew moved away a little, annoyed.

"I'm not after Rebel raiders or any other," Matthew said shortly.

"I'm just going to protect myself, that's all. If anyone takes a shot at me, I'll have something to answer with. That's all."

The Cuban's eyebrows climbed. "Ah?" he said. Then he brought his thick lips close to Steel's ear. "Why take that chance? Do what I did—what a lot of smart men are doing. Change your registry. Sail under another flag. Confederates won't bother you, then, or the Northern Navy either." He chuckled. "That's why Hite asked me if I'd have gin and bitters—an English drink. The *Annie B.* is flying the Union Jack now. Better protection than guns!"

He winked broadly. Matthew turned and looked at him with distaste. Damned coward, he thought, hiding behind another flag. Like hiding behind a woman's skirts. Fernando would lie like hell to save his own dirty hide. God damn it, if I sail at all I'll sail under my true colors. That *Annie B.* is a speedy ship, she'd make a good privateer. Matthew's eyes narrowed. Fernando was the kind of a crook to watch. It was not unlikely the Union Jack would come down and the Confederate flag go up, if it were to the man's advantage. The man's skin was oily and shiny, his brutal little eyes were deep-set, his loose lips were curled in a satisfied grin.

Hite set two identical glasses of whisky before Steel and Fernando.

"Two of a kind," Hite remarked casually and turned away.

[11]

CASS BLAKE was drunk. He stood in one corner of the music room, his back to the wall, a champagne glass in his hand. The music room was one step higher than the Blake drawing room beyond it, and Cass, through fog, could see Serena and James Thurlow, bride and groom, still standing near the doorway, greeting late guests. The rooms already were crowded. Among the silks and laces, velvets and ribbons of pretty girls and matrons, Cass occasionally glimpsed the blurred green sash of an Army surgeon;

and here and there a flash of gold on the shoulders of a Navy officer swam and quivered and disappeared in the throng.

Cass braced himself against the piano. He raised his eyebrows and blinked rapidly, trying to clear his vision. He saw Loyalty, a hazy, ethereal Loyalty, enter the room on the arm of Henry Austin. Henry, like James Thurlow and William Hastings and most of the other young men in the room, stood straight and proud in his Army uniform, a crimson sash slashing across his waist. Henry clasped James' hand and Cass fancied he could see the two friends grinning at each other in the special comradeship of Army men. Henry had shaken Cass' hand, too, and so had Thurlow, but only with politeness. They reserved that special warmth for their fellow soldiers.

Automatically Cass bowed to guests who glanced his way and he was ready with his usual quick smile and ofttimes a word of eager greeting was on his lips, but the guests turned away before he could speak the words and after a while his smile grew thin. He stood alone, listening to snatches of talk.

People were saying it was nice to see Loyalty and Henry together again and there were whispers that Loyalty was well rid of that mercenary Matthew Steel. Matthew Steel—another pariah like himself, Cass thought. He remembered reading that Steel's ship lay at the foot of Beekman Street, ready to clear for Liverpool. Liverpool was a long way from the wedding reception in the Blake house for Serena and James Thurlow.

For a minute Cass stood very still, deep in thought, and then he whirled suddenly and made his way to his own room.

He closed the door behind him and pulled a suitcase from his closet and threw a few articles of clothing into it. He stripped his formal clothes from him and tossed them in a heap on his bed in a kind of feverish haste. From downstairs he heard laughter and then music, gay and light-hearted, and Cass hurried as though eager to escape it.

He picked up a heavy jacket and cap and then he fumbled in a drawer for a bottle of whisky and he slid it under his coat. He went to the door and opened it and the music and voices from below increased in volume; he scanned the empty hall and then he slipped out and down the back stairs leading to the kitchen.

He attracted little attention as he let himself out into the alley way. A long line of carriages stretched far down the street and coachmen and footmen talked together in pleasant little groups. Cass recognized a fat and red-faced figure leaning against a near-by carriage. He whistled and Bennett turned and quickly threw open the door of the shabby vehicle and bowed in recognition to Cass.

Cass slid into the seat and immediately, with desperate haste, began to uncork the whisky bottle. Bennett watched him indulgently and then asked good-naturedly: "Where to, Mr. Cass?" Cass glanced up, his lips wet, and he began to laugh but there was no humor in it.

"Pier 23, Bennett," he gasped. "I don't know why—I just supposed you knew. That's it, Bennett, Pier 23, at the foot of Beekman."

[12]

THE *Loyalty* was ready and her master was ready and she waited only on the tide. The passengers' quarters were filled to capacity and the hold of the ship was crammed with corn and wheat—a welcome cargo in Liverpool. The only cargo which would be more welcome, Matthew thought, was one of Southern cotton. Cotton prices were going up and before the Rebellion was over would reach an all-time peak, and profits would be enormous. It was a temptation to a man.

He put his signature to the last paper on the stack before him and handed them to a waiting clerk. His first officer waited, tense and alert as he always was at sailing time. Matthew nodded to the clerk and turned his attention to the officer. He was not as skillful a seaman, nor as pleasant a companion aboard as Jules Descase. Matthew had a moment's uneasiness, thinking of Jules. Jules carried a valuable cargo on the *Messenger*, and it would be a rich prize for a Rebel raider, and it was a long way from San Francisco to New York. However, it was too late now to change his orders, even if he wished. The *Messenger* was well on her way toward Cape Horn, answering his summons, and the *Comet*, under his command, should have touched San Francisco, unloaded, and headed back toward Shanghai by now.

As far as business went, Matthew had no cause for worry. Although he had been forced to pay more than it was worth, by hard negotiating he had secured a warehouse on South Street. He could now afford to import and hold his goods for higher markets, if it seemed wise. He need no longer dispose of his shipments the moment he docked, in order to have money to pay his crew and to buy a new cargo. It was another long-planned advance. This time he'd choose his homecoming cargo carefully, machinery, war materials and cotton goods, and hold it till the need was greater and the prices higher. In a few months such articles would command a record figure. Bringing the *Messenger* to the East coast was another bid for high stakes.

The officer ducked his head and raised his fingers in a semblance of a salute.

"All ready, sir. Not much of a crew—but the best I can do. Old men and young ones, mostly, but enough. One young fellow just came aboard. Drunk as a lord, sir, and soft, but he'll make a hand, once he's sober. Looks like a deserter."

Matthew jerked his head. "All right. Anything else?"

"Gentleman to see you, sir. Graham White."

"I'll see him." He looked at his watch. "Thirty minutes?"

"Right, sir."

The seaman left and Matthew, for a minute, was alone. Old men, boys, Army deserters—Lord, what a crew! Once it had been a mark of distinction to sail on Matthew Steel's ship. But few men would go to sea now, with better paying employment ashore; and even if that were not the case, the better seamen would not appear at Steel's ship now and ask to be signed. The South Street grapevine had been thorough. Matthew Steel was no longer its hero. There had been rumors that there was heated talk—even petitions, in the capital to force Matthew to give up his ships to the government, but Matthew had discounted them, for no actual pressure had yet been brought to bear. He presumed the government could commandeer his vessels if it wished; but likely there would be warning first. Perhaps Graham White brought that warning.

Matthew stood as the older man entered and he waited until Graham White offered his hand. Matthew had learned in the last week not to be the first to offer his hand, even to men who did business with him. It was too apt to be refused. But now Mr. White extended his as he had always done and Matthew clasped it and pushed a chair toward him.

"I'm on my usual errand, Captain Steel," Mr. White said easily. "I'll make it brief," he promised. "We are in need of information—in greater need now than ever before. The leaders of both sides, both Federals and Rebels, are sending dozens of men to Europe to gather information and to act as propagandists to attempt to influence public opinion and government policies there. No doubt you carry some of them as passengers. It seems that many men in the government are sending their own private informants abroad. Unfortunately, even in Washington, our leaders are not all of one mind. There are many different opinions on policy abroad, and of course it is charged that President Lincoln's foreign policy has not crystallized, and no one knows exactly what will happen next."

Matthew nodded. The Rebels were ahead of the Federals on that score, too. Newspapers revealed that already brilliant Rebel leaders were in England, France and Spain, attempting, with considerable success, to win support of government leaders.

"Why come to me, Mr. White?" Matthew said bluntly.

Graham White met his bold stare. "One reason, Captain Steel, is that your previous reports have been candid and honest. Another is that you are a keen observer—if you choose to be. The third, and most important, is that you seem to be more or less unbiased—at least at the moment. I believe that your reports of the attitudes in England will not be colored by wishful thinking. We can send many zealous patriots abroad. But they are apt, despite themselves, to see and hear only things favorable to the Union. I do not believe that you will sugar-coat any news you might gather, to make it palatable to the North. Am I not correct?"

Graham White was smiling and Matthew laughed shortly. Then White looked beyond Matthew at a chart on the wall and his face was expressionless. "We are prepared to pay for your services," he said, courteously.

For some reason Matthew was angered. He stood up and the older man rose, too. White looked at Matthew Steel's jutting chin and waited.

"All right," Matthew said finally. "I guess we understand one another."

Without haste Graham White left the ship. On the pier he paused. It was always a thrill to see a great ship leave the dock, he thought, and he waited for the music that was sure to come.

He stepped back out of the way of the crowds, waiting. For just a moment, he recalled, when he offered to pay him, Matthew Steel almost refused. Graham White smiled. If he hired the man to gather information for him, it was another step toward his eventual conversion to the Union cause. It would be easy enough to check the truth of his reports—but Graham White had no doubt of Matthew Steel's honesty. As long as Matthew sailed under the Stars and Stripes he would not betray the flag. It was White's job to keep Matthew sailing under the Stars and Stripes.

Graham White had sought this assignment. He had seen the first crack in Matthew's armor when he had promised him payment for his aid to the Union. Play on that string a little more, he thought, and the man will begin to protest his loyalty. There were many men of value to the North who were yet to be convinced. The President, through cautious, considered moves, was trying to influence large groups of them at once to rally behind the flag, and gradually he was succeeding, for the Northern front was stronger now than it had been only a few weeks ago. The government also was attempting to win the support of entire nations. It was all part of the giant plan for ending the Rebellion; and some men, like Matthew Steel, must be won singly. It took patience, but it was worth it, White believed, and voluntarily, Matthew Steel could be of greatest value. For this reason he had asked that no pressure be brought upon Captain Steel officially, and that his ships not be seized until all else failed.

The chantey had at last begun and Graham White stood still, listening. He had seen many ships sail, in his years of service on the waterfront. But this time there seemed something lacking. There was no easy, light-hearted lilt to the sailors' voices. A few more years, Mr. White mused regretfully, and there would be no chanteys at all on the waterfront. The rhythm of the old songs meant to lighten the labors of men would be lost forever, along with the white sails that harnessed the winds.

Mr. White sighed, and watched the *Loyalty,* easing from her berth. It seemed that even this was the beginning of the end of the chantey, for this song was more a lament than a prelude to roaming. And then he realized what was missing in the song that was sending the *Loyalty* on her way. Matthew Steel's rich, strong voice was absent. For the first time he was not telling South Street good-by with a laugh and a song, with a rakish tilt to his cap and a gay wave of his hand.

White looked about him, expecting the usual South Street faces there to tell the *Loyalty* good-by. But the people on the pier were unfamiliar, well-dressed friends and relatives of the paying passengers, not the South Street people who had always before gathered to wish Matthew Steel Godspeed. Where were Old Dan and Patrick Draddy and Mrs. Doughty, and Hite and Morton from the Cock and Bull? Where was Lexie, and why was Cromwell, the carver, not there to look with admiring eyes on the *Loyalty's* figurehead, whose beauty was still unchallenged?

None of them had come to Pier 23 to watch the *Loyalty* sail.

CHAPTER V

THE FORECASTLE of the *Loyalty* was filled with ill-smelling, ill-assorted men who seemed to speak all languages but English. Cass, lying sick and miserable in a narrow bunk, opened his eyes to them and closed them at once, appalled at what he saw. The lantern swung easily and sickeningly with the rhythmic motion of the ship, shedding only a small sickly circle of light; the tiny space allotted each seaman was crammed with blankets and seabags and the hulks of the men themselves. The sober realization that he had condemned himself to two weeks of this, before he could set foot on land again, turned Cass' stomach. The air was foul; the close confinement was worse than any jail, for this cell was not still. It moved with the vessel and the creaks and moans of straining timbers and the unfamiliar damp, the fishy, salty, waterfront odor, hung heavily in every corner and seemed to permeate his clothing and make him one with his unwashed shipmates.

Any illusions Cass might have had about the color and romance of sea-roving were forgotten now in his discomfort and disgust. The impulse to flee that had driven him to Matthew Steel's ship had faded; he longed bitterly to be back in his own room at home. And then he remembered the faces of his father and his sisters and again he shrank from them. But when he opened his eyes again and saw the beady, black eyes of a Liverpool seaman bending over him curiously, noticed the bearded, ferret-like face peering at him, he turned his face away and gave himself over to misery.

The Englishman spoke to him but Cass heard him only dimly and did not answer. The man tugged at him and Cass rolled over and jerked himself away.

"Cap'n's orders, boy," the seaman was saying cheerfully.

"Tell him to go to hell," Cass answered.

There was a moment's silence, and then the man moved away and Cass had a moment's respite. But not for long. He had signed aboard Steel's ship as seaman and a seaman he became. Under the eye of the mate the men worked swiftly. Cass was hauled unceremoniously from his bunk. On the deck the last fumes of the wedding champagne were washed away from him by bucketfuls of stinging sea water. And Cass, sobered and shaky, found himself eased into place, one of a team of working men.

His stomach refused the ship's rations at first and weakness succeeded nausea. His hands bled from rope burns and his back ached from unaccustomed labor and the muscles of his arms and legs felt as though they had been thoroughly beaten by mallets. When he crawled back to his bunk he found that the last of the bottle of whisky which he had depended upon for comfort had mysteriously disappeared and only fatigue was left to dull him to the discomfort of his quarters. He lay, venting his rage in hate for Matthew Steel, for the ship's four officers, for the men who were jammed into the crew's quarters with him.

But within a few days Cass began to eat, and his skin, raw from wind and sun and spray, began to darken. He worked doggedly, hating it all, watching from the corner of his eye for the appearance of Matthew Steel, determined that the man should not find him lacking in performance of his duties. His days were confused, divided into watches instead of days and nights; but now when he collapsed on his bunk and dragged his one blanket over him he slept as he never had slept before, regardless of the snores and grunts, wheezes and mumbles of the men about him.

Gradually, to Cass the men became individuals. There was a brawny, blond, young Englishman by name of Cannon from Manchester, slow to anger and slow to speech, who finally confided he was working his way back home, to visit his family and persuade his younger brothers to return to America with him. The man was quiet, good natured and likable; but he was certainly a fool, Cass thought, to return to a country embroiled in civil war.

In the far end of the crew's quarters was a small island, one man apart from the rest. The bunks on either side of him and above him were unoccupied, and he sat alone, ate alone, and seldom took part in any of the forecastle talk. The man's name was Webb—whether it was his first or last name Cass never learned—and he was black. But when an argument broke out, and it often did, Webb had only to rise and stand, his great bare arms and swelling biceps polished and glistening with sweat in the dim light—and order was restored. The white men in the *Loyalty's* crew might avoid Webb because he was a Negro; but they respected his strength.

There were a Portuguese, who often sang himself to sleep, and a Greek, dark-faced and sullen, who carried a knife in his belt, and whose language seemed mostly grunts; there were an Italian or two, and a gray-haired American, whose hacking cough punctuated the nights. There was an imbecilic hulk of man of doubtful ancestry, whose main job seemed to be to empty slops and polish brass work; and there were a score or more of others who came and went, indistinguishable one from the other.

Of them all, Webb interested Cass most. For Webb was a friend to all and his great strength eased the labors of weaker men, including Cass, when they were at work side by side. It was Webb whose big, black hands guided Cass' inexperienced ones in handling the ropes; it was Webb whose quick movements covered Cass' bungling and averted disasters; it was Webb who explained instructions and patiently demonstrated, until Cass understood. Webb's deep voice was like music, and when at last he came quietly into the crew's quarters and went to his own isolated corner and stretched his great body out to rest, Cass heard him sigh; and it seemed to Cass that the weariness of laborers all the world over were in the black man's patient sigh before he slept.

Cass saw Captain Steel only from a distance. Orders came through the ship's officers. Now and then he saw Steel on the deck, talking to a passenger. Cass judged the first-class passengers were businessmen and politicians. Only the steerage was not overcrowded. Coming back, Cannon said, the order would be reversed, steerage would be crowded and perhaps the more expensive quarters would go begging for occupants. It was always like that, Cannon said; immigrants coming to America.

The tension of war hung heavy over the ship. "It's those guns," Cannon volunteered. "If it weren't for the guns aboard we'd not be thinking of privateers."

There were practice drills at the guns and the men did not acquit themselves well. Of them all, Cannon and Webb were the best of the lot. But the *Loyalty*, with her present crew, would not be a formidable foe for any Rebel raider. Captain Steel, the mate said in disgust, might as well have saved himself the time and expense of arming the ship.

Every man aboard was glad at voyage's end. The ship came to anchor in the river and a river boat came out to remove passengers and crew. Cass, standing at the rail, watched the eager departures. This trip of the *Loyalty* had been monotonous, dangerous work. Pushing a ship back and forth across the Atlantic in wartime, with the perils of the sea multiplied by the danger from Rebel raiders, took endurance and stamina and courage.

Cass watched Cannon lower himself into the river boat. He was at home, he had some place to go, some place where he would be welcome. Webb, big and black, followed; he, too, knew this port well. Cass' tired young-old eyes left them and swept over the ship and he saw Matthew Steel, surrounded by a knot of men from the port. A new and grudging respect for the man stirred within Cass. Matthew Steel had endured the hardships of a seaman for many years, he had saved from his small wages, gambled, invested, learned, endured, and climbed, doggedly, up the ladder. No wonder the man was reluctant now to give up what he had earned. It seemed to Cass that Matthew's face had thinned and the lines about his mouth and eyes had deepened. Cass had not thought, before, that a man as flint-like as Captain Steel might suffer silently, too. But Cass had learned much on this voyage, and he was seeing many things for the first time. It had been a revelation to him to see what sweat and weariness thousands of men must endure for the sole, doubtful privilege of survival.

"Come with us, Blake?"

Cannon was calling to him and Cass brought his eyes back to his shipmates. A small, surprised smile twitched his lips and then he, too, went quickly down the ship's ladder to the waiting small boat.

[2]

MATTHEW saw Cass leave the *Loyalty* and he had a moment's anxiety. The boy was inexperienced in seaports and might well come to harm. The least he would do would be to get drunk again, and likely robbed. If he were lucky, some other member of the crew might haul him aboard at sailing time. But deliberately Matthew put Cass from his mind. He had plenty of work to do and he had no time to play nursemaid to Cass Blake. The young man's appearance on his ship had startled and irritated him. But he had signed on as seaman. There would be no coddling of a weakling aboard Matthew Steel's ship, no privileges because he bore the name of Blake.

Matthew was still burning with anger and disappointment at Loyalty's refusal of him and he was not unaffected by the change of sentiment toward him on South Street. But stubbornly he refused to permit either event to influence him and he hewed strictly to the line he had laid down for himself. To gather information for Graham White worked well with his own plans, for he must also study the sentiment of the English in regard to the war between the states if he were to guess the final outcome correctly.

Accordingly he wasted no time in handling his regular ship's affairs, and then decided that time spent in sampling British opinion would be well invested. He roamed the waterfront. He talked and listened to shipping men and merchants in Waterloo Inn, and he spent long evenings with former shipmates and old acquaintances in other nooks and crannies seldom frequented by foreigners. He visited business establishments uptown and talked to men in dignified, wood-paneled offices, and he sampled opinion in the city's homes as well. He was adept at leading questions, and he was careful in his summing up of the information he gathered.

It did not take a man trained in espionage to discover immediately that Liverpool was almost solidly Secessionist and that shipping and business circles, throughout England, were warmly pro-Southern. If Liverpool itself were a fair example of the sentiment of all England and of the English government, there was no question that the Rebels had the strong support of at least one foreign power.

Matthew checked and rechecked on his findings. Goods for export to the United States were piled high on the wharves and little of it was going out in American vessels. British freighters were having a field day and he saw many a familiar ship, formerly flying the Stars and Stripes, now displaying the British flag. Hundreds of American vessels, he learned, were being transferred to British and French registry. It was easy to see what the war between the states already was doing to America's merchant marine.

And British shipyards were humming. Shipbuilders on both sides of the Atlantic, apparently, had most to gain from the Rebellion. English yards were turning out ships new and improved in design—ships designed particularly for Rebel use, fast vessels designed for the shallow inlets and sounds and inner channels of the South; already an iron steamer, the *Bermuda,* had slipped out of an English shipyard and was in use by the Confederates, and a second large vessel, heavily loaded with munitions, was said to have followed the *Bermuda* to sea by only a few days. Foremost in negotiating contracts for these Confederate ships was a man named Bulloch, a brilliant Northerner, a New Yorker, who had cast his lot with the South.

Shipowners with whom Matthew had gambled in the past were openly gleeful now and they rubbed their hands together in anticipation, predicting the English-built ships were faster and more rugged than any American ship afloat. Matthew baited them and listened and made notes in his journal aboard the *Loyalty.*

"Recognition of the South by England might well be not far off," Matthew wrote thoughtfully. "England has everything to gain by the war; war profits—and permanent division of the Union. The upper classes also see in democracy a threat to their way of life and find more in common with Southern land-owners. Many speeches in Parliament are strongly pro-Southern. It is evident that Napoleon of France is also watching the struggle greedily and makes every attempt to discredit democracy as a form of government. France, Britain and Spain are preparing to invade Mexico—ostensibly to collect their debts. Such an invasion is, of course, a direct violation of the Monroe Doctrine. But it is as Captain Scripliff said: it is a good time for these European powers to return to get another foothold on the American continent. From Mexico it would be but a step for France to reannex the Louisiana territory. All signs in England—so far—point to strong Southern support. . . . Looking back over the notes I made after my talks with Scripliff, I wonder, perhaps, if the Russians do not understand the British and interpret their aims better than most Americans. . . .

"Britain is also preparing to send soldiers into Canada to gather on the northern border of the United States. Men say they are only replacements—but they have their tongues in their cheeks when they say it. . . .

"Cotton prices are climbing. The mills are already slowing and merchants predict that unless the sea-lanes are kept open to the cotton ports of the United States the mills will soon stop entirely and suffering will be acute. They believe unemployment both in England and France will bring about a demand by the people for a recognition of the Confederacy. Districts like Manchester and Lancashire, Birmingham, Rochdale and Bradford will feel the pinch when the mills close."

If all these rumors proved true, Matthew mused, and they seemed well founded, if British and French troops were massed on both borders, the North would be squeezed in a giant pincers that might end the conflict soon, and on terms dictated by the Confederacy. Only master diplomats who could persuade the European powers not to recognize the Confederacy, an unbreakable chain of ships that would firmly isolate the South from European munition makers, and an Army that could meet the Rebels and vanquish them on land, could save the United States from permanent division.

Summing it up, it looked to Matthew like an almost hopeless cause for the Union. In this first year of war, the Rebels had every advantage. Humming shipyards, heated, biased speeches in Parliament, newspaper reports, statements from Napoleon, the demand for cotton, the prosperity that came with the new monopoly of Southern markets and the new dealings in materials of war, the removal of American ships from the world trade marts, all spoke for a Southern victory in the diplomatic war in Europe. Southern propagandists declared that not slavery, but the tariff, was the issue. And defeats of the Federal Army at Wilson's Creek in Missouri and the rout of the Federals at Ball's Bluff, Virginia, were followed by an immediate spurt of pro-Southern articles in the British press.

On the opposite side of the ledger, however, Matthew listed four things. First, there were rumbles of trouble in Poland, between Russia and England and France. It was the ever-present, age-old problem, but the kettle was boiling again and he recalled Captain Scripliff's prediction of another war; a war in Poland might occupy Britain and France so they would take no active part in the Rebellion in the United States. Surely the European powers did not desire more than one war at a time—any more than did the United States. Secondly, there was Russia's frank friendliness to the Federal government. Russians had always believed in a strong United States as a curb to over-ambitious Britain, her old-time enemy. Any increase in British strength, on land or sea, periled Russia. If the United States were divided into two important nations, or two American nations and a flock of British, French and Spanish protectorates, Russia would stand alone against Britain in future conflicts. Russia, Matthew believed, would stand by the North, and news dispatches from Russia, reprinted in unfriendly English papers, supported this opinion. There was much talk of Alexander II liberating the serfs, and the Russian emancipation was heralded by all liberals the world over. It was considered another spiritual tie with the Free North of the United States, and parallels between the Great Emancipator of Russia, the Emperor Alexander II, and President Lincoln were drawn.

Third, there were the surprisingly successful operations of the United States Navy. Forts Hatteras and Clark on the North Carolina coast had been taken in the first Federal victory of the war and there were signs of increased effectiveness of the blockade. And fourth, there was also in England a liberal group, laborers and intellectuals, who supported the Union cause. They had fewer spokesmen and fewer publications to air their views. But a word here and there to Matthew had revealed a strong undercurrent that excited his curiosity.

It was hardly conceivable, however, Matthew thought, that the workers of England, who stood to suffer most from the cotton shortage, would long support the North. To judge for himself how strong were the sentiments of the laboring class, Matthew decided to attend a workers' meeting in Manchester.

He had two surprises.

He stood on the fringe of the crowd, silently studying the speaker and the reaction of the audience. The vehemence with which the leader spoke in passionate defense of the Union, and the huge crowd's intense concentration and low rumbles of approval amazed him.

America, the speaker said, was the hope of the workers' world. In America, a laborer had a chance to become a capitalist. Free enterprise, freedom of speech, freedom of religion, a government of the people and by the people—where a workingman's vote was as good as a millionaire's; America, where there was a chance for all. The Union stood for freedom, the speaker said, the South for slavery. It was the Rebellion of the Southern landowners which was causing the shortage of cotton and the specter of hardship and starvation hovering over workers in England. Division of the Union would not mean more cotton for England. Only the preservation of the Union, the preservation of democracy in the United States was the salvation for English workers—for workers the world over. Democracy threatened the way of life of English aristocrats. But it was the hope of the world for the common people. It must be defended.

The deadly seriousness on the faces of these men and women, frugal, work-hardened, was new to Matthew Steel. Many a man spoke, to add his bit to the resolve of England's workers. Abolish slavery, they urged, support the Union. Prepare to sacrifice, until the Rebellion in the United States could be ended and the flow of American products to English mills be resumed. Don't believe the propaganda of the gentry!

Listening, Matthew Steel frowned. There was something familiar to him in the faces of these people. It was the look on the faces of all workers the world over, men and women. He had been one of them for many years. Mary Steel had been one of them. Her small, gentle hands had been large-veined and the joints were knotted and her face had the same patient, tired lines. Matthew moved uncomfortably. He had not thought of his mother nor remembered her so vividly for a long time. He could see her plainly, as plainly as though she stood here beside him, slight and wiry and strong. She would have fitted easily into this group; her head would have nodded now and then in agreement.

But Mary Steel had been deluded. It was not American citizenship, but wealth, that made a man free. Matthew had discovered that. . . . He brought his attention back to the matter in hand.

Yes, the determination of these people was a surprise. Even if their beliefs were as mistaken as Mary Steel's, they were strong, and their influence on English policy would be hard to determine. It must not be discounted.

Matthew received his second shock when he glanced across the meeting hall and saw Cass Blake.

He had expected Cass to be dead drunk in some waterfront dive. But he was standing there on the edge of the crowd, listening intently, and his thin face was tense with strain. Cannon stood beside him. Cass, clean and shaven but plainly dressed, his eyes wide awake and intent, stood among the working men of England, listening to their impassioned speeches for preservation of American democracy and one inseparable American nation.

Matthew went back to his ship and incorporated in his report some of the statements of the English liberals. Cass Blake came quietly back to the vessel in time for sailing, and Webb and Cannon followed. They were only two days out from port when Matthew saw, through his glass, a British ship, and as their paths came closer together he saw British soldiers lining the rails. He knew where they were headed. The rumors that Britain was sending troops to Canada had proven correct.

Matthew, lowering his glass, trying to add this bit of concrete evidence to the information he had already gathered, and to weigh its effect on the Rebellion, noticed Cass Blake standing on the deck, and he also was staring at the British ship. He did not see Captain Steel, who passed close behind him. But Matthew heard Cass swearing under his breath.

[3]

IF MATTHEW STEEL was floundering, searching for truth, Cass Blake was searching, too. Aboard the ship Cass had worked with his hands for the first time in his life, and he had found in it a deep satisfaction. He had been awkward and inexperienced and ashamed of his ignorance and his lack of strength. He had learned from Cannon and Webb, the Negro. It was a new sensation to learn a new skill and he found unexpected pleasure in being one of a team of men. He was earning his own keep, without privileges accorded him because of wealth or background or the magic name of Thaddeus Blake. Cass' self-respect had been stripped from him at Bull Run. But little by little, in the ship and sea and the men with whom he worked, he began to find a tiny grain of confidence again.

The old Cass, cocky and arrogant, would not have shared quarters with a Negro; he would not have welcomed advice from an English seaman, son of a workman. But the new Cass was more malleable and receptive and he gratefully accepted Cannon's help and Webb's quiet friendliness in the spirit in which they were meant.

They asked him no questions. When men are reared in poverty and have seen much disease of mind and body, Cass reasoned, they accepted imperfections tolerantly. And they were good medicine for Cass Blake. They seemed even to find something in Cass which they liked—which surprised Cass, in his new humbleness. When Cannon turned from the river boat and spoke to him: "Come with us, Blake?" it was a short invitation but the most welcome Cass had ever received. He had accepted it gladly, surprised and pleased.

Visiting Liverpool and then Manchester with Cannon had been a revelation. Cass had met Cannon's two husky younger brothers and he had sat with them while Cannon extolled the advantages of America. Cannon pointed out to them the possibilities of making a comfortable living in New York, and, later on, of going West and taking up some land. There was no limit, he said, to how far a man could go in America. Listening silently, Cass learned more of his own country from these English workers than he had ever known before.

Cass met Cannon's girl, too. She was a pale-haired girl with a quick smile and there was eagerness in her eyes when Cannon talked of the United States. Cass watched Cannon's glance stray to her, all the while he told his brothers of the beauties and wonders of the United States.

They'd be coming, sure enough they'd be coming, just as soon as they could scrape a little money together. Times were going to be hard in the mill districts this winter, harder still a year from now, they prophesied; the mills would close if the war between the states continued. Some cotton was being held back by speculators, the young men said; the speculators would wait until people felt hunger before the cotton would come out of hiding. Then the mills would roll again for a little while. But people would manage, they guessed.

The brothers suggested they attend a liberals' meeting to hear speakers talk about the Rebellion in America. They were anxious to prove to Cass and to Cannon that they understood the issues involved and were heartily behind the Federals, too.

So Cass stood beside Cannon and his brothers. Like Matthew Steel, he looked at the faces about him and to him, too, they were strangely familiar. It was from these people—England's middle-class, that many Americans came, Cass told himself. That is why they seemed so familiar. There were blood ties between them and Americans, which only great strain could ever break. There was fortitude and endurance and courage in their faces—such as there must have been in those of the first colonists. Cass thought: "This is the heart of England, the conscience of England, and all the fine talk of the aristocrats cannot move them. These people will suffer when the mills close, but personal hardships will never make them falter in what they believe is right." Watching them, something within him that had been hurting him for a long time began to soften a little, to break up and dissolve and give him a little relief and a warm, new feeling of peace.

He listened intently to the speakers. The preservation of the Union, the preservation of Democracy—the hope of the world! He had heard those words before, passionate words, and it was Loyalty who had spoken them. He could close his eyes, here in this tense, crowded room, and see his sister again and hear her voice, and the hard thing within him continued to crumble and melt until it was almost gone. Here, among these people, steadfast in the face of sacrifice, he felt strong. Their eyes were wide open to the cost, they were looking toward the United States to uphold the dreams of freedom-loving people throughout the world. They talked of it without self-consciousness. The South was for bondage, the speaker said, the North for freedom.

The meeting ended on a prayer. "God bless and strengthen the North. Give victory to their arms!" And Cass found his own lips moving with a thousand others in the rumbling "Amen."

Liverpool was a notorious Secessionist hole, the Cannon brothers warned him comfortably, talking to him as to one of themselves. There was much talk about immediate war between England and the United States over the Trent affair. But John Bright and Richard Cobden and W. E. Forster, the great liberal leaders, would fight such a move. It was inconceivable that English workers would support a war that would uphold slavery.

Cass, heading back toward South Street aboard Steel's ship, turned the subject over in his mind. One thing greatly troubled him. President Lincoln had said time and again that his purpose was to preserve the Union and uphold the Constitution. But he had not promised freedom to the slaves. And if the issue were not slavery, then the great English middle-class would not long curb the government and prevent British recognition of the Confederacy.

The immigrants aboard the *Loyalty* had hope in their faces and hope in their hearts, too. Cass, torn with worry and the birth of understanding, watched them covertly. They had been coming in a steady stream, as long as ships had been sailing back and forth across the Atlantic. Such a faith as these people had in the United States must be preserved. It was such a simple faith. America, to them, meant freedom.

But it could not all come at once, Cass thought uneasily. The ending of the Rebellion must come first, and then the gradual emancipation of the slaves. The patient man in the White House cautioned Abolitionists and Radicals to make haste slowly. He wanted to free the slaves gradually and compensate their owners, and prepare a colony or a homeland for the freed men. The President knew that a legislative act or a proclamation would not necessarily mean freedom. For instance, Cass considered, Webb, born a slave, had bought his freedom—but he was not truly free, nor had he achieved equaliy. It will take time and work, Cass thought.

Cass wanted to fight. He wanted to give everything he had in defense of the flag and all it stood for. He knew, now, what it was all about, even though no single issue was as yet clear-cut. They were all interwoven, so you could not untangle them and say, "This is the reason for the war—this is the cause of the Rebellion—this is the issue." They all overlapped, a way of life, the Union, emancipation, equality of opportunity, and the United States flag, the symbol of freedom to the little people of the world.

But Cass still had a private war to win. At the workers' meeting the strength he needed had almost come to him. But when he was alone the knot inside hardened again and paralyzed his will. It was even worse to bear now when he had something concrete and great to fight for and it was clearly before his eyes each day in the pathetically hopeful faces in steerage. But when he thought of the battlefield again the old horror came back; men with their limbs shot away, men lying still and watching themselves bleed to death; a doctor testing a knife on his thumb before an amputation; disease and filth and thirst, noise and exhaustion and the cartridge taste . . .

The knot inside him, which had begun to break a little when he heard the final prayer at the meeting in Manchester, was cowardice and he had not yet conquered it. *I'll keep on sailing on the Loyalty,* he decided. *I'll go back to England again, to Manchester and Lancashire and Rochdale and London, and perhaps somewhere, among the workers, I'll find the courage I need to fight again.*

[4]

GLOOM hung over the North like a heavy cloud-bank throughout the long months of 1862. Hopes rose with minor victories, plunged with great defeats. Men talked loudly and optimistically as Federal military leaders, McDowell, Pope, Hooker and Burnside took the spotlight, and they waited for a hero to emerge; and, with their failures, hope ebbed again. The Southern tide was coming in, and it seemed that nothing the Northern armies could do could turn it. McClellan failed in the Virginia peninsula in the Battles of the Seven Days; Pope took defeat in the Second Battle of Bull Run. The armies were improving, authorities said; McClellan's men bore little resemblance to the early volunteers who had fought at the first Bull Run. But that was not enough. The expedition of France, Britain and Spain into Mexico materialized and the North grew tense. The threat of intervention by England grew with each Southern victory, and was evidenced by the massing of English troops on the Canadian border. Matthew Steel and Cass Blake saw increasing evidence of it as they crossed and recrossed the Atlantic, wondering, each time they arrived in England, if they would be greeted by the news of a declaration of war between the two countries, or would hear of a truce and attempt at compromise, or a Southern victory which would end the war.

Ship after ship, built in British yards by British workers, eluded the authorities, who were profuse in their regrets, and slipped out to sea to join the increasing fleet of Rebel raiders. By New Year's Day, 1862, it was reported that one raider alone had sunk sixteen Northern vessels; and each month, as the *Loyalty* gingerly felt her way through the hostile waters of the Atlantic, the danger increased.

Arsenals were busy in England. Blockade runners were thick; in May cotton reached its peak in price—thirteen pence per pound. And in England and in France mills slowed and finally ground to a complete stop, and hunger and poverty moved into the mill districts.

The passenger list of the *Loyalty* on her return trips to America swelled. Men, women and children clamored for passage. They did not care that the United States was ravished by war; men had heard of the bounty money for volunteer fighters for the Union. Lincoln had called for hundreds of thousands of men; the ranks of laboring men were depleted as hundreds laid down their tools and picked up guns. There was work for everyone and more, in the United States, and those who did not work could fight. The specter of famine hovered over the textile workers in England and in France and more and more of them turned their faces westward. "Go to America or upon the parish," they told one another.

By midsummer, England's aristocratic leaders stated frankly that the success of the Southern states was a certainty. Jefferson Davis, they said, and other Southerners, had built an army; they were also making a navy. And they had, apparently, made a nation. France urged England to recognition of the Confederates, suggesting that Southern victories entitled them to it. And, pointing to the suffering in the manufacturing districts, leaders urged intervention in favor of the South, to bring prosperity at once to districts full of privation.

The only things to ease the burden on Northern hearts during those dark months were the Navy's success in opening the cotton port of New Orleans, the good news of the campaigns in the West, and the amazing fortitude of the workers of England, which not even starvation could break.

But Matthew and Cass, too, began to catch tiny cracks of suspicion appearing in the workers' speeches. Southern propagandists, increasingly bold with each new victory, declared that slavery was not an issue. To suffer and starve for freedom for slaves was one thing; to suffer only for the perpetuation of the North's economic stranglehold on the South was another.

Matthew incorporated this opinion in every report he made to Graham White. He harped on this theme stubbornly; if the support of England's suffering workers was to be kept—and that support was vitally essential to the battered North—they must be assured that freedom for all men was the Union's aim.

Matthew, keeping his ear to the ground in England, watching headlines and reading reports after defeats of the Northern Army, continued to see increasing evidence of the Navy's growing strength. The fleet was an ill-assorted one, for the Navy had pressed into service every likely vessel. Yankee ingenuity had been taxed to build a fleet, for supplies in the navy yards had been allowed to dwindle to a dangerous point before the war began. Government machine shops were small and without adequate tools and expert mechanics could not be made of inexperienced laborers overnight. Poor workmanship and poor materials would weaken the fleet. But merchants' yards and thousands of civilians had rallied behind the government and little by little the United States Navy was swelling and strengthening and was making its new power felt. If foreign intervention could be delayed long enough, the great productive power of free men might overwhelm the Confederates and their wealthy British aides; a solid wall of ships would cut off the Rebels from outside help and hold the South in a grip it could not break. And the most brilliant Southern leaders and finest armies could not continue to win victories without munitions and supplies.

The *Messenger* had been long delayed in leaving San Francisco. Slow repairs and difficulties of recruiting a crew had held Jules Descase in port over long. This word, awaiting Matthew Steel in his office at his South Street warehouse, caused him great concern. The Confederate privateer *Alabama* was prowling the sea-lanes; the notorious *Florida* was taking high toll of American merchantmen. If Jules Descase's chances of a safe voyage around the Horn were slim in the winter of 1861, the odds against him increased a hundred-fold six months later.

In the first week of September Loyalty returned from one of her periodic trips to Washington. It was late at night when she let herself into the quiet house. She used her own latchkey. The shortage of servants had been felt in the Blake household.

Loyalty was so weary her flesh felt numb and her mind was dulled. Her work was a link between the U.S. Sanitary Commission offices in Washington and the women volunteers in New York. The horrors of the sights she had witnessed in the capital, after the Second Bull Run, had been their own anaesthetic. She was used to such sights now. But the men who were hauled back to the capital after Second Bull Run had brought back to her too clearly her first experience in Alexandria. She heard the same mutterings—the fight had been over the same terrain, the same railroads had been the prize. Almost involuntarily she had looked for Cass among the wounded, for it seemed to her the miracle of evil history repeating itself. But there was no Cass and no Captain Steel to come to her aid. This time she had made the railroad trip alone, except for the convalescents she was helping to move to hospitals in the Northern cities.

She set her little portmanteau on one of the great carved chairs of the familiar hallway and glanced at the clock. It was after eleven. A light shone from the library and she approached it quietly. Thaddeus sat alone and he looked up from his desk as she entered.

She dropped into a chair and pulled the little Shepherdess hat from her head. She managed a little smile for Thaddeus.

"You are very late, Loyalty."

"The train was late. And then we had a dozen men to settle in the hospitals first."

"A dozen? Last time you accompanied only five."

"We needed their beds in Washington." Her lips firmed. "Father—it's much worse than the papers report. It is the worst it has yet been. There were hundreds, thousands, perhaps tens of thousands wounded at Bull Run. Every available building, churches, the College, even the halls and rotunda of the Capitol, are being used to house the wounded. And their needs are enormous! They have nothing—not enough chloroform, not enough morphine, not enough sheets or bandages or lint. Surgeons are working everywhere, under the most appalling conditions of filth; and corpses are prepared for burial out in the open, on vacant lots, where anyone—including children—may see. There aren't enough nurses, the convalescents who were helping are not strong enough to do much. And there seem as many suffering with disease as with wounds. There is a shortage of smallpox vaccine and malaria is gaining. Father, the people do not know how bad it is—if they did, not a man or woman in the North could sleep! The capital is again in danger, and what grave danger! The wounded are still coming in—by wagon, and railroad and river steamer, and there is no place prepared for them, no place to put them, nothing with which to treat them. They are grateful for any help, those poor, suffering souls!"

She leaned her head against the back of her chair and closed her eyes. "They wouldn't let me stay," she finished wearily. "They said I must come back and try to get more help—contributions, supplies. Father, the men themselves say that Pope had a hundred thousand men at Bull Run and the Rebels only about half that number—and yet Pope failed. What is to be the end of it? And these men were not green troops—they were seasoned fighters. But the soldiers themselves are losing heart, with defeat following defeat, and there are said to be many desertions. And the dead—they are still moving them from the battlefield, trying to identify them. Father—what is going to happen to us?"

Thaddeus took a deep breath. "I don't know, Loyalty," he said. "I declare, I don't know. I think the people should be told the truth—the entire, terrible truth. Perhaps it would arouse them to action. But others think that the truth would discourage them and start a great drive for a compromise, and cause even more dissension, for Lincoln will never compromise—never! If we can just hang on, surely it's bound to turn, in a little while, if only we can avoid foreign intervention. In the West—"

Suddenly, through the night quiet, the doorbell pealed. The chill of fear swept over her as she ran down the hallway and threw open the door and faced Serena.

Serena had a dark cloak over her white dress. She stood like a sleepwalker, looking at her sister, her uncovered, golden hair glinting in the faint light from the street lamp behind her. Loyalty put her arms around her and drew her inside.

"James?" Loyalty half-whispered. Serena's head nodded. She stared at Loyalty, her eyes blank, her lips quiet. She held a piece of paper in her cold fingers and Loyalty pried it loose from them, gently and spread it out and held it to the gaslight.

James was one of the fourteen thousand Union men to fall at Second Bull Run.

Thaddeus' arms encircled his elder daughter. Loyalty stood with the paper in her hand, staring at it. That's the second man Bull Run has taken from us, Loyalty whispered. Cass was the first.

[5]

THERE were no stars but the wind was fresh and strong with a hint of rain in it. The *Loyalty* skimmed the water easily, her great sails spread to the wind, and she steered with only a touch of Matthew's fingers. The ship seemed alone and safe and unthreatened in her own natural element; the watch was alert and the ship was quiet, and she was straight on her course. The passengers slept, for the ship kept an even, rhythmic motion, with no pitching or rolling. Matthew could feel the great ship's perfect balance beneath his feet, feel her power in her speed, feel her perfection of design in the way she cut the waves and her quick response to his will. Wooden sailing ships were giving way to steamships clad with iron; but there would never be another ship like the *Loyalty*.

He had been unable to sleep tonight and now, near dawn, had come to take the wheel himself. It used to bring him peace, to get the feel of his ship, alone and in the night, and he was in need of peace. But of late there was little rest for him. The hundred-odd souls aboard were his responsibility. He found it difficult, these nights, to sleep, knowing these waters were infested with privateers. And tonight his feeling of danger was unreasonably acute.

He had been very fortunate so far. But his mathematical mind had figured the chances on the *Loyalty* staying afloat; and it was possible but not probable that she should continue shuttling back and forth along these sea-lanes much longer without encountering a predatory Rebel. The *Loyalty* would be a rich prize; and, once captured, she might make a blockade runner or privateer herself. A hundred-and-fifty-pounder or an eleven-inch gun or both could make the *Loyalty* an unpleasant adversary even for a ship mounting an entire broadside of the light cannon of the old style of armament. And the *Loyalty* could take the hundred-and-fifty-pounder well.

Suddenly Matthew grinned. To get the most from the *Loyalty*, however, the Rebels would have to take her master with her. No one knew the ship as he did; she might respond poorly to another. And of course she was not as easily maneuvered, not as fast in some weathers, as a steam-driven vessel. It was on long, round-the-world hauls, in all kinds of weather, in all zones and seasons, that the *Loyalty* ran up a magnificent, over-all record. In short, sharp engagements, in darting runs, she would be at a disadvantage. She had not been built for such work. She had been built to roam, and to exchange one nation's treasures for another's. He must not let his love for his ship magnify her virtues. . . . Well, then, a privateer, not wanting the *Loyalty* as a prize, would strike to sink or burn her.

But tonight there was nothing to mar the peace. If only it could go on like this, Matthew thought, without sea prowlers, if only a man could go about his work trading, shipping, hauling passengers, with a home to go to and people who loved him waiting for him at the end of a voyage. A man could ask for no better life than that. As always, his thoughts went back to Loyalty Blake. If she were waiting for him at journey's end, no danger would matter. Time had done little to ease his longing for her. Lately he had become victim to black moods new to him, and periods of indecision disturbed him greatly. His need for Loyalty gnawed at him like a canker and he tortured himself with memories of her and doubt for his future nagged him, too.

He was prepared for bad news concerning the *Messenger* when he arrived in New York again, for the ship was long overdue. He was glad luck had permitted him to make this many successful Atlantic crossings, for he would have need of this year's profits if the *Messenger* had come to harm. It was also time he had a message from the *Comet*. His mind touched these things, went on. The war news was bad for the North. Black despond had settled over the United States. Men were calling for an investigation into the conduct of the war, were clamoring for a military leader who could win a victory, and Southerners were jubilant.

Perhaps the sensible thing to do was to cast his lot with the Rebels. But if he turned Confederate he'd be exchanging the danger from raiders only for the danger from the United States Navy—no pleasant thought. Nevertheless, it looked as if he'd have to change, if he were going to be on the side of the final victor, as he had promised himself he would be.

Yet he hesitated. Perhaps it was his constant exposure to the workers of England, for he had attended the workers' meetings as religiously as he had talked with the Southern sympathizers of Liverpool and London. It was still a paradox to him that those who suffered most from the war in the United States were the Union's staunchest supporters abroad. In any event, it disturbed him, now when the North's hopes were darkest, that he found himself listening more sympathetically to the speeches of the liberals. He had promised himself to keep out of this conflict, to use it only as a means to further his own ends. Sentiment ought not to cloud a man's common sense.

But at the last meeting he had attended the speech might have been written by Loyalty. It had made him think of her longingly, with deep desire. The familiar ring to the words of the workers had moved him and he realized that he had not given Loyalty full credit for her sincerity or her knowledge. He had been a fool, he thought, to have left her so abruptly, in anger at being crossed. If he had stayed, listened to her, tried to understand, they might have come to some common meeting ground. But his emotions had been too close to the surface where she was concerned. He had been furious that politics should enter into their relationship. He was beginning, very slowly now, to see also that she was right in her refusal of him. There could have been no lasting happiness between them, regardless of the great strength of their love, if they held different ideologies and with war over those beliefs raging throughout the nation and the waters which bordered it. Perfect understanding was essential between them, or the very power of their love would have destroyed them. Loyalty had been wiser than he knew.

The rain was coming in great soft blobs like an early snow. Matthew peered into the darkness and about him, on the ship, other watchful men squinted into the dusky blanket of old night. There were no lights, nothing in the way of the *Loyalty*. She would make good time on this crossing, never impeded by darkness. The *Loyalty* was alone on the sea, roughening now, and the rain, suddenly serious, sharp and slanting and fierce, made tiny knife thrusts at the ship.

But suddenly Matthew knew the *Loyalty* was not alone. It might have been a sound, a smell, a different air current as a ship neared or passed. Whatever it was, he trusted the instinctive warning completely, for that warning had saved him before when he had skirted too close to a reef, or when a bullet or a blow had been aimed his way. He followed that impulse for caution now, and he whistled, sharp and clear, knowing there was some threat out there in the darkness. His men came running, bewildered, and Matthew turned the wheel over to an officer and reached for his glass, wishing for the dawn. Light would come at any moment—enough to outline the danger out there in the wind and rain. He knew the threat was there; he questioned only the direction from which the attack would come.

"Sound the alarm."

He stood at the rail, trying to penetrate the darkness, listening with every nerve, feeling, with every inch of his body's surface. In the east there was a streak of light and against it he knew the *Loyalty's* sails gleamed white. He held his breath. The ship's rattle sounded, jarring his men from sleep.

And then the raider struck. One minute the *Loyalty* was alone in the night. And the next the raider separated itself from the darkness and loomed huge and ugly, almost alongside. She seemed to come out of the night or up from the sea, phantomlike, a nightmare materializing. There was a thunderclap; a sharp crack, a smell of smoke and powder and the *Loyalty* seemed to hesitate, and then to plunge, and to shudder from stem to stern.

In the forecastle the demoniac clattering of the hand rattle had brought the men rolling out of their berths. Cass heard it, through the thick cotton-wool of sleep, and then he was awake, sitting up, his teeth chattering with nervous excitement, and he was paralyzed for a moment, unable to move. That sound—God, how it brought back Bull Run! There were lanterns like fire-flies, and rushing bodies and curses, and the forecastle emptied. Webb went by him, shirtless, the muscles across his black back shining; Cannon was gone before him, and the other men, until Cass was alone, in his berth, shaking.

The ship paused, shivered, plunged on again, and again there was the thunderclap. Cass forced himself to the edge of his bed, shoving the blanket from him, but it seemed to curl around his legs and cling to him, holding him back. He reached for his trousers and pulled them on, and he tried to make himself stand. He could not. His hands froze, clinging to the sides of the bunk, and they were like the fingers of a corpse, rigid and clamped. There was bedlam from above him; the ship lurched, turning, he heard another sound—the *Loyalty* was returning fire. Cass should be there, at his gun station, and he knew it, and he could not force himself to get up out of his bunk. If I drown here, he thought, if water starts pouring in through the hatchway—

The thought terrified him. Drowning, like a rat in a trap, was worse than being on deck, where he might, at least, have a chance. His fingers loosened and he staggered to his feet. His teeth were playing a tattoo; but he wanted to run—out of this underwater trap, away from this devilish cacophony; the powder smell came thickly to his nostrils and made his stomach cramp and twist. His heart pounded so violently it seemed it would burst from his body and his blood beat in his ears and he heard his own voice, whimpering. He moved, somehow, out of the forecastle, he gained the deck, and he was thrown flat on his face as the ship changed course, abrupt, sharp, a movement that would have strained and broken a less agile craft; the deck came up to meet him and slapped him in the face and for a minute he lay still and he felt himself sliding and he clutched for something to stop him. His hand caught a rope, and he raised himself, bruised and bleeding, and his wild eyes took in the scene about him.

The raider was close, very close, almost on top of them. She was firing but the *Loyalty's* men were returning every shot. Matthew Steel stood among them, his feet wide apart, his voice shouting orders, and Cass could see Webb and Cannon at the guns, where he should have been. Weakly, he began to sidle his way toward his post, shamed, scared, his stomach sick, his head throbbing wildly, the hot, sticky feeling of blood dribbling from the small cut on his forehead. As Cass watched, the distance between the *Loyalty* and the raider widened a little. Steel's men were straining at the ropes, shifting the great ship's sails, and while Cass stood, unable to make his feet move toward his post at the gun, the ship seemed to give a little leap ahead. He saw Matthew lift his hand and bring it down in sharp signal and the guns of the *Loyalty* barked again.

The light was stronger now and the raider a little farther away. Cass stared at it, fascinated, and its flag caught his eye. It was the Union Jack. Cass made a noise somewhere down in his chest, an exclamation of surprise and fury. He started forward and found relief in action. "Why, they can't do that," he said aloud, wonderingly. "They can't do that!" He stumbled on, and a crash, deafening and horrible, threw him again to the deck. He heard the men shout and he raised his head and saw a mast cracking, toppling, falling with a sickening, tearing sound, taking ropes and canvas with it. He clambered to his feet and ran a few steps, still watching the raider, unable to drag his eyes away, and he saw the Union Jack descending, rapidly, disappearing into the muddled darkness of the ship itself. The distance between them still widened, the raider itself pulling away. The light swelled. And then, as if by magic, another flag flew above the privateer. It was of the familiar colors, red, white and blue, but in a new pattern—that of the Confederacy.

Cass hunched over, to still the violent cramping of his stomach. He inched his way through the men, through the debris, he even managed to run a little, toward his post.

Cass smelt it first, and then he heard it—above the roar of the sea and all the racket of the laboring ship, as the thunder of the guns died, he smelt the smoke, and then he heard the crackling of a fierce fire. And right on top of it, crowding the sound of the flames, he heard the screams.

Cass did not wait for Matthew Steel's shout. He was ahead of the rest, straight toward the companionway. Down there in the bowels of the ship were steerage passengers, and a wall of flame was between them and the deck. He forgot the raider. He forgot the guns behind him, where he should have been; he even forgot the tightness of his stomach. There were only the screams of the trapped passengers aboard the *Loyalty,* there were the flames, and there was the triumphant, tardy, brazen ascent of the Confederate flag on the ship that had struck and run. It seemed to Cass that the imprint of the Confederate flag on the privateer had been burned on his eyeballs, and it was there now, in the flames that licked at the companionway. Anger rose in Cass, a thick, hot wave of it. His arms began to move, his hands were quick, he was beating at the flames with his bare hands. The smoke choked him and he raised his head and turned and ran back a step or two and drew deep into his smarting lungs a full, life-giving breath of air. A seaman was running toward him and he had a bag in his hands, wet and dripping with salt water, and Cass grabbed it and went again into the companionway and began beating at the licking flames. There were others crowding behind him now, passing him weapons—water, sacks, an ax; Cass hacked and fought and worked like a hundred men, and the flames licked at him while he beat his way through the entranceway to the panic stricken passengers beyond.

After a long time the smoke died, the clouds broke. The *Loyalty* lay upon the sea, her deck scarred and charred, one mast shot away. The sun played upon her mercilessly, throwing her wounds into bold relief. The stench of ashes still hung over her, and smoke and powder, but she was still afloat.

Passengers milled about the deck, gathered in little groups, scanning the horizon anxiously, chattering, repeating themselves in the way of all people after a sudden tragedy, a little important, now that the danger was past, of their part in it; still shivering in remembrance, sobered a little by their narrow brush with death, fearful of another stab by the enemy. But the seas, calm again, showed no sails nor smoke. Again the *Loyalty* was alone, and only her scars and those of her men showed that the raider had struck at dawn—struck and run, not following to claim her victim.

There were injured lying in the passenger cabins, thrown open for the wounded. An aged woman, her thin, white skin almost transparent, her toothless mouth still trembling with shock, plucked nervously with old fingers at her bed-coverings. And a younger woman lay still, staring at the wall before her, only now and then silently twisting when a spasm of pain rocked her and the bed beneath her. Her child would be born soon now, and before its time.

Matthew Steel had attended his passengers first. Quickly he inspected the damage to his ship, fearing fire in the hold. A quick examination proved to him that the *Loyalty* had taken her punishment well, like the champion she was. Then he strode toward the forecastle, but men, a solid block of them, barred his way.

Their backs were to him and he pushed among them, and recognizing their captain they made way for him. There were groans and curses from several of the berths on which men were stretched, but there was no sound from Cass Blake's, about which other men were huddled. Webb and Cannon stood beside him. On Webb's forearms were bleeding wounds, and the big Negro did not notice. Cannon's face was burned and his hair and brows were singed and his eyes were rapidly closing. But Cannon made no complaint. About them crowded other men with other injuries, but they made no sound, for all of them were looking at Cass Blake, lying silent on his bed.

Webb had placed him there. Webb had picked him up and carried him, trying not to slough off any of the burned flesh. Cass' face was almost unrecognizable as a face. His chest was burned deep, the skin gone, the muscles bared; his hands lay in pools of blood and his bare feet were charred, cooked and twisted. But there was still life in him. The slit that was his mouth moved a little as he grimaced, and his breath came from it in little gasps, whistling.

Matthew motioned the silent men back a little. They seemed to press so close upon Cass Blake. He leaned over Cass, wishing he could touch him, let him know that he was not alone. But there was no place on his body that a touch would not bring greater pain.

"God!" Matthew said. The word came involuntarily, through his clenched teeth. He hoped Cass was unconscious. No man should be damned to such living hell as this. Cass' body twitched a little.

"Matthew?"

"Yes, Cass."

"The fire—"

"It's out, Cass. Thanks to you."

Cass' breath came short and hard. "Don't thank me," he gasped. He managed to turn his head a little, toward the sound of Matthew's voice and his words came fast. "I didn't do it for you. I didn't care if you lost your ship, or your cargo, or your life. It was the immigrants, the people in the steerage—"

"Yes, Cass." Matthew's voice was deep and gentle. It took all his strength to look at Cass, Cass Blake, lying there like that, trying to talk, trying to argue with him, explaining to him, hating him, in his last breath. Jesus God Almighty, he said under his breath. He clenched the side of the bunk with both his hands. Over his shoulder he could hear Webb's breathing, heavy, as if he had been running, and the slight shuffle of the feet of the other men who waited and listened and watched.

"That Confederate flag on that ship—God damn them to hell." Cass' body jerked, straightened again. "I'm going to die, Matthew," he said, his words suddenly clear. "I wish I'd died fighting for the Union—not for you! I was fighting—for the immigrants—the people who believe in—the people who have faith—" His voice trailed off.

"The American eagle," he said, after a little silence. "You don't love the eagle, Matthew Steel, unless it's on a coin. . . . You're a capitalist now, but you used to be one of them. You couldn't have done that, anywhere else, except the United States, in a democracy. . . . Ask them in steerage."

The ship rocked easily, the familiar creaks of her sharp as pistol shots in the silence. There was no sound for a long time and then a man's voice, desperate, broke into it: "Isn't there anything we can do?" Silence was the answer. Another tried. "Some liquor for him?" And again there was silence. Then a man standing near the berth turned his head toward the speaker. "He couldn't swallow it," he said laconically.

"You could do such a lot, Matthew," Cass said, almost in a whisper. "As Loyalty said, she was right, Matthew." His lips moved a little longer but no sound came from them. His eyes stayed on Captain Steel.

Matthew did not know whether Cass could hear, but he hoped he could, perhaps he could.

"You did fight for the Union, Cass," he said clearly. "You did fight for the Union—the good fight. You're a good soldier, Cass, a good soldier."

Captain Steel stood erect. He looked down at Cass' body and the lines about his eyes and mouth cut deep. He folded his lips tightly. Webb raised his big hand and passed it over his face. Someone cleared his throat.

"That's something for you to remember," Matthew said finally, to his men. Captain Steel was not one to show emotion and he bit the words off sharply. "We sailed with Cass Blake. And Cass Blake was the bravest man we'll ever know."

[6]

IT DISTURBED Matthew deeply that Loyalty would learn of Cass' death through the newspapers or some other source, before he could reach port. Sympathy and love for her consumed him. When he was met by a tender carrying a health officer and other officials and newspaper reporters, and he foresaw additional delay in docking, he was hard put to it to control his impatience. But the captain of the *Loyalty* had maintained a steady hand on ship, crew and passengers, had prevented hysteria and quieted fears and herded the vessel safely into East River. He could not relax that hand now. He moved carefully, concentrating on the business in hand, courteous to the representatives of the press, giving considered replies to official questions. But when he saw a familiar, dark, wide face among the crowd of men who came aboard the ship from a tugboat, he excused himself abruptly and went to him.

Jules Descase, watching Captain Steel avidly and trying to make his way toward him, leaped to meet him. The Frenchman looked like a sick man, thin and anxious. He clasped Matthew's hand in both his own and searched his employer's face carefully and imploringly with his small, bright eyes. He began to talk in four languages, and his sentences were liberally spiced with profanity. The words spilled out, and Matthew stopped them only by tightening his hand on his arm.

"Wait, Jules," he said. "I'll hear the details later. The *Messenger* —where is she?"

Jules shrugged and spread his hands. "It was a privateer—off the coast of Brazil—"

"Did they sink her or capture her?"

"Captured her. Sent a prize crew aboard—took me and my men and a long time later landed us some place on the Southern coast. They took us to a prison camp in Macon and finally sent us up to Libby Prison in Richmond with some political prisoners. There were plenty of Frenchmen about and they aided me . . ." Jules shrugged again and breathed a curse. "I tried to send you word. It's bad luck, Captain Steel, and now the *Loyalty*—but there was nothing I could do—nothing! *Mon dieu!* Her bow was ironed and she could have cut us down like a paper toy. We saw the smoke first, and then the smoke stacks and the long black hull. She was flying the English flag. They came alongside us easily—they could do at least twelve knots under steam, and very well under canvas. They hailed us where from and bound, her crew was all at quarters and port guns fronted to the ship. We hove tc—what else could we do? The steamer lay on our starboard quarter and they sent a boat with an armed crew. You have never seen men so armed! They went over the *Messenger* thoroughly and took everything of value, sextants, charts, papers, instruments. One of them said they had orders to destroy and burn all American ships, but after they looked us over they had a conference and decided to delay. They said the *Messenger* would make a fine privateer, they would put three or four guns aboard her and a crew and they'd have another raider. They boast their ships and crews are of the finest and they laughed. They say the Federals are sending only old propellers and salt tubs after them! They claim they have a vessel capable of capturing any vessel short of a frigate in our Navy. The only consolation is that the *Messenger* will not be converted into a coal barge. Some ships captured have been stripped and are towed behind the privateers to carry coal and supplies." Jules wrapped his arms around his head and groaned. "The disgrace of it, Captain Steel—and there we were, helpless—"

Matthew rubbed his hand hard over his mouth and chin. Then he put his hand on Jules' shoulder for an instant. "All right, Jules," he said quietly, and the man's face came up in gratitude and relief. "You did the best you could. It can't be helped. We're in a war. You're all right?"

Jules grimaced. "My stomach is sick from the food in the Southern camps. Flour full of maggots—hard crackers, and not enough of that. God! Traveling in box cars, they exhibited us like monkeys in a circus at every stop, and the heat and bad water gave me fever and flux. Now, though, I shall be well again. I had to come to tell you, Captain, and then I will volunteer to fight those Rebel devils!"

There was a crowd of curious to watch the stricken *Loyalty* dock. Jules was relieved to be given work to do and he leaped eagerly to his tasks and Matthew was glad to turn the vessel over to the Frenchman's capable hands. Matthew left the ship almost at once. He had a small packet under his arm, and he hailed a hack and gave the address of Thaddeus Blake.

Matthew walked up the steps and faced the door. A wreath, stiff and without beauty and tied with crepe, hung upon it. He reached for the bell handle and pulled it briefly. The door opened almost at once and an elderly servant stood there, his face remote and guarded, but his eyes widened ever so little, betraying him, as he faced Captain Steel.

"I should like to see Mr. Blake," Matthew said.

The man hesitated and then he bowed slightly. "If you will wait, please, I will see if Mr. Blake is in." The door swung shut, clicked gently, and Matthew waited, staring at the mourning wreath. He was near to Loyalty now and his heart was pounding and his mouth felt dry. The door opened again and the servant looked stonily over Matthew's shoulder as he spoke. "I am sorry, sir, Mr. Blake is not at home."

"Miss Loyalty, then?" Matthew's voice was a little husky as he spoke her name.

"I am sorry, sir. Miss Loyalty is not at home."

Matthew measured the man with his eye. Beyond him he caught a glimpse of the long, luxurious hallway, silent and deserted. But he knew that both Thaddeus and Loyalty were in that quiet house. His chin firmed. The door was closing, slowly, and he put out his hand to stop it, and then he withdrew it. The door clicked shut again, softly, barring him, shutting him out, and the crepe fluttered a little and was motionless again. Matthew glanced at the little packet he held and hesitated a moment and then he turned and walked slowly down the steps and reentered the carriage.

The driver waited and Matthew was lost in thought. Serena—perhaps Serena would see him. It should be to some member of the family that he presented this little packet, and told them what he had to say. He gave the driver the address of the new home that James Thurlow had built for Serena, but when they drew up before it he saw that the curtains were drawn and there was no light. It looked deserted, but he went to the door and pulled the bell anyway, and waited a long time. There was no answer to his ring. There was a wreath and crepe on that door as well.

Slowly he returned to the rig and he stopped with his foot on the step, biting his lip and frowning. He turned to the driver finally and asked: "Do you know where Judge Austin, Judge Henry Austin, lives?" The driver nodded and Matthew stepped into the carriage again. When at last they drew up before an impressive entranceway, Matthew saw that the house was softly lighted and a carriage stood at the door. At least some member of the Austin family was at home and perhaps he would be received. At one time the Austins had been close associates of Thaddeus Blake. They, at least, would have entry to the Blake house now, direct access to the family. Wealth surrounded and protected people in their grief, he thought, but some way he must penetrate that shield.

Again Matthew rang the doorbell deliberately and the door was promptly opened to him.

"My name is Matthew Steel. I would like to see Judge Austin on a matter of great importance."

The servant bowed courteously. "I am sorry, Mr. Steel, but Judge Austin is not at home. A tragedy in the home of a friend has called him there."

"Then Henry Austin—the son?"

"Yes, sir. Major Austin is in. I will see if he will receive you."

The door was left ajar and Matthew waited. It seemed to him he waited a very long time, but finally the man came back and opened the door for him to enter. Matthew stepped inside. From a room opening from the hallway Henry Austin appeared. He was in uniform and he walked with a cane, his foot dragging. He nodded to Matthew but he did not offer his hand.

"You wished to see me?"

"Yes."

Henry stood back and motioned for Matthew to precede him into the drawing room. He followed, moving painfully, and steadied himself by holding the back of a chair. "Will you sit down?"

Matthew's glance dropped from Henry's face to his leg and he took the offered chair but he did not relax. He leaned forward and waited until Henry had eased himself into a high-backed chair, facing him. He looks a little like a judge on a bench, Matthew thought, and perhaps, in a way, that is what he is. He's improved; he's matured. He's no doubt an excellent officer, deliberate and cool under fire. He looks like a good man. His eyes are not shifty and he sits quietly.

"I tried to see Mr. Blake—or Loyalty," Matthew said bluntly. "They would not receive me. I called at Mrs. Thurlow's home, but there seemed to be no one there."

"Perhaps you do not know that Captain Thurlow was killed at Second Bull Run. Mrs. Thurlow has returned to the Blake home."

Matthew started. "No, I did not know. . . . Cass' death, then, was a double blow."

"Yes." Henry's voice was cold. "However, Captain Thurlow died a soldier's death. That has been of consolation to his widow."

Matthew looked at Henry sharply and Henry met his gaze steadily.

"When disgrace is added to grief it is, of course, doubly hard," Matthew said plainly. "What I wished to say to Mr. Blake, if he had seen fit to see me, was that his son died a hero. I think the Blake family should know that, Major Austin, and it might bring them some comfort now. Cass was a sick man, mentally sick, when he came back from the first Bull Run. He was cured—he cured himself, of that illness. I believe that his family, and perhaps his former friends, thought Cass a coward. I made that mistake myself. I learned differently."

Henry Austin's hand tightened on the head of his cane. For the first time he noticed the dark smudge beneath Matthew Steel's eyes, the deep lines in his gray, weary face. The man's face was lean and hard and there was still the stubborn set to his chin, but there had been a change in him, a subtle change that Henry could not define. He was warmer, more human, more approachable, and Henry felt his resentment and dislike thawing a little. Matthew Steel could be a very likeable man, Henry found himself thinking, if he would permit himself to be. His words carried conviction. It must have cost him dearly to come here, to ask me to go to Loyalty for him. When had Matthew Steel ever before admitted failure? When has he done a thing he did not want to do, to help someone else? It's a sea-change, Henry thought. The man is different. Something has touched him at last, dug clear into the sensitive core of him, and he is not sparing himself . . .

Matthew's voice went on. When at last he was finished he nodded to Henry, strode down the hallway and let himself out. From the window Henry watched. Matthew spoke shortly to the driver and was on his way, a man who knew exactly where he was going. He looked exhausted, Henry thought, and yet Henry did not believe that Matthew was thinking of rest. He apparently had another important errand tonight.

[7]

GRAHAM WHITE dropped his newspaper and leaned his head against the back of his chair and closed his eyes. It was late and he needed sleep, but it was hard for a man to rest in these troubled times . . . He must see Captain Steel tomorrow, secure his latest report. His reports had been faithful and accurate. They followed to the letter the pattern that other reports painted, and occasionally there was some bit of genuine importance. They had been valuable, but Graham White was doubtful whether employing Captain Steel as agent for him had served the main purpose he intended—to bring the man into the Union camp.

With headlines reporting disastrous defeats, with the scales tipping more and more heavily in favor of the South, Graham White considered anxiously his own assignment regarding Captain Steel. He was forced to admit that he had not been successful so far. And the chances of Steel now declaring his allegiance were slimmer than ever. He said he'd pick the winner and put his money on him. It was about time, Graham White thought wearily, for Steel to turn Confederate.

The loss of his ship, the *Messenger,* also reported at length in today's news columns, and the attack on the *Loyalty* might, however, give the man a personal score to settle with the Rebels. Graham's eyes flew open and he sat erect. If Matthew Steel's anger were aroused, he might be willing, now, to fight. On the other hand, angry or no, Steel would consider carefully not revenge, but reparations for the damage done him. Would he stand a better chance of being compensated for his losses, if he joined the blockade-runners? There was some chance of that. It would be a dollars-and-cents decision, if Matthew Steel made it; Graham White would bank on that.

There was a sharp rap on the door and White called, "Come in." The door opened and Captain Steel entered. White went to meet him, holding out his hand, but when he saw Steel's face an exclamation broke from his lips.

"Captain Steel! Are you sick, man?"

Matthew shook his head. "A little tired, maybe."

White shoved a chair toward him and Matthew dropped into it. "I wanted to see you tonight," Matthew said. White frowned and he turned to a table and poured a glass of whisky and handed it to Matthew. Matthew took it and gulped it and handed the glass back. "Thanks."

Here it comes, White thought. The man is deserting and his conscience is driving him wild. White sat down, his face stony, waiting. The man should not have come here, he thought swiftly. Why torture himself and me with a confessional?

"Well, Captain?"

Matthew ignored White's unusual coolness. He was thinking intently, searching for the right words to say. He looked at his hands, clasped between his knees, and only now and then glanced at White. It was almost as though he were talking to himself. He spoke swiftly, as though his time were short.

"I won't be bringing you any more reports, Mr. White," he said. Despite himself, White's lip curled. Matthew did not notice. "I'm not making any more runs to England. I am offering the *Loyalty* —and the *Comet*—if she's still afloat, though she's slow in reporting—and my own services to the Navy." A half-grin twisted his lips. "I don't know if they'll have me now, but I'm at their service. I saw how ineffective a wooden sailing vessel without steam auxiliary is against the Confederate steamers. She hasn't got the chance of a snowball in hell. The *Loyalty's* not a fighting ship, but maybe she can contribute something—and maybe I can, too. I'd like to fight, if they'll let me. If they want the *Loyalty* for a transport or supply ship or hospital ship, they can have her. But I'd like to get into action, a gunboat, anything, any capacity. Maybe I can relieve one of the men who's been out there, doing my fighting for me this past year."

Graham White sat frozen in his chair. Matthew stood, not noticing, and began to pace the floor. "But there's something that has to be done, Mr. White. You've got to make the government—whoever is the head of those things down there in Washington, understand the importance of it. Don't take my word for it—just ask any of the men who've been in Europe, and have seen it, and talked to people, as I have. The Union has two friends in Europe. Russia —and the liberals of England and France. Russia's all right so far. It is to her advantage to be. She won't intervene in our Civil War, as England and France want her to, as long as we likewise refuse to join England and France and intervene in Poland. A Russian always decides an issue with one idea in mind—whether it is to his advantage. Russians aren't charitable, you know, unless it furthers their own interests. Oh, sure, individual Russians like us, all right. But as a nation—as a people, they decide everything from one point of view and one only, what's best for them.

"But the English liberals, the working class, they are the ones. England is closer right now to recognizing the Confederacy than she has ever been. Gladstone himself is declaring a Southern victory is assured. Shipping men all over England speak of it openly. But the liberals—the only thing that can keep them supporting the North, Mr. White, is to make slavery the issue. To *make* slavery the issue—whether it was in the beginning or not."

Matthew turned his eyes on Graham White and they were burning as with fever. White stood up and took his arms. He had to look up, to meet the younger man's gaze.

"Captain Steel," White began. His hands tightened. "Captain Steel—" White was smiling and there was a proud, triumphant light in his face. Seeing it, Matthew relaxed a little, his shoulders drooped slightly and his own lips softened in a grin.

"I know what you're thinking, Mr. White," Matthew said finally, more quietly. "I don't blame you. You think because the Rebels got the *Messenger,* and fired on the *Loyalty,* that I want revenge. All right. Many people will think that, and that's all right with me." His chin grew stubborn again, more familiar to White. "But I'd like you to know that isn't true. I don't give a damn about the ships. I'll admit that I did—up until a few days ago. They were mighty important to me. Now I don't care. Never mind why. That's not important. But things look mighty black for the North right now and she needs all the help she can get. Effective help. Power and guns."

White nodded. Excitement flooded him and he leaned forward eagerly, his white head near to Matthew's dark one, not wanting to stop the flow of words from Matthew Steel's lips. If only all the North, all the die-hards, the critics of the administration, the powerful war profiteers, the strong youth, the experienced elders of the Union would suddenly throw their entire united weight into the battle, as Matthew Steel was doing—then the Union had a chance. Perhaps Matthew Steel was a symbol, Graham White thought hopefully, of the change in sentiment that would bring about a change in the fortunes of the North. A Yankee never knows when he is licked, he thought proudly; when times are darkest and their backs are to the wall, then their true strength is displayed. A flush of personal pride and pleasure that his plan had worked, that Matthew Steel had been delivered into his hands, a valuable ally, touched Graham White.

"It's good to hear, Captain Steel," he said. "It's good to hear."

"Somewhere I read that Charles Sumner said this war might be won or lost abroad," Matthew continued. "I think he is right. Forgive me, if I harp on the same string. But I haven't much time. I want to get into action. I've waited too long as it is. So there's only one more thing I want to say. First—make slavery an issue, for God's sake make it an issue! By that one fact you can hold the support of workers the world over, men who'll fight against bondage in any way they can, and curb their governments from supporting the South actively. And, God help us, we need them! And keep Russia's support. That's my final report, Mr. White."

Matthew started for the door but White stopped him. "Wait a minute. I know you're in a hurry to enlist." A broad smile broke over White's face. "But wait—just a few days longer. First you're coming with me to Washington."

[8]

THE purpose of the statesman was to draw people out—not to divulge information. Charles Sumner, statesman extraordinary, was glad to meet Matthew Steel again, happier still that the man emphatically repeated his own theory; that in lieu of a great military victory, English intervention could be forestalled now only by announcing to the world that a victorious Union would assure that the United States would be forever free.

But Matthew Steel's burning earnestness reached the Senator, and he complimented Steel by admitting him to the inner circle. He cautioned Matthew that everything said here in this small, smoke-filled hotel room, was in strictest confidence. The three others present, including Graham White, already were aware of what he would say; government employes or elected representatives, they were seasoned politicians and they knew, before the public did, of coming events. Matthew's conviction of the necessity of stressing slavery as the issue in the war, was echoed by thousands, hundreds of thousands. Great pressure had been brought to bear upon the President for many months, and now, with military defeats enhancing the danger of foreign intervention, President Lincoln had at last begun to give a little. Of course the President hated slavery. In the President's own words, "As I would not be a slave, so I would not be a master." He said also that he believed the government could not endure permanently half slave and half free; but his paramount purpose was to save the Union, not to save or destroy slavery. He had declared if he could save the Union without freeing any slave he would do it; and if he could do it by freeing all the slaves he would do it—and if he could save it by freeing some and leaving others alone, he would also do that. So, if he were convinced that to save the Union the slaves must be freed, then he would do so. But the President favored a slower change, so that provision for the freed men could be made. Freeing them, in one great move, would be a magnificent gesture; but the President did not feel it would be the wise or prudent course. Colonies should be provided for the freed blacks; they should be aided and taught how to handle their new independence.

But, Sumner said, he was glad to report confidentially that the President had now begun to see the necessity of a blanket proclamation of emancipation of all the slaves of the Rebels. The Senator predicted that in a very short time—perhaps within the week, certainly within the month, the President would announce his plan for emancipation. Actual emancipation would likely take place within a few months. The announcement would come at any moment, and might avert a crisis with England. Matthew's reports, coupled with hundreds of similar vein from abroad, had pointed the urgency of such a move.

The talk went on and it veered around to Russia. Questions flew thick and fast around Matthew's head, and other men came and went, taking part in the discussion, or listening quietly.

"You have friends in Russia, do you not, Captain Steel?"

Matthew nodded. "A few."

"You speak the Russian language?"

"Yes—fairly well. Enough to understand and be understood."

"You have also had business dealings with them. Successful ones, I understand. How did you manage to come out ahead, financially?"

The Senator was smiling a little and Matthew grinned, too. The other men laughed a little. They confessed they didn't understand the Russians, a suspicious race.

"Well, I've always found that the way to get what you want from a Russian is to show him how it will benefit him," Matthew said. "For instance—they don't care how badly you may need money or goods. But if they are in desperate need of what you have to give, you can persuade them to buy at your figure. You must simply convince them their need is as great as the price you ask."

The men laughed. "That takes a good salesman."

"It seems to work. They are a very literal people. They are not easily swayed by emotion. They are friendly toward the United States, for we have much in common. But if suddenly conditions changed so our friendship was no longer of value to them, I think they would not offer concessions to us, out of the kindness of their hearts. I think that to the Russians every day is a new day, a clean slate. What happened yesterday, any deals you may have had, were concluded then. No obligations, on either side, seem to carry over. You can't expect a favor from a Russian because you once did a favor for him. You must prove each time that by doing what you wish he will benefit. If you've nothing with which to repay him, now or in the future, he'll refuse you. And it won't worry him at all. Moreover, they are intensely patriotic. They are sensitive people, extremely so when it comes to their own country. They want to be recognized, given credit for their own worth, not looked down upon or underrated. They haven't the finesse in diplomacy that the British have. The British have bested them diplomatically time and again. The Russians know the British are ahead of them when it comes to innuendo and maneuverings. The only way the Russians know how to combat that is with strength. They are not a subtle people. Perhaps they will be, a few generations from now, for they have the Oriental habit of observing and copying anything that is proven good or clever, and they are not stupid. They are very ambitious and they are learning, I think, a great deal from the British, but they have a long way yet to go. Meanwhile, they are trying to hold their power by pure numbers and brute strength, to make up for their shortcomings in strategy.

They have great endurance, as much tenacity, I believe, as any race, and certainly their share of courage. But you can't be subtle with a Russian. Maybe suave diplomats can work in Great Britain and in the court of France, but Russians prefer more direct dealings. Their intrigues, generally, when they attempt them, are pretty heavy-footed, and an American can sense them a mile away. But you cannot embarrass them, or hurt their pride, or trick them, and keep them as friends. You must deliver exactly what you promise, and they will pay to the exact penny what they have agreed. They fear England—"

Suddenly Matthew's voice stopped. He was frowning in thought and he had forgotten the men around him. There was silence in the room for a minute and then he spoke again, slowly. "The problem, though, is not to get Russia in the war. It's to keep the English and French out of it."

He stood up and crossed the room in three long strides and came back again.

"Russia's fleet was bottled up in her own ports during the Crimean War," he said slowly. Still frowning, he rubbed his chin, thinking deeply. "Our ports—San Francisco—New York—are in danger of Rebel raiders. We need protection. . . . Russia's fleet is said to be second largest in the world, but I doubt it, from what I have observed of it in Kronstadt and in the Pacific. . . . Russia's naval power would be multiplied a thousandfold if her ships were in friendly ports where they would be in a position to strike at British shipping if—"

Matthew Steel began to grin. For the first time since he had come to Graham White's hotel room there was the spark of the old Captain Steel, the gambler, the trader, the gay adventurer, in his face. The room was silent, except for the ticking of a clock, and then one of the men swore softly, as the magnitude of the idea came to him.

"Why doesn't someone—" Matthew began impulsively and then stopped. All eyes in the room were upon him. "Well," he added, after a pause, "that's all I have to say. I wish to enlist at once."

But Matthew Steel was detained in the capital for other meetings and further discussions. When he left Washington for New

York again he was not in naval uniform. Matthew Steel, private citizen, was starting on the biggest trading venture of his career.

[9]

THERE was a neat stack of cards and notes on the table in the Blake hallway, Henry Austin noticed. There had been many callers offering condolences on this day. But not only the mourning wreath on the door, the stack of snowy cards, and the butler's quiet voice told Henry that death had entered this house. It seemed to him the thick carpets muffled his steps more than usual, as he limped toward the drawing-room door; it seemed that the gas lights did not burn quite so brightly, and the colors in carpets and hangings were more subdued. The tick of the great clock was louder, for a heavy silence had descended over the house. It is, of course, just my imagination, Henry told himself; the very knowledge that Cass will never again come striding in, whistling, tossing his hat and gloves and stick to the old servant—just that knowledge makes me feel there is a change in the place.

He stopped in the doorway, balancing himself with his cane, a package in his other hand, and quietly surveyed the room before him. A long table had been set up in the Blake drawing room, and on it were stacked piles of towels, small books, neat little packets. Serena sat beside a low fire, sewing, and Loyalty was bending over the table, counting some articles and making notes on a paper before her. Judge Austin and Thaddeus Blake sat near Serena, smoking and talking.

For several weeks now Serena had been wearing mourning and Henry had become accustomed to the girl's white face above the dull black of her dress. Serena's face had thinned and her eyes were shadowed and she seemed smaller, more helpless than ever before. But when Loyalty glanced up to see him in the doorway, Henry caught his breath. He had never seen Loyalty in black before. The stiff bombazine of her gown was softened only by a deep, tucked yoke of light crepe and it was edged at the neck with a tiny ruffle of lace. Against it, Loyalty's white skin was flawless, and her gleaming hair, pinned back from her small, heart-shaped face was no lighter than her dress. There was no color in Loyalty's face, and her eyes were soft, glistening, as though they had been washed by many hours of tears; but she was composed and her movements were carefully deliberate as she worked. She was very weary, Henry knew, for there had been little sleep in this household last night and the shock of Cass' death had been to Loyalty a staggering blow. Watching her, his heart ached, for her pathetic little face was turned toward him in welcome and she straightened and held out her hand to him across the table.

Henry hobbled toward her, half-smiling. God, how he wished he could help her! He would give his whole life to making her happy, he thought. Perhaps tonight, telling the story he had to tell, he could really bring her a measure of peace, and he would see some of that stark suffering in her face lift. But—and here Henry's heart sank again—though he was bringing her comfort he was acting only as a messenger for Captain Steel.

In spite of that he could not deny her the knowledge that had come to him. He took a deep breath and glanced also at Thaddeus and Serena, and pity for them strengthened him. He nodded to his father.

"It is good of you to come, Henry," Thaddeus said, and held a chair for him.

"Not at all," Henry said easily. "What's all this, Loyalty?" He gestured to the table.

"We are assembling comfort bags. Volunteers from Boston are passing through at noon tomorrow. They will be given luncheon at the Astor House, and each is to be given a comfort bag and an overcoat. We have one hundred and ninety-four bags here, isn't that right, Serena?"

"Yes. Three more towels to finish, and then everything is complete!"

With her quill Loyalty tapped the various items. "Handkerchiefs—three for each bag; buttons, needles and scissors. I am glad the New Testaments came. See, Henry, tiny ones, gilt-edged and bound in leather. There is a place in each for a picture, and a place for name and address." She held one of the small books toward him.

Henry put the packet he carried beside him in the chair and took the little Testament and leafed through it. "Very nice, Loyalty."

"But the material they gave us for toweling!" Serena said in disgust. "Look at it. It makes me ill, it's so coarse and stiff."

"We were lucky to get that," Loyalty answered firmly. "When I think of all the hours of sewing and the good material that went into useless things at the beginning of the war—just because willing women volunteers didn't know what the men would need—it is such a shame!" Loyalty dropped into a chair and sighed. "You remember, Henry, all those silly havelocks that women made at the beginning? As if men could wear them in that dreadful heat at Bull Run—"

Thaddeus moved a little in his chair. "What's the packet, Henry?" he asked idly. Henry took the packet in his hands and looked at Thaddeus for a long instant before replying. He glanced at his father thoughtfully as though seeking his understanding and the Judge sat a little straighter. Loyalty noticed the exchange of glances and she bent forward, knowing now that Henry's call was not without a purpose. Only Serena continued to sew, her eyes on her work.

"That is what I came about," Henry said slowly. "I hardly know if this is the time—but—"

"What is it, boy?" Thaddeus asked quickly.

"I have some word of Cass," Henry said finally. "I thought I should bring it to you." Deliberately he laid the packet, still wrapped, upon the table, putting it from him as a messenger might. "Believe me, sir," he said sincerely, "I would not do this if I did not think it was right."

"Of course not, Henry. What is it?"

"I had a caller tonight. Captain Matthew Steel."

Loyalty started. She gripped her hands together tightly in her lap and waited. Thaddeus' face darkened a little and Judge Austin stood, his back to the fire, watching his son keenly. Henry looked at his hands and his lips straightened. He began to talk slowly and his words dropped in the quiet room like beads on a tile floor, each one clear and distinct.

He was a conscientious reporter. He left out nothing. His story did not take long. "This packet contains the few of Cass' things that were left," he finished. "The money he earned—Captain Steel said a seaman's wages are not high, but he thought Cass was proud of it. And—the flag which covered his body as it slipped into the sea. Captain Steel said he deserved that honor, that he deserved full military rites, but they did the best they could."

Thaddeus turned his face away. Serena had buried her face in her hands, but Loyalty faced Henry squarely. Tears glistened on her eyelashes and her cheeks were white but she was smiling, a tremulous smile of thankfulness and pride. Henry moistened his lips. He had been remembering Matthew Steel's face as he talked. It had been an ordeal for Captain Steel to come to Austin, but Steel had not avoided it. Henry would be no less strong. Captain Steel had trampled on his own pride and his own desires and offered his gift, without strings attached, to Austin, in order that the woman he loved, and who needed it, might have it.

"He wanted you to be sure to know that Cass did not die in vain and that he died a hero's death, for his country," Henry added. "Moreover, the stories of Cass' heroism, not only from Captain Steel but from the crew and passengers, and tributes to him, have been given to all the newspapers and they are making much of it."

Thaddeus shielded his eyes with his hand. "I see no reason to disbelieve Captain Steel," he said finally, carefully controlling his voice. "It is not hard to believe that my son—"

"Of course it's true," Judge Austin assured him. "Cass had the heritage, Thaddeus, and he proved it. Moreover, no man could fake such a tale. You've every right to be proud, immensely proud of Cass."

Thaddeus nodded. He, too, was smiling as he dropped his hand. Serena wiped her face. It seemed to Henry that all in the room relaxed, drew closer together. Now they could talk easily of Cass, discuss his death, remember him with love and pride, find release for their sorrow in natural discussion unhampered by shame. That is the way death ought to be, Henry thought, only a separation, not shameful tragedy. What a great difference it made!

Loyalty slowly reached for the packet. She took up a pair of scissors and cut the cord which bound it. There were a few small articles in a large paper and she laid them aside. There was a small, dog-eared journal and an envelope in which was a slip of paper bearing dates and figures, and some coins. And there was the flag.

The flag was a large one, hand-sewn, and it was of a rough woolen material like serge, a flag made to stand the sun and wind and rain and spray, heavy, its colors brilliant. Loyalty held it on her lap, smoothing it, feeling its rough texture.

"We misjudged Cass," Henry said. "All of us. For that we should be blamed. I told Captain Steel that." He set his teeth. "I think, sir, that it is possible that we also misjudged Captain Steel."

Loyalty's hand, stroking the flag, stopped. Thaddeus' face hardened a little as he turned to Henry.

"Do you think, perhaps, that my son's death has converted Captain Steel to the Union cause?"

Loyalty held her breath. Henry nodded slowly. "Yes, sir, I believe it has. He is a changed man. He is—different—I can hardly describe the change. But I believe he became very fond of Cass, and he admired him greatly. He acts to me, sir, like a man whose eyes are opened at last." Henry turned to Loyalty. "I do not think the change has come with an idea of a reward. He indicated to me that he would make no attempt to see you, or any member of your family again. I do not know what his plans are—we discussed only Cass. But I think it quite possible that Cass is responsible for bringing Captain Steel into the Union camp. The word seems incompatible with Captain Steel—" a flicker of a smile touched Henry's face—"but it seems to me that the man has learned humility. And Cass has taught it to him."

Thaddeus nodded shortly. "We shall see," he said crisply. "Undoubtedly, the emotion of the moment, the heroism of my son, would affect even Captain Steel. But whether it is lasting is another question. I still think a leopard does not change his spots."

Loyalty's eyes flashed but she said nothing. A silent, passionate prayer of petition repeated itself over and over within her; let it be true. Let Matthew Steel see and understand, she prayed. Let this be the time, as Henry thinks it is, when Matthew Steel emerges, when he sees the worth of the Union cause, when he sees the need of his country and answers it.

Later, alone in her room, Loyalty indulged in dreams. Her refusal of Captain Steel had been right. This long denial, the heartache and loneliness must not be in vain. And Cass' death. Surely that, and her prayers, would change Captain Steel. Even now. she thought, he might be joining the service, ready, willing, anxious to fight, eager to make up for his long delay. There would be no more epithets thrown his way—slacker, mercenary, war profiteer, Copperhead. He would prove himself, and then, some day, in the not so distant future, he would come back to her—or she would seek him out. She must hang on to that belief, keep her faith strong.

But less than two weeks later Thaddeus handed her a paper open to Marine Intelligence. The notice leaped out at her from the page. The *Loyalty,* Matthew Steel, Captain and Owner, would sail for St. Petersburg.

"He has a rich cargo," Thaddeus said flatly. "Even some cotton and tobacco—though Heaven knows where he got it. He'll make up his losses on this voyage, with good fortune." Thaddeus' nostrils flared in disgust and he turned on his daughter with unusual urgency. "Loyalty—forget him! He'll never be anything else than what he is. Even Cass' death couldn't change him. He's money-mad, that's all. Sailing to St. Petersburg in the fall. A profitable voyage, and he'll be ice-bound there for the winter. As safe a place —and as far from the fighting as a man can get."

For once Loyalty could not answer. She had been so sure. But the black type staring at her from the paper did not lie. A mercenary? Why else would a man turn his back on the suffering Union and take a valuable cargo of goods to St. Petersburg in this dark fall of 1862, if not to make money?

[10]

MATTHEW STEEL and Jules Descase walked together down Cherry Street. A fine, cold rain darkened the walk, intensified the gutter odors, dimmed the lights. But in spite of it Jules was thinking of Cherry Street and South Street and all the area between with fondness. It was always thus on the eve of sailing.

Jules glanced at Captain Steel's face and sighed. He would have sworn that he knew Matthew Steel as well as any man. But he did not know the man who strode beside him tonight. Resentment stirred within Jules. He had not wanted to go with Captain Steel on this voyage to St. Petersburg. He had repeated his desire to join the United States Navy, to strike back at the Rebels who had taken his ship and held him prisoner. But Captain Steel had deliberately prevented him.

It was true that Steel had not blamed him for the loss of the *Messenger*, and he had generously paid him his entire salary, even for the time he was a prisoner of the Rebels. But Matthew had insisted that Jules remain with him for one more voyage. Surely, he told the Frenchman, Jules owed him that much. He needed him for this trip. It was, Jules thought, taking unfair advantage of their long and close friendship and it was moreover unlike the Captain Steel he had known. Steel had struck many a hard bargain as a trader. But he had never before, to Jules' knowledge, put heavy pressure on a friend to further his own interests.

Jules had finally been persuaded, but the relationship between him and Captain Steel was strained. It seemed to make no difference to Steel. Once Jules was committed to his employ for the St. Petersburg venture, Matthew dismissed the matter entirely. He did not seek Jules' companionship. He did not confide in him. He worked like a machine, sparing of speech, careful of his time and energy, meticulous about the repairs and loading of his ship.

And now at last they were ready again to sail, but Jules, despite all his efforts, had been able to recruit only a skeleton crew. He had finally announced the fact to Matthew, and the Captain had immediately pushed his paper work aside, reached for his coat, and started out with Jules along the waterfront, searching for more men.

The cargo in the *Loyalty* was indeed a valuable one. How Matthew had secured it was a subject of discussion in every South Street tavern and coffee house. The voyage, this late in the season, would be a long and hard one. To have any margin of safety, more men were needed, and Matthew Steel, a believer in careful preparation to cut down risk, was out to get them.

For two hours now the two men had called at taverns and boarding houses. Jules was not slow to sense the animosity of the waterfront toward Captain Steel. No one could have ignored it. There were not only dark glances and mutterings toward the Captain of the *Loyalty,* but open remarks, cutting, slurring insults, to which Steel turned a deaf ear.

That puzzled Jules still more. In the old days Steel had marched forward brashly and boldly, not giving a damn about anyone or anything outside his own desires and his own good fortune, but he had been quick to defend his good name. Now he was still looking out for Matthew Steel's pocketbook, but he seemed to hold little animosity toward those who reviled him. And once in a while Jules had caught a new look on Matthew's face when he was rebuffed. Captain Steel never lost his temper, he never slowed his pace, never allowed his personal feelings to interfere with his work and progress toward his goal. But once or twice Jules saw on the Captain's face an expression that would have meant hurt on the face of any other man. At long last it seemed that the hostility of the waterfront had pierced Matthew Steel's armor, and the prick of it was causing him discomfort if not actual suffering.

More often than not they were met only with silence and stares, when Matthew announced to a group of men that he was looking for able seamen. Once in a while a man followed them to the street and agreed to sail with them. When there was no response Matthew turned on his heel in silence and went on to the next place, his chin set.

They were before Mrs. Doughty's Boarding House for Seamen now and Matthew mounted the steps. Mrs. Doughty herself answered their ring, but when she saw who it was she pushed the door closed again, but Matthew's boot was quick and the door did not latch.

"I don't want a room, Mrs. Doughty," Matthew said quietly. "I'm looking for men." Calmly he forced the door open and the big woman fell back, breathing heavily.

"And if there's any boarders here who'll sail with you, Matthew Steel, then it's good riddance!" she snapped.

Matthew ignored her and went to the dining room. Lexie Small, who was serving the dozen or so men around the bare board table, froze in her tracks, her mouth open, and watched Matthew as he spoke. Matthew went through his usual ritual. He was leaving tomorrow for St. Petersburg. The ship would winter there and the crew would be paid during the time in port. Food was good. The ship was in perfect sailing condition.

One man arose finally and uncomfortably. "I'll go, Captain Steel," he said. Matthew's sharp eyes bored into him and he shook his head.

"Sorry. My men must have a clean bill of health." The fellow slunk back to his place at the table. There was silence in the room and Matthew studied the faces about the table and then he turned to go. Another voice stopped him.

"I'd sail, Captain, but I owe money—to Mrs. Doughty and to Jimmy From Town." Another spoke around the food in his mouth. "So would I, Captain—but Jimmy Burns—"

Jules watched Captain Steel. The two men were healthy, husky seamen, valuable men. Matthew's eyebrows drew together as he regarded them, and then he jerked his head shortly.

"All right. I'll advance the money." He whirled and started for the door. A hiss followed him.

"You've sunk a long way, Matthew Steel," Mrs. Doughty rasped. "And so Jimmy From Town is your friend now! Birds of a feather!"

It was as if Matthew had not heard. Jules followed him from the building, and, on the street again, Captain Steel threw back his head, searching the sky, letting the rain fall on his face. What had come over him, to forsake the decent things he had been fighting for, only to line his pockets further? Jules' face twisted in distress and worry and he shook his head slowly. There was no use questioning Matthew Steel.

It was a queer way to start a voyage, the Frenchman thought. Reared on superstitions of the sea, he was uneasy that the *Loyalty* would sail with curses following her. It was no secret that dozens of people fervently hoped the ship and her master would meet disaster. It was not good to dare the ocean and the elements without prayers for their safety following them.

"I guess that's enough, Jules," Captain Steel said finally. "Webb is to bring two more free Negroes—he vouches for their strength and character. Webb is a good man. I trust him."

Jules nodded. Yes, the crew would be all right, with these new recruits. The ship was in good shape, the cargo was properly stowed. But the heavy weight of impending disaster still lay upon the Frenchman's shoulders and he could not shake it off.

South Street had come to life, as it always did with darkness. Bawdy and raucous, it nevertheless looked beautiful to Jules, and he wished he need never leave it. He looked again at Captain Steel and was surprised to see that Steel's face had softened, too, as he walked down the street, past the familiar signs, the familiar shop fronts. He feels it, too, Jules thought; he doesn't want to leave port any more than I. He loves the waterfront, he always has, since he was a boy, and he loves it even now, when it is against him. But his desire for money is an obsession; he's a man driven by something outside himself. He is like a man with a sickness, for which he is not to blame. Jules' short, wide, monkey face saddened. He felt a twinge of pity for the strong man striding beside him. Approval and respect must mean much to Captain Steel, and yet he had lost them, and he had only his wealth left and money could not buy him friendships.

Old Dan sat on his usual corner, his hunched shoulders damp from the rain, his head bowed, his chin nestled against his old fiddle, and his aged dog danced shakily on her hind legs, pathetic and pleading. Captain Steel stopped and dropped a coin into the old fellow's cup. The beggar squinted up at him in the dim light.

"Thank 'ee—" he began his usual whine, and then he arose shakily, bringing his old face close to Matthew Steel, straining his weak eyes to see. "Is't you, Matthew Steel?"

"Yes, Old Dan."

Old Dan's toothless mouth worked frantically and his words came at first with an effort and then with a rush. He was shaking violently, the bow knocking against the fiddle, his dirty rags fluttering like those on a scarecrow. He fumbled in his cup for the biggest coin and he held it out to Matthew in his grimy fingers.

"Take it back, Matthew Steel," he quavered, his voice a treble in his fury. "I'll have none of yer dirty money! Nor would ye want to give it me, if ye knew where't went! Every penny other'n for my bread goes to the widows and children of fighting men—and ye'd not be wanting to be helping them any, now would ye, boy-o? Take it back, I tell ye!"

The crowds on the sidewalk halted and watched as the old voice rose to a scream. Matthew stood as though turned to stone and the old man threw the coin on the ground at his feet and spat. He fumbled for his little stool again and sat down, his wasted, misshapen body shaking, tears flowing from his eyes. He wiped his slobbering mouth on his greasy cuff.

"There's a word for the rotten stuff crooks are turning out for the Army—I heared it!" Old Dan's shrill, accusing voice went on. "It's the word for ye, Matthew Steel. Shoddy! Shoddy! That's it—that's what ye turned out to be—shoddy! Ye and yer money—take it and be damned to ye!"

There was a rumble and a movement in the crowd about the excited old man. Matthew Steel glanced about him and then he turned away and without a word he pushed through the crowd and went on toward his ship.

It was then that Jules crossed himself. To take a ship to sea with the curse of a beggar—it was a bad start to a voyage.

[11]

EACH night was colder. Matthew could feel the breath of approaching winter as the *Loyalty* widened the distance between her and her home port. But despite Jules' forebodings the winds and tides were with the *Loyalty*, and she sailed smoothly and swiftly toward St. Petersburg, racing with the ice that would imprison her for the winter in that port. Jules had molded his crew into a coordinated team more quickly than most, and no rebel raiders were sighted. Tension eased as each day passed with no new danger and it was easy for the men to forget the threat of disaster which hung over them. There were laughter and even songs in the forecastle, and it was easy to be lulled into a sense of security, and to imagine that this trip was like those gay, adventurous early ones of the *Loyalty* under Captain Steel's command.

Often, for a little while Jules forgot his resentment toward Captain Steel and permitted himself to enjoy the smoothness of the voyage. Sometimes Matthew, too, looked up at the stout sails and towering masts, so skillfully harnessing the winds, and smiled. The *Loyalty* was no fighting ship. But she had no rival in the business for which she was designed.

Webb, the Negro, and his two colored friends were the backbone of the crew. It was their voices also which led the songs in the forecastle. And Webb, taking his turn at the wheel, often sang to himself, the wind and the waves and the slap and rattle of canvas his accompaniment. Sometimes Matthew came beside him, leaned on the rail, listening, and Webb would flash his white teeth in a happy grin and go on with his song. Often it was the mournful *Reuben Ranzo,* which seemed to have no end. "*He learnt to write on Wednesday, he learnt to fight on Thursday, on Friday he beat the master—*"

Matthew liked to hear him, for Webb was a happy man, without a care in the world, and his was the happiness of understanding and acceptance, not of ignorance. It was good to find something in the world that seemed normal and right, Matthew thought, and beneath the blue sky, with the sea beneath them, with the vessel on her course, and with Webb singing the old songs of the sea, he could forget the purpose of his voyage and all that had gone before it.

"When did you first go to sea, Webb?" Matthew asked him.

"When I was a little fellow, suh—well, not so little, I guess. I got my growth early. But I wasn't very old. I worked on the docks, down in Carolina—and I'd go out on the boats whenever the master'd let me. That Carolina coast! Always changing, it was, with the winds and tides, and the sands filling one channel, opening another. It was fascinating, like a puzzle. I know that Carolina coast like I know my own hand, suh. I've often wondered, how's the Northern men, who ain't been around there much, keep it blockaded? Seems to me I could take a vessel in or out of there any time, slip her in, some of those channels. Of course, most of the channels that shift are shallow—not big enough for a real ship like the *Loyalty,* suh, but there's one in particular I used to like to pass through, because it was a hidden place. It would let any ship through—if you knowed it well; you know how boys like to have secret hiding places—secret doors—"

Webb rolled his eyes around at Matthew and the Captain nodded, smiling.

"I've always thought I'd like to go down along the Carolina coast again, and just snoop around. These blockaders and privateers that's gettin' loose—they ain't comin' out of the regular harbors—or if they is, they ain't comin' by the regular channels. I'd make a good blockade runner, Mr. Steel, suh!" His booming laugh rang out. "I bet I knows ways to get a ship in there that the Federals never dreamed of. Sometimes it looks like you're goin' straight on the rocks for sure—but at high tide even a big vessel can squeeze through. I remember one place, I sounded it a hundred times, I reckon, and I took ships through, big ones and little ones, just for fun, and because sometimes it's shorter. Those Southern boys know that coastline, Mr. Steel. No wonder to me they go and come, even if there is a blockade."

Matthew regarded the black man thoughtfully. Webb fell silent, lost in memories, smiling happily to himself, and then his big voice began again, at first a hum, deep as organ music, and then the round, full rich tones that no white man could imitate, as he followed the adventures of *Reuben Ranzo.* "*The mate he was a good man, he taught him navigation, now he's captain of a whaler and married the captain's daughter—*"

But despite the peace in the forecastle there was little rest for the *Loyalty's* master. He missed Jules' companionship, and he deeply regretted the fact that he had had to use pressure to keep the man with him. But this trip was important—God, how important it was! And he had used any means at his disposal to find the proper men to man his ship. It had been hard also to compromise with his hatred of Jimmy Burns and his methods. But delay was dangerous and expensive and a few strong men, even if they were bought, meant a margin of safety for the ship which he desperately needed. It was, in fact, a political move, Matthew thought; and he remembered the government men he had met, who admitted that many times they had to sacrifice small ideals, small secret hopes, to bring about a greater good. No wonder those men were harassed and tormented, with the decisions they had to make, the weighing, the continual compromises, the distasteful deals that were necessary to reach a worthwhile goal.

Matthew was convinced that this voyage, if successful, was worth almost any sacrifice of lesser things on his part. His chance of success was slim—so slim in fact that sometimes he cursed himself for starting on a wild goose chase, and an expensive, time-consuming one at that. Then his thoughts came back, optimistically, to success. Suppose he were successful, by a roundabout means, of bringing the Russian fleet to the ports of the United States. Jesus God, what results that would have!

If the Russian fleet quietly appeared in New York and San Francisco harbors, guns unveiled, Great Britain and France were bound to hesitate and think again before they recognized the Confederacy. It should, of course, be announced that it would be only a friendly call, a visit to friendly ports. But England and France had long suspected a secret alliance between the great powers of the United States and Russia, providing for Russian armies to join the North, if England and France threw their lot with the South. Matthew had been assured that no such alliance existed and he believed that was so. But England and France might well do some fancy guessing, if Russia's fleets were safe in United States ports.

Sweat broke out all over Matthew's body when he thought of it. The appearance of the Russian men-of-war in New York and San Francisco would also remove another imminent danger. No Rebel privateer, even Captain Semmes himself, would dare to strike at a Northern port—if the Russians already were there. While every available vessel of the United States was joining the blockade fleet or aiding in opening the Mississippi, the great might of Russia would protect the vulnerable Northern ports from attack!

Moreover, the gesture of friendship on the part of Russia, when all the rest of the world seemed against the North, would greatly encourage the people, and they needed encouragement now. Their own defeats and the troops of England on the Canadian border and the soldiers of France in Mexico frightened them, as well they might; and the thought of the United States being the battle-ground for the great armies of the Old World likewise made Matthew shudder. In Europe itself, countless wars had been fought over some nations—Poland, the Balkans; and the land and the people had been ravished, impoverished, again and again. That the wars of Europe should ever extend to the soil of his own country made Matthew physically ill.

There was, of course, the danger that Great Britain and France would consider the appearance of the Russian fleet in United States port as an act of war. If there were the faintest rumor that the affair had been planned by the two governments, or that an American official had anything whatever to do with the plan, it might well be considered a challenge to war. That suggestion had been made and discussed at great length in the conferences in Washington. But it was the belief of the majority that Britain would hesitate before declaring war, if the Russian fleet were free and in a position to strike at her shipping, and was not bottled up in her own ports as it was during the Crimean conflict.

But absolute secrecy was a necessity. Matthew would have liked to have regained Jules' respect and confidence by telling him that sailing aboard the *Loyalty* on this voyage was, in reality, striking a blow for his adopted country. He could not. It was true, as Jules believed, that the criticism and slander of his old friends had got under Matthew's skin, and, quite humanly, he would have liked to have cleared himself by letting them know what he was attempting. But his lips were forever sealed. Not now, or ever, must it be known that he was attempting to persuade the Russian fleets to visit American ports, at this most crucial moment in the War Between the States.

It was his cross to bear, and it was a heavy price to pay. Once understanding had come to him—and it had come, crystal-clear and with a great impact—with Cass Blake's death, he had wanted only to get into the fighting as rapidly as possible, to redeem himself if he could and make up for his long delay. He had told Graham White he was eager and willing to serve in any capacity. He had meant that. It was to his credit that he made no protest when he was asked to do this job, though it meant carrying with him forever the stigma of mercenary and slacker.

It is the price I have to pay for my stupidity, Matthew told himself, and it is just. It was easier, too, now that he was right, within himself. It made a great difference when a man was at peace with his conscience.

There was not a man in Washington who would admit, now or ever, that he had any knowledge of Matthew Steel's mission. If he were successful, and the fleet of Russia appeared in New York and San Francisco, on a good-will tour, the event would go down in history as a remarkable and fortunate coincidence. But the coming of the Russian fleet, following the emancipation proclamation, might be the additional weight that would tip the scales in favor of the North, and change the entire course of the war.

It was worth fighting for. Deliberately Matthew smothered the one tormenting thought that, above all others, tortured him day and night. If only Loyalty Blake might know that her faith in him had not been misplaced. But that, of course, was impossible, and he must take that also as part of the cost.

Meanwhile, as the *Loyalty* sped on, Captain Steel sat in his cabin and planned his strategy. He had thought first not to delay to load the *Loyalty,* but to sail only with ballast, but that, he realized, would be a sad mistake. With his valuable cargo—and he had emptied his own warehouse and paid immense prices to others to secure it—he had a good excuse for arriving and wintering in St. Petersburg. As a trader, interested in profits only, and a man who had so far had no part whatever in the war, he would certainly not be suspected of ulterior motives. The thing he must do was to make no mistakes.

Again and again he went over his knowledge of the Russian people, and of the individuals he would seek. Thilo Kalin, Peter Segonov, Lesovsky, and their friends. He would avoid public officials. Admiral Popov likely would not be in Kronstadt, but a letter to him, carefully worded, might help. A seed must be planted—carelessly. It must be casually nourished and watched, while he idled in St. Petersburg.

It was a great challenge to a man and one that Matthew Steel relished.

[12]

THE heavy plain board table before him was scarred by a thousand knives and bottles and ashes from cigars and pipes; it had been scoured by a hundred barmaids, and darkened by years of smoke, spilled liquor and the rubbing sleeves of countless men. In fact, this inn had served the men of several generations and the father and grandfather and great-grandfather of the present proprietor had no doubt laid logs in the great fireplace, trimmed the wicks, changed the candles, and greeted guests in this very place. That feeling of age and permanence gave it a charm all its own, and Matthew liked to come here, in early evening, and eat and drink his fill.

It was in this inn also that naval men from Kronstadt gathered. There were at least seven naval vessels laid up at Kronstadt, Matthew had learned, for the winter. And this particular tavern served as a rendezvous, an unofficial club, for the junior officers and sometimes the older officers as well.

Tonight Matthew had come early, for he had a stack of American and English newspapers with him. It was good to see papers from home, even though they were weeks old. Carefully he had sorted them by date, and he started to read the older ones first, to bring himself up to date on important events. Dispatches in Russian papers had told him the most outstanding events of the United States and Europe; but these detailed accounts, plus the editorial comments, gave him a more complete picture.

It had been a dark winter for the North. France declared the battle of Fredericksburg, in December, was in reality the end of the war. Ten thousand Federals were dead, and the North, it was said, was stricken with anguish and discouragement. It had been an unhappy Christmas for the North and the New Year had dawned no more brightly.

But on New Year's day President Lincoln had signed the Emancipation Proclamation. The papers were wild with delight. Surely now, the editors screamed, Great Britain and France could not recognize the Confederacy, when the War Between the States was in reality a war of liberation! But military victories of the South still loomed large to British statesmen. They had their eye on Southern markets, for if the South became a strong nation in its own right—as everything indicated it would—it would be good to be its friend. There were border incidents. A skirmish on the Canadian border was explained by the English blandly. The British soldiers were there to protect Canada from invasion by the Northern forces! Matthew snorted in disgust.

The more he read the more uneasy he became. The Emancipation Proclamation—a great, magnificent, beautiful gesture, a proclamation that freed an entire race. It had brought celebrations in St. Petersburg, too, and the Russians had pointed out to him the similarity in the problems of the two nations, for Alexander had freed the serfs and now Lincoln had freed the blacks. A great step forward, the Russians declared. And in England, where people were starving while the mills lay idle, it had been heralded by liberals with great joy also. It was true that the act would be a curb, at least for a little while, on the British government.

Matthew thought of Cass Blake again and the workers' meetings in England. Yes, emancipation would foster their simple belief that America was a refuge for the oppressed; it would lighten the hearts of all the downtrodden of the earth. But it must have caused the President great worry when he signed the actual document. The President's far-seeing wisdom would not be heeded, nor would he be remembered for his wise counseling on the question of freeing the Negroes. The public, at home and abroad, saw only the great, broad, dramatic strokes.

Looking behind the headlines Matthew could see that minor victories had been attained. The groundwork had been laid, men had been trained, ships had been built, supplies secured, munition plants and depots restocked; a great organization to supply troops had been put into operation and even the machinery for care of the wounded had been improved. But the people did not see these things. They saw only headlines, not the fine print. Smashing victories. The Emancipation Proclamation! Those things would strengthen the morale of the North, bring her friends abroad. The drum beat, not the fine, perfect melody of a violin, roused men to battle.

It was too bad, Matthew thought, that a move to go down in history as the greatest reform of the century was in reality only a political expedient. Unfortunately, many social reforms, before and after Lincoln, would undoubtedly be similarly inspired, as falsely interpreted and as widely heralded. But perhaps, Matthew thought, to comfort himself, in the final summary, the good accomplished justified the means. Only Lincoln's own plan, for gradual freedom and compensation, along with education and preparation for care of the freed men, would have been so much the better course. This move might drain the South of manpower, delay foreign intervention. But the problems that would arise from it might well widen the breach between the North and South till it was almost beyond healing. Military victories before this would have made it unnecessary; but desperate measures were required now if the Union was to be saved.

And it definitely had stalled British recognition of the South. The arrival of the Russian fleet would cause a similar delay.

Matthew put down the papers. He had long ago learned the Russian habit of eating while he drank. He was not fond of vodka and now he called for hot rum. He ate and drank slowly, reviewing the progress—if it was progress—that he had made here in Russia.

His welcome had been heart-warming. The Segonov household had been most hospitable and he spent much time there, not only because he liked the family itself and Peter in particular, but because many persons of importance were among their guests. But at the Segonov galas there was little time for talk. Even though he was their guest for weeks at a time he found he had more intimate conversation with men in this little inn near the river.

Tonight he was not disappointed. He had barely begun his meal when the door opened and an icy blast of air blew in Thilo Kalin and a superior officer, Captain Lesovsky. Thilo's face mirrored his pleasure as he approached Matthew and Captain Lesovsky also smiled. Both men unwrapped themselves from their heavy gray, fur-colored overcoats. Matthew shoved the papers out of the way and made room for them. He felt a sudden stirring of excitement within him. He had been in St. Petersburg for many weeks now, listening, judging, feeling out the temper of the people, and he had made no positive moves of his own. Anyone sent from the United States for a specific purpose would certainly have begun his work before this, the Russians would think. There was no suspicion attached to him, and there must not be. But he had waited long enough. Soon it would be spring, the harbor would be open, the ships lying at Kronstadt would be readied for sea. The time was ripe and his position was perfect. He could feel his stomach muscles contract a little, his pulse quicken. It would take only a few words—one evening of conversation, perhaps. On that the success or failure of his entire venture would depend. The long voyage, months in this harbor for himself and his crew were all for this one night, this one conversation, which must bear fruit.

He greeted the men pleasantly and they sat gratefully and waited for their drinks.

"And so you catch up on the news, eh?" Thilo said, gesturing toward the papers.

"Yes. And it is not so pleasant."

"The North, the dispatches say, cannot win a victory on land or sea," Captain Lesovsky said seriously. He shook his head. "It looks very, very bad."

"Yes." Matthew looked down at his plate. "Our countries have more in common than emancipation. It is said here that all Poland is in a state of siege. Do you really think war will come for you also?"

Lesovsky nodded. "It seems inevitable."

Matthew took a sip of rum and put down his cup. "Well, then, we'll have still more in common—common enemies." He grinned. "But why talk of war? I have just read all these papers and they are full of it. Rebel raiders—my God, the toll they take of our shipping!"

"They are skillful sailors and they must have good officers."

"Yes. And their strategy is good. Despite the fact that they have few ships—I do not know how many privateers there are, but there are not a great many, in spite of the English—they have done tremendous harm. Being in a position to strike at our shipping gives them great advantage. And they can coal and supply and repair in any English or French or Spanish port. A small number of ships can cause much trouble and great losses that way."

The men agreed. "You will have a dangerous trip home," Thilo observed.

Matthew nodded. "Yes. But I have a good crew, and ofttimes one ship can slip through while a fleet cannot. I'll be leaving as soon as possible. It has been a pleasant winter here, one I will not soon forget. Why do you not visit us in America, Captain, and give me an opportunity to repay you? Thilo will tell you New York is most hospitable."

Captain Lesovsky laughed. "That would be more pleasant, certainly, in case of war, than to be caught here again in Kronstadt."

Matthew glanced at him in sudden interest. "Why, of course." He chuckled. "What a joke—and what a surprise to Britain, if, instead of in Kronstadt, you had your ships in a neutral port at the beginning of hostilities—if, of course it comes to that. You might take a page from the Rebels' book and pounce on British shipping. They are smug about their Navy. But how it would hurt them to have you attack their merchant ships!"

He turned to his plate and began to eat. Captain Lesovsky raised his glass and drank and when he put it down he was frowning thoughtfully. Thilo Kalin also seemed absent-minded.

"My only regret about this pleasant winter," Matthew went on, as though changing the subject, "was not to find Popov here. But he always yearned to be Admiral of the Pacific fleet, and I am very glad for his appointment to that post. Where is he now, Captain?"

"Popov?" Lesovsky's attention came back to Matthew. "He's off in the Southern Hemisphere somewhere, looking over the colonies of the European sea powers."

"Ah. I'd like to send him greetings and congratulations on his appointment, but I suppose I could not reach him."

"But that can be arranged. He'll be at Nikolayevsk on the Amur in the spring—about the time you start homeward. We have a telegraph line only to Omsk, and a post, via Irkutsk, from there. It is slow—but he would receive your message eventually. Popov was fond of you, Steel. He'd be glad to have your message."

"Then I shall do that. He is a good man. It would make Popov furious to be blocked into a port in time of war. What will he do, do you think? Make his headquarters at Kodiak, or some other Russian base?"

Lesovsky shrugged his shoulders. "That I cannot say. There are not sufficient supplies at Kodiak, or any other Russian Pacific base, for a fleet. He has five sloops of war, four clippers and one boat of the Siberian flotilla—it would take quite a harbor for all of them. He would scatter them, I suppose, probably keep one ship in Shanghai."

"But the British would bottle that one up quickly enough. The English have the Bombay post, and telegraph to Calcutta. Then by warship—they could get news of a declaration of war two or three weeks earlier than Popov would have it. It would put him in a bad position. Central and South America and Mexico—Spanish, Portuguese and Dutch—all those ports would be the same for they are all friendly to England and France. Captain, I'm no naval strategist, but it surely looks to me like you are in the same position we are in. We've no friends in the world except each other!"

Matthew laughed and went on with his dinner with a relish.

"You are not a Navy man, so you can eat," Lesovsky said wearily, pushing his plate from him. "This is a serious matter, Steel. You have some good ideas. Being an outsider, you can see the whole picture, perhaps. Tell me, Captain Steel. If you were commander of the Russian Navy, and war was declared between Great Britain and her allies, and us—how would you deploy your vessels?"

"What a question from a man of your rank! Are you serious, sir?"

"Of course."

Matthew put down his fork and wiped his mouth. "Well—being a civilian, and a foreigner, I suppose it does no harm for me to talk. I think, however, I'd take no chances on my fleet being shut in my own ports this time. I'd get my ships out, secretly, long before the British or French suspected anything, and I'd get them to a neutral port, where communications were such that I would hear, as quickly as my enemies, of a declaration of war. Then—of course I do not know the strength of your Navy, Captain, but if my ships were fewer in number than the British, or less well-manned, I'd follow the system that has proven so successful for the Rebels."

With his fork Matthew drew a little map in the soft wood of the table top.

"I'd send one ship to prey on shipping between Liverpool and South America—the hit-and-run type of fighting on merchant ships. I'd send another to harass ships going from England to the East Indies, say, and another south of the equator. Oh, it would take some thought, to plan it well. But I'd use a ship on each of the main trade routes, and I'd slash their merchant shipping to hell. It would do them more damage than naval engagements. The Rebels have taught us that."

Lesovsky stroked his chin. Matthew shook his head, as though to brush the subject aside. "But perhaps it won't come to war. Great Britain and France vacillate. Let's talk of something more pleasant. Thilo, are you to arrange the trip to Moscow you promised me?"

The talk veered into other channels. It was late when the men finally arose, stretched their legs, and buttoned themselves into their heavy coats. God, a St. Petersburg winter! Matthew thought, as he let himself out of the comfortable inn. But inside him he was warm and content. His words had not fallen on deaf ears. It had been good fortune, too, to be able to talk directly to Lesovsky himself, an ambitious fellow who had the ear of Vice Admiral Krabbe, Minister of the Marine. In his own bed, Matthew could not sleep. He went back over his conversation with Lesovsky. Had he said too much—not enough? Never a word, of course, about the aid the Russian fleet could give to the Northern cause. That would have carried no weight with a Russian, might well have defeated his purpose. Had he been impersonal, offhand enough? The idea itself was sound, and Lesovsky's intense interest proved that the naval officer saw the sense of it, daring as it was. If Lesovsky presented the idea to Krabbe, it would be as his own idea, and that was the way it should be. Matthew grinned into the darkness. The truth was, such a move was all to Russia's benefit. It might even avert a war over Poland. A neutral port, Matthew had specified—one with good communications. Well, what neutral ports were there where Russian fleets would be welcome, and where facilities were adequate, besides those of the United States? And for Admiral Popov, what better Pacific port than San Francisco, where he had always been welcome, and which could easily accommodate his entire squadron?

His work in St. Petersburg was done. His conversation had not taken more than an hour. He could say no more. It would be folly to bring the subject up again. He was eager now to go home. He would run the gauntlet of Rebel raiders again, God willing, and be back on South Street in early summer. Whether this voyage bore fruit made no difference now, for the die was cast. Once the ice moved and the *Loyalty* was freed, he'd head homeward, and he'd pray to God the Russian fleet followed him. And he, at last, could join the fight. If only he were not too late. The papers had said the North was cracking, that the war would be over in a matter of months. He moved uneasily in his bed.

Only President Lincoln would not quit. He'd fight on, till the last man was gone, before he would let one inch of the republic be torn away, before he would let the United States be permanently divided. Providence had provided the man Lincoln in this hour. The nation had reeled through two dark years, but advances had been made, and if only foreign intervention could be delayed long enough—

It was hard to put those headlines out of his head so he could sleep. Fredericksburg, the failure of the thrust against Vicksburg, the long casualty lists . . .

He tossed in his bed. He hoped with all his heart that Lesovsky approved and embraced his plan, and presented it to his superiors as his own. If Lesovsky saw merit in it, he would do just that, and a promotion for him might result if the plan were approved. It was an opportunity for the Russian naval officer, and Matthew did not believe that Lesovsky would pass it by.

And now he could go home.

CHAPTER VI

BENNETT LOWERED himself gingerly to a straight-backed chair near the stable entrance and carefully unbuttoned his coat and waistcoat beneath it. He breathed noisily, puffing through his mouth, enjoying the freedom of his loosened clothing around his great middle. He rested a minute, and then he awkwardly pulled off his shining boots and wriggled his toes in pleasure and rested his pudgy hands, small for so large a man, on his big thighs, and permitted the roll of fat across his shoulders and the back of his neck to show as he slumped comfortably in his seat.

He closed his small eyes and a little smile, that of a benign and not very intelligent cherub, curved his mouth. His chins and his jowls shone with sweat. A small breeze from the open doorway fanned him pleasantly, causing his sparse white hair to rise and fall over his pink scalp. Ah, he thought, July in New York! The heat, even in early morning, was oppressive. He was glad for the short quarter hour he had to rest before he appeared at the Blake door to take Mr. Blake to his office.

He thought longingly of ale, cold and foam-topped, and a dark, cool drinking house. Even in the morning—sometimes most of all in the mornings—his mouth felt dry. He swallowed painfully. But he could not drink. He had promised, on his word of honor, if Miss Loyalty employed him, that he would maintain strict sobriety during working hours.

It had been a pleasure to work for a fine family again. He had thought he would never again have that chance. But the Blake coachman had gone to war and men were hard to find. True, the coachman had returned, wounded, and Miss Loyalty explained that when the man was able to work again—in just a few weeks, now—he was to have his old job back. But in the meantime Bennett, providing he could maintain proper dignity, could have the position.

It had been almost too good to be true. Bennett had no illusions about himself. He knew that once he had been the finest coachman in all New York, and he knew also that he had deteriorated into a lazy, drunken sot. That Miss Loyalty had recognized his former skill, and had given him an opportunity to regain his lost self-respect, had been the greatest of gifts to Bennett. He had conscientiously garbed himself properly and the fine, unspotted uniform of dove gray, the shining boots, had taken years off his age and made it easier for him to assume again the proper manner.

It had not been easy work. Despite the fact that they were in mourning, Miss Loyalty and Miss Serena were very busy and their war work and charities took them all over the city, at all hours of the day and evening. Mr. Blake also had a crowded schedule, and Bennett had to step lively, sometimes, to fill all their demands. He was proud to exhibit his skill as driver, the way he could sift in and out of traffic, his knowledge of streets and quick, less-traveled routes, his punctuality, his perfect form. He had been sharp with the footman assigned him, a spare, cocky little creature by the name of Slade. He had checked the grooms severely also, and the turn-out now was quite to his satisfaction, the carriage gleaming, the harness perfect, the horses fine and cared for. Ah, it was a fine thing, at his age, to have a second chance to prove his worth!

A fly settled on the top of his head and he brushed it off. The heavy, ammoniac smell of the stables behind him curled his nostrils and he sighed wearily and reached for his boots. He must go to the Blake entrance now and take the master down to Wall Street and his office. Then he would return and drive Miss Loyalty and Miss Serena to Grace Church for a noon wedding, and secure his orders for the day.

He tugged at his boots. He had one on and the other partly on when there was a commotion in the doorway. His own carriage and team had been led out, into the alley, awaiting him, and now an incoming carriage careened by it, so close the team leaped and it seemed the wheels scraped. Bennett stomped his foot into the boot and stood up, shaking his fist.

"You sonofabitch," he shouted at the driver, but the driver ignored him. The team was foam-flecked and both men on the box were so excited their eyes seemed ready to pop from their sockets. The horses reared, came to a standstill, and the men were off the box, and grooms and other coachmen and stable boys came running. Monday morning, Bennett muttered, buttoning his waistcoat. Fine thing, to be drunk on Monday morning, and to run their horses as if they were being chased by the devil himself. The new generation of coachmen had no sense at all. They did not know how to care for animals or equipment, they raced around like madmen, forgetful of decorum, interested only in speed, a foolish lot.

Bennett waddled toward them, his face crimson with heat, the tightness of his coat, and his annoyance. The men were shouting, gesturing and their excitement was contagious and the voices of all the group rose.

"It's a revolution! It started early this morning. The mobs are gathering all over town, and there is no militia to stop them! They started to gather when the draft drawing began and it's getting worse. There is a mob from Five Points, and they are moving along the waterfront in the warehouse district and forcing workers to join them. They've sacked several places already, and are growing more violent, setting fires and breaking windows, and the post office is barricaded—"

"Brokers and businessmen are forming volunteer groups to try to maintain order. You never saw anything like it! If it keeps up the omnibuses and horse cars will all be stopped. They are carrying placards and they are shouting blasphemy toward Lincoln and blaming the Negroes for the war—"

Bennett came closer, frowning, trying to make sense from what the men were saying. He kept saying, "What—what?" and plucking at the sleeve of the man next him. Finally the fellow turned and, recognizing Bennett, he grinned good-humoredly.

"It's the draft riot, Grandpa," he said, disrespectfully, and Bennett drew himself up, puffing his cheeks. "The drawing for the draft began Saturday, you know, and trouble was in the offing—and this morning they tried to go on with the drawing and all hell broke loose. Southern sympathizers and draft dodgers and all the rabble that's got nothing else to do has decided to take over the city." He poked Bennett playfully in the ribs. "Better go find yourself a nice chair in a drinking house, Grandpa, and have yourself a vacation. There won't be many venturing out today. Most businessmen are barricading themselves in their own homes, fearful of the mob."

"Mob?" Bennett spat the word. "A bunch of trouble-makers! Hah!" He strode to his carriage with what dignity he could muster. Rabble-rousers, alarmists, those fools back there. As if any such disgraceful doings could halt the daily work of a man like Thaddeus Blake.

The footman was beside him, tense with excitement, and Bennett swung the carriage round and brought it neatly to a stop at the Blake entrance. There were more carriages than usual on Fifth Avenue this early morning, and they seemed in a hurry, and down the street were unaccustomed little knots of pedestrians. Slade leaped down and ran up the steps and rang the Blake doorbell. He waited several minutes before it was answered and he raised his eyebrows questioningly at Bennett. But at last it opened and Thaddeus Blake and Christensen appeared. Mr. Blake carried a satchel of papers and he was as calm as usual. Bennett permitted himself a little snort of contempt for the excited men in the stable block.

"Good morning, Bennett," Blake said, as usual.

"Good morning, sir," Bennett replied. Everything was quite the same. But Mr. Blake and Christensen stopped on the walk before they entered the carriage.

"I wish you'd reconsider, Mr. Blake." Christensen's voice was hurried and urgent. "I was at the police station early and they cannot spare a man for protection of one family. But they urged me to persuade you to leave the city, and to take the young ladies with you until the trouble blows over, or until the militia has the situation under control. You are too prominent in Union activities, Mr. Blake. They fear you'll be singled out for attack. Really, sir, the situation is serious."

Mr. Blake frowned; his thin face was troubled. "I left word for Loyalty and Serena to stay indoors with the curtains drawn and the doors bolted. I am sure they will be safe enough. You heard Loyalty's reaction, Christensen. She flatly refused to leave. I agree with her. We can't permit a mob to oust us from our homes. Let's get on to the office. There may be need of special precautions there."

Still Christensen hesitated. "There's pillaging and robbing and plundering going on right now, Mr. Blake, and not so many blocks from here, either. The mob is gathering on Broadway, and though now they seem to be surging up toward Union Place, and toward East River, it's but a step over here to Fifth Avenue. There are not enough policemen in the city, sir, the mob numbers in the thousands. They are setting fires—"

"We'll go to the office, Christensen."

Mr. Blake took his place in the carriage and Christensen followed. Slade closed the door behind him and mounted the box. He spoke to Bennett from the corner of his mouth as the carriage moved away. Bennett started the team smoothly, with never a jerk, flicked them with a whip till they gained a fast clip, and swept east toward Broadway.

"We may never make it," Slade said in a low voice. "They say you can walk as fast as you can drive down Broadway. I heard Mr. Christensen say at the door they was stopping carriages and taking the horses, these mobsters. Jesus!"

Bennett pursed his lips. "I've been driving the streets of New York for twenty-five years, through fires, through storms, through fever and cholera epidemics, and I have never yet been stopped."

"There's always a first time," Slade mumbled. He folded his arms stiffly before Bennett could reprimand him and sat ramrod straight. He sat on the edge of the seat, his eyes rolling to right and left. "Jesus!" he said again. Then: "Sonofabitch! A fine time for a riot, just when the militia have been called away. Do you suppose they planned it that way?"

Bennett did not reply. He knew that Lee was invading Pennsylvania and the governor of that state had called upon New York to aid him, and the Seventh and Seventy-first regiments of the state militia had left for Harrisburg. It was an unfortunate coincidence that Lincoln had called just now for three hundred thousand men, and that the draft would have to be enforced during this absence of the militia. Naturally, the city's scum would take that opportunity to riot. Had it not been for the numerous Federal defeats the draft would not have been necessary, Bennett reasoned. But the North knew the fear of invasion now, for the South boasted Lee would take Philadelphia, New York and the capital; and few volunteers were answering the call to colors, to fight for what appeared to be a losing cause. The draft had not been popular anywhere in the North, but the first day of the drawing had gone by without incident, and it had been hoped that the rumors of revolt were false. But of course law and order would triumph.

Yet Broadway had never been like this before. The walks were crowded, as they were occasionally for a great parade, but this was not a peaceful, holiday crowd. There was a menacing rumble of voices and shouts, angry, threatening, and it seemed to sweep down the street like the first low, warning wind of approaching storm. Traffic moved slowly, hacks and drays and private carriages, heavy wagons and even pedestrians, moving among them with fine disregard for regulations. There were no policemen to straighten out the mess. Bennett was annoyed. Every morning he had dashed down Broadway to Wall, coming to a halt in front of Blake's office exactly on time, without hindrance or accident. His record was about to be ruined now and he took it as a personal insult. Many of these men clogging legitimate traffic were nothing but drunken bums. Here and there one leaned from a hack, a bottle in his hand, and shouted something obscene, a curse on Lincoln, a damnation on the draft. In the mobs on the walks also were women, shrill-voiced, dissipated, ragged and dirty old harridans, drawn out of their hovels, intoxicated by the prospect of violence and possible plunder; and in the mob, too, were children, ragged, skinny little boys with ferret faces, little girls with matted hair and wide, staring eyes.

Bennett took a firmer grip on the reins. Ahead of him traffic had slowed and stopped and he saw hoodlums approach a fine carriage and grab at the horses' bits. In a few minutes, amidst much shouting, the team had been freed from the carriage and two disreputable, unshaven men were astride the animals, hooting and hollering, riding them back up the street, leaving the carriage stranded and the coachman standing beside it, bewildered and afraid. The crowd whooped and yelled in delight and there was in their shouts something sinister and it made Bennett tingle with apprehension. His team reared a little, pulled at their bits, but Bennett's hand steadied them. From the corner of his eye he saw men advancing toward him, and he knew they intended to follow the lead of the others who had stolen the horses from the carriage ahead of him. Slade was muttering and he was trembling. "Oh, Jesus," he kept saying. "Oh, Jesus, the bastards, what'll we do, Bennett, what'll we do? Better let them take them, Bennett, better let them have their way. It's no use trying to fight a mob, Bennett," he babbled.

Bennett gripped his long whip. Suddenly he stood a little and the whip barely touched his team. The beautifully trained animals had been awaiting just that signal and now they whirled in an incredibly small space, their sharp, flying hoofs plowing the air before them. The carriage turned sharply in the middle of the street, and Bennett's whip was working, and it sang and whistled as it came down through the air. The horses knew the sound, they trembled, fearing the lash upon them, and they raced, their hoofs beating a deadly tattoo on the pavement. Again and again Bennett's whip came down mercilessly on men who attempted to grab the harness or the carriage door handles, and sometimes the whip found its mark and a man's howl and another's curse rang out, and a thousand stopped to watch. Others raced toward the carriage, but none wanted to come within the range of those delicate, sharp hoofs, nor under the lash of Bennett's flailing whip.

Slade clung to the box, his dignity and his training forgotten. Bennett's face was grim, but he handled his team well. A tiny smile of satisfaction curled one corner of his mouth as he saw a path opening for him. The team gained speed. Bennett turned off Broadway, raced east to Mercer, and swept around the corner at a dead run, heading south, and his pursuers were lost.

Mercer Street, compared to Broadway, was almost deserted. Bennett slowed his team a little, but gradually, quieting the animals with his skillful hand on the rein and his steady, coaxing voice. Again he held his whip at the prescribed angle. He glanced at Slade sharply and Slade sheepishly let go his frenzied hold on the seat and regained the proper posture. At Canal Street Bennett turned west again, and continued south on Church Street to Vesey, and then, cautiously, he turned back to Broadway again.

There were soldiers in City Hall Park, and around the Astor House were policemen and special guards and a great crowd of well-dressed men who were undoubtedly from the offices and warehouses of the lower city. But this group was peaceful. Beads of sweat were standing out on Bennett's big face, rolling down his cheeks and soaking into his collar, but the carriage proceeded slowly, in regulated traffic, south toward Wall, and in a few moments he turned east again and drew up in front of Mr. Blake's office.

He stared ahead as Slade slid shakily from the box and opened the carriage door. But he rolled his eyes around to catch a glimpse of Mr. Blake and Christensen as they emerged. The two men stood on the walk and then Blake walked forward and looked up at his coachman.

"That was well done, Bennett. Very well done," Thaddeus said. Bennett's chest swelled a little. "Take the horses back, Bennett, and get them out of sight. It seems the rioters intend to form a cavalry regiment and I understand they are taking all the animals they can get, including those from horse cars. Put the carriage up until further orders." Blake stroked his chin. "But wait. I want you to take a note back to Miss Loyalty."

He hurried into his office, motioning Slade to follow him, and in a few moments Slade returned and handed Bennett an envelope. The coachman tucked it carefully inside his coat. Slade leaped quickly to the box.

Bennett slipped across Broadway at the first opportunity and headed North again. He heard fire bells pealing, he heard the shouts and howls of a growing mob. A knot of men armed only with stones surged out into the street ahead of him, holding up their arms to block his progress, but Bennett neither slowed nor stopped. The team plunged on and the men fell back, but they sent a rain of rocks toward the carriage.

When at last he pulled up at the stables his team was streaked with sweat and flecks of foam and they were trembling like race horses at the starting gate. Bennett clambered down from the box slowly and stroked the horses, quieting them. Then, with great dignity, he turned toward the rear entrance of the Blake house to deliver Mr. Blake's message himself to Miss Loyalty.

The sun beat down upon him unmercifully, and the dust curled around his shining boots. He was puffing from the exertion and the heat, but he did not loosen his coat or waistcoat. The respectful eyes of grooms and stable boys bored into his back. A deep satisfaction, sweet and heady, had come to Bennett. Old he might be, fat and unlovely to look upon. But he had delivered Mr. Blake to his office, and almost on time.

[2]

A NAVAL vessel had sighted the *Loyalty* two hundred miles off the coast and warned her to be on close watch. A Boston dispatch had said the pirate *Florida* was seen the day before eighty miles southwest of Gay Head, burning a brig and a fishing schooner. Matthew was relieved when they neared Sandy Hook, but he was surprised at how few pilot and tugboats came to meet him. Usually the little boats made the sea look like regatta-day. But now only a few old faithfuls met the *Loyalty*.

"I'd not dock if I were you, Captain Steel," the pilot warned. "There's no labor on the docks nor in the shipyards; everything's closed up tight and the mob loots a ship if it has half a chance. With Negroes aboard—" the pilot glanced meaningly at Webb—"you'd be taking a terrible chance. Negroes are streaming out of the city in all directions—them as can get out. I saw them on 33rd Street—the rioters built up a barricade of wagons across 33rd and Sixth Avenue, and then they burned the Negro homes. They let a few women and children escape—but no men. They didn't get off with a quick and easy death, either. There was a Negro killed on

Pier 4 at the foot of Morris Street on North River this morning."

"Who's the leader?"

"Man named Andrews is said to be the head of it. He's got the people so worked up now nothing will stop them. The Mayor has been pleading for troops, but with the militia in Pennsylvania he's not having much luck. Some think this is part of a Rebel plot, with Lee pushing into Pennsylvania, to take over the city, and then they'll be ready to welcome Lee when he moves in. But they used the draft as a reason to start it. Under the law a man has to serve if his name is drawn, unless he pays three hundred dollars or provides a substitute. The leaders of the riot claim it's a draft of poor men, and the rich can get out of fighting, and so they started out by rioting around the places where the drawings were being held and smashing all the buildings and the equipment to bits and then they set fire to it. It's a wonder the whole city didn't burn. Plenty of tenements are leveled, and there were bodies of children lying in the street and people walked right by them, paying no mind. It's as if they were clean mad, Captain Steel. Colonel O'Brien was beaten and hung, and then today his house was looted, and you'll see his clothing or his wife's on men and women in the mob. They're after the Mayor and Union leaders, men like Horace Greeley and Thaddeus Blake—"

Matthew snapped to attention. "Blake? Has his house been—"

The pilot shook his head. "So far as I know they haven't got Blake yet, nor the Mayor either, though they tried to gut the Mayor's house, which isn't far from Blake's on Fifth Avenue. At O'Brien's it took three hundred police to drive the mob off, and they went into other houses near by, and the police used clubs on any of them they could reach. It took a detachment of the Eleventh Regiment to clear them out. The Ferry House at the foot of 42nd Street was fired this morning, too. They said that friends of the Mayor armed themselves and stayed in his house and drove off the mob. Some of the soldiers at first used blank cartridges—that was yesterday. But not now. They fire to kill. They're using grape and cannister and bayonets. The Hudson River Railroad tracks were torn up, and they're being repaired, under the protection of gunboats in the river and a couple of howitzers loaded with cannister."

It seemed to Matthew an interminable time until the *Loyalty* was finally at anchor in mid-channel. He left the vessel in Jules' charge, and gave strict orders to Webb and his two Negro friends to stay aboard and out of sight. One look at Webb's mask-like face made him doubt that he would be obeyed. The Negro had heard some of the pilot's account, and the word had sifted down through the ship, into the forecastle.

Matthew quietly threaded a knife scabbard on his belt and slipped a small pistol inside his coat. He went ashore on the tug, and as he approached the pier he could already see evidence of the revolution, now nearing the end of its second day. The accounts he had heard, the mention of the name of Thaddeus Blake, filled him with anxiety and fury. He could not permit himself to think of Loyalty being endangered by a howling, crazy mob. He stepped ashore, and went down South Street toward the foot of Catharine.

Glass lay like snow upon the one walk of South Street and had been ground to powder in the street itself. Great gaping holes and empty show windows of silent, empty shops leered at him. Down the street smoke still drifted from a deserted, fire-blackened building. The street was unnaturally quiet, but from no great distance Matthew heard the sounds of voices raised in wild shouts.

He glanced up Catharine Street. Before a hardware store a crowd had gathered and it moved, as one man, out into the street, then, with a rush, toward the shop. They had made of themselves a battering ram, and as Matthew watched he heard the door give way with a crash and the men poured into the shop. In a few minutes they emerged. They brandished knives, brand-new and glistening, and a few had guns, which they were loading, gloating over them, waving them, shouting hoarsely. As Matthew approached them he saw that the faces of many of the men were crimson, their eyes bloodshot, their foreheads dripping sweat. They looked drunk, as though they had not slept. They had been continuing this carnival of destruction for almost thirty-six hours.

Automatically, as the dangerous crowd surged out into Catharine Street and turned northward, Matthew stepped back into a doorway. The clothes of the mobsters were ragged and dirty and some wore no shirts at all. Matthew waited, watching them surge forward, and then he saw a familiar figure.

Old Dan had been at his usual corner, and now when the mob parted, Matthew saw him still sitting there on his small stool, his fiddle hugged close against his thin old chest, his dog cringing close to his knees. Matthew could not see the old fellow's face, but he seemed to be making himself as small and inconspicuous as possible, eager to avoid notice. Then one of the men who had run from the shop flourishing a new and gleaming knife saw him.

With one swift, horrible motion the knife descended. The dog's shrill yelp of terror and pain cut through the crowd's roar. Matthew saw the animal give one wild leap, saw the long line of crimson and raw, red flesh the whole length of it, heard the attacker's shout. Matthew started to run toward the old beggar, but the distance was too great. Old Dan had struggled to his feet, and he was shaking his fist at the mob, and the man with the knife heard him and turned back. He slashed again, and Old Dan fell, his fiddle beneath him, and the man turned and ran after the others, up Catharine Street, leaving Old Dan where he lay.

The dog was still groveling in the gutter, his legs twitching a little, the blood flowing from the long wound in his side. Matthew reached for his own knife and then he saw the animal give one last jerk and lie still. Matthew turned Old Dan over, felt for his heartbeat. Old Dan had too fragile a grip on life, and the neck wound was deep. He did not open his eyes nor speak. Matthew straightened him as best he could and stopped the blood with part of Old Dan's ragged jacket.

The mob was completely out of sight, headed, Matthew supposed, for the sink-hole of Five Points. Across the street the doors of a saloon opened wide, and in the dim interior Matthew could see a few men sitting, their heads on the tables, asleep or drunk.

He stood up and raised the body of Old Dan in his arms. It was only a few blocks to the Cock and Bull and Old Dan's wasted body was light. Matthew strode forward, and the few stragglers on the street stepped out of his way.

The doors of the Cock and Bull were wide open, too, and Hite and Morton were behind the bar. Their faces were haggard with loss of sleep. They were shoving food and drink to the men clustered about them. Many of the men, Matthew noticed, in one swift glance, were shipyard workers, many of them middle-aged or gray-haired, looking bewildered, uncertain. With the yards closed they had no other place to go. But also at the bar, or sleeping, heads on the tables, were men who had obviously been in the mob.

Matthew walked through the barroom, toward the familiar door at the back. Hite glanced up and saw him and his mouth fell open, and many customers followed his glance. Hite left the bar and half-ran to the door, and he reached it at the same time as Matthew.

"Jesus, Joseph and Mary!" Hite breathed. "Matthew—is Old Dan—"

"He's dead," Matthew said tightly. Hite opened the door and Matthew went into the dim room beyond and shoved the door shut behind him with his foot, cutting off the stares of the curious. Carefully he laid the old man's body on the floor, and then he arose and wiped his face on his sleeve. "I saw the bastard that killed him. I'd like to get my hands on that—"

Hite rubbed his thighs with his hands. In the silence Matthew could hear the man's palms rasping on the rough cloth of his trousers. The rubbing went on and on, and then Matthew looked up and his eyes were dangerous. Nervously Hite pulled a cloth from a table, upsetting an empty glass as he did so, and placed it gently over Old Dan's body.

"How far's this riot gone, Hite?" Matthew asked.

"Too damned far. The Governor made a speech this afternoon, said the draft would be called off. They won that point, anyway. They attacked the Seventh Avenue arsenal, but some soldiers met them with four- and twelve-pound howitzers. It's spread to Staten Island, and they sacked the Lyceum there and attacked the Marine Hospital. Some say they got five hundred muskets and plenty of ammunition there. They've attacked the brothels on Greenwich—and—it was pretty bad. They burned one, and let no one escape from the building—cooked them alive; and wrecked others. They've burned Negro houses by the dozens and plundered drinking shops. The Negroes have been horribly tortured in Brooklyn, and it took grape and cannister to stop them. They got the home of David Dudley Field—and Mayor Opdyke's. But the worst thing they've done, I think, is to burn the Colored Children's Orphanage. Poor little black devils—

"There's been thousands of families leave the city. I'd like to shut up shop, but they won't let me. They'd mob the place and take it over. As long as we keep open and keep serving the bastards—" Hite wiped his gray face and reached out to the table for support. Then he glanced at Matthew sharply and his face hardened. "Are you joining the mob?" he asked harshly. "Your friend Jimmy Burns is in the middle of it."

Matthew hitched up his belt and Hite noted the scabbard. Matthew's face had whitened and he was biting his lip at Hite's thrust. His fist clenched, but after a minute it loosened and he nodded toward the white-covered object on the floor. "See that he gets a decent burial. I'll pay for it," he said.

"There's been messages for you," Hite said grudgingly. "Tessa Dunn's back. She's at the Irving House. And your ship, the *Comet*, is lost." It gave him pleasure to report the last.

Matthew hesitated just an instant, his hand on the door, and then he nodded shortly and was gone.

[3]

THE quick, sharp end to the riot, with the arrival of troops, had come just in time to save the city, men said. And, as if a merciful power were watching over them, the news of the Northern victory at Gettysburg swept over the shocked, scarred city, to salve its wounds and draw the minds of its people from the shameful days just passed. By common consent the women of New York did not discuss the riot. There was a limit to what people could endure, and they tried hard to forget. They talked instead of Gettysburg, and little by little the glorious meaning of that great victory came home to them. It had, indeed, been the crisis. Lee was turned back, Lee was beaten, Lee's great bid for victory had failed. He would never again have another such chance to beat the North to its knees. The Federal line, after all, had held. The back of the Rebellion had at last been broken.

The rioters had crawled back into the nooks and crannies from which they had emerged and they were again the nondescript, single souls they had been before they had been transformed into a destroying force. Their leaders were whisked away. With Gettysburg, and then Vicksburg, came new hope to the North, and once again men began to dream of victory and a united, unbroken nation.

The only hope for the Rebels now, men declared openly, was foreign intervention. The victory at Gettysburg had helped to stay Britain's recognition of the Confederacy once again and the liberals of England were standing firm in their friendship toward the Union. But if Britain and France hoped to see the South as an independent nation, as indeed they did, now was the time for them to send real aid. Eyes turned toward the governments of Europe, watchful, defiant.

In New York, in newspaper offices, in the room of Graham White at the Astor House, in government offices in the capital, men speculated about foreign intervention. Too bad, men said, that the Federals had not followed up Lee's retreat, and forced his surrender at once. As it was, it looked like a long war still. But the Northern armies at last had proven they had become a fighting unit. The South was sufficiently weakened so other victories were not only possible but probable. Only one tremendous threat remained—the intervention of England and France.

The British parliament would vote again, soon, on the question of recognizing the South. But suddenly another incident occurred to give the British a subject on which to speculate, and to give them pause.

Graham White, reading of it, smiled quietly to himself. So did Charles Sumner. The outcome of Matthew Steel's mission to Russia would not be known, for certain, for some time yet, for the Russians confided their plans to no one. But at any rate, so far, the news was encouraging, and it had, apparently, caused the English some concern. What were the Russians up to, British editors asked? Were they sending their fleet into the Mediterranean, perhaps?

For dispatches from St. Petersburg said simply that the great Russian fleets had put to sea.

CHAPTER VII

"YOU CHOSE a bad time to return to New York, Tess."

"Yes. I'd have liked to have missed the riot." Tessa shivered. "I stayed here in my rooms as long as I could, and grew more and more terrified. Then I joined the crowds in the lobby, and saw women much more hysterical than I, and I suppose that made me feel better." Tessa smiled, her slow, lazy smile. She glanced at Matthew, her narrow eyes brilliant beneath the long lashes. "I was hoping you'd come, Matthew."

Matthew pushed his chair back from the table and looked at Tessa thoughtfully. As a matter of fact he had not even thought of Tessa's safety, during the wild hours when hoodlums roared through the city. He had been thinking only of Loyalty, though Tessa was alone in New York and Loyalty had a family and friends and all the power of Thaddeus Blake to protect her. Nevertheless, he had walked and run and shoved and finally slugged his way up Broadway and to the block on Fifth Avenue in which the Blake home stood. He had never known relief like that which came to him when he saw the Blake house solidly guarded by dozens of well-armed soldiers. After the attack on the Mayor's house and open threats against Thaddeus Blake, the men had told him, the heavy guard had been thrown about Blake's home; and inside the great, solid, safe-looking house friends and employes sat, armed and ready to shoot to kill. Loyalty was safe in a small fort of her own; but Matthew stayed near by throughout the rest of the night, till morning brought a lull in the mob's activities and fresh troops brought the situation finally under control.

Now he grinned at Tessa, half-teasing. "I guess I figured you could take care of yourself, Tess," he said easily. "You seem to do pretty well."

Tessa's cheeks grew a little pink. "Yes, I've done all right," she said carelessly. Her long fingers stroked a glass in front of her, feeling its smoothness, seeming to seek an imperfection. "But—how about you? I've heard of your losses, Matthew, and I'm sorry. I've heard also that you've lost a lot of friends on South Street."

Matthew's face sobered. "Yes," he said. The way his lips clamped down on the word was familiar. Tess knew it would do no good to question him further on that subject.

She still was sensitive to Matthew's every gesture, every tone. Swiftly she took a new tack.

"You look well in a Naval uniform. It was a big surprise to me."

"And to others, I reckon," he said a little shortly. Again his lips straightened and he looked down at his plate. Tessa feasted her eyes on his face. She wanted to reach across the table and run her hands along his stubborn jaw, urge him to tell her the whole story. His same old charm for her was there and it would be easy to let it overpower her. She frowned, resentful toward those former friends who had deserted him.

"Damn Hite and Morton," she said. "Hasn't a man got a right to look out for himself?" She leaned across the table and her hand slipped over his. I want so much just to touch him, she thought; despite herself her voice dropped, grew a little unsteady. "Matthew, I would not have cared, whether you joined the service or whether you were a Copperhead."

Matthew looked at her without raising his head and grinned slightly. "Same old Tessa," he said. He withdrew his hand and felt in his pocket for a cigar. Tessa leaned back and bit her lip and clasped her hands tightly beneath the table. Matthew, not looking at her, knew that he had been abrupt and he made an effort, now, to talk more easily with her. He did not want to hurt her needlessly. "The fact remains that now I am in the Navy. Me—and the *Loyalty*, and Jules and Webb. They let Jules and Webb stay with me and the ship—but the rest of my men!" He raised his eyebrows and shook his head, half-laughing at himself, half-disgusted. "The highest honor a sailor can have is to serve with the attacking fleet, and they need good, trained men on the blockaders, too. The rest of them, the very young ones, the very old ones, those who are gun-shy, they put on ships like the *Loyalty*. We'll have a job making seamen of them. And when we do they'll take them away from us and give us some more green ones, probably. I joined the Navy—and what do I do? End up as a God damned messenger boy for the ships in the blockade fleet, shuttling back and forth between the Navy Yard and the ships."

Tessa laughed. She looked ten years younger, Matthew thought, when she laughed like that. When he first had met her tonight he had been struck by the hard, brittle polish she had acquired. Her mannerisms were the result of practice, even her fluid grace which had been her greatest beauty had become a little exaggerated, so it seemed more a pose than a natural gift. The sophistication that was Tessa Dunn's protected her and was valuable in her profession, but it might well bruise any man with whom she came in contact. He had liked her old half-awkward girlishness better. He was glad to see it shining through the veneer now.

"And you'd rather be just one jump ahead of Farragut."

"Well, I'd like to be in the attacking fleet, or at least to be a blockader, where I might have a slim chance of mixing with a Rebel ship. I joined the service to fight. But that isn't my job. It's not my business to guard the Rebel coast, nor to grapple with a blockade runner or a privateer. I'm supposed to keep out of trouble, if possible, for the *Loyalty* is considered no fighting ship, no fitting match for a well-armed Rebel vessel. My guns are short-range; I've no iron on the *Loyalty* and no steam power. So they assign her to supply, carrying medicines and munitions and mail to the ships that do the work." Matthew gritted his teeth. "And it's my own fault. If I'd gone into this in the beginning, when they needed ships so badly, they'd have sent the *Loyalty* into the blockade fleet at once, with the best armament they had. They've got every kind of vessel in the fleet, Tessa; it's a sight to see. There are wooden frigates, stripped to the girt line, clean for action, stripped of everything that seems like extra rigging, and with their bows heavily ironed to cut down the enemy. There are transports and puffing little tugs and big store ships and dirty coal vessels; schooners, barges, mortar boats, trading drafts, square riggers. The *Loyalty* could have been among them. But not now. The yards are turning out new vessels especially designed for fighting. It's better to equip them and send them in to do the real fighting and let old ships like the *Loyalty* supply them. And I've no one to blame but myself, but it is a damned monotonous job."

"I don't see why you joined the service, Matthew," Tessa said. "It isn't as if you couldn't afford three hundred dollars, even if you were drafted. Surely because Hite and Morton and some of the others on South Street—"

Matthew's look was sharp. "I joined because I have a job to do," he said shortly. "I'll do it—even if I don't like it." He was silent a moment, then he said suddenly: "Tessa, do you remember Cass Blake?"

Tessa nodded. Matthew told her a little of Cass' death and Tessa sat silent, a little shaken, not only at the story but at the effect it had evidently had on Matthew Steel. As a child, as a girl, growing up, she had adored him, partly because of his arrogance, his damn-your-eyes and to-hell-with-you attitude. He had lost some of that now. Tessa tipped her head, her narrow eyes measuring him. He had great financial losses, and did not discuss them. Was he going to take a beating without protest? He had lost friends on South Street and instead of standing up to them and going his own stubborn way he had joined the service. And now he was talking about Cass, and English workmen, and ideals, strange talk for Matthew Steel. Tessa was not sure that she liked the change and certainly she did not understand it. It seemed to widen the gap between them—the gap she had thought she was closing when she had become wealthy and successful and assured.

And she still loved him. If he were to beckon her she would be swift to go straight into his arms and to forget these new doubts and perhaps to win him back to the reckless way he used to be. She thought of these things as Matthew talked, half following his words but in no way sensing the meaning underlying them.

Finally Matthew paused. Tessa had not understood what he was trying to say, Matthew knew. She had heard the news of Cass' death and the manner of it, but the knowledge that had come to him as a result escaped her completely. He found himself pitying her. Poor Tessa, he said to himself, she'll never change. She's gone as far as she will ever go, and it is foolish to try to take her farther, to show her what's ahead of us all.

He leaned back and raised his glass. "Let's have a toast, Tess, and stop all the serious talk. Tomorrow I go to sea again, and this is a night for celebration." Gratefully Tessa raised her own glass. This was more like it. She remembered now her decision in San Francisco, her plan to offer him money. She glanced at him over the rim of her glass. Money was hard to come by, and she valued it. But when she met Matthew's eyes she knew that anything she had that Matthew Steel wanted, now or ever, she would give to him.

"Matthew," she said, a little awkward in her attempts to be casual, "I know you don't like to talk of the loss of the *Messenger* and the *Comet*—but it must have hit you pretty hard." She pleated the tablecloth carefully with her slender fingers and kept her eyes upon it. "I thought—well, you gave me those lots in San Francisco. They turned out to be very valuable. I made other investments. I found I was a pretty good business woman—and I had some good advisers. I'd like to return what you gave me, now, if you'll—"

Her fingers were working fast, nervously, and she stopped and swallowed. Matthew sat still and after a minute she forced herself to look at him. He was smiling, his face was gentle. This time it was Matthew who reached across the table and stopped her restless fingers.

"Thanks, Tess," he said simply. Suddenly Tessa felt her eyes smart and her throat hurt. Damn it, she thought, when his voice is like that I can't resist him. I never could. When he's gentle and tender, when his voice is deep and rich and personal and his attention is really all for me, he does something to me that no one else can. "Did you come from San Francisco to offer me that?"

He sees through me like a window-glass, she thought, half-angered. She sighed and then, half-sullenly, resentfully, she nodded.

"Tess, you're kinder than I deserve. I can't thank you. I can't tell you what such a gesture means. But Tess, I don't want money

—and I couldn't take yours, if I did need it." She flicked a side-wise glance at him.

"Why? Why couldn't we be—sort of partners?"

Matthew gave her hand a reassuring, impersonal little pat and grinned. He tipped back in his chair.

"Honey—you keep your money," he said. "Listen, Tess. Maybe it's hard for you to believe. It's even hard for me to believe, some-times. I've lost my ships—yes. They represented a lot of money and years of work. But I never felt better in my life. I never felt richer."

She looked at him suspiciously. "Something's happened to you, Matthew," she said finally. "Maybe you've figured a way to get along without money. But suppose some day you . . . marry, and have sons of your own. How about them?"

"Hell, Tessa, they can start out the way I did," Matthew an-swered impatiently. "What's wrong with that?" He glared at her. "If they haven't got the guts to fight for it, as I did—as you did—" He stopped. "That's the beauty of being an American," he said slowly. "Every boy has a chance. Oh, I don't say they're equal chances—not yet. But a fellow has a better chance here than any-where else. Only, if we lose the war, Tess, if the Union is broken up, there won't be that chance. This won't be a strong nation any more, able to hold her own with the rest of the world. She'll be a bunch of little puppet states, governed by the European powers, and they'll bring their class-consciousness and their intolerance over here. Our only salvation is to save the Union, make this country strong and independent and make democracy work, im-prove it, make this equality business true. It's worth fighting a war for. But war is a costly business. Take the merchant marine for in-stance—it will be years, generations, if ever, before we win back supremacy again. I'd like my sons, if ever I have any, to take part in that. What better thing could I give them than that chance? Money wouldn't make men out of them. Look at Cass. Was it money that gave him triumph over fear? Don't you see, Tess? Don't you understand?"

"No," Tessa said bluntly. The word fell heavily into the silence. Matthew turned away and picked up his cap. He turned it over in his hands, staring at it, smoothing the black visor with his thumb. His face was closed again and Tessa knew that she had lost the moment's intimacy. She rose and stood facing him. Her hands went out to his chest and then they crept over his shoulders, fingering the shoulder straps, touching the silver eagle in the center of the silver anchor. "Matthew," she tried again. She arched her body a little, in invitation. "The money—it's all yours, if you want it."

He took her wrists firmly in both hands and again he shook his head. "Thanks, Tess," he said again. "It was great of you to come to offer it. But I don't need it."

"Then this last trip to Russia—it was very successful?"

Surprisingly he smiled and his eyes grew bright and shining.

"I don't know for sure yet, Tessa," he said slowly. He looked over her head, at the window of her sitting room. Tessa watched him, puzzled. "But I think—I hope—it may turn out to be the best trip I ever made."

Tessa relaxed suddenly, letting her whole body go limp with relief. So that was it. The old gambler, the old trader in Matthew was still working. He was doing all right, she'd had no need to worry about him. He hadn't changed at all. No doubt this war business was a carefully planned move to further his fortunes. He was still the man she loved, selfish, stubborn, ambitious, reckless, but still Matthew Steel.

She raised her lips. Matthew's hands closed on her shoulders and he shook her a little, laughing, and then he kissed her once and the door closed behind him.

[2]

For hours Captain Matthew Steel had kept a glass screwed to his eye. He must know every inch of the Carolina coast by now, the crew thought, watching him. Each time the *Loyalty* reached this area the Captain slowed her speed, and often, against his usual custom, he ordered the ship hove to overnight. Dawn found him and the Negro, Webb, studying the coastline with the glass and once the Captain had a jolly-boat lowered and he and Webb and a few strong men to row had gone close to the rocks, standing like crags and castles, huge and jagged at low tide, off which the *Loyalty* was anchored. Captain Steel had spent considerable time skirting that reef, and the men with him had declared that Webb had pointed out to him a well-concealed channel, deep and wide enough for a good-sized vessel to pass through at high tide. The reef, they said, was not a continuous one, as it appeared from off-shore; it was two, over-lapping, one running behind the other, forming a carefully hidden entrance to the bay which extended inland and whose entrance, thirty miles down the coast, was carefully guarded by vessels of the blockade fleet.

These frequent hesitations along the Carolina coast were the only break in the tedious routine of the ship's work. There was much speculation about them among the crew. Any valuable information Captain Steel gathered would be relayed to the proper places, the men said, and that would be the end of it. But the Captain's preoccupation with this particular area gave the crew a welcome topic for discussion. It had been going on for weeks now, but on this trip the *Loyalty* again had been ordered halted—and this in broad daylight.

There were wounded aboard, men suffering from dark blue welts beneath their skin, welts and ridges made by unburnt cubes of cannon powder that felt like red-hot bullets. The pain was enough to make them curse and pace in agony, but they were not stretcher cases and so they were going back to Northern hospitals for treatment and they traveled on the *Loyalty,* no hospital ship. They muttered at this delay and questioned the crew. But Captain Steel did not make known his purpose. He stood on deck, studying the shoreline, and then he turned the glass over to Webb and went to his cabin and the men could do nothing but wait.

The wounded, men who had seen actual fighting, were heroes to the crew members of the *Loyalty.* Not a one of them but envied the fighting men. But at the same time none would join with the passengers in complaint. The *esprit de corps* built up in a few weeks aboard the *Loyalty* would be the envy of any fighting vessel. Anything Captain Steel did would be defended to the death by his men.

The *Loyalty* had been assigned a menial job and she was outmoded, compared to the formidable fighting ships now being developed. But by some means or other the men who served aboard her had come to love her, and they had great admiration for her master. How it had come about no one knew for certain; the officers of other vessels would have liked to know. Something in the attitude of the Captain toward his ship, and of Jules Descase and Webb, had seeped into the crew, and they had learned respect for the beautiful, gallant old clipper. Pride in the *Loyalty* had likewise spread from them to other men in the fleet, and when she appeared, with something besides coffee and hard-tack for the men, with messages and newspapers from home, she was welcomed with cheers. Her speed records in her class had preceded her and men of the sea knew her and her history and that of her master well. Like a celebrated beauty, in spite of her age, the *Loyalty* could not help but be conspicuous. She was one of those colorful champions that could not, even in the most commonplace job, go unnoticed, and gradually, as the weeks went on and the *Loyalty* faithfully, unwaveringly discharged her duties, affection for the vessel among Navy men had deepened.

About her master, too, was an aura of mystery and romance. A well-known, successful shipowner, who had at first refused his support, had done a complete about-face, and finally had offered his vessel to the government, not for sale, but as a gift. Legends had always been quick to grow about the *Loyalty* and her captain and they did not cease now. It was too bad, men said, that Captain Steel couldn't actually get into battle. That would be something to see. But they respected the fact that he accepted his tiresome assignment without protest and discharged it faithfully. Because of its monotony, it was not an easy job.

Matthew had tried to ease his own restlessness by picking up what information and new skills he could. It was second nature for him to note and file away landmarks in his memory. Years of sailing had made him a keen observer. He zealously prodded Webb for information about the Southern coast and found the man's knowledge was sound, his memory accurate. Whether this information would ever be of value was doubtful; but Matthew was not one to pass up an opportunity for new knowledge. He likewise mastered the new flag signals developed since the war began, and he studied naval history and naval customs and followed the strategy of the naval leaders.

But this time Matthew Steel did not linger off the coast simply to break the boredom or gain a little information that might, or might not, some day prove valuable. He had been warned to watch for a privateer operating in these waters, an elusive ship that struck and then disappeared, and had so far successfully evaded all pursuers. When Matthew had seen the map that had been prepared, with pins marking the exact positions of the ships that had been attacked, and of the directions in which the vessel had fled, he had, at first, opened his lips to speak. Then he had thought better of it. Theories, unless there were facts behind them, were not welcome in the Navy. An independent operator like Matthew Steel had learned that in his first few days as a member of the service. But he was in the Navy to win the war, and if, by a little independent sleuthing, he were able to contribute actual information of value, it would undoubtedly be received with pleasure.

He had, moreover, a more than usual interest in this particular privateer. It was said that she strongly resembled the old slaver, the *Annie B.*

Matthew Steel, in his own quarters, studied his charts. The vessel had struck here, and here; he tapped the map with his finger. The Cuban, Fernando, captain of the *Annie B.*, had been engaged in the dirtiest of all commerce, slaving, before the war. He knew this coast as well as Webb.

The *Annie B.* was known to have run the blockade successfully more than once and she had carried the most valuable of all cargoes—munitions. Each time he thought of Fernando and the *Annie B.*, Matthew's mind also slid back to another picture, the Pond's rifle which Cass Blake had carried with him back from Bull Run.

The *Annie B.*, emboldened by her successes, no doubt, had been strengthened and ironed, in some British yard, perhaps; and she had turned privateer. She had struck at a fishing schooner, at two vessels in the supply fleet, and at merchant ships. Fernando would like nothing better than to claim the *Loyalty* as a prize. Matthew, too, would welcome an engagement with Fernando; he'd prefer a hand-to-hand battle with the oily turn-coat himself.

But he would not have that chance. The *Loyalty's* wooden hull had no iron sheath. Her guns were less adequate than those that would be mounted on the vicious *Annie B.* The *Loyalty* had no steam power. She'd be a poor match for the privateer. Matthew clenched his fists. "Damn it," he said aloud. "I'd like to meet Fernando, the dirty, slippery—"

But he had a job to do. He had no right, unless he was attacked, to endanger the lives of his crew and the wounded men aboard. He had no right even to be attacked, if he could avoid it. His orders were to pick up and deliver, to leave the fighting to more able vessels. Yet some sixth sense that had served him well in the past told him that he had stumbled on to the *Annie B.'s* base. Her depredations, her quick disappearance, her sudden reappearance, and then her fading away again like a phantom ship, all within a small area, were evidence in Matthew's mind. He checked tide charts and hours of daylight and he figured again and the answer came out the same each time. The *Annie B.* could strike exactly where she had struck, and she could regain the shelter of this particular inlet before her pursuers could catch her. Her base was not a far-off, foreign one. It was right here on the Carolina coast, in one of the most heavily guarded inlets of the Southern states.

And the doorway to it—Matthew was certain of it—was the hidden channel, the fault in the rock reef, that Webb had shown him.

Blockaders, armed to meet pirates like the *Annie B.*, lay off the natural entrance to the inlet. The privateer would never enter or leave that harbor under their menacing guns. But she could leave it, and reenter it, under the skillful seamanship of Fernando, by the little channel that Webb had discovered.

Matthew had no proof that the *Annie B.* lay concealed there within that inlet. It was not his job to seek her out. He was not sure that any vessel as large as the *Annie B.* had ever slipped through that small channel. It would take a master pilot to take a vessel through. But it was possible—he had assured himself of that, and Fernando's seamanship was noted. The evidence—and instinct—was enough for Matthew, though it might not be enough for more seasoned members of the Navy.

Suppose his hunch was right, and the *Annie B.* did lie there, within the inlet? It was his duty, obviously, to report it to the blockaders, to ships equipped to meet her, and it was his job to sail on, back to the Navy Yard, on his usual freighting trip.

But suppose the *Annie B.* lay there, and she slipped out again on this very night, to strike again? Matthew had seen the damage one privateer could do and it made him sick to think of it. In one excursion the *Annie B.* could sink or damage several ships; in a few months her victims would number in the dozens. And Matthew knew too well what a shipload of English rifles could do in Rebel hands. The quicker the *Annie B.* was stopped, the more lives were saved.

He might be overstepping his orders, if he chose to grapple with the *Annie B.* But morally, if he could stop one privateer, at any cost, he would be right. Matthew had been his own master too long to worry much about red tape. He was in this job to help win the war, and that meant engaging the enemy wherever and whenever he met him, not running from him because his assignment was to deliver mail instead of to fight.

Matthew's hand balled into a fist, and he pounded it lightly in the palm of his other hand. He walked across his quarters, three steps forward, three steps back. No, he had no right to endanger his men or the ship, which now, rightfully, belonged to his government and not to him. But he couldn't let a bastard like Fernando, with a devilish instrument for destruction like the *Annie B.*, get away, could he? No man ever won a battle by sitting with his hands folded.

The truth was—and he must be very careful in his reasoning, Matthew cautioned himself—he was itching to fight. It would give him great personal satisfaction to meet Fernando face to face. But he must not consider that. He must judge, impersonally, what his chances were of victory in a battle with the *Annie B.* They were not, he admitted truthfully, very good. In fact, they were damned poor.

Matthew put his foot on a chair and leaned against his knee, chewing his lip. If there were only himself he'd wade into the battle for the pure pleasure of knocking a privateer to hell, or trying to; he'd take his chances, slim as they were.

He took a deep breath and straightened. It was a great temptation, but his duty was clear. If only the *Loyalty* were armored. If only he had the guns! If only he had a crew such as he had in the ship's younger days, not a bunch of boys or old men, faithful and diligent but untrained for warfare, and a handful of wounded. If he had big, tough sailors, who loved to fight—like the men who had sailed with him on his China voyages; if he had the guns, the ammunition, the armor, he'd rip the *Annie B.* to ribbons.

Matthew strode back to the deck and took the glass from Webb. There was no sign of any wisp of smoke, nor the outline of any vessel anywhere in the inlet. But it was not yet high tide. It would be several hours yet before that channel was a safe exit for a ship like the *Annie B.* High tide would come with dusk. The *Annie B.* could slip out into deep water, and darkness would come down to safeguard her, and she would be ready to strike again.

It wouldn't do any harm, Matthew thought finally, to wait a little, anyway. It would be madness to engage the *Annie B.*, but the *Loyalty* could still outrun her. There'd be time, after he sighted her, if he was fortunate enough to see her, to escape, and to report her to the next vessel he contacted.

But Matthew's blood tingled. He knew that if the outlines of the *Annie B.* appeared in his glass, the *Loyalty* would not run.

He waited, and the crew waited with him. This was something more than a cursory examination of the coastline. The men sensed it. Captain Steel's face was closed, stony, and what was going on behind it they did not know, but a breathless uneasiness, the sense of something about to happen, settled over the ship. The wounded men felt it; it was the familiar tightening of nerves and muscles, the sharpened consciousness, that came before a battle. Quiet moved over the *Loyalty*, and men began to speak in low voices.

Captain Steel paced the deck and as dusk approached his tenseness became more evident. There had been no orders to prepare for a battle. There was only the waiting.

If the *Annie B.* came through that channel, Matthew was thinking, she'd have to choose the exact moment—the one moment when the tide was high and the light was still strong. She'd never risk it if the light were too dim, for she had a mighty small margin of safety. He checked his position. The *Loyalty* could lie hidden behind the rocks and islets a little way down the coast. The pirate would be near to the channel when she sighted the *Loyalty;* she would open up with her guns then and she'd fight her way out, for she would know her hiding place had been discovered and she could not afford to let the *Loyalty,* with that knowledge, escape her. The men aboard the *Annie B.* would be on the alert, ready for action; the destruction of the *Loyalty* would mean their only chance for escape and survival.

The proper thing for him to do was to get out of here, put as much distance between himself and the inlet as he could, and pray that the *Annie B.* did not overtake him and pounce on him during the night. He should report his suspicions to a patrol vessel, and leave it up to them. In the meantime, before the *Annie B.* was caught, how many ships would be sunk, how many lives lost?

Again he paced the deck, came back to his vantage point. Damned if he'd let that ship out—if she was in there. He'd know, in just a little while now, if the *Annie B.* was there, taking refuge under Rebel shore guns, and if she would try, tonight, to slip to the open sea and make another raid.

Suddenly Matthew Steel's body froze. There was a movement in his glass. A wisp of smoke. He knew, for a certainty that it would grow larger, that the ship would take on the familiar outlines of the nefarious steam sloop, the *Annie B.* He could see it growing, in his mind's eye, coming so close he could make out the features of Fernando himself. In the glass, actually, the ship was still a tiny speck, indistinguishable to any but trained eyes. Matthew Steel felt that speck was the pirate; every nerve in his body told him so. Reason seconded instinct. It was the logical place for the wily privateer to be.

And at the same moment he knew what he was going to do.

[3]

THE lifeboats lay in the shelter of the rocks, safe from the guns of the approaching *Annie B.*, and the men in them were silent, resting on their oars, watching the Loyalty. Even the wounded men were silent, forgetting their own torment. Captain Steel had moved swiftly and cleanly, once he had sighted and identified the *Annie B.*, and knew that she was headed for the channel. The lifeboats had been lowered and filled, and only Webb, and Jules Descase, and a handful of other carefully picked men, were now aboard the *Loyalty* with Captain Steel.

The ship's papers, a few instruments, and some few personal belongings of the Captain had been shoved into a sea-bag, and it lay now in the stern of one of the lifeboats, safe between a seaman's feet. Captain Steel himself was at the wheel of his ship. The men in the lifeboats could not see him, but they knew he was there. When they had abandoned the vessel, at his orders, they had seen him take the helm. They had seen his face as he watched until they were free of the ship. They had heard his voice as he had given his final orders. And now, waiting, watching the white sails of the *Loyalty*, seeing beyond her, across the rock-reef, the growing silhouette of the *Annie B.*, the men held their breath.

Aboard the *Loyalty*, Matthew Steel's hands were strong and steady on the helm. He held the vessel straight on the course he had chosen. The ugly shape of the *Annie B.* was plainly visible now, even without the glass, and she was headed, of course, not down the inlet where the blockaders awaited her, but toward the channel. The smoke from her stained the crimson sky behind her. She knew that she had been sighted by the *Loyalty*, and she knew that she was trapped.

For it was evident now, to Fernando, furious and cursing, aboard the *Annie B.*, and to the men of the *Loyalty* in the lifeboats, waiting, and to Jules Descase and to Webb, standing near to Matthew Steel, what Matthew was going to do. The men aboard the *Loyalty* were braced for the impact. The men in the lifeboats were braced, too. Matthew Steel was braced. His face was set, his teeth clenched tight together, his eyes straight and steady. The wind was with him, the tide swept him onward, and the waves dashed high over the jagged rocks. Matthew's head was lowered a little, as though he awaited a blow. His feet were widespread, to take the shock. The setting sun caught in the brasswork of the beautiful ship, the brass caps on the lanyard knots and the ends of the rigging and the heavy brass railing, bright as burnished gold around her quarter-deck; and the deck itself, scraped bright and shellac-coated, was never before so smooth and gleaming. The sails had never seemed so white, so flawlessly cut, so strong, spread to the breeze; she had never sailed so evenly before, without a quaver, responding to her master's hand.

She was no fighting ship, they said, for she was a wooden ship, powered only by the wind and the will of her commander. But the *Loyalty* could defeat the black, armored, machine-driven *Annie B.*, and the Navy would say it was a good exchange. What ship in the blockade fleet would not have been sacrificed to halt that privateer?

The *Loyalty* gained speed, sailing before the wind. The rocks loomed large and ugly before her. Matthew's lips drew back from his teeth and he held the wheel, tight, and the rocks came close.

The channel through which the *Annie B.* had planned to steal was directly before him. A minute ago the privateer, steaming confidently out to sea, had been a dangerous and wicked thing. Now she was impotent, wasted. For the channel was no longer open—nor would it ever be, again. The hands of the master of the *Loyalty* had moved, and then it came, the sickening, murderous sound of stout wood splintering, tearing, crashing; the suck and bubble and rush of water, the shudder of the ship, the creak of the straining masts, the snap and then the rip of canvas, as Matthew slammed her, slantingly, into the channel, onto the rocks.

At the beginning of the war, Charleston harbor had been blocked by sunken ships. Now the *Loyalty* was solidly impaled, closing the narrow entrance to the inlet, and she shivered, from stem to stern. The whistle of the wind and the water and the pounding of the surf hid Webb's shout as she crashed. The ship reeled, crazily, the wheel spun, the masts dipped, she made one glorious effort to right herself. A piece of her figurehead broke, floated away, disappeared. And then, very slowly, the *Loyalty* began to settle, and a wave washed over her deck, hid it for a moment, receded, and then came back again.

As he had been told, Webb lowered the Stars and Stripes swiftly and he handed the flag, uninjured, to Jules Descase. Then another flag appeared, and a shout went up from the men in the lifeboats, watching. It was the black and white and scarlet house flag of Matthew Steel, that the *Loyalty* had carried proudly to every corner of the globe, flying defiantly; Matthew Steel's signature, eloquent as a clenched fist.

A little later, while he and his men fought with the oars to a lifeboat, drawing away from the ship, Matthew looked up and he could still see his flag. The figurehead, the beautiful, fabled figurehead, was completly gone now. After a while the flag, too, would disappear. The sea would beat the *Loyalty,* carrying away her rigging piecemeal, but the great solid hull of her would lie forever in the channel.

Matthew was glad that his flag was there. It was like leaving a little bit of himself aboard the beloved ship that he had sent to her doom. Perhaps it was not the Navy custom. Matthew didn't know. He swallowed and his throat was dry and tight as he watched the vessel list, shake, seeming to shudder at the surprise and suddenness of his desertion.

The quarterdeck was awash now, the light of the brasswork put out by the hungry sea. How often had he stood on that deck, a deck level as a ballroom floor in the calm and stillness of a tropic night, and looked up at the riding light, competing with the stars? How often had he and the *Loyalty* fought fierce seas, taking the punishment with a fierce, triumphant joy at their endurance? How often had he crowded on sail, for the pure joy of a race, confident his faultless ship would not fail him?

His cabin would be filled now, the cabin that had been home. Water would have rushed in through the open port, pounded on his chart table, sent his chair, smooth from the outlines of his own body, crashing against his bed. The staterooms, the galley, from which Webb had often brought him steaming, early-morning coffee; the hold, which still bore, deep within it, the magic odors of the priceless cargoes she had carried, a lingering scent of spices, a whiff of tea, somehow still there despite the new odors of gunpowder and the musty scent of sackcloth and bamboo wrappings; the sea would have her way there at last. Breakers would roar around the *Loyalty's* stout hull, pounding, demanding admittance, and in low tide waves would whisper around her, like the rustle of the fine silks she once had carried. Water, so carefully denied the *Loyalty's* hold, so carefully kept away from the Steinway Grand that made music for the customers of the Bella Union on the California coast—now it would flow, unresisted, and the awful weight of it would pull her down till she rested, at last, on the ocean floor.

The worst tempests the Horn had been able to produce had not vanquished the *Loyalty*. Time and the competition of machines had not dimmed her performance. It was Matthew Steel, the man who loved and knew her best, who had finally, deliberately, sent her down.

There was silence in the small boats as the men of the *Loyalty* watched the doomed ship. They watched the *Annie B.* withdraw, also, fading back into the shoreline from which she had emerged. She would no longer be a menace to sailing men. The *Loyalty*—who said she was no fighting ship?—had defeated the privateer; she had closed the channel, and those who knew the stoutness of her knew that she would never give way.

Watching, some sailors rested on their oars and when they moved again their rhythm was uneven. Suddenly, to put them on the beat again, Webb's deep voice rose in a chantey, and other voices joined him, and the oars in the Captain's boat immediately settled into smooth and perfect accompaniment.

It was a song that for ages had lightened the labors of sailing men, and had been heard often aboard the *Loyalty*, putting new strength into cold and exhausted men, bone-weary from their battle with the sea. It was a long pull song, and Webb's voice measured it now to the dip of the oars. "*Oh, shake her up and away we'll go, So handy, my girls, so handy. Up aloft from down below, So handy, my girls, so handy—*

The men glanced at Matthew Steel and then they glanced away.

[4]

THERE was a good feeling of fall in the air when Matthew came back to South Street. It was stimulating, brisk, after the heavy heat of summer. Matthew and his men had been picked up and brought back to the Brooklyn Navy Yard aboard one of the blockaders, heading back for repairs after a long vigil on the Confederate coast.

It had seemed strange to be only a passenger aboard a ship that put into New York harbor, and he felt a little lost and very much alone. The war news was good and ordinarily he would have cause for personal rejoicing, for the Russian Atlantic Squadron lay, in all its might and glory, off Pier 23 in North River.

There were three frigates, he had been told, in the Russian fleet—including the *Alexander Nevsky*, flagship for Rear-Admiral Lesovsky. So Lesovsky had been promoted, Matthew had thought, with satisfaction. No doubt his promotion had come because he had proposed this expedition and convinced his superiors of the worth of it. The other two frigates—his informers had trouble with the Russian names—were undoubtedly the *Peresvyet* and the *Oslyabya*, most sea-worthy of the squadron, though the *Oslyabya* had been in Greek waters when he had last heard of her. There were two sloops of war. Those, Matthew figured, would be the *Varyaga* and the *Vityaz;* and two clippers, the *Almaz* and the *Isumrud*. The *Zhemchug*, as Matthew had surmised when last he had seen that aged vessel, was not hardy enough to make this voyage. And Popov, in the Pacific, at the same time had herded his warships into San Francisco Bay.

The Russian fleet had received an elaborate, almost a hysterical, public reception in New York. There had been a large official delegation to greet the distinguished, well-armed foreign visitors, and the ensuing triumphal parade, with a glittering military escort and lively bands, had been all the celebration-loving Russians could wish. The American people had immediately jumped to the conclusion that the Russians had come for the sole purpose of aiding them against the Rebels by this demonstration of their friendship and readiness, and they had taken them to their hearts. The Russians, if Matthew knew them, would revel in this, and they would say nothing to dispel that illusion.

Even if a man sought to correct that impression, and shouted from the housetops that Russian warships lay in New York and San Francisco harbors solely because it was to their greatest benefit to be there, the American people would not now listen. God, Matthew thought, how people do go from one extreme to the other. If a man is on your side he is a hero, and can do no wrong. If he is on the other he is the devil incarnate. But perhaps it was not really important, except that in future dealings with the Russian people the American public might be disillusioned, because they had misinterpreted this gesture as generosity.

However, the coming of the Russians had admirably served the intended present purpose. No danger now of a Rebel privateer making one last vicious thrust at a Northern port—not while the Muscovite guns glistened there in the sunlight! And, likewise, Great Britain and France, for the first time since the start of the war, had stopped talking of intervention. They were making decidedly friendly overtures to the representatives of the United States government abroad, and the Rebel diplomats were finding themselves eased out, gradually, politely, but completely, as only British diplomats could do it.

Yes, that was a great satisfaction. But it was not quite enough to overcome the feeling of loneliness that came over him now. He was not sorry he had sunk the *Loyalty* and defeated Fernando. But the *Loyalty* had long been at his command, and it seemed to him, aboard a steamer, that her ending had been not only that of one ship, but of the whole era of sailing ships. Traveling away from her on a steam-propelled vessel had seemed to put a final, finishing farewell to days he had loved and days that would never come again.

After his story had once been told to officers of the rescue vessel, Matthew had been left much alone on the return trip to New York. He had reported to his superiors, answering questions crisply but completely. He had been given a three-day leave, and then he would report back for a new command—if he was to be given any.

Perhaps the Navy would not agree with him that his judgment had been right.

And now he was back on South Street again, his sea-bag over his shoulder. Just like any one of thousands of homecoming sailormen he had watched during the years, as he himself had come, countless times, so many years ago. His face was weathered and lined, a young-old face. His uniform was faded and worn, but it looked well on his hard, straight body. He walked slowly, steadily, thinking, *I'm right back where I started.*

But as he walked, with no particular destination in mind, he began to feel a new peace. He had time again to note the familiar signs, the store fronts, that he had loved and thrilled to, as a boy. Brokers' offices, sailmakers, dealers in ships' instruments, liquors, importers, turpentine distillers, dealers in naval stores, notaries, a clothing store, blockmakers, storage houses, junk shops, stevedore's offices, importers of brandy and wine, dealers in copper, shipwrights, wood-carvers, markets and sugar refiners, the tobacco inspection warehouse, all the little shops and big ones, the familiar signs and sights and smells that made up South Street.

He lingered for a moment at an intersection. The docks were crowded with vessels of all sizes. The piers groaned with merchandise and with people, longshoremen, draymen, all the familiar hodgepodge that he had known. Only the ships from the cotton ports were missing, a great many tugs had gone to other harbors, and there was more smoke and much less canvas. . . . A few boys hung on the outskirts, watching, ducking drays and cargo slings. As he watched, two of them darted across the street toward him, and as they neared him they turned to each other and spoke, and then they came on and slowed, half-shy, half-bold, their bright eyes in their brown faces appraising him. Boys still found magic in the waterfront, Matthew thought, easing his sea-bag to the walk beside him. That was good. These boys would be sailors themselves one day—but not aboard clipper ships. Would there be the same magic to steam vessels? They'd never bring a steamer home to a working song, and perhaps the music of the clippers, already fading, would one day be completely forgotten. Too bad these lads would miss the beauty and the thrill of it.

"Say," one of the boys spoke to him. It was the uniform, of course. Faded as it was it still bore the insignia of an officer. He waited. "Aren't you Captain Steel?"

"Yes." The momentary pleasure he had felt left him and his voice was crisp. For a long time now the name of Captain Steel on South Street had been almost an epithet. He looked away, his lips set. The boys circled him, came around to stare at his face, and he was surprised that their eyes widened and they were breathless—with what? he asked himself. Excitement, he supposed, as though they had met a notorious convict. He reached for his sea-bag, prepared to move on. "Jesus!" one of the boys breathed, but it was not profanity.

"Could I carry your bag, Captain Steel?" the youngster asked. Puzzled, Matthew shook his head, silently. "Aw, please, Captain Steel, I'd be awful careful of it, sure. Hey!" he shouted to a friend across the street, cupping his mouth with one hand, pointing frantically to Matthew with the other. "Captain Steel! Captain Steel!"

Matthew's face crimsoned, but in spite of himself he grinned. He moved off swiftly, leaving the boys in a small group, staring after him and chattering. He had stood that way himself once, he remembered, staring admiringly at the captains of sailing vessels home at the end of a voyage. These boys knew only that he had captained the *Loyalty;* he was glad for their admiration. It gave him a warm, rich feeling, and he felt a little shaken, too. He was not accustomed to it.

Ahead of him, moving slowly across the street to the land side, staying close together, was a strange little group. There was talking and laughter and weeping among them. Their clothing was strange. The women wore shawls about their heads and carried bundles and the men also were heavily laden. Immigrants, foreign-born, just arriving on American soil. Again Matthew stopped, watching them. They passed him, still talking, their eyes a little frightened, flicking him with friendly, shy glances. Among them was a young girl, her plain face very white. Her worn cloak did not conceal her advanced pregnancy. She clutched a bundle very firmly. Matthew waited until the group had passed him, and he glanced over his shoulder at the girl; her slim shoulders were very straight, her head high. She might have been Mary Steel.

Automatically he headed toward Catharine Street and Cherry, the old district of sailors' boarding houses. Mrs. Doughty would not take him in, however, he remembered, and indeed there was no need for him to go back there. True, he had lost his three vessels; he was no longer a wealthy man. But he could afford decent lodgings in a decent hotel for the three days of his leave. Money seemed mighty unimportant now. He'd have to start over, when the war had ended. He'd have to learn more about steamships. They were efficient, all right, and fast, and Matthew liked speed and appreciated efficiency. But he wondered if those ships would ever seem to be a friend to their masters—or if they would be, always and forever, machines.

Dover Street, Roosevelt, James, Oliver, he could call the streets like a boyish, unrhymed chant. At Catharine Slip the two-hundred block would begin. Funny, how a man remembered things like that, that he had learned so thoroughly in his boyhood, and then, for a time, forgot. Liquors, grindstones, storage, blacksmith, iron, grocer, shipjoiner. He had not been away from South Street very long, he reminded himself, but it seemed to him now he was more conscious of it than he had been since his boyhood. He had taken it all for granted, he had not really seen it, he thought, since the early years when he had discovered it for himself.

All right—so his steam sloop lay at the bottom of the Atlantic; the *Loyalty* was impaled on a rock off the Southern coast, and the *Comet* flew the British flag. What the hell difference did it make?

He walked on. Tessa Dunn would still be waiting at the Irving House. In an hour or so he could be sitting across the table from her, drinking champagne, striving to be gay. He put the thought out of his mind. It was a circle, a tortuous circle, like a treadmill, reaching nowhere. Well, after the war, he'd start over again. In America a man could start over.

He took a deep breath and set his chin. Yearning for Loyalty Blake nagged at him. What was she doing now, tonight? At least she was safe, no longer threatened by a wild mob. The memory of the riot, and of his fears for Loyalty, sharp and torturing as they had been, struck him, and he shoved it away from him. He must think of something else, where he would go, how he would spend his leave, for instance.

If there were messages for him—but who would send him messages now? He was no longer a shipowner with a warehouse of valuable goods and a huge bank account. Anyway, if there should be a message, from a creditor, for instance, it would be at the Cock and Bull. Hite and Morton might respect his uniform, even if they still had no use for him. He'd try it, anyway. He'd go to the Cock and Bull and have one drink, for memory's sake, and then he'd go on uptown and find a hotel room and have a bath and change to his one other uniform which he carried in his sea-bag.

A big man was coming toward him and he recognized Big Wayne, the stevedore. The large-featured, plain face was turned toward him, but Matthew knew better than to speak first. He kept walking, ready to meet the man's eye, waiting to have his glance slide uncomfortably away from him, as it had last time they had met. But suddenly Big Wayne's face cracked in a huge smile and he hastened his pace, and came to Matthew, his huge, ham-like hand outstretched.

"Cap'n Steel," the man said. "How are ya?" He gripped Matthew's hand and Matthew returned the greeting. Big Wayne let go his hand but he continued to stare and his regard was friendly. "I heard about the ship, Cap'n," he said, and he ducked his head in a sort of salute. "I felt mighty bad."

Matthew thanked him and moved on. He rubbed his hand over his face, a little confused. Big Wayne loved the ship almost as much as I did, he thought. It was he who made it possible for me to buy the *Loyalty* in the first place. He stopped, looked over his shoulder, thinking he would like to go back and talk to Big Wayne, to talk to him for a long time over a drink and food, to tell him all about the ship, all her long, gallant performance. But the stevedore had been lost in the crowd. Anyway, that would be a fool thing to do, Matthew told himself, just because a man speaks a friendly word to you—

Three men were lounging at the door to the Cock and Bull, and they stepped aside as Matthew approached. One of them was familiar, but he paid no attention to him, until the man came forward and stopped him. It was Cannon, the Englishman, who had sailed with him and Cass Blake, and he was holding out his hand.

"We been hoping you'd come, Captain Steel," Cannon said, his face glowing with pleasure. "We been sort of hanging around the Cock and Bull here, when we had some time off, sort of hoping you'd show up. We'd like to talk to you when you have some time free, sir—we're a kind of committee; we are talking of forming a sort of seamen's organization, with hiring halls, to get out from under Jimmy Burns and the other crimps who make their living stealing seamen. We'd like your advice, sir, when you can spare the time. And we're sorry about the *Loyalty,* Cap'n and we're proud, too, all of us, who sailed aboard her—mighty proud. Fixed that privateer for fair, didn't you, sir?"

After a little Matthew moved on into the Cock and Bull. It was a funny thing, he thought, just when a man gives up everything, then all the things he really wants seem to come back to him with a rush. He had lost his ships and his money, and suddenly when he thought he was finished, when he thought he was just another of those who had made a try for success and failed, people began to reach out toward him in friendship. Gratitude welled up within him. When a man least expected it, he thought, things came to him. Take Cannon, now; that was a good idea, a seaman's organization, with their own agencies for employment, their own hospitals, perhaps, and later on funds to care for the disabled and aged men who had followed the sea and the families of men who were lost. After the war was over the merchant marine would need strengthening and it would not be easy to get young men to go to sea, when there were so many opportunities ashore, in the cities, in the new territories of the west, in the reconstruction of all the war's havoc. A seaman's organization, with proper benefits, well managed, to correct the abuses of seamen ashore and at sea, would do much. It was a fine idea.

Matthew dropped his sea-bag in the corner and moved up to the bar. It was not crowded this early in the evening. Hite, filling orders, had aged, Matthew noticed. His movements were not as quick and automatic as they used to be. He had used to be the best bartender in the business and he had not lost his skill but he had definitely slowed. Hite and Morton were really a comical pair, he thought with affection, the one short and rotund, despite his age, the other tall and cadaverous. They were a part of South Street.

Hite turned toward him and his moon face crumpled. With one movement he picked up a glass and a bottle of whiskey and rolled toward Matthew. He placed them before him and said clearly: "On the house. So you're back, Matthew. God be praised, boy, God be praised."

Slowly, Matthew picked up the bottle and poured himself a drink. He held it for a little while before he raised it to his lips. He was not sure that his hand was quite steady.

Hite scrubbed his nose and his mouth and chin with his hand and turned away. He had said enough. Matthew raised the glass and drank. Never had a drink tasted so good. Morton moved toward him and filled his glass again, his saturnine face softened with a grin.

"Glad you're back, Matthew," he said briefly. "Damned glad you're back. People been driving us crazy, asking for you."

Matthew raised an eyebrow. He felt warm and comfortable and at home. These men would not mention his ship. They were letting him know, by their manner and their gentle jokes, that he was home again. Along the bar, men craned their necks to see him and Matthew did not care. He had not felt like this for years—not since before the war. He pushed his cap on the back of his head and his forehead wrinkled as he grinned.

"Who's been asking for me?"

"It's those damned Russians." Morton put his hands on his hips. "Thilo Kalin's been in here a hundred times, demanding we produce you—pluck you out of the air, I reckon. And the sailors themselves, not only the officers. Thilo can't keep them out of the station house. They drink ale and gin, damn their souls, and nobody can understand their lingo, and the only English they know is 'Captain Steel.'" Morton grinned and moved away to attend his customers and then he was back. "Been a couple of other fellows in here, too—Graham White was one—said he wanted to shake your hand." Morton had a white envelope in his hand and he wiped his hand on his trousers before he handed it to

Matthew. "Maybe a little dirty, Cap'n," he apologized. He had never called Matthew captain before. "But it's been right here so I wouldn't forget to give it to you if you should come in. It's an invitation," he confided. "A big doings for the Russian officers. Both the Russians and some fellow from the City Council was in, wanted us to be sure and get it to you, and Graham White said so, too. Hell—how'd we know where to find you? Said they'd tried the Navy. Navy couldn't tell them anything, and it was Tess who told them to leave a message here." Morton flung up his head. "By Jesus, Tess left a note, too." He bustled off, hunting among the bottles and glasses for the message.

Matthew broke the seal on the envelope and looked at the enclosed card with little interest. It was a carefully written, formal invitation to the banquet and ball in honor of the officers of the Russian Atlantic Squadron, at the Astor House, and the date was tonight, October 2nd. Matthew read it slowly. He would like to see Thilo and Peter and Lesovsky again. It would do no harm to appear and to shake their hands. After all, he had invited them, hadn't he? And his city was certainly honoring them, as he had promised. He pushed the card back in the envelope and glanced at his watch. Even if he hurried, however, he could not appear at the banquet. But, knowing the Russians, he knew that none of them would leave the celebration as long as music played, or a drop of liquor flowed. They would be at the Astor House till dawn. He had plenty of time. Meanwhile it was good to sit here, to be welcome, to exchange words with Hite and Morton when they had time between customers. A three-day pass was not bad, he decided, not bad at all.

Morton put another envelope before him and Matthew picked it up. His name on it was in Tessa's handwriting. Funny, looking at it, he had no feeling at all, not of excitement nor even of curiosity. He thought a lot of Tess, though; she was a good friend. There weren't many women who'd cross a continent to offer money to a man when they heard he'd had bad fortune.

"And so I am off to Europe—on a British steamer, and they promise me I will not have to endure being at sea more than eleven days—thirteen at the very most—" Tess had written. "I have a fine contract, and after all I must do what I can while I'm still young. Entertainers don't have too long a professional life. It's a glorious opportunity. I heard about your ship and while I think that was a crazy thing for you to have done, I admire you for it. The papers certainly gave the story a great deal of space. I heard also you gave your ship to the Navy instead of selling it. I don't understand that, but I suppose you know what you are doing. . . ."

Matthew folded the note and tucked it back in the envelope, smiling. Tess was happy and he was glad for that. She was off on another chase for money and glory and he hoped it was successful, and, knowing Tessa, he knew that it would be.

Almost reluctantly he moved back from the bar, raised his hand in salute to Hite and Morton, picked up his sea-bag and went to the street. He looked around for a hack for hire. He might as well go directly to the Astor House and take a room there and when he was ready he'd join the great celebration for the Russians.

He stepped to the curb, watching the traffic, waiting for an empty carriage. He saw one approaching and he raised his hand, and then, recognizing the driver, he let his hand fall, and he looked on, beyond him. There was no use signaling Bennett.

To his surprise the carriage came close to the curb, and in a minute Bennett was off the box and standing beside him. His face was red, but he stood stiff and straight. His buff-colored coat would not quite button over his stomach and his waistcoat showed through, but it was clean and his boots had been recently polished. He wore a high, starched, white collar and a four-in-hand cravat; Matthew remembered him wearing those things when he had been the autocrat of Washington Mews, but he had not worn them in later years when he had become the slovenly, drunken driver of a carriage for hire. He was holding the lash whip in his right hand, the prescribed two feet from the butt, which rested on his right leg, the whip pointing out at an exact forty-five-degree angle. Matthew did not laugh. He had seen the old coachman stand like that hundreds of times in his boyhood. Mary Steel had praised his stance and livery as perfection in his trade and said it was right to take a pride in one's work. Bennett had taught many a young man that proper posture and the proper expression to wear when he waited for the master or mistress of the house. But Matthew knew that strict, rigid formula which Bennett so valued had been saved only for the select. Never, in the years he had driven a hack for hire, had Matthew seen him put on his old dignity. He had never treated his casual fares—certainly not Matthew Steel—as he had his employers—his betters, in Bennett's code—in the old days.

And he was working hard for that old manner now. His eyes were straight ahead but he could not keep them there. They rolled around to watch Matthew Steel, though his head did not move.

"I'd be proud to drive you, Captain Steel," he said.

Matthew took a step or two towards him. He found he had to swallow to loosen a sudden tightening of his throat. Bennett turned his eyes straight front again.

"To wherever you want to go, Captain Steel," he said quickly. He waited, and still Matthew watched him. Once he had refused to drive Matthew to the Blakes', though he had driven Matthew and the red-haired Tessa Dunn. He wanted now to make his position quite clear. "To wherever you want to go, Captain Steel," he repeated firmly.

A ragged urchin, looking for a coin, stood at the horse's head. Matthew did not insult Bennett by picking up his own sea-bag. He left it lying on the walk for the coachman to place in the carriage. He nodded, and Bennett flung open the door with a flourish and Matthew stepped inside. He did not speak until he could control his voice.

"To the Astor House, Bennett," he said steadily.

[5]

It was good to sit at a glittering banquet table again, among distinguished men and beautiful women, to hear laughter and light conversation, to see happiness and optimism on the faces of her friends. Loyalty put down her water glass and rested her hands in her lap, and took pleasure in watching those about her.

Directly across the table from her was a handsome young Russian lieutenant, Peter Segonov. He was a good-natured and alert young man and he found it difficult to keep his eyes from wandering to Loyalty again and again. Once she had caught him staring at her openly and she had, quite without thinking, smiled in most friendly fashion, and a great, delighted grin had broken over his face. He was relieved that she was not annoyed.

Thereafter, it seemed to her that his eyes danced each time he looked at her. Lieutenant Segonov, for all he was a foreigner, had a sense of humor, Loyalty decided. She liked these Russians. She glanced to the head of the table, near which sat the guest of honor, Admiral Lesovsky, in command of the Atlantic Squadron of the Russian fleet. The Russian fleet—how good it made her feel to think of it lying out there in the bay! And to know that the Pacific Squadron of the Russians was at this very moment guarding San Francisco's Golden Gate.

The Admiral looked more like a Russian should look, she thought, with heavily gilded epaulets and many decorations on his green uniform. His face was dark and grim and very earnest, except when he smiled, and tonight he smiled more often than usual. Everyone was in the highest spirits. The welcome to the Russian fleet had seldom been surpassed in New York's history. Not since the ball for the Prince of Wales, before the war, had there been such a distinguished gathering.

Everyone of prominence in the city is here, Loyalty thought, her eyes moving from one table to another. All the city officials, government representatives from the capital and from other states. Graham White sat a few places away, near her father. Judge Austin was there, and his wife, handsome in evening dress. Alice

Hastings and her husband. She stole a look at Henry beside her, thin and distinguished in his Army uniform, and at Serena, on his other side. Serena wore silver gray, not a festive color, but with her gold hair it was very beautiful. She looked like a cameo, her sister thought, and she was glad to see her out of deep mourning once again.

But now the banquet was over and Captain Eads of St. Louis, the gunboat-builder, was on his feet, proposing a toast to the Czar. Loyalty liked Captain Eads, but she wished he would not talk so long. His deep voice rang out over the room: "To one whose virtues I feel totally incompetent to express, to one who has shown himself in the march of human progress far ahead of all others, one whose sagacity, whose statesmanship and many Christian virtues fill not only his own land but the whole world with his fame—"

There was more, but Loyalty did not listen. She amused herself watching the expressions on the faces around her. Peter Segonov was politely interested. The Russian Admiral scowled into his glass, but he emptied it with one quick motion when the time came, and then, in accented but quite clear English he began to speak.

"I regret very much that I cannot express as I would wish all the feelings of gratitudes which the speech of our friend Mr. Eads has produced on all of us. The praise which he gave to our Emperor is really deserved by him—"

There was a gust of cheers and Loyalty felt that others in the big room also were restless, anxious to express themselves in some way, if only by cheers. Next time there are huzzahs, I shall join them, even if I am a lady, Loyalty thought, in satisfaction.

"I assure you gentlemen, that from the beginning of these difficulties of yours our people have followed with deep interest and at the same time with sorrow the trials through which you are passing, but we expect that the talents and energy of the heroes who have already made themselves immortal will save your country—"

How good that sounded! Loyalty's restless fingers tightened on the little scent-box in her lap. What a wonderful surge of confidence had followed the coming of the Russians. When it seemed there was no friend in the world for the North the Russians had come, quietly but in all their might, in open defiance and warning to the British and French. A good-will visit, they announced carefully, but the papers openly proclaimed their unheralded coming as an act of friendship, a gesture that put new life and hope into the battered North. The appearance of the Russian Atlantic Squadron in New York, and the Pacific Squadron in San Francisco, had shocked and stunned the British and French. Loyalty chuckled, thinking of it. Surely this is truly the decisive point of the war—Vicksburg, Gettysburg—and now the coming of the Russians, with their ships and their guns!

"Let us drink to the health of the President of the United States!"

The gentlemen were on their feet again and now General Walbridge was going to speak. Loyalty pursed her pretty lips. Parke Godwin would be next, for he was already flushing a little and clearing his throat to himself, sure signs that he was soon to take the floor. A dimple appeared in Loyalty's cheek as she suppressed a giggle.

There was beneath the gaiety of the occasion a deeper, stronger happiness, and Loyalty knew it well, but she did not want to examine it now, for it was almost too great, too intense. She had discussed with no one the end of the ship named for her. There was no need to discuss it. It had been a magnificent gesture, one that neither her father nor any other critic of Matthew Steel could ever underrate, and he deserved all the praise that the press and public had heaped upon him. *The Loyalty would know no other master,* he said. He had been a true prophet. Where was he now, she wondered? Her fingers caressed the scent-box, as though it were a link with him, and her face sobered. She raised her head, deliberately tried to recapture the excitement she had felt at the glitter of the uniforms and gold braid, at the feel of celebration and victory in the air.

The room was warm; despite the fact that her curls were pinned high upon her head—chignons had climbed each year—the few that touched the back of her neck felt warm. She raised her kerchief to her lips daintily and placed the scent-box on the table where her plate had been. From the tiny perfume-scented sponge within it a delicate odor drifted.

The Admiral was speaking again and Loyalty fastened her attention upon him.

"The Emperor from the beginning of his reign sought only peace. . . . But I believe it the duty of every people to defend its integrity, either to live as a nation or to die. There is no middle ground. I hope that the present circumstances will end peacefully, but we are ready now for any sacrifice. If foreign nations are for peace with us we shall receive it on honorable terms and bless our God for that peace—"

The applause was deafening and Loyalty joined it. Henry Austin turned and smiled at her and Serena bent forward so she, too, might exchange happy smiles with her sister. It was good to see Serena enjoying herself, Loyalty thought, with a rush of love for her. She glanced at her father and he smiled and nodded to her, too; he looks so old, she thought, but tonight he is happy and relaxed and unworried. This has done so much for us. The coming of the Russians—even if it gave us only this one night as holiday and change from all the hard anxious days—has meant so much to us all. What a fortunate coincidence that they happened to come at this particular time! And why did they come? The papers declared it purely an expression of friendship toward us. Yet everyone is surprised that it happened now. What was it Graham White had said, more emphatically than she had ever heard him speak: "Nothing like it in diplomatic history!"

At any rate it was—how had her father put it so aptly? A great victory in psychological warfare.

The people were standing at last, and Loyalty was conscious of Peter Segonov, standing stiff and unmoving across the table from her. He was flushed and excited, and he bent toward her and pointed to the little scent-box.

"But of course! You are Loyalty! I should have known!"

A puzzled little frown creased Loyalty's forehead. She picked up the scent-box, the tiny thing almost like something alive in her hand, and held it out to the Russian.

"Is it not beautiful? It is from your country, Lieutenant—a valued gift."

"Yes, yes, I know." Peter lapsed into Russian in his excitement, and he turned to call over his shoulder. "Thilo—Thilo—here!" Lieutenant Thilo Kalin joined him, glancing a little shyly at Loyalty as he did so. "Thilo—the scent-box! She is Loyalty, Matthew Steel's sweetheart. The box—you see, Thilo—it was Madam's, my grandmother's. It was a gift from the Empress to her mother, a lady-in-waiting!"

Thilo bowed to Loyalty. The name of Matthew Steel had struck her and she stood still, staring at the Russians, trying to understand Peter's mixture of English and Russian. Lieutenant Kalin glanced at the box in Loyalty's palm and then he reached over and picked it up, without so much as asking permission. But Loyalty did not protest. This man knew Matthew Steel. Suddenly Loyalty's mind flashed back—the last trip the ship *Loyalty* had made under Matthew Steel's house flag had been to St. Petersburg. Somewhere, in the depths of her consciousness, an idea stirred, came to life. She caught her breath. Matthew Steel had been in Russia last winter; he had returned just before the Russian fleet put to sea. He was a friend of these Naval officers. Was there any connection between him and the coming of the Russian fleet?

The other members of her immediate party gathered about her now; Serena and Henry, her father and Judge Austin, and Graham White. With another bow Thilo returned the box to her.

"Your pardon, Madam," he said. "You see—" his English was better than Peter's—"we are friends, very good friends, of Matthew Steel. This little box once belonged to the grandmother of my friend, Lieutenant Segonov. Peter remembers well when Madam Segonova presented it to Captain Steel, to bring to his sweetheart in America. It was one of their family treasures. We did not realize that you were the one—though we should have, eh, Peter? Captain Steel always said she was the most beautiful in all New York!"

Loyalty's face flushed crimson but she could not suppress a smile. The Russians certainly made no attempts to be subtle, but their compliments were sincere. The thought, however, kept nagging her—Matthew Steel and these men—they seemed to know him well.

"I am proud to have it, Lieutenant," she answered quickly,

closing her fingers about the box. "I did not know its story. But if it has been in your family a long time—is that not where it belongs? I should be glad to return it to you now, as a gesture of our friendship—"

Peter Segonov was scandalized. "No, indeed! We are honored, and I am delighted to meet you." Peter bowed formally. "But Captain Steel—where is he, why is he not here? What a man and what a hero! The Russians love him, Madam, we owe him much. And he invited us here. He spent last winter with us. He promised to return our hospitality." Peter was in high good humor and he threw his head back and laughed. "And now we come—but Captain Steel is nowhere to be found. He is too busy winning the war. But the ship, ah, Madam, there will be many a tear spilled in St. Petersburg for the death of the ship! She was a beautiful vessel and he loved her like a sweetheart!"

Thilo took Peter's arm. "But she had a noble ending, Peter," he said quietly. "Forgive us, Madam." He bowed to Loyalty and again to Serena, and, less elaborately, to the gentlemen of the party. "We are at your service, Madam—Miss—" he added sincerely to Loyalty, and then, taking Peter's arm, he withdrew. After an instant Loyalty looked around at her father and then at Graham White. Mr. White's face was impassive. It was not like him, Loyalty thought, to be so much on guard. Now, catching her glance, he smiled a little and was in haste to speak.

"Interesting people, aren't they?" he began, but Loyalty did not smile.

"Yes," she said. She faced Graham White squarely but she said nothing more. Henry took her arm.

"There's music, Loyalty," he said gently.

Obediently Loyalty went with him and Serena toward the ballroom. Ahead of her she saw the broad shoulders of the two Russian officers. Their heads were close together and they were talking animatedly. Friends of Matthew Steel—

This box came to me such a long while ago, Loyalty thought, and it was then I knew I loved him. It has always seemed like a tie between us. How strange that now, tonight, I should find out whence it came. It is like a bond, leading from Matthew Steel to me, to the Russians—a talisman, perhaps. Perhaps, too, she thought yearningly, it will lead me back to him.

Henry bent his head to Serena, and Serena looked up at him with a smile and some light remark. How beautiful she is tonight, Loyalty thought, and how kind Henry is to her. Loyalty felt apart from them, as she must always feel apart, from everyone, for she had walked alone now for a long while. But this was a night for playtime and gaiety. Time enough tomorrow to take up the burdens of work again. There would be plenty of work for women for a long while to come, even after the war was won. Women always had to clean up the debris after a man's war—to try to heal the wounds and work for order again. How could women remain cloistered and idle in their homes, Loyalty thought, when there was so much work for them to do! But tonight was for play.

She swept into the ballroom as she had in the happy old days before the war; vivid and radiant, her eyes sparkling, her curls gleaming, the beautiful, rich folds of her garnet-red gown whispering about her. She would savor every rich moment of this night of laughter. The music made her pulse race. With a quick little gesture she flipped open her small fan and fluttered it before her flushed face, and she watched the dancers, her own body unconsciously swaying, ever so little, to the rhythm of the music.

Thilo and Peter were joining a group of Russians clustered around the entrance and as she watched they stopped, talked together and glanced back to Loyalty with wide grins. Bless me, she thought, mustering a polite little smile, are they going to ask me to dance? Do the Russians know our dances? Laughter bubbled up within her and she fluttered her fan a little more.

The crowd thinned a little as couples moved to the dance floor. Henry turned to speak to Loyalty, Serena's hand on his arm. As he did so Loyalty's fan stopped suddenly and she stood motionless and the color drained from her face. Henry followed her glance.

There was a newcomer among the Russian officers around the entrance, a tall officer of the United States Navy. The Russians gathered thickly about him. It was obviously a reunion of old friends and there was much laughter and back-slapping and hand-shaking.

"Loyalty, you'll excuse us—" Henry began and then he stopped.

He smiled at Serena and he led her to the floor. Loyalty did not hear him, nor see him go.

Thilo and Peter were beside the American officer now, and they were grinning broadly and gesturing toward Loyalty. The American's face turned from them and he looked beyond the Russians to Loyalty, and his smile faded.

Loyalty's hand, holding her fan, dropped to her side and she stood very still. She saw Admiral Lesovsky touch Matthew Steel's arm, and she watched Matthew turn, almost absent-mindedly, and take his hand and speak to him, and she could even hear the Russian words of greeting Matthew spoke, across the little space that separated them. It is good to see him smile, she thought. He is so at ease with these people, their respect and friendship for him is so genuine. He is thinner, his face is more bronzed. He is a little older—and the arrogance that he used to carry, half defiantly, has gone from him. But his eyes are still direct and unwavering, and there is a new understanding in them, too. He is everything that I dreamed he would be, that I knew he would be, she thought, and there was glory in her face.

Matthew Steel turned away from the Admiral and Captain Eads was there to take his hand, and then General Walbridge, and then he turned toward Loyalty. Loyalty was not conscious of the hundreds of eyes upon her, watching the last act of the drama being played here in the Astor House ballroom. She only knew that this was no time for artifice or pretense. Henry Austin, glancing over Serena's shoulder as they danced, saw, and looked away. Thaddeus Blake left a sentence hanging unfinished, in mid-air, and Graham White, to whom he was speaking, did not notice. A woman's intuition, Graham White thought, smiling. A woman as sensitive and intelligent as Loyalty Blake would not be misled. She had guessed there was a connection between the Russian arrival and Matthew Steel and now she saw her suspicion verified. He could almost see her quick mind assemble the evidence and come swiftly and correctly to a conclusion. She knew the man she loved and she knew how to judge him. But Loyalty was not troubled by political machinations now. She seemed unaware that there was anyone besides Matthew Steel in the room, and Graham White's face sobered as he watched. What unwavering faith she had in him, White thought, almost reverently, what God-given trust!

Captain Steel paused, a few steps from Loyalty. He said nothing but his eyes spoke for him. He searched her face, and, as it had always been, it seemed to Loyalty he held out his arms to her.

It was Loyalty who went to him and silently took his arm. The Russians made a lane for them and quietly Matthew Steel and Loyalty Blake went from the ballroom and down the long stairs, and to the entrance. The music followed them, dimmed, but Loyalty did not know. She could not look at Matthew Steel now, she could not speak, for her heart was too full, and tears pressed too close against her eyelids. She felt the warmth of his hard arm through his sleeve, and, halfway down the stairs, his right hand came down over hers on his arm, strong and warm and tight, in a grip that almost hurt.

The doors opened for them and they were on the walk and the air was sweet and fresh, an autumn night in New York. There was a closed carriage-for-hire at the curb and the driver opened its door and stood at attention as they approached. Loyalty entered it, thinking vaguely, *I've left my cloak*—and it did not matter at all. She heard Matthew Steel's quiet voice. "Thank you, Bennett," he said.

Matthew Steel was beside her then and Bennett carefully closed the carriage door.

POSTSCRIPT

It is, of course, true that in the fall of 1863, when Great Britain seemed about to recognize the Confederacy, the Atlantic Squadron of the Russian Imperial Navy appeared unexpectedly in New York harbor; and Russia's Pacific Squadron paid a "good-will visit" to San Francisco Bay.

Historians agree that this appearance of Russia's warships in United States ports helped to turn the tide of the War Between the States. But why they happened to come at that crucial time has long been the subject of rumor and legend and debate.

One theory is that the then Secretary of State William Seward arranged with the Czar to have the fleet winter in American waters, and agreed to pay all costs of the expedition; and that payment for this demonstration was included in the $7,200,000 which the United States later paid to Russia for the territory of Alaska. Alaska, it is said, cost only $1,400,000 and the other $5,800,000 was for the carefully timed visit of the Russian fleet.

The World Almanac in 1944, in dealing with U.S. territorial expansion, supports this view and gives as its authority "government reports." But the 1945 edition of the World Almanac revises the paragraph and deletes mention of a secret deal and payment for the visit of the Russian fleet. The revision, according to E. Eastman Irvine, Editor, is from data furnished by the Governor of Alaska.

There are other theories on why the Russians came to the United States at that particular time. Oliver Wendell Holmes praised the Russians in verse, indicating that they extended a helping hand to the North as a gallant, unselfish gesture of friendship. Newspaper accounts of the actual visit and reception of the Russians indicate this view was generally held throughout the North by the delighted American hosts.

But two scholars, F. A. Golder ("The Russian Fleet and the Civil War," *American Historical Review*, July, 1915) and Foster Rhea Dulles (*The Road to Teheran*) advance a more thoughtful theory, and point to actual Russian documents to support it: that Russia's fleet came to American harbors because Russia feared a war of her own with England and France on the Polish question and sought neutral ports as havens for her ships—ports from which she could strike at her enemy's merchant shipping if hostilities actually began.

Whether it was a secret arrangement, bought and paid for in some manner by the United States government; whether it was a purely magnanimous and friendly gesture on the part of Russia; whether it was a fortunate and unparalleled historical coincidence, may never be actually decided and agreed upon by all historians. And it may never be known who—Russian or Yankee—originated the idea and made the arrangements.

Accordingly, I have taken the liberty of writing this story, *Praise At Morning*, about a Yankee trader who might have been the unknown negotiator responsible for Russia's significant and history-making naval demonstration in New York and San Francisco harbors in 1863.

MILDRED MASTERSON MCNEILLY

ACKNOWLEDGMENTS

FOR their aid in securing the material for the historical background of this book I wish to express my thanks to librarians of the New York Public Library, who aided me by providing newspapers, early histories, maps, street directories and pictures of New York, 1854-1863; of the Library of Congress, Washington, D.C., for bibliographies on foreign relations during the Crimean and Civil Wars; the Map and Photostatic Divisions of the Library of Congress for copies of Confederate and Federal maps of the Bull Run battlefield and of San Francisco a century ago; to the staff of the Bancroft Library, University of California, Berkeley, for permitting me access to Golder's "Russian-American Relations During the Crimean War," *American Historical Review*, Vol. 31, 1926; "The Russian Fleet and the Civil War," *American Historical Review*, July, 1915; and Adamov's "Russia and the United States at the time of the Civil War," *Journal of Modern History*, 1930; to the excellent staffs of the Alameda Free Library and the San Francisco Public Library, for their untiring aid in securing general material and early copies of the *Alta California;* to George Willard Bowen of Seattle for early maps of New York City; to Major Joseph Mills Hanson, Custodian, Manassas National Battlefield Park, Manassas, Virginia, and to the numerous friends who have provided unpublished private journals of Civil War and clipper-ship days.

M. M. McN.

COURTNEY
ALLEN